Ancients and Moderns

For Stephanie Lian

Ancients and Moderns

William Crotch and the Development of
Classical Music

HOWARD IRVING

Ashgate

Aldershot • Brookfield USA • Singapore • Sydney

Published by
Ashgate Publishing Limited
Gower House
Croft Road
Aldershot
Hants GU11 3HR
England

Ashgate Publishing Company
Old Post Road
Brookfield
Vermont 05036–9704
USA

The author has asserted his moral right under the Copyright, Designs and Patents Act, 1988, to be identified as the author of this work.

British Library Cataloguing in Publication Data

Irving, Howard
    Ancients and Moderns: William Crotch and the Development
    of Classical Music.
    (Music in Nineteenth-Century Britain)
    1. Crotch, William, 1775–1847.   2. Music—Great Britain—19th
    century.
    I. Title.
    780.9'2

Library of Congress Cataloging-in-Publication Data

Irving, Howard Lee, 1951–
    Ancients and moderns: William Crotch and the development of
    classical music/Howard Irving.
        (Music in Nineteenth-Century Britain)
        Includes bibliographical references and index.
        ISBN 1–84014–604–4 (hc.)
        1. Music—England—18th century—History and criticism.
    2. Musical canon.   3. Crotch, William, 1775–1847.   I. Title.
    II. Series.
    ML286.3.I78   1999
    780'.941'09033—dc21   98–54372
                                                                      CIP
                                                                      MN

ISBN 1 84014 604 4

This book is printed on acid free paper

Typeset in Sabon by Manton Typesetters, 5–7 Eastfield Road, Louth, Lincs, LN11 7AJ

Printed and bound in Great Britain by MPG Books Ltd, Bodmin, Cornwall

Contents

General Editor's Preface

At the turn of the last century the factionalism engendered by attitudes towards ancient and modern music was, and still is now, a critical focal point for gauging musical values and tastes of the time. Not, however, that early attitudes were invariably partisan. Amongst some contemporary figures the portrayal of the parties as mutually exclusive was nothing more than a politicizing gesture. But in others the controversy was more immediately heartfelt, and in any event the representation of the quarrel, as Howard Irving calls it, is multi-faceted. It runs from the most vituperative and closed-minded denunciations to the clearest expressions of impartiality and disinterestedness. For modern musicologists trying to assess the language of the quarrel, as well as its inevitable influence on the development of a canonic repertoire, ascertaining its aesthetic and ideological nature and establishing its context is of paramount concern. Howard Irving's book addresses just this concern, and it does so in three ways: firstly, by evaluating relevant writings of William Crotch and others in light of the ancient–modern quarrel; secondly, by placing this evaluation into an alternative reading of the theories of William Weber; and thirdly, by providing a valuable transcription of Crotch's illuminating set of eight 1818 lectures. The reader can therefore judge for himself/herself not only Crotch's disposition towards music generally and the ancient–modern quarrel more specifically, but whether this accords with the views of modern musicologists on this and related topics. In this sense *Ancients and Moderns* sheds light as much on current values and tastes as it does on those of the eighteenth and nineteenth centuries.

Bennett Zon

University of Hull

Acknowledgements

Several individuals and institutions helped to make this book possible. I am indebted, first, to Lars Troide and Stewart Cooke of the Burney Project at McGill University for putting the Project's substantial collection of Burney materials completely at my disposal. Both Stephen Parks, curator of the Osborn Collection at Yale, and Miss Jean Kennedy MBE, the former County Archivist of the Norfolk Record Office, supplied me with much needed materials. I have relied on the interlibrary loan department at the University of Alabama at Birmingham, especially Eddie Luster, Marilyn Grush and the late Tinker Dunbar.

This book was written with the assistance of grants from the Graduate School of the University of Alabama at Birmingham (UAB) and the National Endowment for the Humanities. William Crotch's lectures and other materials are quoted with the permission of Norfolk Record Office, Gildengate House, Anglia Square, Upper Green Lane, Norwich. Letters by Charles Burney that are held in the Barrett Collection are quoted by permission of the British Library. Burney's letters and other materials in the Berg Collection are quoted with the permission of the Henry W. and Albert A. Berg Collection, The New York Public Library, Astor, Lenox and Tilden Foundations. Burney materials held in the Osborn Collection are quoted with the permission of The James Marshall and Marie-Louise Osborn Collection, Yale University Library. Parts of Chapter 3 appeared in an earlier form as 'Classic and Gothic: Charles Burney on Ancient Music' in *Studies in Eighteenth Century Culture*, **23** (1993), 243–63.

Several colleagues and friends either read and commented on parts of the manuscript or helped me develop ideas that appear in this book. Like many musicologists who work in small departments, I have enjoyed the intellectual support and nurture of individuals outside my field, especially George Graham, James Rachels and Scott Arnold in the Department of Philosophy at UAB. Within musicology, special thanks are due Kerry Grant both for advice and encouragement at a crucial stage in this project. I have received invaluable critical guidance from two other sources. First, the skilful and sensitive editing of series editor Bennett Zon has made this a far better book than it would otherwise have been. In addition, I owe a substantial debt to anonymous referees who offered detailed and constructive comments on this and related manuscripts.

Abbreviations

Barrett	Barrett Collection
Berg	Berg Collection
BL	British Library
BM	British Museum
CB	Charles Burney
Correspondence	NRO, MS 11214–1126
DNB	*Dictionary of National Biography*
FB	Frances Burney
General Account	NRO, MS 11230
GM	*Gentleman's Magazine*
Lectures	NRO, MS 11229
Memoirs	NRO, MS 11244
NRO	Norfolk Record Office
NYPL	New York Public Library
Osborn	Osborn Collection
QMMR	*The Quarterly Musical Magazine and Review*
RMA	Royal Musical Association
TT	Thomas Twining
WC	William Crotch
YUL	Yale University Library

PART ONE
Ancients and Moderns

Introduction

In a lecture series first read at the Surrey Institution in 1818, Oxford University's Heather Professor of music William Crotch surveys British musical life over the preceding four decades. Crotch describes a period of great change from the concert world he had entered as a celebrated child prodigy in the final quarter of the eighteenth century. During the eventful 40 years surrounding the turn of the century, trained musicians are said to have displaced connoisseurs as the accepted arbiters of musical taste and the rightful leaders of musical institutions. Audiences, at the same time, learned to display a new reverence both for musicians and their creative efforts. Crotch notes that by the second decade of the nineteenth century concerts were often attended with a respectful attention that might have been found in Crotch's youth only at the élite Concert of Ancient Music. Unlike the Ancient Concert, however, the programmes of groups such as the newly formed Philharmonic Society are cited for their mixture of old and recent music, a tendency Crotch welcomes. Indeed, Crotch acknowledges the appearance of a new kind of contemporary musical masterpiece that combines the best qualities of ancient and modern music. The excellence of this new musical species is susceptible to analysis by skilled critics and requires no validation by the Ancient Concert's well-known formula limiting programmes to music at least 20 years old.

These changes took place in Crotch's scenario against the background of a great conflict of musical ideologies that pitted advocates of ancient and modern music in a bitter struggle for dominance. The initial result of the ancient–modern quarrel was a deep division in British concert life and an extended period of musical decline. Earlier advocates of ancient music might have charged the decline of British music to the introduction of a decadent 'modern style', but Crotch – who had become the *de facto* spokesman for the ancient-music community – contends instead that the ancient–modern dispute itself caused a musical depression. Public taste was compromised by the blindness of both factions to the genuine merits of the other style and by the fact that concerts were restricted to a single musical species. The ancient–modern quarrel is said to have been resolved shortly before Crotch's 1818 lectures by the belated introduction of certain music by Mozart that offered a synthesis of the two approaches. The model for this synthesis is a work whose London première the previous year had done much to encourage a change in Crotch's thinking about the modern style and its partisans, Mozart's *Don Giovanni*.

The evolutionary process by which the new system of institutions and values Crotch describes in his 1818 lecture series came into being is the subject of this study. Part Two of the present volume makes available the text of Crotch's 1818 lecture series for the first time in a modern edition. Part One introduces these lectures by examining Crotch's lecturing career, by exploring certain issues facing the professional critic at a vital juncture in the history of music criticism and, most importantly, by examining the ancient–modern quarrel that Crotch treats as the most compelling feature of musical life around the turn of the century.

As other lectures by Crotch clarify, the quarrel described above is part of a much more extensive conflict that began in the seventeenth century and continued in some form even after an early nineteenth-century *rapprochement* between the contending parties.[1] On the surface, the central issue of the debate was the contrast of harmony and melody. This is often expressed by writers on the ancient side, such as Christopher Simpson in 1674, by the comparison of music that is 'most excellent, for Art and Contrivance' with a more generally pleasing but inferior variety of 'light and airy Musick'.[2] A number of other issues were closely bound up with the melody–harmony debate, however: should music be regarded as a mere gratification of the sense of hearing or can it somehow be an intellectual art form, comparable in significance to poetry or painting? This question is central, in turn, to the matter of whether music can have the intellectual substance necessary for it to achieve classical status and thereby avoid the continual cycle of celebrity and obsolescence that is the fate of lesser arts. The melody–harmony debate was also enlisted in an argument over whether music has a moral purpose or effect and whether this effect is a function of its form or its content.

---

[1] Crotch places the revolution that produced a new modern style at several different points in different lectures. The earliest point in the area of sacred music is the music of Francesco Durante (1684–1755) (cf. NRO, MS 11232/1, where Durante is called 'the father of the modern school'). Recent scholarship places the beginning of the ancient–modern polemic in British sacred music somewhat earlier, around the time of the Restoration. Ruth M. Wilson traces the origin of the notion of ancient music back to around this point in *Anglican Chant and Chanting in England, Scotland, and America 1660 to 1820* (Oxford: Clarendon Press, 1996), p. 162, where she finds the beginnings of the idea in the writings of Henry Aldrich (d. 1710), Thomas Tudway (d. 1726), and Arthur Bedford (d. 1745). In NRO, MS 11232/2, reprinted in Part Two below, Crotch allows that the ancient–modern divide continued after 1818 but adds that the differences between the parties 'are no longer, as formerly, advanced in the way of opposition and hostility to each other'. Recent scholarship by Bennett Zon traces the ancient–modern polemic through the end of the nineteenth century. See B. Zon, *The English Plainchant Revival* (Oxford: Clarendon Press, 1998).

[2] Christopher Simpson *A Compendium: or Introduction to Practical Music. In Five Parts* (London, 1678; 6th edn, London, 1714), p. 115.

Some of the critical writing upon which the present study is based treats the aesthetic issues of the ancient–modern quarrel in a distinctly ideological context. The issue of progress is the most obvious ideological dividing line between the two sides, but this is not the only issue or even, in many cases, the most important one. The ancient faction crusades for musical classics, but its preference for form over content also leads it to promote self-referential musical values that can be appreciated at their highest levels only by specialists and connoisseurs. The ancient side, accordingly, tends to be viewed by moderns as exclusive and authoritarian in addition to reactionary. Moderns almost invariably endorse a view that progress in the arts is possible if not inevitable and desirable but, in addition, tend to view musical complication as an impediment to clear communication and to stress instead the content that music has the power to convey or express as an approachable musical quality that can have positive social effects even on the uninitiated.

Different aspects of this long controversy have been investigated in some detail.[3] This is especially true of the seventeenth century origins of the concept of ancient music as that notion developed in its natural birthplace of sacred music.[4] Similarly, the intellectual background for the first recorded exchanges between the two factions, which took place

---

[3] H. M. Schueller's 'The Quarrel of the Ancients and the Moderns', *Music and Letters*, 41 (1960): 313–30, remains in many ways the most comprehensive study to date, tracing the ancient–modern polarity from its seventeenth-century origins through the end of the eighteenth century. J. C. Kassler's introduction to R. North, *Roger North's The Musicall Grammarian 1728*, eds Mary Chan and J. C. Kassler (Cambridge: Cambridge University Press, 1990), pp. 3–17, offers a valuable discussion of the intellectual roots of the dispute. Studies of the late eighteenth-century phase of the quarrel include C. L. Cudworth, 'An Essay by John Marsh', *Music and Letters*, 36 (1955): 155–64 and Cudworth's edition of J. Marsh, 'Hints to Young Composers of Instrumental Music', *Galpin Society Journal*, 18 (1965), 57–71; Thomas McGeary's chapter on 'Music Literature' in *The Blackwell History of Music in Britain*, vol. 4 *The Eighteenth Century*, eds H. Diack Johnstone and Roger Fisk (Oxford and Cambridge, Blackwell, 1990), pp. 397–421, and Thomas B. Milligan's *The Concerto and London's Musical Culture in the Late Eighteenth Century* (Ann Arbor, MI: UMI Research Press, 1983), pp. 3–5. Most of the important issues of the quarrel are discussed in detail in the introduction to Enrico Fubini, *Music and Culture in Eighteenth-Century Europe: A Source Book*, trans. Wolfgang Fries, Lisa Basbarrone and Michael Louis Leone, eds, Bonnie J. Blackburn (Chicago and London: University of Chicago Press, 1994). The ancient–modern polemic is also a recurrent theme in Wilson, *Anglican Chant*, and Zon's *English Plainchant*. Additional references to an ancient–modern divide include Stanley Sadie, 'Concert Life in Eighteenth Century England', *Proceedings of the Royal Musical Association*, 85 (1958–59), 17–30, and Nicholas Temperley, 'Handel's Influence on English Music', *The Monthly Musical Record*, 90 (1960), 163–74.

[4] William Weber, *The Rise of Musical Classics in Eighteenth-Century England: A Study of Canon, Ritual, and Ideology* (Oxford: Clarendon Press, 1992), pp. 25–74; See also, Wilson, *Anglican Chant* and Zon, *English Plainchant*.

in the seventeenth century, before either side regularly employed the words 'ancient' and 'modern' in this context, have been explored.[5] Still other scholars have examined a related ancient–modern quarrel from the late seventeenth century waged by parties that *did* identify themselves as ancients and moderns. Although the words 'ancient' and 'modern' did not have the same meaning then that they did later, the famous international ancient–modern quarrel of the seventeenth century concerned – to the limited extent that music was involved – the same issues of form versus content that persisted as a central issue of music criticism a century later.[6]

Two aspects of the ancient–modern debate have received substantially less attention. First, while an ideology of ancient music has been described in careful detail,[7] the ideology of the moderns and in particular the moderns of the later eighteenth century has scarcely been delineated beyond a basic advocacy of some form of the notion of progress.[8] Closely related is the fact that too little attention has been focused on the ancient–modern debate as it applies to concert music in particular and to the time period, stretching into the nineteenth century, that Crotch discusses. When the quarrel surfaces in recent scholarship

---

[5] By far the best and most extensive presentation of the seventeenth-century intellectual origins of the ancient–modern divide is found in J. C. Kassler's introduction to North's *Musicall Grammarian*, especially pp. 5–17.

[6] Music is overlooked in the most extensive studies of the seventeenth-century ancient–modern quarrel by Joseph M. Levine, *The Battle of the Books: History and Literature in the Augustan Age* (Ithaca, NY: Cornell University Press, 1991); *idem*, 'Ancients and Moderns Reconsidered', *Eighteenth-Century Studies*, 15 (1981), 72–89 and *idem*, 'Edward Gibbon and the Quarrel between the Ancients and the Moderns', *Humanism and History: Origins of Modern English Historiography* (Ithaca, NY: Cornell University Press, 1987), pp. 178–89. H. M. Schueller deals with music in the context of the Battle of the Books, however, in 'The Quarrel of the Ancients and the Moderns', especially p. 18. A useful treatment of relevant musical issues of the seventeenth and early eighteenth centuries is found in D. T. Mace, 'Musical Humanism, the Doctrine of Rhythmus, and the Saint Cecilia Odes of Dryden', *Journal of the Warburg and Courtauld Institute*, 27 (1963), 251–92.

[7] Weber, *Rise of Musical Classics*, especially in the chapter 'The Ideology of Ancient Music', pp. 198–222.

[8] Kassler discusses the ideology of the seventeenth century moderns in her introduction to North's *Musicall Grammarian*, pp. 7–11. In many ways the ideologies of the two sides in this earlier period resemble their counterparts a century later. Kassler notes that the late seventeenth-century 'ancients', much like the most militant ancient supporters in the later eighteenth century 'were concerned to preserve the status quo', and that 'their most prominent spokesmen tended to be high-church clerics, relentless foes of Latitudinarianism and dissent, enemies of toleration and comprehension, staunch Royalists and Tories'. The moderns were divided into two camps, one advocating radical reform of the educational system and Utopian planning and the other more accepting of traditional social values.

there is a tendency to interpret it as a purely eighteenth-century phenomenon and as a simple case of reactionaries struggling with
progressives.[9] This approach overlooks the complex and sometimes
self-contradictory web of related issues that tend to accompany contemporary writing on the subject.

There are good reasons for giving the late eighteenth-century phase of
the quarrel special attention. First, the several late eighteenth-century
writers whose critical ideas are examined here knew each other and –
especially when they could do so anonymously – responded in print to
each other's ideas. There is, therefore, much more of the effect of a
dialogue or exchange in their writing than is usually true in British
music criticism. Their critical writing also appears at an important
point in the development of music criticism itself. British music criticism, as Charles Burney explained in 1789, had only come into being a
half-century before Crotch began lecturing.[10] By the early nineteenth
century this new critical discipline was only beginning to develop the
self-awareness to look back on its brief history and assess its future
prospects. As many have noted, the middle of the eighteenth century
marks the birth of this new branch of criticism with a shift in writing
about music from a pastime of literary men mainly interested in the
mythical music of the ancient Greeks to a field led by professional
musicians with more practical interests.[11] But after an initial burst of
activity that produced Charles Avison's *Essay on Musical Expression*
(2nd edn, London, 1753) and Charles Burney's *General History of
Music* (1776–89), critical writing on music seemed to fall into neglect.
A perception of neglect, in fact, was part of the rationale offered for the
introduction in the year after Crotch's 1818 lecture series of the first
successful British musical periodical in which criticism was regularly
featured, *The Quarterly Musical Magazine and Review (QMMR)*.[12]

---

[9] Fubini's introduction to *Music and Culture*, pp. 28–30, for example, discusses ancient–modern tensions in the context of the Burney–Hawkins dispute, contrasting Burney
the progressive empiricist with Hawkins the reactionary rationalist. In much the same
way, Kerry S. Grant views Burney in *Dr. Burney as Critic and Historian of Music* (Ann
Arbor, MI: UMI Research Press, 1983) as a straightforward progressive in his dealings
with the Handelian faction.

[10] C. Burney, 'Essay on Musical Criticism', *A General History of Music*, with critical
and historical notes by Frank Mercer (London, 1935; New York: Dover, 1957) (hereafter *General History*), vol. 2, p. 7.

[11] For example, Schueller, 'The Quarrel of the Ancients and the Moderns': 324;
Lawrence Lipking, *The Ordering of the Arts in Eighteenth-Century England* (Princeton,
NJ: Princeton University Press, 1970), pp. 211–14.

[12] The place of *The Quarterly Musical Magazine and Review* in British criticism is
discussed in Jamie Croy Kassler, *The Science of Music in Britain 1714–1830: a Catalogue of Writings, Lectures, and Inventions*, 2 vols (New York: Garland, 1979) and in

The most important reason for giving Crotch's account of an ancient–modern quarrel a hearing is that it bears on the question of the origins and development of the notion of classical music and of a canon of respected master works. Others – in particular William Weber – have identified the British ancient-music community as the source both for a canon of widely accepted, frequently performed secular masterpieces and for the social rituals, institutions and aesthetic values that make up the notion of classical music. Research into both canon formation and the development of classical music has been limited by the arbitrary boundary marked by the end of the eighteenth century, however. Many of the processes that helped form later notions of classical music had only been set into motion at the eighteenth century's end and therefore need to be followed into the early years of the new century.

Crotch's interpretation of the events of his time does not always mesh comfortably with certain other evidence of contemporary London concert life. This is most noticeable when he asserts a resolution to the ancient–modern conflict in 1818, much earlier than would seem justified by other evidence. The public concerts that Crotch cites in his 1818 lecture (i.e., the Philharmonic Society) do not yet exhibit the balance of old and new that Crotch, in his idealism, is eager to pronounce as normative. In the area of sacred music, the ancient–modern polemic has been shown to have continued long after the truce Crotch proclaims. Indeed, Crotch's own later correspondence on this subject continues the rhetoric of ancient–modern division.[13] More generally, many of the phenomena Crotch describes as innovations in 1818 – the conspicuous demonstrations of respect afforded performers, the respectful silence at modern-music concerts, and the mixed ancient–modern programme – have been detected long before the period Crotch discusses.[14] It is important to keep in mind, however, that Crotch speaks in his lectures of changes in particular spheres of musical activity – primarily opera, concert and chamber music – and that his remarks concern the general acceptance of a new way of looking at music and its institutions among the cross-section of London society that formed his lecture audience. Viewed as merely one stage in the long evolution of a concept, his lectures offer an important contemporary account of the development

---

Leanne Langley, 'The English Musical Journal in the Early Nineteenth Century' (PhD, University of North Carolina, Chapel Hill, NC, 1983), pp. 54 and 195.

[13] In his *History of English Cathedral Music 1549–1889*, vol. 2, p. 370 (2 vols, London: T. Werner Laurie, 1908), John S. Bumpus quotes from a letter Crotch wrote to the founder of the Gresham Prize for sacred music in 1833 in which Crotch complains of 'the decay so long apparent in our Church music'.

[14] Simon McVeigh, *Concert Life in London from Mozart to Haydn*, (Cambridge and New York: Cambridge University Press, 1993), pp. 62–3.

of classical music by an active, well read and unusually gifted contemporary observer.

Who was William Crotch?

The name William Crotch is most likely to be encountered today in a few specific contexts. Many know him as a celebrated infant prodigy whose gifts were carefully documented in the last quarter of the eighteenth century in long essays by Daines Barrington and music historian Charles Burney.[15] He is also familiar in British choral music circles as a minor early nineteenth-century composer of oratorios, anthems and service music.[16] Still others know him from Handel studies or even as an accomplished water colourist.[17] Above all, Crotch has been identified for nearly 200 years as a distinguished academic. He succeeded Philip Hayes as Oxford University's Heather Professor in 1797 and served as the first Principal of the Royal Academy of Music when it was founded in 1822. Consistent with his status as primarily an educator, Crotch's publications are mostly intended for amateurs and students. These include a few rudiments texts, a considerable body of piano transcriptions, a book summarizing his three decades as a popular public lecturer that was published under the title *Substance of Several Courses of Lectures on Music* (London, 1831), and a three-volume anthology of the music performed at these lecture-recital programmes, published as *Specimens of Various Styles of Music Referred to in a Course of Lectures read at Oxford and London* (London, c. 1806).

Crotch has probably attracted less scholarly attention in his role as critic than as an educator and composer, or so one might judge from the absence of any large-scale study of his critical activities and by the fact that most of his lectures have still not been made available in a modern

---

[15] Daines Barrington, 'Some Account of Little Crotch', in *Miscellanies* (London, 1781), pp. 311–25; Burney, 'Account of an Infant Musician', in *Philsophical Transactions of the Royal Society of London*, 69 (1779), 183–206. See also, Michael Raeburn, 'Dr Burney, Mozart, and Crotch', *The Musical Times*, 97 (October 1956), 519–20.

[16] Jonathan Rennert, 'William Crotch (1775–1847) – Worth Reviving?' *The Consort*, 31 (1975), 116–25, and *idem*, 'William Crotch, 1775–1847', *Musical Times*, 116 (1975), 622–3.

[17] For Crotch's place in Handel criticism, see, among others, George J. Buelow, 'The Case for Handel's Borrowings: the Judgment of Three Centuries', in Stanley Sadie and Anthony Hicks, eds, *Handel Tercentenary Collection* (Ann Arbor, MI: UMI Research Press, 1987), pp. 61–82. I. Fleming-Williams, 'William Crotch, Member of the Oxford School and Friend of Constable', *The Connoisseur*, 159 (1963), 140.

edition.[18] That may be caused by a regrettable and incomplete impression of him as a pedagogue and reactionary. The above mentioned *Substance of Several Courses of Lectures on Music* may be to blame for this. The public lectures Crotch summarizes in this book, like the 15 *Discourses on Art* of his acknowledged model Sir Joshua Reynolds, were intended to have a critical as well as a pedagogical function. A major portion of each of the original lectures involved the performance and criticism of specific examples, some of which were either new at the time or at least new to the British audience. The *Substance* – a condensation of 30 years of lectures – is, by contrast, justifiably regarded as a pedagogical work[19] because its focus is squarely on the music of an earlier time and its character therefore more that of a presentation of well-established truth than an exploration of new music or a practical guide to uncharted aesthetic territory. In the *Substance* Crotch dispatches recent figures like Mendelssohn, Spohr and Weber in a single sentence, devoting the bulk of his attention to the period before about 1760. The *Substance* also imitates Reynolds's *Discourses* in its preference for statements of general aesthetic principle over the detailed criticism of particular examples. The aesthetic principles summarized in the *Substance*, however, were far from new even 60 years earlier when Reynolds first began to set into crystallized form the collection of widely held opinions about art that make up much of neo-classical aesthetic theory.

The *Substance*'s fixation on the music and ideas of an earlier time is a reflection of the fact that it was written at the end of Crotch's career. His best and most original critical ideas came early, like his celebrated performance ability. The theory of art that Crotch first adapted and developed as a young lecturer at Oxford had never before been consistently applied to music criticism by his few professional predecessors in this critical discipline. Music was very much in need of a critical writer with a status and credibility as a practitioner, comparable to that which Reynolds enjoyed in painting, to explain how it might fit into the aesthetic systems of the eighteenth century. Had Crotch been more assertive when he first began his lecturing career in 1798, a year after Edmond Malone's first complete edition of Reynolds's *Discourses*, he might have fulfilled this role.[20] Unfortunately, for reasons that can be considered shortly, the *Substance* was delayed for 25 years from the point at which Crotch

---

[18] One of the most extensive discussions of Crotch's role as a lecturer and author is found in Kassler, *The Science of Music in Britain*, vol. 1, pp. 229–44.

[19] A reprint of the *Substance* has been issued by Boethius Press (Clarabricken, Co Kilkenny, Ireland, 1986) in a series of 'Classic Texts in Music Education'.

[20] Reynolds's *Discourses on Art* were published individually between 1769 and 1790 as they were read at annual (later semi-annual) prize-giving ceremonies at the Royal Academy of Art. In addition, a collection of the first seven of the *Discourses* was

probably first intended to offer it. And since the *Substance*, as the only accessible source of Crotch's ideas, has been the primary source for nearly all that has been written about him for well over a century, Crotch has seemed more intensely preoccupied with the past than he actually was during his most influential years as a public lecturer.

The manuscript lectures reprinted in their original form for the first time in this volume were written a year after the belated first London performances of *Don Giovanni* in 1817. They show a very different side of Crotch from the later book and from many of his earlier lectures. Much of this series is not devoted to a pre-1760 golden age but rather to introducing British listeners to challenging new music and to preparing the way for the new musical system mentioned above. This new system as Crotch describes it is profoundly different from the musical infrastructure of his youth in the way music is expected to be heard and the way musical institutions are to be managed. Crotch speaks of a new kind of professionally managed concert, accessible to the general audience, in which old music is mixed with contemporary master-works in such a way as to entertain as well as edify. His introductory lecture in 1818 describes, then, a system of institutions and values that is consistent with the culture of classical music but different in many ways from that of the ancient music community. Although the intellectual starting-point of Crotch's lectures is the earlier critical tradition of ancient music as it is found in the writing of figures like William Jones of Nayland and Sir John Hawkins, Crotch extends and modifies commonplace assumptions of this tradition in fundamental ways.

Crotch's lectures

Publishing a first-person account of pivotal socio-cultural developments by a reliable contemporary observer who was both a gifted musician and a competent aesthetician requires little justification. But since Crotch's lecture notes have already been gleaned once by their author for the above mentioned *Substance*, there may be a need to explain further not only why they need to be reproduced in their original form but also why this particular set has been chosen from the considerable body of available material, why they have been arranged in this particular order and why it is necessary to preface Crotch's text with the extended introduction that forms Part One of this book.

---

published in 1778. It was from this second, incomplete collection that Crotch first became acquainted with Reynolds's ideas in 1790, as Crotch relates in his *Memoirs*, NRO, MS 11244, p. 75.

First, the present edition was made possible by the discovery some years ago of a number of bound volumes containing materials by Crotch in the archives of the Norfolk Record Office (NRO).[21] The NRO volumes, which include more than 1 000 pages of lecture notes as well as correspondence, Crotch's *Memoirs*, and other valuable papers, were assembled near the beginning of the present century by Cambridge scholar A. H. Mann in preparation for a book on Crotch that was never written. Mann's several volumes are not publishable in their present state, nor would they be even with substantial editing. As Mann himself observed, the lectures were placed in their present binding not because they were 'an actual series of such works, but a miscellaneous lot, bound together to preserve them'.[22] At the same time, one can see from lectures that once served to introduce or conclude a series that Crotch often intended to develop a central theme through the several lectures that made up his classes, and these themes are not easy to follow in the disarray of the NRO volumes.

Mann's decision not to arrange the lectures in a systematic ordering that would reflect the way they were actually heard by Crotch's audiences no doubt has to do with the constant editing and reuse to which these notes were subjected over a period of 30 years or more. It is often not easy even with the aid of the *General Account of all the Courses of Lectures*[23] that Crotch prepared near the end of his career to identify or date individual lectures because of changes made much later that can obscure their origins. The most extensive changes appear, of course, in connection with relatively recent figures like Haydn, whose fortunes varied considerably during the years Crotch lectured in response to rapidly shifting aesthetic values. Crotch's alterations are, therefore, of some interest in themselves in connection with Haydn's reception history. Still, together with different versions of individual lectures prepared to accommodate the purposes of different lecture series, these alterations complicate considerably the task of putting together an edition of the lectures that might be for music what Reynolds's *Discourses* are to painting.

While in many cases it is not profitable to try to identify a definitive version of Crotch's lectures or to put them into an ordered sequence,

---

[21] See, C. B. Oldman, 'Dr Burney and Mozart', in *Mozart Jahrbuch 1962–1963*, pp. 75–81 (Kassel: Internationale Stiftung Mozarteum Salzburg, 1964), and *idem*, 'Dr Burney and Mozart: Addenda and Corrigenda', *Mozart Jahrbuch 1964*, pp. 109–10 (Kassel: Internationale Stiftung Mozarteum Salzburg, 1964). Mann's notes on the lectures are found on the covers of individual volumes and in NRO, MS 11210.

[22] NRO, MS 11210.

[23] Crotch's *General Account of the Lectures* (hereafter *General Account*) is inserted between the seventh and eighth lectures of NRO, MS 11230.

the present set of eight forms a cohesive whole that is an important exception to this pattern. These notes date from a period of change in Crotch's thinking and, accordingly, from a time of renewed productivity after two decades during which he added little to the stock of ideas he had been expressing from some of the same yellowed pages since his earliest Oxford presentations. Crotch's *General Account* shows that the years 1817 and 1818 produced a remarkable total of 16 new lectures. However, it is not the number of new contributions that is of greatest interest here but a new focus. The *General Account* describes a group of lectures from 1808 as 'in a great measure new, being written after a *re*perusal of Sir Joshua Reynolds Lectures & Price on the Picturesque', but most of what was new had to do with minor points of aesthetic theory. These 1808 lectures still concentrate on the same body of seventeenth- and early eighteenth-century music that Crotch had made the centrepiece of his lecturing career from the beginning.

In the 1817 and 1818 lectures, by contrast, there is a much greater representation of more recent music, including works like *Don Giovanni*, *La clemenza di Tito*, Mozart's quartets K. 421 and 387, Haydn's *The Creation*, his 'London' symphonies and Op. 76 quartets, and Clementi's *Gradus ad Parnassum*. These lectures also take a significantly more critical look at earlier figures including Handel. Crotch's 1818 treatment of the *Dettingen Te Deum* includes his condemnation of a specific act of borrowing by Handel, a rarity to say the least for this usually stalwart defender of Handel's practices. One of the 1817 lectures is similarly candid in its evaluation of *Judas Maccabaeus*, going so far as to brand some of its movements 'contemptible to the refined taste of the judicious critic'.[24] At the same time, Crotch is so generous in his praise of music in the modern style and of Mozart in particular that the second lecture of his 1818 series concludes with reassurance for the regulars in Crotch's class that despite appearances his basic principles and values remained unchanged. The shift in Crotch's thinking that forced him to accept the role of balanced critic over that of defender of ancient music also prompted him to offer with greater clarity and directness a message that is often implicit in his earlier work: that modern music had improved considerably from a point he identifies as the period of its greatest decline in the late 1770s and that this improvement is the direct result of efforts by the best modern composers to buttress the modern style through the self-conscious adaptation of values and stylistic elements Crotch associates with ancient music.

Nearly all of Crotch's detailed discussions of specific works in the modern style were omitted from the later *Substance*, either because the

---

[24] *Lectures*, NRO, MS 11229/7.

music in question was no longer contemporary enough in 1831 to merit close attention as new music, because a concentration on the particular distracted from his larger purpose of offering statements of general truth, or simply because of a regrettable terseness that characterizes much of Crotch's published writing. This last characteristic, together with an unfortunate tendency to take for granted that contemporary audiences would share an admittedly dated aesthetic well into the nineteenth century, makes his writing unusually liable to misunderstanding and very much in need of introduction and clarification.[25]

Another reason for choosing these particular lectures has to do with the fact that the years spanned by Crotch's lectures are both important in the history of musical canon formation and otherwise relatively poor in published critical writing on music by professionals. In the inaugural issue of *QMMR*, editor Richard Mackenzie Bacon charges that musicians characteristically avoided writing about their art except for 'a few (and they are a very few) regular treatises on the more abstruse branches' of the science.[26] In making this observation he perhaps tactfully overlooks unsuccessful recent attempts at published music criticism by professionals such as German-born A. F. C. Kollmann's *Quarterly Musical Register*. Kollmann's valuable journal had failed after only two issues a few years before *QMMR*'s appearance, probably because of a popular bias against professionals that was quick to brand their writing inelegant and self-serving.[27] Bacon's assessment of the state of music criticism, however, overlooks oral presentations of the kind Crotch had pioneered a dozen years earlier as a legitimate alternative to the printed word. In fact, the opportunity that lecture-recital programmes like Crotch's offered for the illustration of important points through the performance of musical examples made them arguably a superior, though admittedly a more ephemeral, vehicle for criticism in any case.

There had been music lectures in and around London long before Crotch, but they had never featured performance to the same extent nor

---

[25] Some possible causes of later writers' frequent misunderstandings of Crotch's treatment of Handel are explored in Howard Irving, 'William Crotch on Borrowing', *The Music Review*, 53 (1992), 237–54.

[26] 'Plan of the Work', *QMMR*, 1 (1818–19), 1–2. Noting that 'it is rather a matter of wonder we have no periodical work exclusively devoted to [music]' Bacon suggests a reason: 'practical musicians very much disregard such attempts. It should almost seem that the symbols by which we express the objects of our other faculties are considered to be inapplicable to our appreciation of sounds, and that words in their combinations could do nothing, either to improve the practice or to increase the enjoyment of the art'.

[27] See an anonymous review of Kollmann's journal in 'Review of New Musical Publications', *Gentleman's Magazine* (hereafter *GM*), 83 (1813), 354–6.

had they surveyed the broad range of musical styles and periods that his did.[28] In many cases the performance of examples may have been limited by the difficulty and expense of hiring a professional ensemble. J. R. S. Stevens, Professor of Music at Gresham College, notes that at the well-known musical lecture series at his institution lectures were supposed to be 'half an hour Theoretical, and half an hour Practical' but that his predecessor in the position, a Dr Aylward, had ignored performance altogether. Stevens tried to 'revive in some degree the neglected custom' of performance and, on 13 May 1801, he 'read the life of Agostino Steffani, and exhibited some of his works'. The examples in this case were all duets performed by two male singers with Stevens at the piano. Stevens observes that 'the Novelty of such an Exhibition at this place attracted an audience of 64 persons', a respectable if, perhaps, atypical crowd by the standards of his later efforts. This lecture, in fact, set a pattern for Stevens's subsequent programmes, all of which had to rely on vocal ensembles made up of his church-music colleagues and acquaintances for the performance of examples. This, of course, limited considerably the range of Stevens's lectures and precluded critical discussion of recent instrumental music.[29]

Crotch circumvented the problem of limited performance resources in his London lectures by playing lengthy musical 'specimens' himself on either the organ, piano or harpsichord. These examples, drawn from a full range of musical genres, made up roughly half of each hour-long programme.[30] Although he initially objected to this approach as unsatisfactory by comparison with the full orchestra he had enjoyed in his first lecturers in Oxford's Music Room,[31] Crotch's remarkable facility for reproducing orchestral effects at the keyboard from open score was

---

[28] Other music lectures are discussed in J. C. Kassler, 'British Writings on Music, 1760–1830: a Systematic Essay toward a philosophy of Selected Writings' (PhD, Columbia University, New York, 1971), pp. 280–91.

[29] R. J. S. Stevens, *Recollections of R. J. S. Stevens, an Organist in Georgian London*, ed. Mark Argent (Carbondale, IL: Southern Illinois University Press, 1992), pp. 120–21.

[30] Crotch's lecture notes sometimes specify which instruments were used for particular examples. See Howard Irving, 'William Crotch on *The Creation*', *Music and Letters*, 75 (1994), 548–60. Kassler provides further information about the mechanics of Crotch's lectures in 'The Royal Institution Music Lectures, 1800–1831: a Preliminary Study', *The Royal Musical Association Research Chronicle*, 19 (1983–85), 13–21.

[31] Crotch's *Correspondence* includes a letter addressed to 'Rev. Dr. Jowett/Trinity Hall/Cambridge' dated 17 December 1804 in which Crotch discusses his upcoming lecture series at the Royal Institution. With regard to the musical examples, Crotch remarks, 'I represented the stupidity of [not having an orchestra] as strongly as I could, to the managers but they wished me to perform my examples myself ... '. He indicates that both a piano and a harpsichord were to be available for the January 1805 lecture series.

often remembered by contemporaries and students.[32] His lecture-recitals, then, formed a kind of hybrid presentation of arts and letters that replaced traditional complaints about the musician's narrowness and awkwardness with language with a new strength and fed on the contemporary popularity of transcriptions. In so doing, Crotch helped to define in the public mind a new conception of the skill and preparation required for credible music criticism. By 1829, *The Harmonicon* accepted his lecture-recital format as the definitive plan for a serious public presentation on music.[33] The influence Crotch's lectures had in nineteenth-century musical life is indicated by the extent to which his ideas and terminology were adopted by others at the time and by the fact that they continued to be remembered at the end of the century by individuals like J. S. Shedlock, William H. Husk and Sir George Grove.[34]

Crotch's lectures can help fill a lacuna that now exists in studies of the development of musical classics. Attention has mostly been focused on two points, the beginnings of classical music in the ancient-music

---

[32] See, Anonymous, 'Memoir of William Crotch, Mus. Doc.', *The Harmonicon*, 9 (1831), 4. 'Dr. Crotch's talents as an organist or piano-forte player, which are of the highest order, has, with the exception of his performance at his Lectures, been chiefly confined to the circle of his private friends. His particular merit consists in score-playing and giving the effect of a full band on an organ or piano-forte.' See also, J. R. Sterndale Bennett, *The Life of William Sterndale Bennett* (Cambridge: Cambridge University Press, 1907), p. 27. 'A great musical treat, often enjoyed by his class [at the Royal Academy of Music], was his playing from memory a series of the Choruses of Handel, which he could select with endless variety.' J. R. S. Stevens also speaks highly of Crotch's abilities in *Recollections*, pp. 179 and 187.

[33] Anonymous, 'Dr. Crotch's Lectures' *The Harmonicon* 7 (1829), 160. 'As practical examples of various composers, nothing could have been better calculated for the purpose than those produced and performed by the highly-gifted professor; but in a scientific institution, and one that ranks so high, we have always thought that the science of music, strictly so called, should at least divide the lecture with the practice'.

[34] See, Bernarr Rainbow *The Choral Revival in the Anglican Church 1839–1872* (New York: Oxford University Press, 1970). Rainbow notes (pp. 61–2) that Thomas Helmore, an important figure in the Tractarian Movement and in the revival choral of the choral tradition, also lectured on church music and used Crotch's terminology. Samuel Wesley also adopted Crotch's division of music into the 'sublime', the 'beautiful' and the 'ornamental' styles, though he seems to have misunderstood partially Crotch's meaning. Some of Wesley's lectures are contained in the British Museum (BM Add. Ms 35.014). Crotch's lectures are mentioned by Shedlock in J. S. Shedlock. 'Handel's Borrowings', *The Musical Times*, 42 (1901), 450–51, 526–7, 596–8, and by William Henry Husk in 'Crotch, William', Sir George Grove, ed. *A Dictionary of Music and Musicians* (London, 1899), vol. 1, p. 420. Grove himself included 'Specimens, Crotch's' as a separate entry in his *Dictionary* and listed the individual titles of the examples contained therein. See, Nicholas Temperley, introduction to William Crotch *Symphony in F Major*, in Barry Brook and Barbara B. Heyman, eds, *The Symphony: 1720–1840*, 60 vols (New York: Garland, 1984), pp. ix–xiii.

movement before 1800 and the period after 1850, by which point the notion of a musical canon and the institutions that serve to perpetuate it were in place in a recognizable form.[35] There are good reasons for interest in these two points, although certain aspects of British ancient-music culture urge wariness in embracing this particular old-music tradition as a straightforward beginning for a musical canon. Still, any insecurities here may be overshadowed by a great many points of similarity between ancient-music culture and the classical tradition. Above all, the essence of classical music in the minds of many may be the spectacle of a social élite listening attentively to old music and thinking of it as morally and aesthetically superior to the products of popular culture. This is a picture that develops clearly well before the year 1800, and it is probably with this image in mind that some studies choose to focus exclusively on the eighteenth century.

The year 1800 marks a point at which attention naturally shifts away from England and the works of Handel, Corelli and others towards a later and more glamorous stage of canon formation centring on the German-speaking countries and the Viennese classics and beginning in the 1820s. British traditions may seem to have little to offer at this point, since the ideology of ancient music as it has been described in the writing of men like William Jones of Nayland and Sir John Hawkins specifically rejects stylistic features of the music of moderns like Haydn, Mozart and Beethoven as inconsistent with, and even antithetical to, the principles that made music worthy of preservation and classical status in the first place.[36] Despite some discomfort with what are viewed

---

[35] See, for example, William Weber 'Wagner, Wagnerism, and Musical Idealism', in David C. Large and William Weber, eds, *Wagnerism in European Culture and Politics* (Ithaca, NY and London: Cornell University Press, 1984), pp. 28–71, and 'The Rise of the Classical Repertoire in Nineteenth-Century Orchestral Concerts', in Joan Peyser, ed., *The Orchestra: Origins and Transformations* (New York: Charles Scribner's Sons, 1986), pp. 361–86.

[36] Briefly, a central theme of Weber's chapter 'The Ideology of Ancient Music' (*Rise of Musical Classics*, pp. 198–222) is that the modern style lacks substance. The most musically sophisticated individuals Weber cites depict the modern style as discursive and disorderly and complain that it makes too little use of the musical elements of counterpoint or 'harmony' that give music its substance and integrity. In his *A Treatise on the Art of Music, in which the Elements of HARMONY and AIR are Practically Considered* ... (Colchester, 1784), p. 49, William Jones (of Nayland) cites Haydn in particular for these faults. In the writings of Burney, another of the individuals Weber uses to establish an ancient ideology, counterpoint or harmony is treated as the primary musical element that gives music longevity and therefore makes it eligible for a status as classical. Burney's thinking on this subject is explored in Howard Irving, 'Classic and Gothic: Charles Burney on Ancient Music', *Studies in Eighteenth Century Culture*, 23 (1993), 243–63.

as the extremes of the German style, Crotch's lectures serve a valuable purpose by connecting the ancient-music tradition with the later Viennese classics-based canon. In the process of making this connection, Crotch clarified certain principles on which the idea of classical music rests and opened the concept, at least in theory, to the possibility of the contemporary master-work that continues to be an important part of this notion.

The moderns

The voice of the moderns is less clear in this study than that of the ancients. One reason for this is inherent in the notion of 'modern music' itself, any conception of which necessarily lacks the relative stability of an established repertory and tradition. The situation of the particular group of moderns that is of interest here was especially difficult because their conception of modern music did not even come from a clearly defined repertory on whose stylistic principles all could agree. Instead, it came from an aesthetic ideal with ideological overtones that was derived from Neapolitan opera, a music that could itself no longer be viewed as modern. Further, during the period that Crotch surveys in his 1818 lectures the homophonic instrumental style that was 'modern' by comparison with Handel was well advanced in its evolution into something very different from its aesthetic roots in Neapolitan opera.

The moderns also lacked a candid and effective spokesman. The most familiar name in the modern camp, Charles Burney, can be found on both sides of the ancient–modern divide. In some ways the distinction of forthright modern should instead go to Burney's occasional friend and correspondent, the Reverend William Mason. Mason – a poet, political figure, Preceptor of York Minster and, above all, quintessential dilettante – was, more than any other individual considered here, the kind of person Burney must have visualized when he imagined a partisan for modern music and its values. Like many others identified here as moderns, Mason was not merely a literary critic of music but something of a practical musician as well. Burney once wrote that he could, play 'very well the Harp^d & knows the thing thoroughly'.[37] Mason was also a composer, especially of a few stage works, and the inventor of a new musical instrument, the celestinette. Horace Walpole called it 'a copulation of a harpsichord and a violin' in which 'one hand strikes the keys

[37] Charles Burney (hereafter CB) to Elizabeth (Mrs Stephen) Allen *c*. 20 April 1764 in Alvaro S. J. Ribeiro, ed., *The Letters of Dr Charles Burney*, vol. 1, *1751–1784* (Oxford, Clarendon Press, 1991), pp. 39–40.

and the other draws the bow'. 'The sounds are prolonged', Walpole reports, 'and it is the softest and most touching melody I ever heard.'[38]

Mason knew and maintained a correspondence with most of the important figures in the arts and letters, though his politics left him estranged from many in the Johnsonian circle. As a writer on music, his most substantial contributions are his four *Essays, Historical and Critical on English Church Music*, published as a set at the end of his life in 1795. The *Essays* are not of interest here because they are brilliant, original, or even carefully researched and unusually well written. For that matter, even the most sympathetic study of Mason to date – published in 1924, when interest in his poetry was, perhaps, at a lower point that it is now – does not justify itself on the basis of Mason's value as a critic or poet. Instead, John Draper's book on Mason is 'A Study in Eighteenth Century Culture', valuing Mason's very commonplaceness and his role as 'a lively embodiment, of the culture of his class and age'.[39] In much the same way, his significance as a music critic comes from the fact that his *Essays* summarize in a more frank, concise and overtly partisan manner than Burney's writing, a collection of familiar ideas and points of view that directly oppose both the aesthetic and the ideology of the critical tradition of ancient music.

Mason's contributions to the ancient–modern quarrel are not limited to the *Essays*. By the time the *Essays* appeared late in the century, their message was already well on its way towards being irrelevant. Besides, the *Essays* are addressed to a limited although ideologically significant corner of the musical world in church music. They do not specifically take on the secular ancient music culture of the last quarter of the eighteenth century, although they are filled with aesthetic pronouncements that have a broader application than Mason's nominal area of interest. Instead, Mason's greatest influence on music criticism came from his role as correspondent and informal adviser to the first professional music critics, Charles Avison and Charles Burney. In this capacity, Mason was able to shape the issues and interests of music criticism. In fact, the most important evidence for Mason's influence – aside from surviving correspondence that documents his exchanges with both of the men named above – is the existence of plainly contradictory points of view within the writing of Avison and Burney, one of which is obviously in line with Mason's *Essays*.

---

[38] Walpole to Sir William Hamilton, 19 June 1774 in Horace Walpole, *The Yale Edition of Horace Walpole's Correspondence*, ed. W. S. Lewis (New Haven, CT, 1937–83), vol. 35, p. 423.

[39] John Draper, *William Mason: a Study in Eighteenth-Century Culture* (New York: New York University Press, 1924), p. 15.

Burney certainly had his differences with Mason over the specific area of church music. But in letters to Mason and in the second volume of the *General History* Burney still repeatedly defers to Mason's judgement on the important aesthetic issue of the ancient–modern quarrel, the question of whether music should be judged according to the content it can convey or express or by virtue of purely musical values.[40] Only in a lengthy anonymous review of Mason's book did Burney address candidly their real differences on music. In this late source, as in many other reviews from the 1790s, Burney's candour was assisted by the fact that his anxieties over the hostilities in France had caused him to back away from what he often called in correspondence his 'liberal principles'. For most of his career Burney thought of Mason as the epitome of a cultivated man who was 'nearly as good a Musician & Painter as Poet'.[41]

The contemporary assessment of Mason may be less favourable. The picture of Mason that emerges from Draper's careful study does not inspire confidence in Mason's musical opinions, especially when Draper describes him as 'not sufficiently deep-rooted intellectually to hold very firmly to principles, literary or otherwise, in opposition to the spirit of the age' so that 'with an unconscious ease, he naturally shifted his sails to any wind that blew'.[42] The most uncomfortable aspect of this characterization is that it sounds all too close to Charles Burney himself. At the same time, one can apply to both men – as well as most of the other modern partisans considered here – Draper's pre-emptive defense against an inevitable charge of their superficiality: 'if one sneers at Mason, one must sneer at the age'.[43]

Charles Burney and the quarrel

The figure on the modern side whose thinking is most in need of close examination is Burney himself. Burney continues to be depicted in

---

[40] In *General History*, vol. 2, p. 125, Burney approves of Mason's censure of 'Bird, and other old masters' in 'his excellent *Essay on Church-Music*' for their 'inattention to prosody, accent, and quantity, in setting English words'. Likewise, in correspondence with Mason (Ribeiro, *Letters*, p. 340), Burney is prepared to concede the 'absurdity of Fugue, Canon, & other Gothic Contrivances, in rendering the words of vocal music unintelligible'. But in his review of Mason's *Essays* in *Monthly Review*, 20 (1796): 403, Burney is more supportive of cathedral music and more willing to accept that texts could indeed be intelligible in fugues if they were set carefully.

[41] CB to Elizabeth (Mrs Stephen) Allen, c. 20 April 1764, in Ribeiro, *Letters*, p. 39.

[42] Draper, *William Mason*, p. 95.

[43] Ibid.

recent scholarship on both sides of an ideological fence: as a staunch
Tory who, as Samuel Johnson defined Toryism, ought to be an advocate
of the *status quo*, but at the same time as an unashamed progressive in
music and a champion of innovation; as a vigorous opponent of counterpoint but also a dedicated Handel supporter; and as a frequent
attender of the Concerts of Ancient Music but an ardent disciple of
Haydn. Reconciling these positions will require exploring an area that
some Burney scholars have cautiously avoided, the question of his
intellectual influences.[44]

Burney's interactions with Crotch can help reveal his otherwise ambiguous musical values by illuminating a side of the music historian's
personality that is seldom seen. Crotch and his mentor, patron and,
ultimately, opponent were the most respected musical figures in England at the dawn of the new century. Their lives intersect symbiotically
at several points. In his later years, Crotch consistently referred to
Burney as 'my patron thro' life', but there is reason to suspect this view
was one-sided if not naïve.[45] As long as Crotch's activities were limited
to lecturing on music within the confines of the Music Room at the
conservative stronghold of Oxford he offered Burney no reason to fear
for the prosperity of the modern style. Oxford offered no formal course
of study in music when Crotch assumed the Heather Professorship, and
even the occasional lectures that had been intended in the bequest that
established the post in 1626 had been allowed to lapse.[46] After being
encouraged by an Oxford colleague to resume the practice of music
lectures, and after testing the waters with a tentative introductory talk

---

[44] As Kerry Grant remarks in *Dr. Burney as Critic*, p. 20, eighteenth-century aesthetic
theory consists of 'an immense literature filled with contradictory conclusions drawn
from the same evidence'. Grant, therefore, leaves 'to more intrepid scholars the task of
sorting out the attendant philosophical and aesthetic influences' on Burney.

[45] A. H. Mann, 'Notes to Crotch's Memoirs', NRO, MS 11200, p. 9, quotes from
Memoirs: 'he became my patron thro' life. He drew up a letter giving an account of my
early musical talents to D. Hunter who inserted it in the Philosophical Transactions vol.
69 part I'. Mann further remarks that 'Dr. Burney received several of the particulars
about Crotch from Robert Partridge Esq, one of the corporation of Norwich'.

[46] The original bequest is described in Sir John Hawkins, *A General History of the
Science and Practice of Music*, ed. Othmar Wesley (2 vols, London, 1776; London, 1875;
Graz, Akademische Druck- u. Verlagsanstalt, 1969), vol. 2, p. 572. Hawkins notes that
Dr William Heyther gave an endowment to the university beginning in 1626 of which £3
'is to be employed upon one that shall read the theory of music once every term, or
oftner, and make an English music-lecture at the Act time'. Hawkins continues, 'It
further appears ... that Dr. Heyther's professor was required to hold a musical praxis in
the music-school every Thursday afternoon, between the hours of one and three, except
during the time of Lent ... ' See also, Susan Wollenberg, 'Music in 18th-Century Oxford',
Proceedings of the Royal Musical Association [RMA], **107** (1981–82), 70.

in 1798, Crotch began giving regular classes to interested amateurs and students in November 1800.[47] Musical examples were performed by the Music Room Band under the direction of John Malchair.

After a few years of this schedule Crotch found it necessary to resign from most of his Oxford appointments, possibly because of a disagreement with the Dean of Christ Church.[48] He retained the Professorship itself, which did not require his continuous presence at Oxford, and dutifully performed the limited tasks of his office until his death in 1847. But the remaining 25 years of his career were spent teaching and lecturing at venues in and around London, especially at the famous Royal Institution and its several imitators.[49] Soon after his relocation, Crotch and Burney found themselves on opposite sides of an ideological divide that is documented by an exchange of letters beginning in the early spring of 1805.[50] Burney, in fact, probably engaged in covert actions to suppress Crotch's ideas because of a point of view he interpreted as anti-modern and implacably opposed to all innovation.[51] It

---

[47] See Crotch's *General Account*: 'My friend Mr. Roberts, a miniature painter at Oxford had often endeavoured to persuade my predecessor Dr. Philip Hayes to write lectures on music and this communicated to me might (with the perusal at Bath, on a last visit to my sick friend & patron Revd A Schomberg of Sir Joshua Reynolds' lectures on painting) be considered as the origin of these lectures ... Dec'. 4th 1798 I read my introductory lecture alone as a public gratuitous lecture, in order to announce my intention of reading a course to subscribers. In this I was aided by the music room band.'

[48] Rainbow *The Choral Revival*, p. 205. See also, Bumpus, *A History of English Cathedral Music*, 2, pp. 446–7, and Watkins Shaw, *The Succession of Organists of the Chapel Royal and the Cathedrals of England and Wales from c.1538* (Oxford: Clarendon Press, 1991), pp. 213–14. Shaw indicates (p. 214) that Crotch must have left Oxford in late 1806 and cites notices in *Jackson's Oxford Journal* for 27 December 1806 and 11 April 1807.

[49] The origins and early history of the Royal Institution are discussed in Kassler, 'The Royal Institution Music Lectures, 1800–1831', 1–30.

[50] Some of this correspondence is reprinted in *General History*. In an appendix, Mercer reprints a letter from Burney to Crotch, pp. 1032–6, and a response by Crotch, pp. 1037–9. A more candid statement of Burney's feelings about Crotch can be found in a draft of a note to Christian Ignatius Latrobe that Burney hastily scrawled on the back of a note from Mr and Mrs and Miss Maling in the Yale University Library (hereafter YUL) Osborn Collection (hereafter Osborn). Burney confides his displeasure with Crotch's public statements on Haydn and Mozart and concludes: 'I wish not to quarrel with my countryman [Crotch was from Norwich and Burney lived for several years in the town of King's Lynn], with whom I have long lived in peace though not amity – and therefore, *Mum* is the word, ab' all these matters. C. has foolishly excited a rage in all those who most admire, and best understand the great musical phenomenon, Mozart, who died Oct' 1791, at 34. Excuse paper, haste, & bad writing ... .'

[51] The evidence for Burney's probable actions against Crotch is documented in Jamie Croy Kassler, 'The Royal Institution Music Lectures, 1800–1831: a Preliminary Study', *The Royal Musical Association Research Chronicle*, 19 (1983–85), pp. 5–9.

may be a result of Burney's objections that Crotch did not publish the above mentioned *Substance* until the end of his career in 1831.

While Burney is a thoroughgoing modern in his correspondence with Crotch, other sources reveal a more confusing pattern of allegiances that seem to justify the conflicting positions briefly set forth above. Indeed, the inconsistency of this individual has contributed much to a general state of confusion on the quarrel. The well-documented deliberate insincerities with which Burney attempted to placate the powerful ancient music faction in his *General History of Music* and *Account of the Musical Performances in Westminster-Abbey*[52] are not the only source of difficulty as one tries to approach his honest sympathies. Although he is more candid in his correspondence, it is not always easy in unguarded private writing to find the real Charles Burney, nor can one necessarily even identify exchanges that are related to the sensitive issues of ancient versus modern music without some awareness of its most common stereotypes and loaded expressions.

One reads in a letter Burney wrote to Montagu North in the summer of 1771, for example, a statement that North must 'have thought so much & so deeply & discriminately upon the subject [of music] yourself, that I have the advantage at least of being understood by you in many things wch will escape others'.[53] He adds that North 'must clearly have seen my discontent [in Burney's recently published book, *The Present State of Music in France and Italy*] through all the soft & civil Terms I was able to give it, both with respect to composing & performing of Vocal Music'.[54] Although one can sense from his conspiratorial tone that Burney is speaking frankly to a kindred spirit, it might take a sensitivity to the discourse of ancient-versus-modern music to associate the remainder of his remarks with the quarrel. In his next sentence, Burney resorts to the quarrel's standard melody-versus-harmony opposition to complain that 'the Voice already corrupted & vitiate in its Intonations by the Temperament of modern Instruments is overcharged with Harmony & suffocated by Instrumental performers who seem ambitious of being heard even when they have nothing to say'.[55] That this should be taken as a broad ideological statement rather than a passing commentary on contemporary performance practice may still not be particularly apparent unless this letter is seen in the context of a series of similar communications written that spring and summer to Baron d'Holbach, Jean-Baptiste-Antoine Suard, Diderot and his friend

---

[52] See, Grant, *Dr. Burney as Critic*, especially pp. 240–43.
[53] Ribeiro, *Letters*, pp. 95–6.
[54] Ibid., p. 96.
[55] Ibid.

Samuel Crisp and with the aid of unguarded remarks in his later publications.[56]

At times Burney's musical correspondence can take on the cryptic character of a secret society, with a catalogue of objections to ancient music that did not need to be spelled out and even a private vocabulary. In a letter to his intimate friend and co-conspirator Thomas Twining, Burney complains of having to waste his time poking and poring 'over English Fogrums of the last Century'.[57] 'Fogrum' is a word Burney is said to have picked up in his youth from his rakish patron Fulke Greville. Fanny Burney defines the word as synonymous with bad taste,[58] but in practice it seems to have had a variety of related meanings, some of which are anything but clear to the modern reader. Fanny herself notes that Greville's 'esteem for virtue was never pronounced, lest it should pass for pedantry; and his scorn for vice was studiously disguised, lest he should be set down himself for a Fogrum',[59] giving the word a colouring that resembles the later 'Victorian'. This is one of the few recorded uses of 'fogrum' that is not directly related to music and to the ancient–modern quarrel. It may not have been priggishness, however, but a more straightforward pedantry Dr Burney had in mind when he dismissed Jones of Nayland to Twining as 'a mere *Grumbling Fogrum*' because of the dullness of Jones's writing and interests.[60] Twining, on the other hand, puts a slightly different spin on the word when he speaks of Lord Monboddo as 'a simple, fogrum kind of antient-led good man' who is like 'the blind horse in the mill, that thinks he is going forward all the time'.[61]

Jones and Monboddo may have had other qualities in common as fogrums, but if this word has anything to do with being 'ancient-led', Monboddo suffered from the fault in a very different sense from Jones. When Twining describes Monboddo as 'ancient-led' he refers to the *real* ancients, the Greeks of antiquity. Jones, however, studied the ancients only in the more recent musical sense of Handel, Corelli and Geminiani. It is characteristic of Twining to conflate the ancients of antiquity and the eighteenth-century musical variety, suggesting that at bottom

[56] See Ribeiro, *Letters*, p. 79 (to Baron d'Holbach, 23 May 1771); pp. 81–2 (to Jean-Baptiste-Antoine Suard, 24 May 1771); pp. 83–5 (to Diderot, 27 May 1771); and pp. 89–90 (to Samuel Crisp, late May 1771).

[57] CB to Thomas Twining (hereafter TT) 10–12 November 1783 in Ribeiro, *Letters*, p. 387.

[58] Percy A. Scholes, *The Great Dr. Burney*, 2 vols (Oxford, 1948), vol. 2, p. 41 n. 1.

[59] Frances (Burney) d'Arblay, *Memoirs of Doctor Burney*, 3 vols (London, 1832), vol. 1, p. 55.

[60] CB to TT 6 September 1783, in Ribeiro, *Letters*, p. 379.

[61] TT to CB 9 February 1776 in BM Add Ms 39929, ff. 73–5.

music's quarrel of ancients and moderns had to do with the same issues as the more familiar international ancient–modern quarrel of the previous century. This, however, can make it difficult to know with certainty at any given point which ancients and moderns Twining means.

'Fogrum', to offer one final use of the word, could refer not only to people but to music itself. In this case, however, it was not a simple matter of old-style versus new-style or progressive-versus-reactionary but instead had something to do with unnecessary complication in the music of any age. In a letter to Burney, Twining suggests that Corelli, one of the archetypal composers of ancient music, was in fact *not* fogrum; his music, by virtue of a desirable simplicity, had managed to avoid becoming dated. 'How impossible', Twining notes in the course of speculating that music in the modern style might share with Corelli's works the quality of simplicity that produces musical longevity, 'if one tries ever so, to get the least idea of a modern overture become fogrum?'[62] And how optimistic, from our point of view, to hope to understand a dispute in which the vocabulary can be unique, undefined and presupposes a shifting background of assumptions that vary radically with the speaker. Even Twining and Burney could not always communicate safely. When Twining congratulated his friend on the progress of the *General History* by remarking on the excellence of the 'articles that relate to your principal object, the history of *modern* music', he was forced to follow 'modern' with an explanatory 'I mean as distinguish'd from the Greek &c' that he would not have had to add if he had been corresponding with a true man of letters like himself.[63]

In the discussion of the modern faction in Chapter 2, Burney is presented as an individual with deep and interrelated conflicts in both his aesthetic and political philosophies. These conflicts are highlighted by a comparison of his thinking not only with that of militant moderns including Mason, but also with Crotch, a relatively moderate ancient sympathizer. Examining Burney's criticism in this context illustrates tensions between competing ideological points of view and illuminates the difficult situation of the professional music critic in eighteenth-century Britain. Chapter 2 also shows that even though the moderns were deeply fragmented and uncertain of their values – just as

---

[62] TT to CB 16 October 1773 in Ribeiro, *Letters*, p. 164. See also, *General History*, vol. 2, p. 77, n. (k): 'The simplicity of Corelli's style has doubtless greatly contributed to the longevity of his compositions; and it seems as if the more transient general use and favour of Purcell's productions, who flourished about the same time, may be ascribed to the temporary graces and embellishments with which, for the use of ignorant singers, he loaded his melodies, which his other excellencies of invention, modulation, and expression of words could not save from neglect.'

[63] Ribeiro, *Letters*, p. 141, n.16.

supporters of ancient music reveal a similar uncertainty through much of the eighteenth century – they had in common a central core of values with a pronounced aesthetic component.

Factions supporting ancient and modern music were strongly influenced by their interactions with prominent men of letters at the end of the eighteenth century. For several reasons, however, the modern side was more sensitive to the literary community and more inclined to seek its approval. Ancient music had on its side a century-long tradition and a greater confidence in music's value and fitness to be accepted as an art worthy of classical status. Because of this confidence, Crotch, the most influential spokesman for ancient music after the turn of the century, was able to insist that music be accepted on its own terms. He thereby avoided the complications that can result from detailed explanations of how central concepts of eighteenth-century aesthetic theory might apply to music. The same was not true, however, of the most articulate authority on the modern side, Charles Burney. In Chapter 3, complex issues of the relationship between musicians and men of letters are revealed in Burney's largely unsuccessful attempts to apply pervasive aesthetic mythology of the eighteenth century to music criticism.

CHAPTER ONE

William Crotch and the quarrel of ancients and moderns

Introduction: Crotch and Charles Burney

Although William Crotch's role as apologist for ancient music actually began at Oxford seven years earlier, it is appropriate to begin this examination of his lecturing career with his first appearance in London in 1805 and with an argument that erupted soon after between Crotch and his erstwhile mentor Charles Burney. In a letter to Crotch dated 17 February, Burney speaks of being troubled by 'severe, and even, contemptuous remarks' about Haydn that his young colleague was supposed to have made a month earlier in the last instalment of a lecture series at the Royal Institution in Arlbemarle Street.[1] Burney was then entering his seventy-ninth year and living quietly at Chelsea College. He did not attend these lectures himself but instead heard complaints from what he calls 'some Germans & good judges of Music who have kept pace with the times, without being insensible to the merit of old masters'. Aside from his well-known affection for the modern style, Burney was ready to come to the defence of his favourite composer one last time because it was widely rumoured during that winter that Haydn was dead.[2]

But another reason for the uncharacteristic venom of his letter can also be detected: Burney treats young Crotch not as an individual but as the representative of a powerful ancient-music faction with which one can sense the older man has had a long history. A pattern can be seen when this letter is viewed alongside others letters quoted below, the remarkably frank articles he wrote shortly before for Abraham Rees's

---

[1] Burney's comments come from an exchange of letters with Crotch that is reprinted in C. Burney, *A General History of Music*, with critical and historical notes by Frank Mercer (2 vols, London, 1935; New York: Dover, 1957) (hereafter *General History*), vol. 2, pp. 1032–6 and 1037–9. In addition, Burney wrote to Crotch again on this subject on 4 November 1805. Crotch's original letter in reply to Burney's complaints, dated 4 March 1805, does not survive. Burney's initial letter of 17 February is held in the Gerald Coke Collection, Jenkyn Place, Bentley, Hampshire, England. A draft of his second letter is in YUL, Osborn.

[2] In his letter to Crotch of 17 February, Burney writes that his unidentified informants are disturbed by Crotch's remarks on Haydn, 'and at a time too when all the musical world is lamenting his loss and singing *Requiem* to his soul'.

Cyclopaedia; or, Universal Dictionary of Arts, Sciences, and Literature,
Burney's diary entries for 1805, and his earlier anonymous book reviews for the *Monthly Review* and *Critical Review*. Despite his Tory
politics and his many social contacts in the world of old music, this
increasingly outspoken old historian's tolerance was wearing thin for
what he might have called the 'bigoted devotion to the exclusive merit
of Handel'. Besides, ancient music had never before had on its side a
musician-critic with the credibility of Crotch, who was still remembered
as a boy wonder, and it must have seemed to Burney, as it did to others,
that the modern style itself was in jeopardy.

The exchange of letters resulting from this dispute includes some of
Burney's most colourful and frequently quoted aphorisms, but the ideas
expressed therein are on the whole predictable and uninteresting.[3] These
and other letters are useful for the present purposes because they reveal
more clearly than is usually true in Burney's cautious writing his tendency to see several old-music groups as a single enemy camp with a
united purpose of stamping out innovation. The letters also show a
tendency on the part of both respected authorities to view their art in
terms of a deep, bitter and persistent ancient–modern division. Seeing
these individuals in a rare moment of candour bears, in turn, on a
matter that must be considered before music's quarrel of ancients and
moderns is examined further: was there in fact a pervasive ancient–
modern division in the late eighteenth century? And if there was, should
it be viewed as the compelling aspect of musical life Crotch indicates in
his 1818 lecture series?

William Weber and the ancient–modern quarrel

Ancient–modern polarity surfaces only tangentially in the most important recent research into the phenomenon of ancient music and the
development of a musical canon by William Weber. Moreover, Weber's
conclusions minimize the possibility of a pervasive ancient–modern
division and discourage Crotch's view that ancient music needs to be
examined in binary opposition with the modern style to account for its
role in the development of musical classics. Before old music became a
fashionable upper-class pursuit, Burney sometimes depicted the ancient-

---

[3] Burney's parting advice to Crotch urges the younger man to 'Praise when you can;
play the best productions of gifted men; and let alone the spots in the sun which are
invisible to common eyes and you will not find it impossible to please a whole audience.'
See, Lawrence Lipking, *The Ordering of the Arts in Eighteenth-Century England*
(Princeton, NJ: Princeton University Press, 1970), p. 234.

music movement as a divisive force, promoted by bigoted, illiberal and highly disagreeable men like Hawkins who were out of step with prevailing tastes.[4] This point of view is shaped by a common French sentiment, most apparent in the writing of Rousseau that strongly influenced Burney's aesthetic, that values the universal intelligibility of a simple, homophonic style as consistent with the legendary music of antiquity and dismisses counterpoint as an élitist Gothic contaminant. Accordingly, the preface to Jean François Le Seur's *Mort d'Adam* of 1798 claims the composer 'avoided all semblance of the musical Gothic and followed only the grand taste of the antique, so that the work was not directed to one country, or one people, but rather to the brotherhood of the human race'.[5] Weber shows convincingly, however, that ancient music functioned in England as just the reverse of Burney's earlier assessment: it was a unifying agent, whose broad popular acceptance helped knit together the British state itself during a period of constitutional crisis and external threat.[6]

Weber acknowledges some of the more militant and divisive rhetoric by militant ancient partisans – for example, Jones of Nayland's incendiary pronouncement in the introduction to his *Treatise on Harmony* that 'we are now divided into Parties for the Old and the New in Music' – but he believes this statement to have been made with 'considerable exaggeration'.[7] Instead, Weber stresses the universality of ancient music, noting that in the programmes of the Concert of Ancient Music 'for the first time the society as a whole conceived old works as a special corpus of music, to be performed systematically and reverentially in a public context'.[8] In music, he suggests, just as in political life, party affiliation became a secondary concern, 'replaced by a new political

---

[4] Thus, Burney wrote of Marpurg that 'he is a favourer of the old fashion'd french Music, & consequently has but little toleration for other kinds. He treats with contempt due only to Ignorance & Dulness, some of the best modern Composers of Italy' (CB to Baron d'Holbach 2 June 1772 in Alvaro S. J. Ribeiro, ed., *The Letters of Dr Charles Burney*, vol. 1, *1751–1784* (Oxford, Clarendon Press, 1991), p. 113). With regard to Hawkins, Burney wrote to Twining (April, 1773 in Ribeiro, *Letters*, p. 125) that 'Modern Music & Musicians are likely to have little Quarter from such a writer, who besides his little knowledge in practice, delights so much in old musty Conundrums that he will not give a hearing to anything better'.

[5] Quoted in Daniel Heartz, 'Classical', *The New Grove Dictionary of Music and Musicians*, ed. Stanley Sadie, 20 vols (London: Macmillan Publishers Ltd, 1980), vol. 3, p. 453.

[6] W. Weber, *The Rise of Musical Classics in Eighteenth-Century England: a Study of Canon, Ritual, and Ideology*, (Oxford: Clarendon Press, 1992), p. 14 and 'The 1784 Handel Commemoration as Political Ritual', *Journal of British Studies*, 28 (1989), 43–69.

[7] Weber, *Rise of Musical Classics*, pp. 202–3.

[8] Ibid., p. 168.

structure – a kind of broad-based Establishment that masked its own internal divisions'.[9] 'In such a way did the new political order and the musical canon take root in close relationship to each other', Weber notes, adding that 'by the end of the eighteenth century, Anglicans and Dissenters were able to sit down together in public halls – in some instances even in churches and cathedrals – to hear Handel's oratorios, odes, and masques'.[10]

The different understandings of the state of ancient–modern relations and of the role played by ancient music that are reflected in Weber's analysis and the writings of Burney and Crotch are not as irreconcilable as they may appear. Which is valid might depend on the precise time period and on the particular audience in question. By Crotch's account, the ancient–modern quarrel began well before 1800, the end of the period Weber considers, but its existence was not widely acknowledged by the concert-going public until well into the nineteenth century. This timetable is reflected in Crotch's lectures. Although Crotch assumes an ancient–modern dichotomy in lectures before 1818, it was only then that he was prepared to speak openly of 'a division of the musical world into two great parties'. 'Why then', this same lecture questions after describing a prolonged musical schism beginning in the 1770s, 'it may be asked was [the existence of an ancient–modern polarization] not generally admitted *till lately?*'[11] The question is a good one, for he seems to mean that the general public had only recently become aware of a division that professional musicians had long taken for granted. In the present study the individuals who write openly of ancient–modern conflict – Burney, Crotch, solicitor John Marsh, organists William Jones of Nayland and William Jackson of Exeter, divine William Mason, naturalist Benjamin Stillingfleet and others – are all either professionals or unusually sophisticated amateurs. On the other hand, it is not common to find direct references to an ancient–modern schism in media intended for the non-specialist reader such as newspapers.

If the perception of division may have varied among different groups, then it is important to consider more carefully what segments of society Crotch and Weber have in mind when they arrive at such different interpretations of the ancient–modern quarrel. First, Weber's conception of the ancient-music audience, the group within which ancient music might be said to have had a unifying effect, is remarkably inclusive by comparison with Crotch's simplistic black-and-white caricature of the

---

[9] Ibid., p. 14.
[10] Ibid.
[11] NRO MS 11232/2.

two sides. Weber's 'ancients' – if, for convenience, that term can be extended to include both composers and partisans – include even an individual now often viewed as the quintessential modern, Charles Burney, together with Burney's arch-enemy Sir John Hawkins.[12] Weber's most extended construction of the ancient-music movement includes an assortment of performance traditions, both sacred and secular, instrumental and vocal, and a wide cross-section of social strata. The diversity of this following is itself compelling evidence of ancient music's power to bind together disparate groups under a common banner. Disciples of ancient music in some sense of that expression include Oxford academics like Dean Henry Aldrich, the middle-class antiquarians of the Academy of Ancient Music, conservative divines including Bishop of Norwich George Horne, and church musicians such as William Jones of Nayland.

It should be noted, however, that the ancient-music following that was most visible during the time period Crotch identifies with ancient–modern tensions, and at the same time was most directly responsible for creating the first musical canon, was considerably less socially heterogeneous than the broader cross-section of individuals who might be associated with old music. Music's first canon of regularly performed master works is identified in the programmes of the Concert of Ancient Music or, as it liked to call itself, 'Antient Concert'.[13] This venerable concert association, formed almost 30 years before Crotch's altercation with Burney, was the creation of John Montagu, fourth Earl of Sandwich, and a small group composed mostly of nobles. It was, therefore, associated in the minds of many with the nobility, who remained in its effective control through Crotch's day, and was therefore more liable than less prestigious ancient-music groups like the earlier and more distinctly middle-class Academy of Ancient Music to be viewed as a

---

[12] Two recent studies discuss Burney's role as a music historian primarily in the context of his progressive leanings as contrasted with Hawkins. See, Enrico Fubini, *Music and Culture in Eighteenth-Century Europe: a Source Book*, trans. Wolfgang Fries, Lisa Basbarrone and Michael Louis Leone, ed. Bonnie J. Blackburn (Chicago and London: University of Chicago Press, 1994), and Thomas McGeary, 'Music Literature', *The Blackwell History of Music in Britain*, vol. 4 *The Eighteenth Century*, ed. H. Diack Johnstone and Roger Fisk (Oxford and Cambridge, Blackwell, 1990), pp. 404–5.

[13] Weber, *Rise of Musical Classics*, p. 168: 'The repertory of the Concert of Antient Music furnishes the first instance where we can speak assuredly of a musical canon in the modern sense. Here for the first time the society as a whole conceived old works as a special corpus of music, to be performed systematically and reverentially in a public context. The Ancient Concerts were not an isolated gathering of antiquarians such as the Academy of Ancient Music had become but a secular concert society, led by peers of the realm, the performances of which established a canonic reference point for musical life as a whole.'

controlling social élite.[14] Weber shows that the Ancient Concert's audience included a mix of upper classes with the nobility actually being in the minority. Still, one might safely describe this particular old-music following as homogeneous in its social prominence or ambition, its political conservatism and, above all, in the fact that its members were native-born as opposed to the 'Germans and good judges of music' to which Burney alludes above. The social differences between supporters of the Ancient Concert and the broader ancient-music audience are significant since infrequent public attacks on the old-music movement late in the century often show signs of being aimed at the Ancient Concert in particular and include unmistakable indications of ideological difference.

The precise meaning Weber has in mind for the word 'canon' should also be noted. He refers to a 'repertory of old works that had a common identity' and were 'presented on a conventional basis, though in varying combinations in different places'.[15] He describes, in other words, a 'performed canon' as distinct from a body of music assembled and valued for scholarly or pedagogical purposes.[16] A performed canon as Weber defines it is necessarily the creation of a specific audience more than the scholarly or pedagogical types since such canons develop from individual judgements about specific works rather than any abstract conception of a musical ideal. A scholarly canon, by contrast, might be based on a veneration of erudite practices – for example the practices of the polyphonic tradition – and might therefore need to rely less on the cachet of historical justification.[17]

It is possible for Weber to conceive of the larger set of advocates of ancient music mentioned above in very broad terms because the glue that is supposed to have held together this diverse interest-group – and, at the same time, might have distinguished and divided it from a non-ancient audience – was an ideology of ancient music that could transcend ordinary social and musical boundaries.[18] This belief system has two qualities of interest here. First, the ancient ideology had something of

---

[14] As James E. Matthew notes in 'The Antient Concerts, 1776–1848', *Proceedings of the Royal Musical Association*, 33 (1906), 57, 'The Society throughout its existence maintained a somewhat exclusive and aristocratic position which, in our more democratic days, seems almost comical. To go with your money in your hand was no passport; your social position had to be as carefully vouched for as for a ball at Almacks.'

[15] William Weber, 'The Intellectual Origins of Musical Canon in Eighteenth-Century England', *Journal of the American Musicological Society*, 47 (1994), 488–520.

[16] Weber, 'The Intellectual Origins of Musical Canon', p. 490.

[17] Ibid.

[18] See Weber's chapter 'The Ideology of Ancient Music', in his *Rise of Musical Classics*, pp. 198–222.

an aesthetic component in its subdued, almost academic approach. Weber's analysis of the programmes of the Ancient Concert show an avoidance of ostentatious display arias in favour of slower and more reflective examples. It also reveals a preference for arias that depart from convention by exhibiting 'strong chromatic effects' and variations of da capo form.[19]

At the same time, however, Weber minimizes the role of aesthetics in the creation of the notion of classical music. 'The practice of performing old works did not develop through an aesthetic movement' he observes, or 'a set of ideas involving philosophy or literature, but rather through a gradual expansion of pre-existing musical conventions within contexts of political and social change'.[20] His ideology of ancient music does not, accordingly, reflect the most ubiquitous and divisive aesthetic issues of eighteenth-century critical writing. Foremost among these is the melody-versus-harmony opposition that is inescapable in both continental and British criticism throughout the eighteenth century and beyond.[21] Weber's notion of the ancient-music audience takes in both the die-hard advocates of the contrapuntal style and its vigorous opponents, both the lovers of oratorio and of opera, both champions of instrumental music like Roger North and those who argue for the superiority of vocal music as a medium that combines 'sound' with 'sense'.

In place of such distinctions, Weber's ancients are defined, first, by their interest in a limited variety of non-contemporary music and second, by their tendency to associate this old music with an 'ideological consensus of great unity and strength'[22] that developed in the last quarter of the century over issues of respect for Church and State. Ancient music, in this context, was more than a repertoire of unusual quality, it was a moral force and symbol, the musical embodiment of the dominant culture's social philosophy. As Weber notes, 'the rationale for ancient music was not simply that it was great and immortal, but also that it was beneficial to society, a means of moral regeneration'.[23] 'The movement for ancient music sprang from a moral reaction against luxury and fashion, against the excesses seen in new habits of

---

[19] Weber, *Rise of Musical Classics*, pp. 174–6.

[20] Ibid., p. 3.

[21] See, Edward Lippman, *A History of Western Musical Aesthetics* (Lincoln NB and London: University of Nebraska Press, 1992), especially the chapter on galant aesthetics, pp. 59–82.

[22] J. C. D. Clark, *English Society 1688–1832: Ideology, Social Structure, and Political Practice during the Ancien Regime* (Cambridge: Cambridge University Press, 1985), p. 199.

[23] Weber, *Rise of Musical Classics*, p. 198.

consumption,' Weber observes, concluding that 'its ideological advocates saw ancient music as a force by which not only to improve
musical taste but also to reform and regenerate the society as a whole'.[24]

Recent research by Simon McVeigh seems to support some of Weber's
conclusions.[25] Indeed, if, at some point well before the time Crotch
claims the ancient–modern quarrel became generally acknowledged,
one were to focus on the behavior of the mass audience rather than on
occasional indications of ideology that emerge from published music
criticism and the private correspondence of a few individuals, Weber's
view of ancient–modern conflict as a minor phenomenon in musical life
might indeed appear to be more plausible than Crotch's view of this
same conflict as a pivotal event. Of course, even Crotch only saw the
quarrel as a pivotal event when he could look back on its origins in
hindsight 40 years later. It has been shown that there was no absolute
division between the ancient and modern audiences where eighteenth-
century concert programmes and concert-going behavior are concerned.
It is not at all hard to find the same individuals turning up at both
ancient and modern programmes, and the programmes themselves were
often but not always rigorously one-sided.[26]

There are, at the same time, several ways of accounting for the lack of
ideological conflict these facts may indicate without necessarily tossing
out Crotch's notion of a developing ancient–modern schism. Among
musicians, at the end of the eighteenth century a partisan contemporary
observer named John Marsh suggests that the profit motive transcended
ideology in the case of the London benefit concerts he knew about. In
these vigorously entrepreneurial efforts, a mix of ancient and modern
music is supposed to have satisfied nine out of ten listeners.[27] A combi-

---

[24] Ibid., p. viii.

[25] Simon McVeigh, *Concert Life in London from Mozart to Haydn*, (Cambridge and
New York: Cambridge University Press, 1993), pp. 6–34. Weber, *Rise of Musical Classics*, pp. 202–3.

[26] McVeigh, *Concert Life*, p. 24. Arguing that 'it would be a mistake, however, to
assume that audiences at the Concert and at modern concerts were entirely separate,
different as the two ideologies may have been', McVeigh notes that several of the
directors of the Ancient Concert were in the audience at the first programme of the
Professional Concert in 1788 and that the concerts of this organization were included in
the court calendar. With regard to concerts outside the capital, Stanley Sadie notes in
'Concert Life in Eighteenth Century England', *Proceeding of the Royal Musical Association*, 85 (1958–59), 17–30, that the reduced performance forces of country venues made
an ancient–modern rivalry impractical.

[27] [John Marsh], 'A Comparison Between the Ancient and Modern Styles of Music in
Which the Merits and Demerits of Each are Respectively Pointed Out', *Monthly Magazine*, supplement to vol. 2 (1796): 981. McVeigh observes, however, that the mixture of
ancient and modern works at benefit concerts was a relatively new phenomenon when

nation of economic realities and limited performance forces may also explain the mixture of ancient and modern music at provincial music festivals.[28] Besides, it is not clear that the audiences for ancient and modern music were necessarily always mixed at these two to three-day annual events, since festival programmes typically segregate the modern style into 'Miscellaneous Concerts' given at venues other than those at which the large Handel works that often formed the bulk of the festival were performed.[29] These explanations aside, however, it is reasonable no matter how often known partisans of ancient and modern music appear together to question whether concert-going behaviour and the pragmatic interests of professional musicians are necessarily a reliable guide to the differences of interest here. There are obvious incentives for insincerity on the part of both listeners and, especially, players. Burney cannot have been alone in his ability to enjoy the social advantages of the Ancient Concert while at the same time harbouring, as his correspondence with Thomas Twining and others clearly reveals, a very different orientation in private.

The biggest obstacle to an ideological interpretation of the ancient–modern division is not the fact that ancient and modern advocates could tolerate or even enjoy each other's music but the fact that the social environments of ancient and modern music concert series are uncomfortably alike in some important ways. In particular, it has been shown that the Ancient Concert, despite its reputation for social élitism, was not alone in this regard and that the modern-music concerts of J. P. Salomon and the later Philharmonic Society deliberately cultivated their own image of exclusivity.[30] At the same time, the 'musical Toryism'[31] of the ancient-music movement instinctively prompts a search for an innovative and egalitarian modern-music opposite to serve as its natural foil. There are surely hints in this direction. It is known that the supporters of modern music included radicals like Thomas Holcroft and the Earl of Abingdon and that the latter, through his brief continuation of the

---

Marsh mentioned it and that the number of benefit concerts advertised declined precipitously during the last decade of the century. See McVeigh, *Concert Life*, pp. 102 and 68.

[28] Stanley Sadie makes this argument in 'Concert Life in Eighteenth Century England': 17–30.

[29] Music festivals in selected areas are discussed in Weber, *Rise of Musical Classics*, pp. 103–42. Weber remarks (pp. 126–7) on the tendency of the meetings he surveys to reserve programmes of modern music for the final night of the three-day event.

[30] McVeigh, *Concert Life*, pp. 11–13.

[31] The expression 'musical Toryism' is used by William Weber in 'The 1784 Handel Commemoration as Political Ritual', *Journal of British Studies*, 28 (1989), 51. Weber qualifies this expression by noting that 'musical Toryism' was 'a matter of cultural values more than political party'.

famous Bach-Abel concert series in the 1780s, may have promoted the modern style as a direct challenge to the authority of ancient music's institutions and its intolerant promoters.[32] It is also known that in the German-speaking world a strain of contemporary Haydn criticism conceived his symphonies as a popular music that everyone could understand and appreciate, the perfect counterweight to an exclusive, aristocratic repertory of ancient music.[33] Similar ideas may have circulated among London's significant German-speaking community; certainly Burney treated his young friend and confidant, Moravian minister Christian Ignatius Latrobe as an intellectual fellow-traveller where the modern style is concerned.

Further exploration into the social structure of the British modern-music audience – a task beyond the scope of the present study – may well turn up additional evidence of class struggle and resistance to the cultural domination of an aristocratic ancient-music faction. But for the present, what is needed is not more evidence of class division but some indication of a coherent ideology of modern music that could have been in conflict with the ideology of ancient music that Weber has described so convincingly. As long as Weber's ancient ideology remains unopposed by an alternative point of view there can be no moderns and no ancient–modern quarrel.

It is mainly in the study of music criticism that an ideology of modern music can be identified. When attention is focused on the interests of the relatively small body of specialists and unusually interested parties who wrote critically about music, the reality and importance of conflicting ideologies is inescapable. There is also an undeniable dissonance between the view of ancient music that emerges from the writing of professionals and sophisticated amateurs throughout the period 1770 to 1820, and the function of this music within the social strata served by the Concert of Ancient Music. Apologists of ancient music from Sir John Hawkins, to conservative ideologue William Jones of Nayland, to Crotch himself, do not view themselves as the confident voice of a dominant culture and ideology, but rather as a struggling minority trying, sometimes with scant hope, to preserve artistic continuity and integrity against an overwhelming popular tide of innovation and

---

[32] In *Concert Life*, pp. 15–17, McVeigh comments on the Earl of Abingdon's radical politics and speculates that these concerts 'may well have been a conscious attempt to counteract the aristocratic revivalism of the Concert of Ancient Music; Abingdon went out of his way to obtain and publicize the most modern music (Haydn symphonies) and significantly the principal patron was the Prince of Wales'.

[33] Among the many sources that speak of Haydn's status as a composer for the common man, see a long essay by a writer identified as 'Herr Triest' in *Allgemeine Musikalische Zeitung*, 24 (1801), cols 405–8.

degeneracy. Hawkins, Jones and Crotch also all imagined their interests to be countered by a more or less coherent musical party with radically different values.

What then, were the values of the moderns – a term with other possible uses that was specifically employed by all three of the men named above to refer to living composers in contrast to figures like Handel and Corelli? And beyond what a few conservatives thought, is there, in the broader literature of British music criticism, a collection of musical and social ideas and values that could be called an ideology of modern music? A logical place to look might be in known sources that attack the institutions of old music,[34] but writers of this stamp have not been shown to have shared a consistent aesthetic point of view. On the contrary, there is a notable lack of agreement on musical values among those who line up against the ancients, with some, like cathedral organist William Jackson of Exeter, objecting as much to the music of Haydn as to the music of Handel.

And yet, a not so dissimilar fragmentation has been demonstrated within the diverse ancient-music community itself during its formative years, and the resulting inconsistency in the written record has not prevented the identification of an ideology of ancient music. The history of early ancient-music organizations like the Academy of Ancient Music reveals persistent uncertainty on the very definition of the genre 'ancient music' itself, a concept Weber traces from a point very early in the century. In time, a repertoire of mostly seventeenth and early eighteenth-century music became old enough for age itself to be a defining quality of the type, but before then, and especially while Handel was still alive, some of ancient music's supporters could not agree on the basis of stylistic qualities alone whether the works of even this archetypal figure ought to be accepted as representative.[35] It was only with Crotch, more than a century after the birth of the notion 'ancient music', that a writer finally found it possible to define the type in terms of musical values and, therefore, to separate it, at least in theory, from a specific time and repertoire. An important task for this chapter and the chapters that follow, then, will be to define the values of the two sides more precisely than many of the principals themselves would have been able to do at the time.

To return now to the events of 1805, if Crotch's ancient–modern schism was not important or even apparent to many casual concert-goers, it was very real for the two serious musicians of interest here. Further, both men suggest in their letters the existence of parties or

---

[34] Weber, *Rise of Musical Classics*, pp. 239–42.
[35] Ibid., pp. 65–6.

factions within the British audience who shared their points of view. In a draft of a letter to Crotch in November 1805, Burney's second letter on this subject that year, Crotch is cautioned to 'avoid as much as possible enlist^g on the side of any musical party or faction at the expence of the rest'.[36] Burney does not identify the factions he has in mind, but several old-music interests are named in a letter to Latrobe from the following year. Here, Burney reports (probably unnecessarily, since Latrobe was present at Crotch's first lecture series[37]) that Crotch 'offended Salomon, and lovers of the Germ. school, last year, by his arrogant manner of censuring Haydn, to the great delight of the *exclusive* admirers of Handel, and the English School'.[38] He adds that 'this year he only speaks of Mozart as an innovator and capricious composer, in which he is *hallooed* on by the Catch and Glee singers, and those who regard Dr. C-l — tt [i.e., Dr. John Wall Calcott, a professional musician and "Priviliged member" of the Gentlemen's Catch Club] as a great conjurer'.[39] In doing all this, Crotch has 'foolishly excited a rage in all those who most admire, and best understand the great musical phenomenon, Mozart'. Worse, Burney indicates that 'as C. is going (as they say) to print his lectures, w^d you wish that posterity sh^d regard such men as Haydn & Mozart in no higher light than the lecturer has done, or sh^d think that we did not understand their works?'[40]

Crotch, however, did not publish most of the material in his lectures until a quarter-century later, when his career was behind him and the quarrels of the eighteenth century were of little interest to anyone. The *Eclectic Review* reported the forthcoming publication of 'the lectures

---

[36] CB to William Crotch (hereafter WC), 4 November 1805, *Osborn*.

[37] In a letter to his mentor the Reverend Dr Jowett at Cambridge, dated 24 January 1805 (*Correspondence*), Crotch writes of his first lecture series, 'I am very happy to find Mr. Latrobe could endure my abuse of Haydn's Creation – I wonder how Salomon relishes it – He said after the lecture was over that as to what [I] said of the mixed characters of the symphonies [modern] composers did not think themselves tied down to any rules.'

[38] YUL, Osborn. Extracts from this letter are reprinted in C. B. Oldman, 'Dr. Burney and Mozart', *Mozart Jahrbuch* 1962–1963, (Kassel: Internationale Stiftung Mozarteum Salzburg, 1964), p. 80.

[39] *Lectures*, NRO, MS 11228/11 is probably the lecture to which Burney refers. It is a lecture that considers not only Mozart but Kozeluch and Pleyel. As Crotch wrote in the letter to Dr Jowett cited above, 'my next course will consist of 12 lectures at least and Mozart will have honorable mention but not I think a whole lecture because I have not enough to say about him. At present he, Pleyel & Kozeluch make one lecture'. In the *General Account*, Crotch reports that this lecture was read in a series begun 16 February 1806. Calcott's status in the Catch Club is described in Percy Scholes, *The Great Dr Burney* (2 vols, Oxford: Clarendon Press, 1948), pp. 180–81.

[40] YUL, Osborn.

on Music which [Crotch] delivered at the Royal Institution together with the examples at large' in 1805,[41] but when this book finally appeared in print at least a year or two later[42] it was not the polemic Burney anticipated but the first instalment of a harmless three-volume anthology of musical scores. This first volume of Crotch's *Specimens of Various Styles of Music Referred to in a Course of Lectures read at Oxford and London* is prefaced by a brief and uncontroversial outline of his aesthetic theory and a discussion of the 'national' music it contains. Most of this material comes from the lectures, as does the slightly more provocative commentary on 'scientific' music in the prefaces of the remaining two volumes. But nowhere is there anything like an all-out attack on modern decadence that Burney had come to anticipate from advocates of old music like Hawkins or cathedral organist Jones of Nayland. Nor is there any mention of discrete musical parties supporting ancient and modern music here, as there is in Crotch's *Substance of Several Courses of Lectures on Music* of 1831. Crotch addressed ancient–modern factionalism in the safer medium of the public lecture in the interim between 1805 and 1831, but it was only in the long-delayed *Substance*, the book Burney feared, that Crotch was finally prepared to put into print a candid look at this long controversy.

If Crotch's reluctance to publish an exposé of British factionalism suggests a retreat by this notoriously reticent individual, who is now known at least as well for his diffidence as his public lectures, it is also worth noting that his outspokenness in 1805 may have cost him his position at the Royal Institution. According to the *Manager's Minutes* of the Royal Institution, Crotch was replaced as music lecturer after his altercation with Burney by the same Dr John Wall Calcott Burney mentions in the correspondence above. The *Manager's Minutes* indicate, moreover, that Calcott was to speak, 'on German Music' – a common popular expression for the latest version of the modern style Burney supported – as opposed to the largely ancient-music focus of Crotch's lectures.[43] Indeed, it has been very plausibly speculated that

---

[41] *Eclectic Review*, 1 (March 1805), p. 236, in a list of forthcoming publications.

[42] The first volume of a periodical entitled *The Director*, which appeared in 1807, includes (pp. 60–62) an anonymous account of a course of 13 lectures by Crotch. This article concludes with the observation that 'the specimens performed and referred to in these lectures will shortly be published'. It would appear that somewhere in the time between the *Eclectic Review*'s notice and the present article Crotch scaled down his plans from a comprehensive summary to this safer and less ambitious approach, which involved rather little commentary.

[43] The Royal Institution of Great Britain, *Minutes of the Manager's Meetings 1799– 1900* in facsimile, with an introduction by Frank Greenaway (Menston: Scolar Press, 1971). This statement comes amidst a discussion of the arrangements for the lectures of

Burney, working behind the scenes through connections at the Royal Institution that included his friend Joseph Banks and his son Charles, engineered Crotch's removal.[44]

Crotch's retrospective and a new role for the professional

The questions raised above about the identity and ideology of the moderns form the focus of Chapters 2 and 3. The purpose of this chapter is to clarify Crotch's role in this dispute and to show ways in which his thinking develops, but at the same time diverges, from that of earlier apologists of ancient music. In particular, the origins of Crotch's abstract conception of ancient music as a set of aesthetic values rather than a repertoire of old music need to be identified, since Crotch's flexible conception of ancient music is an obvious model for classical music. Understanding Crotch's conception of ancient music requires surveying an undercurrent of tension that exists from the earliest writing on the ancient–modern quarrel on the question of whether musical style or age should be the test for canonicity. Before looking at definitions of ancient music, however, it is useful to continue the early nineteenth-century history of the quarrel by taking a brief look at Crotch's lectures after his 1805 encounter with Burney.

Crotch's first detailed public acknowledgement of an ancient–modern rift after 1805 can be found in a lecture series begun in February of 1818 at one of the Royal Institution's several imitators, the Surrey Institution. This lecture series clearly marks a turning point for Crotch. In 20 years of public lecturing, starting with his first tentative effort at Oxford the year after his appointment as Heather Professor in 1797, one of Crotch's main messages had been that music was in a prolonged state of decline that followed a still earlier period of greatness stretching

---

the ensuing season to commence on 9 December 1808. Below it in the minutes is a sentence reading '————— [left blank] on the Music of the 18th Century'. In vol. 4, p. 303, the minutes for 4 January 1808, Callcott is said to be scheduled to read his first lecture on Thursday the 14th.

[44] This speculation is offered in Jamie Croy Kassler, 'The Royal Institution Music Lectures, 1800–1831: a Preliminary Study', *The Royal Musical Association Research Chronicle*, **19** (1983–85), 1–30. If Kassler's scenario of behind-the-scenes intrigue is accurate, however, it must also be noted that Burney's machinations had no noticeable long-term effect on Crotch's career, which proceeded on its placid course. He continued to lecture at various other venues, to teach both privately and later at the newly created Royal Academy of Music, of which he was the first Principal, and to retain a tenuous connection with Oxford that did not require his presence at the university. In time, Crotch was asked to resume lecturing at the Royal Institution, and he did so for a considerably higher fee than he had received before.

roughly from Josquin to Handel. This view of a lost golden age continued a line of complaint that began to be voiced in the last quarter of the eighteenth century by well-known advocates of ancient music whom Crotch continued to quote with respect and approval, especially Jones of Nayland.[45] Crotch had been closely allied with the ancient-music movement at Oxford and had been furthered in his career by individuals connected with ancient music, as indeed he was to be once again some four years later when the Royal Academy of Music was formed and he was named its first Principal.[46]

That Crotch was a sincere apologist for ancient music is reinforced by candid correspondence with his mentors, especially the Reverend Dr Jowett at Cambridge. Young Crotch actually seems more inflexible where the modern style is concerned than Jowett, a listed subscriber to Jones's *Treatise on the Art of Music*. In a letter to Jowett from 1804, Crotch reports that he has 'borrowed Haydn's Masses of a Mr. Tripp' and 'tried them and Mozart's', but is 'sorry to say that I cannot agree with you in liking them – no not even *at all*'.[47] Crotch does allow that Mozart's *Requiem* is a favourite of his, adding, however, that the part he likes best is the quartet 'Benedictus qui venit'.[48] Crotch concludes that Mozart, 'is inferior to Hasse and very much to Handel', adding more positively as a postscript that he has 'read a course of lectures this term to a class of 18' in which he speaks 'a little more favorably of Mozart as a vocal composer than I did'.[49] The only statement Crotch makes in this letter that might not seem to be in lock step with partisans of the ancient style concerns a recent concert at Cambridge in which he expresses surprise that 'you should have two concertos of Corelli and but one quartet of Haydn – I have always been of the opinion that one concerto of Corelli is enough for the longest bill'.[50]

---

[45] For example, in *Lectures*, 11231/1, which begins with a quotation from William Jones's (of Nayland) *A Treatise on the Art of Music, in which the Elements of HAR-MONY and AIR are Practically Considered …* (Colchester, 1784).

[46] Thus, in *GM*, 59 (July 1789), p. 610, cathedral organist and well-known ancient advocate Robert Nares takes Charles Burney to task for overlooking Crotch in the *General History*. Concerning Crotch's friends in the ancient-music community at Oxford, in *General Account*, Crotch notes that 'Mr. Crowe [of] the public oratorio of Oxford attended my first classes at Oxford and was the cause of my reading in town in 1805'. Crowe was himself a lecturer at the Royal Institution. In *Archives of the Royal Institution*, vol. 3, p. 284, a list detailing the lecture series read in 1803 includes 'the Rev. Mr. Crowe: a course of 16 or 24 Lectures on History, in March, April, and May, for £50 and the compliment of a Life admission to the Institution'.

[47] *Correspondence*.

[48] Ibid.

[49] Ibid.

[50] Ibid.

Crotch was well known for these sentiments, and it must therefore have come as something of a surprise for some in his audience when he began the introduction to his 1818 lecture series by observing that 'The improvement of modern music, since the period usually assigned to its lowest state of decline, is indescribably great; and the general advancement of the public taste in this country, and especially in this Metropolis, since the commencement of the present century, clearly is perceptible.'[51] He does not say exactly when the nadir of British taste was in this part of the lecture, but in the top margin of his notes he subtracts 40 from 1818 to arrive at 1778. Moreover, Crotch attributes recent improvements he cites to the establishment of well-known professional concert series associated with modern music like '[J. P.] Salomon's and afterwards of the Philharmonic Concert'. These concerts were 'directed by professional musicians' and consisted 'of the music *they* admire and in some degree embracing a variety of excellencies – at least uniting the best Vocal and Instrumental modern music'.[52] 'By making popularity a consideration of inferior moment', Crotch argues, these professionals 'lead instead of following, they correct instead of flattering the public taste'.[53] This, he thinks, is the appropriate role for professionals.

Some, but certainly not all, of the points Crotch makes here are consistent with the ideology of ancient music that Weber outlines. Central themes of the ideology of ancient music are an insistence that music has a more important part to play than mere entertainment, and a belief that appreciating it at this high level necessarily requires preparation and superior judgement. 'If you play an Adagio of Corelli to a person who knows nothing of Harmony', Weber quotes from Jones of Nayland's *A Treatise on the Art of Music*, 'you will raise no Admiration; for the same reason, as if you were to read Milton or Shakespeare to a man who does not understand the Grammar.'[54] The next line of the *Treatise*, which Weber does not quote, continues this line of argument in an overtly partisan manner, 'But a noisy vulgar *allegro*, full of impertinence and repetition, or a common Ballad, will strike the fancy of the one, as a low comedy or a farce is adapted to the capacity of the other.'[55]

If a militant disciple of ancient music like Jones of Nayland might have approved in principle of some of Crotch's ideas, that approval would not then have extended to Crotch's statement about the steady

---

[51] *Lectures*, NRO, MS 11232/2.

[52] Ibid.

[53] Ibid.

[54] Jones, *Treatise*, introduction, p. ii. Weber, *Rise of Musical Classics*, p. 203.

[55] Jones, *Treatise*, introduction, p. ii.

improvement of popular taste as revealed in recent music. Indeed, a common theme of the ideology of ancient music as Weber describes it, a theme evident in Jones of Nayland's remarks quoted above, is the notion that music had been in a prolonged state of decay precisely because it was in the control of an inferior social class which lacked the judgement to reject the specious charms of decadent modern music.[56] That was even true of individuals from higher social classes who patronized the modern style. Weber observes that both Jones and Bishop George Horne saw the ancient concerts 'in political terms, as a bulwark against the erosion of authority', objecting to the 'entertainments of the more frivolous members of the upper classes' as music that 'weakened the social order and demanded the intervention of truer, more enduring models of taste'.[57]

Finally, though the ancient-music movement has been viewed as supportive of what might be called professional values – a quality best revealed in its detailed programmes that supply more information about the music and its composers than is typical[58] – a militant ancient supporter in Crotch's audience might not have welcomed his emphasis on professional management. As his audience did not need to be reminded, the Concert of Ancient Music was by far the most conspicuous musical institution still in the control of amateurs. A few years after Crotch's lecture, in fact, the inadequacy of the Ancient Concert's management scheme of eight distinguished directors was respectfully noted in *The Harmonicon* by a long-time subscriber to the Ancient Concerts who calls for additional professional expertise.[59]

The Philharmonic Society, on the other hand, was an experiment in a new kind of co-operative that gave unprecedented control to professionals themselves. The contrast in management styles of the two organizations is noteworthy. Artistic control in the Ancient Concert rested with an individual director, chosen from the board to wield authoritarian direction over individual concerts. Satires of the Antient Concert caricature its rigid discipline and military-style precision as much as its condescending approach to dealing with rank-and-file musicians. Thus, Peter Pindar depicts Sir Watkin Williams Wynn, a director of the Ancient Concert, as 'The Alexander of the Tottenham troops;/ Who, tutor'd by his stampings, nods, grunts, whoops,/Do wondrous execution with their bows'.[60] Of 'mistress Walsingham', Pindar notes:

---

[56] Ibid., pp. 198–200.
[57] Weber, *Rise of Musical Classics*, p. 205.
[58] Ibid., p. 180.
[59] 'Clio', 'Concert of Ancient Music', *The Harmonicon*, 1 (1823), 56–8.
[60] John Wolcot, *The Works of Peter Pindar, esq.*, vols, London, (1812), vol. 1, p. 416.

Some people by their soul will swear,
That if Musicians miss but half a bar,
Just like an Irishman she starts to *bother*;
And, in the violence of Quaver-madness,
Where nought should reign but harmony and gladness,
She knocks one tuneful head against another:
Then screams in *such* chromatic tones,
Upon Apollo's poor affrighted Sons.[61]

The Philharmonic Society, by contrast, was formed on conspicuously democratic principles. The rules of the Philharmonic prohibited permanent distinctions of rank among the musicians and provided for creative decisions to be made by an elected board of directors. They also required that revenue from concerts be held in common by the society.[62] By the time of Crotch's later *Substance*, the musical world had changed enough that Crotch could insist publicly on professional management in a more direct manner than he was ready to venture even at the Surrey Institution in 1818. In 1831 he added to the remarks on Salomon and the Philharmonic quoted above a sentence commenting that, 'the loss of Salomon's concerts was amply supplied by the establishment of the Philharmonic, directed (as all musical establishments ought to be) by musicians alone'.[63]

Crotch's introductory lecture in 1818 should be read with an awareness of an ideological subtext that can accompany infrequent public attacks on the Ancient Concert around the turn of the century. Some of the earliest criticism of the Ancient Concert appears, first, in a periodical with definite radical sympathies, the *Monthly Magazine*. This periodical, a creation of the 'dirty little Jacobin' Sir Richard Philips, is said to have given 'a power to the Radical press, hitherto unknown'.[64] It is of some interest, in fact, that there is little open criticism of the Ancient Concert, aside from satires by Peter Pindar and the writing of dissident William Mason, until the first year of the *Monthly Magazine*'s publication in 1796. In that year, a long anonymous essay appeared by a solicitor named John Marsh in which the Concert of Ancient Music is cited by name.[65]

---

[61] Ibid., p. 418.

[62] Some of the society's rules are quoted in Myles Birket Foster, *History of the Philharmonic Society of London, 1813–1912: a Record of a Hundred Years Work in the Cause of Music* (London: John Lane, 1912), p. 5.

[63] W. Crotch, *Substance of Several Courses of Lectures on Music* (London, 1831; Clarabricken, Co. Kilkenny, Ireland: Boethius Press, 1986), p. 152.

[64] Walter Graham, *English Literary Periodicals* (New York: Octagon Books, 1966), p. 188–9.

[65] [Marsh], 'Comparison', pp. 981–6; C. L. Cudworth, 'An Essay by John Marsh', *Music and Letters*, 36 (1955), 155–64.

While Marsh's essay is ostensibly a balanced comparison of ancient and modern music, it includes loaded expressions that Crotch, then just beginning his academic career, correctly interpreted as supportive of the moderns.[66] Although Marsh is far from consistent on this issue, some of the points in this essay also reveal anti-élitist sentiments that can be associated in due course with the writings of liberals like Mason and with a liberal ideology of modern music. Though Marsh praises Haydn's 'ingenious modulation, and contrivance' and perversely seems intent on showing that in its own way Haydn's music is as complex and sophisticated as any ancient music, Marsh still argues that 'perhaps the proper test of excellence in [music] should not be, that it affords pleasure to professors and connoisseurs only, but to the greatest number of *amateurs* indiscriminately taken'.[67] His main complaint about Haydn and Pleyel is that they have 'in a great measure departed from that simplicity which alone is capable of giving *general* pleasure'. Marsh concludes that 'it would therefore be well for the state of music in general, if subsequent composers would adhere at all times to *simplicity*, and not attempt to imitate those very elaborate and extravagant compositions, which were merely designed to exhibit the powers of a modern orchestra'.[68]

After the turn of the century, attacks on the Ancient Concert are less guarded than in Marsh's anonymous essay. Marsh himself followed the essay with a volume of *Hints to Young Composers of Instrumental Music, Illustrated with 2 Movements for a Grand Orchestra in Score* (Chichester, n.d.), in which for the first time he used his own name and acknowledged his authorship of the earlier essay – confident, it would seem, that the battle was over and the moderns had won. He was wrong at least in the first of these assumptions. A decade after Marsh's essay but still seven years before Crotch's 1818 lectures, William Gardiner published an article in the *Monthly Magazine* that employs partisan rhetoric to defend Haydn, Mozart and Beethoven against the 'advocates of ancient music' who would 'dictate their own ideas of taste and prescribe the boundaries of science'.[69] Gardiner's article is itself a response to an earlier 'Vindication of Handel' by a correspondent who styles himself 'Oxensis'.[70]

The shift in the role of the professional that is reflected in a comparison of Pindar's satire in 1787 and Crotch's lecture in 1818 needs to be

---

[66] 'W. C.' [William Crotch], 'Remarks on the present State of Music', *Monthly Magazine*, 10 (1800), 125–7 and *Monthly Magazine*, 10 (1801), 505–6.

[67] [Marsh], 'Comparison', p. 984.

[68] Ibid., pp. 985 and 986.

[69] W. G. [William Gardiner], 'Defense of Modern Music', *Monthly Magazine*, 31 (1811), 133.

[70] *Monthly Magazine*, 33 (1812) pp. 12–15.

appreciated in the context of tensions that must have been building for some time between professional musicians and their wealthy benefactors, many of whom were open supporters of old music. These tensions may not have been made public before the turn of the century because there was no forum for the advancement of the professional musician's point of view and because few could have risked offending an important source of patronage. This changed the year after Crotch's 1818 lecture series with the publication of the first issue of *The Quarterly Musical Magazine and Review*, the first successful British music periodical. Aside from the efforts of editor Richard Mackenzie Bacon, a well-known liberal,[71] to champion the interests of the working professional, professionals could, for the first time, express themselves safely through the medium of anonymous letters to the editor. Both *QMMR* and *The Harmonicon* include subdued criticisms of ancient music's most respected institutions, though these never approach the ideological fervour of a few offerings in the *Monthly Magazine*. But there are also contributions by professionals in *QMMR* that ostensibly serve other purposes but still include attacks on ancient-music interests. Accordingly, a professional named F. W. Horncastle offers an essay on 'Plagiarism' in *QMMR* that is in reality a thinly veiled assault on the familiar ancient-music triumvirate of Handel, Corelli and Geminiani.[72] This essay eventually lists 'a few examples of petty larcenies' by moderns, but it is mostly addressed to 'such of your readers as may have been accustomed (like myself) to look up almost with reverence to the abilities of such writers as CORELLI, HANDEL, &c.&c'. Borrowing is a much greater sin for these last composers, who have 'increased the measure of their guilt in proportion as they were more enlightened, more experienced, and more exalted above "petty men," by the splendour of their genius'.[73]

Aside from promoting the interests of musicians and publishing their complaints, Bacon also launched a crusade in the first volume of his journal to promote better understanding between professional musicians and their patrons. He did so out of concern that

---

[71] In *The Science of Music in Britain 1714–1830: a Catalogue of Writings, Lectures, and Inventions*, (2 vols, New York: Garland, 1979), vol. 1, p. 39, J. C. Kassler identifies Bacon with liberal causes. In 1794 Bacon's father became editor of the *Norwich Mercury*, which Kassler identifies as 'one of the leading provincial organs of liberal opinion', and in 1804 Bacon himself assumed this position. Bacon is described as 'an important voice in liberal politics, heard not only through the columns of the NORWICH MERCURY but also in various pamphlets, periodical articles, and speeches written for Edward Harbord, 3d Baron Suffield, and for George Thomas Keppel, 6th Earl Albemarle'.

[72] F. W. H[orncastle], 'Plagiarism', *QMMR*, 4 (1822), pp. 141–7.

[73] Ibid., p. 142.

at present ... the character of the profession [of music] is clouded and obscured by strong facts and by stronger prejudices ... sufficient to close the doors, and to shut the hearts of a great proportion even of liberal persons, against all avoidable intercourse with men and women, who with so much of accomplishment to recommend them, have at the same time among them no small number of examples of laxity of principle to exclude them from society.[74]

Often this crusade employed fictitious 'letters to the editor' written by Bacon himself under various pseudonyms as a means of exposing extreme points of view.[75]

A major part of Bacon's long-term strategy was the creation of a Royal Academy of Music that would offer courses not only in music but in the liberal arts. The latter were necessary, he believed, if musicians were to gain the social standing they needed to be accepted into leadership positions.[76] Bacon was not alone in this; Horncastle contributed his own 'Plan for the Formation of an English Conservatorio' to *QMMR*, in which he also speaks of the need for liberal arts instruction among 'persons not so fortunate'.[77] In any case, Bacon's plan failed when a group made up of prominent members of the Concert of Ancient Music[78] presented as a *fait accompli* an alternative scheme for the academy in which its mission was narrowly limited to musical performance.

Bacon's political orientation is apparent in an angry editorial written shortly after the academy was founded, especially when he speaks of the ruling subcommittee of the newly formed Academy as 'an oligarchy, and an oligarchy almost self-created' and complains that this committee wielded 'absolute authority, without check or limit'.[79] It would be a

---

[74] 'Vetus' [Richard Mackenzie Bacon], 'On the Character of Musicians', *QMMR*, 1 (1818–19), 284–5.

[75] Bacon's practice of using fictitious letters to the editor is mentioned in Leanne Langley, 'The English Musical Journal in the Early Nineteenth Century', PhD, University of North Carolina, Chapel Hill, NC, 1983), pp. 240–42 and in Kassler, *Science*, vol. 1, p. 41. Bacon's practices are examined in Howard Irving, 'Richard Mackenzie Bacon and the Royal Academy of Music', *International Review of the Aesthetics and Sociology of Music*, 21 (1990), 79–90.

[76] This idea was first proposed in [Bacon] 'On the Character of Musicians', p. 292.

[77] 'F. W. H.'[Horncastle], 'Plan for the Formation of an English Conservatorio', *QMMR*, 4 (1822), 129–33. Horncastle notes (p. 133) that 'a liberal education, in the truest sense of the word, is absolutely necessary to form composers of any eminence; it is this that exalts their taste, enlightens their understanding, and assists their judgment. There is a certain refinement, not only in the manners, but in the thoughts of those who have been well educated, that never can be found in persons not so fortunate; it makes a man anxious for the society of his superiors, solicitous for his own improvement and respectability in life'.

[78] Weber, *Rise of Musical Classics*, p. 154.

[79] Anonymous [Richard Mackenzie Bacon] 'The Royal Academy of Music', *QMMR*, 4 (1822), 388.

mistake, however, to dismiss him as a partisan with extreme or atypical views, for on the whole his journal must be counted as a stunning popular success in an unforgiving literary environment that had already seen the failure of a number of earlier attempts at a music periodical. Bacon may refer to social divisions of which his audience was well aware, then, when he writes in his editorial that 'patrons and professors should walk side by side and in complete amity'. He adds, getting to the core of the problem,

> can such amity be expected in an undertaking [i.e., the academy] which estimates even the highest professional ability and character as articles to be bought and commanded, rather than as qualities to be deferred to and as the honourable distinctions of men who must naturally look to be consulted and treated with respect, particularly upon a subject matter which has formed the business of their lives and the object of their worldly affections? We fear not; and thus has crept into the execution of the plan an evil of the greatest magnitude – an evil originating, there is but too much ground to suspect, in an overweening desire to appropriate power.[80]

He complains that the Ancient Concert's plan for the academy 'takes all the power out of the hands of the profession ... while the authority, and with it the bulk of the patronage and controul, is vested in the hands of a few individuals'.[81]

Further, Bacon implies that an alternative scheme he and others were preparing when the Concert of Ancient Music staged its peremptory action had the support of the Philharmonic Society and therefore of an important segment of professional musicians themselves. Crotch's relationship with the Philharmonic Society is of some interest at this juncture. As one of the most respected musicians of the period and an individual of relatively moderate views, Crotch's name and support were sought by both the professionals and their patrons. He eventually developed a connection with the Philharmonic Society and published works like his *Specimens* through the Royal Harmonic Institution, a publishing branch of this professional co-operative. Crotch's name is listed in *QMMR* in 1819 as one of the 50 'members' of the Philharmonic Society, from which a governing body of 12 'Directors' was chosen at annual meetings.[82] The Philharmonic Society also played his music with some regularity for a short time during which it courted him. The programmes of the Philharmonic Society between 1813 and 1815 include his quartet 'Lo, Star-led Chiefs' from the oratorio *Palestine* in 1813, a

---

[80] Ibid., p. 399.

[81] Ibid., p. 396.

[82] Anonymous [Richard Mackenzie Bacon], 'The Philharmonic Society', *QMMR*, 1 (1818–19) pp. 340–50. A list of the society's 'Members' is provided on p. 349.

'Symphony (MS.)' performed at a concert in 1814, and both 'Lo, Cherub Bands' from *Palestine* and 'Lo, Star-led Chiefs' again in 1815. Still, Crotch's correspondence indicates that he gracefully declined the Philharmonic Society's wishes for a more permanent relationship in 1815.[83]

Crotch's moderate image helped him not only to retain the good will of both ancient and modern factions throughout this incident but in time to be named the first Principal of the academy. More generally, one might say that Crotch was to some extent able to play the part of *de facto* mediator during a delicate renegotiation of the roles played by musicians and their benefactors. When the ruling subcommittee of the academy led by John Fane, Lord Burghersh, a Director of the Ancient Concert, heard of Bacon's plans, it sent a circular to professionals that used Crotch's name 'in order, if possible, to repress this hostile demonstration'.[84] 'This judicious and conciliatory letter soon silenced the incipient opposition', the Reverend W. W. Cazalet observes in his mid-nineteenth century history of the academy, since 'the leading Members of the Profession who had hitherto kept aloof, finding that their very first compeers had given in their adhesion, setting aside every other feeling, now cordially co-operated to bring about, as speedily as possible, the establishment of the Academy.'[85] There is in fact nothing conciliatory about the text of this letter, which simply identifies Crotch as the Principal and orders any professionals hoping to work at the academy to rally around him.

With this background in mind, we can return now to Crotch's recitation of recent advances in music in 1818. One of the most significant improvements he cites has to do with a sudden change in the demeanor of audiences at the professionally managed public concerts he describes. In a lecture from 1820, Crotch notes that in only the past few years the symphonies of Haydn had begun to be regarded no longer 'as opportunities for the audience to hold a loud conversation between the vocal pieces of a concert, hurried over in the performance, with no repeats, and the adagios omitted, as was long the case in this nation' but rather

---

[83] Foster, *History of the Philharmonic*, pp. 11, 16, 19, 20. Though Crotch appears as a performer in Philharmonic Society concerts, there are no further performances of his music listed until 1819. Concerning the Philharmonic's wishes in 1815, in a letter addressed to C. J. Ashley and dated 31 May 1815 (*Correspondence*) Crotch writes, 'Residing, as I shall do, the greater part of the year in the country and much employed in professional occupations I cannot tie myself down to any regular engagements to the Philharmonic or any other Society. The concerts for the previous year also being over I beg leave to request the members to accept of my resignation as director.'

[84] Revd W. W. Cazalet, *The History of the Royal Academy of Music* (London: T. Bosworth, 1854), p. 21.

[85] Ibid.

that they are treated as 'the chief objects of attention and admiration so that even the adagios and finales were encored, and every movement was heard with silent rapture'.[86] He sees this new way of listening to relatively recent composers like Haydn as consistent with manners that had been practised for many years before by the devotees of ancient music. He applauds the fact that public concerts had also begun to include a limited repertory of much older music by Handel and other representatives of what he calls the ancient style along with the more challenging efforts of recent and even living composers he thinks share a common approach. Crotch contrasts this new eclecticism with a regrettable earlier segregation of the two musical species of ancient and modern music, in which concerts were invariably exclusive events featuring one or the other.[87]

In the light of remarks quoted above that seem supportive of the moderns and their partisans, and possibly vaguely censorious of the Concert of Ancient Music, Crotch may appear to be something other than an ancient sympathizer in a conflict of musical factions. In fact, however, the moderns are not by any means consistently cited as heros in his 1818 lecture. Crotch resurrects the rhetoric of an earlier period in the history of this long quarrel when he notes, inconsistent with the overall tone and spirit of his message, that the decline of music began in the first place some ten years before his 1778 nadir when 'a great musical revolution was attempted, but, happily, not effected'. This is a reference to the introduction of works in the modern style in the concerts of J. C. Bach and C. F. Abel.

A more subdued treatment of the same ideas appears in the later *Substance*. The *Substance* avoids assigning blame to either side and simply reports that the decline of the art began when 'the musical world of connoisseurs were divided into two opponent parties, the admirers of the ancient and modern styles; the one despising the trifling melodies of the opera, and the other the barbarous and mechanical structure of the fugue'.[88] In other words, Crotch indicates that the ancient–modern quarrel was not a symptom of music's decline but its cause. If so, the quarrel should not be viewed as the valiant crusade to preserve excellence in the face of cultural decay that Jones of Nayland had contended 40 years earlier. Further, Crotch argues that the decline of music began to be reversed with the appearance of works that Jones saw as the epitome of modern corruption. 'The introduction of Boccherini's quintets, of Haydn's quartets, and Clementi's sonatas, into our chambers,

---

[86] *Lectures*, NRO, MS 11063/6.
[87] *Lectures*, NRO, MS 11232/2.
[88] Crotch, *Substance*, pp. 148.

and particularly of Haydn's sinfonias into our concerts stamped a value on modern music which many of the admirers of the ancient school were disposed to acknowledge', Crotch contends, explaining that in this music the 'beauty of melody and scientific harmony' were both apparent.[89] In an often quoted passage from his *Treatise*, by contrast, Jones had given the first two composers Crotch names 'first place among the Moderns for *invention*', but had added that 'they are sometimes so desultory and unaccountable in their way of treating a Subject, that they may be reckoned among the wild warblers of the wood'.[90]

Crotch concludes that it was only 'when Mozart became the universal favourite' that 'the long-desired reconciliation between these parties was easy'.[91] In assigning Mozart the role of bridge between the two camps, Crotch's *Substance* is in agreement with the 1818 lecture in which he first proposed this idea. In the earlier source, Crotch explains that 'the lovers of madrigals, anthems, and choruses eagerly added [the word "admitted" is over-scored] to their former store of amusement, the highly ingenious and elaborate vocal trios, quartets and finales from the operas of this extraordinary composer'.[92] In the context of subsequent lectures in his 1818 series, this is clearly a reference to *Don Giovanni*'s first London performances the previous year. At the same time, Crotch notes – one would think optimistically – that 'on the other hand few, if any, are now found who affect to despise what is scientific and sublime'.[93]

Reconciliation was necessary because in Crotch's view the ancient–modern struggle was bitter. Resuming the partisan rhetoric of militant ancient-music supporters, Crotch notes that in the wake of the modern-music revolution 'the attack [against ancient music] was violent, and the defense vigorous'.[94] The enemy had many faces, but conspicuous among them were 'the admirers of novelty and especially of what they can readily comprehend'.[95] Crotch claims the ancient camp maintained a tenuous foothold against popular opposition because of the

---

[89] In Crotch's first lecture to use this paragraph, NRO 11232/2, the list of composers who redeemed the modern style is slightly different. That lecture reads, in part, 'The introduction of Haydn's music into our concerts and of the productions for the chamber of Boccherini Clementi and Kozeluch, in which harmony and imitation were cultivated, stamped a dignity on modern music which the admirers of the ancient school were disposed to acknowledge.'

[90] Jones, *Treatise*, p. 49.

[91] *Substance*, p. 149.

[92] *Lectures*, NRO, MS 11232/2.

[93] Ibid.

[94] Ibid.

[95] Ibid.

'Performances at Westminster Abbey' – that is, the famous Handel commemoration concerts, given on 26, 27, 29 May and 5 June 1784, to mark the centennial of Handel's birth – and the programmes of the Concert of Ancient Music. In the end, however, the dispute could only achieve its final resolution with Mozart's fusion of the best elements of the two schools.[96]

Crotch and Sir Joshua Reynolds

It is reasonable to question the sincerity of Crotch's conversion experience in 1818, since by this time modern music and especially the music of Mozart was experiencing a surge of popularity. One response to the charge of accommodation is to recall that Crotch's career does not reveal a tendency to court public opinion; on the contrary, in half a lifetime of public exposure as a music critic Crotch had proudly taken the path that led directly away from popular favourites and had in fact viewed public favour almost as evidence in itself of musical inferiority.[97] More importantly, there are indications that Crotch's change of heart in 1818 was not based on a rethinking of his aesthetic position but on a better understanding of the moderns' interests. As he reports in the introductory lecture to his 1818 series, he stands by his earlier positions and thinks it is 'essential to the existence of good taste that they should all continue to be admitted'. What is different is that these positions 'are no longer, as formerly, advanced in the way of opposition and hostility to each other'. Crotch's experiences with the Philharmonic Society in the years before this 1818 lecture series no doubt gave him an appreciation for the best modern music, as did his own composition of a symphony in the modern style for the Philharmonic Society in 1814.[98] But the main argument for Crotch's sincerity as a critic is the fact that from the very beginning of his lecturing career he had advocated a position that is entirely consistent in theory – if not always in practice – with the position of his 1818 lectures. The best way to understand Crotch's 1818 epiphany, then, is to consider

---

[96] Ibid.

[97] As Crotch notes in *Substance*, p. 20, 'were the majority always right, why are the Battle of Prague and Pleyel's Concertante, which they so much admired, now passed into oblivion to make way for similar trash?'

[98] Crotch's symphony in F major has been published with an introduction by Nicholas Temperley in Barry Brook and Barbara B. Heyman, eds, *The Symphony: 1720–1840*, (60 vols, New York: Garland, 1984), Temperley reports, p. xii, that, 'Though it has a number of gestures that recall Beethoven, the general style is modelled on Haydn's and Mozart's, with the first violins still retaining the lion's share of melodic material.'

various sources of influence that contributed to the development of his aesthetic theory.

Two sources of influence contributed to the opinions expressed in Crotch's 1818 series. One is a critical tradition that preceded him in the writing of Jones of Nayland, Hawkins and others. These writers, especially Jones, contributed a network of stereotypes and conventional wisdom that is never far beneath the surface of Crotch's lectures. In fact, in the 1818 lectures in particular the catch-phrases and stereotypes of earlier advocates of ancient music appear as a constant counterpoint to Crotch's main message, a message with which they are often in conflict. Before examining some commonplaces of the literature, it will be useful to consider briefly some consequences of Crotch's use of the ideas of his model in aesthetics, Sir Joshua Reynolds.

Like Reynolds but very much unlike Burney and almost every other contributor to the issues of ancient-versus-modern music, Crotch found it possible to consider music criticism and aesthetics as ends in themselves and to keep both aesthetic speculation and practical criticism largely separate from specific issues of morals, politics and ideology. Glimpses of this ideology are revealed briefly when Crotch speaks in the quotation above of a 'great musical revolution' by the moderns – an idea that Crotch probably took from Marsh's essay – and when he expresses his high-church religious piety. The latter, in a very few exceptional cases, can even lead him to intolerant observations on Roman Catholicism. Even here, however, his remarks are typically couched in terms of practical musical issues and are not gratuitous attacks.[99] In any event, Crotch does not treat the genre of ancient music as a patriotic or cultural symbol, nor does he connect ancient music or, for that matter, cultivated music in general, with issues of social class. His writing is undeniably élitist, but his élite are to be determined not by class or even by class-sensitive issues like general education, but specifically by musical training and ability. In some of his lectures Crotch makes a point of arguing that a 'musical ear' is an essential requisite for the sophisticated listener and that this is 'a possession, neither hereditary nor attainable by riches nor industry; but solely in the disposal of nature'. Paraphrasing an earlier statement by Burney on this point, Crotch insists that 'the

---

[99] A case in point can be found in Crotch's discussion of Haydn's *Seven Last Words* in *Lectures*, 11230/7. Here Crotch observes that 'In a Roman Catholic country' the audience '*is perhaps much engrossed by the excellence of the performance*'. To this he added in an earlier draft, later over scored, 'too little reverence is there I fear paid to sacred subjects even when performed in places of worship – the minds of the audience are wholly occupied with the music and not being permitted to applaud by clapping with the hands they testify their approbation by coughing, scraping with the feet & other irreverent noises'.

opinions of a man, concerning music, who is not possessed of this requisite, can only be compared with those of a blind man on painting'.[100]

Like earlier supporters of ancient music, Crotch thought modern music inferior to music of the golden age and regarded this inferiority as the natural product of a cycle of greatness and decline that he argues all art forms necessarily follow at points in their history. But he does not indicate, as others do, that music's decline mirrored or contributed to a broader pattern of cultural or moral decay. Nor does he usually stress that the decline of music paralleled a simultaneous decline in all other arts resulting from the shallow consumerism of the emerging middle class. He does, however, pass along standard complaints about the fate of some arts without offering an explanation of cause and effect. Like other ancients, he is reflexively sceptical of innovation and prevailing fashion.[101] In the lectures reprinted here he is particularly concerned about the fashion for vapid piano music, a conspicuous product of consumerism and rising middle-class social ambitions that are connected with the piano as an ornamental accomplishment for women.

Consistent with a common position of both ancient music enthusiasts and neo-classical aesthetic theory as it is set forth in Reynolds's *Discourses* and other sources, Crotch's concerns about piano music often stress the fear of deception, of the listener being taken in by impressive-sounding productions that turn out to lack substance.[102] It is not merely the unsophisticated who face this risk. Crotch indicates in the fourth lecture of his 1818 series that he himself no long feels competent to judge some kinds of piano playing because he has 'frequently heard the most difficult music played to perfection by those who were, as I afterwards found, wholly ignorant of what they were doing and incapable of performing the most simple air correctly without the previous instruction of a master and much practice'.[103] Accordingly, he objects

---

[100] *Lectures*, NRO, MS 11064/7. See Burney's review of *Melody the Soul of Music: an Essay towards the improvement of the Musical Art*, by Alexander Molleson, *Monthly Review*, 27 (1798), 190.

[101] For example, Col/7/43: 'How can it be possible that, of all the arts, music alone should be constantly improving from whatever innovation or addition its successive cultivation may choose (I had almost said *happen*) to make? Is Novelty the chief requisite of *our art alone* and originality the chief merit in *her* productions *only*? The ages at which Poetry, Painting, Architecture, & Sculpture arrived at perfection are well known & mentioned without fear of reproach; the causes of their decline have been ascertained, and the means of recovery pointed out.'

[102] Thus, Hugh Honour writes in *Neo-classicism* (New York: Penguin Books, 1977), p. 19, that neo-classicism in painting is characterized by 'A high-minded puritan contempt for the mundane and elegant, a distrust of virtuosity, of being taken in by mere dexterity and deftness of touch ... '.

[103] *Lectures*, NRO, MS 11232/5.

not only to recent piano music but to piano teaching that emphasizes technical facility over utilitarian keyboard skills like score-reading.[104] But unlike earlier writers who voice similar objections, Crotch is not concerned about the unseemliness of personal exhibition or indeed about any attendant social issues raised by piano study but instead discusses only the musical ramifications of this phenomenon.[105]

When Crotch makes occasional statements that seem to reflect an orientation similar to earlier ancient apologists like Jones of Nayland, his opinions need to be read with care. In his reply to Burney's angry letter in 1805, Crotch seems completely in line with earlier advocates of ancient music when he asks, 'is music capable of perpetual improvement in all its branches? The Architecture and Sculpture of ye Moderns is surely not to be compared with those of ye Ancients – Painting too is on the decline'.[106] In other places he adds poetry to his list of declining arts.[107] But he also concludes in the present letter, 'Yet I see with delight that Astronomy, Chemistry, & other Arts & Sciences (& I wish I could add Vocal Music) are daily improving.'[108] His failure to include the arts among his improving areas is revealing, but Crotch seems sincere in the basic principle that underlies his remarks: he acknowledges not only the fact of modern progress but the progress of some branches of music itself. His lecture notes repeatedly stress that his specific area of concern within modern music is the decline of vocal works and particularly sacred music, and that he approves of directions taken in modern instrumental music. At the same time, because vocal music is the highest musical species in a complex hierarchical aesthetic system he developed from the ideas of Reynolds, Crotch could argue that weakness in this particular area indicates an overall decline in music.[109]

---

[104] See the first lecture of Part Two of this volume, *Lectures*, NRO, MS 11232/2.

[105] In Howard Irving, '"Music as a Pursuit for Men": Accompanied Keyboard Music as Domestic Recreation in England', *College Music Symposium*, 30 (1990), 126–37, there is a brief survey of British conduct books on the subject of keyboard playing as an ornamental accomplishment.

[106] Burney, *General History*, vol. 2, p. 1037.

[107] See Crotch's comments in the fourth lecture of Part Two in this volume, *Lectures*, 11232/5.

[108] Burney, *General History*, vol. 2, p. 1037.

[109] See, *Lectures*, NRO, MS 11063/5: 'I shall conclude this lecture with a caution to my auditors not to lose sight of the difference between the improvement of any particular branch of the art and the decay of the art as a whole, as if these were contradictory and incompatible. They must not suppose when I speak of the decline of music that I deny any one merit to the modern school, for which even its warmest champions ought to contend. I admit the superiority of modern instrumental music and even of comic vocal music, though ancient music should be preferred on account of its excelling in the choral, sacred, and sublime styles. An old tree may flourish and send forth new limbs

In short, then, he thinks modern music is doing a good job at what it sets out to do, and he agrees that there is a place for music that does not aspire to what he calls the 'sublime', his highest musical category. The sublime, indeed, was the highest category in all the arts by long tradition in British aesthetic writing going back at least to 1652 with the first British publication of the treatise *Peri Hupsous* by Greek rhetorician Longinus.[110] Crotch unashamedly wrote music himself that does not aspire to his highest subspecies of music, the 'pure sublime', including not only the above mentioned symphony but also, and even more revealingly, sacred music. Later critics, detecting inconsistency between Crotch's theory and practice, interpreted Crotch's sacred music as an indication of a shift in attitude.[111] In this Crotch's intentions are misunderstood in much the same way as Crotch's intellectual model Reynolds – who as a practising artist specialized in portraiture but as a writer on art branded this very genre a lesser sphere of artistic endeavour.[112]

As Reynolds remarked, 'perfection in an inferior style may be reasonably preferred to mediocrity in the highest walks of art'. Hence, then, is 'the necessity of the connoisseur's knowing in what consists the excellency of each class, in order to judge how near it approaches to perfection'. For that matter, 'EVEN in works of the same kind, as in history-painting, which is composed of various parts', Reynolds claims that 'excellence of an inferior species, carried to a very high degree, will

---

when past its full growth and upon the whole in a state of decay. An apology for the repetition of these statements will I trust appear unnecessary when I assure my audience that notwithstanding the frequency with which I have urged and explained these opinions for years past in all my courses of lectures my meaning has been in several instances perverted and misrepresented, or at least not clearly understood.'

[110] Peter Kivy, 'Mainwaring's *Handel*: Its Relation to English Aesthetics' *Journal of the American Musicological Society*, 17 (1964), 170–75. In *The Sublime: a Study of Critical Theories in XVIII-Century England* (Ann Arbor, MI, 1960), 54, Samuel H. Monk attributes to Joseph Addison the distinction of establishing the sublime as a separate category, distinct from the beautiful.

[111] In *A History of English Cathedral Music 1549–1889*, 2 vols (London: T. Werner Laurie, n.d.), John S. Bumpus argues, with reference to the famous Gresham prize for sacred music of which Crotch was a judge, that 'the style recommended by Crotch for the employment of the aspirants for the Gresham Prize Medal is by no means represented in any of these anthems [i.e., 'Sing we merrily', 'How Dear are Thy Counsels', 'O Lord God of hosts', 'Be merciful unto me', all from a collection of *Ten Anthems* published in 1798], for they exhibit "variety", "contrast", "expression", and, in some measure, "novelty" and "originality". His views on the subject of Church music evidently underwent a sudden change'.

[112] As artist William Blake asks in his bitter marginalia to the *Discourses*, if Reynolds valued Rafaelle so much, as he often claims, 'why then did he not follow Rafael's track?' *Complete Writings*, ed. Geoffrey Keynes (London: Oxford University Press, 1966), p. 447.

make a work very valuable, and in some measure compensate for the absence of the higher kinds of merit'.[113] One should not look down at the lesser species of art because, 'both [the greater and lesser styles] have merit', and both 'may be excellent though in different ranks, if uniformity be preserved, and the general and particular ideas of nature be not mixed. Even the meanest of them is difficult enough to attain'.[114]

The division of music into separate branches that aspire to different artistic ends and can be excellent in different ways is the most important element of Crotch's thinking that derives from Reynolds's *Discourses*. Reynolds and Crotch also believe that individual works of art should be judged according to the qualities that are important for their species and to some extent according to the intention of the artist. As Crotch notes in connection with a quality he calls 'design' in music,

> It is scarcely necessary to caution the student against that narrow, though too common prejudice, which, not regarding the general character of a movement, exclaims against one species of music because it is not another, complains that a movement is slow or quick or chromatic or noisy without considering the author's intention. Though the same persons would readily perceive the absurdity of objecting that a tragedy were not a comedy, or an elegy an epic poem. Before any composition therefore is censured, let the meaning of the author be considered.[115]

There are, of course, limits to the freedom he would allow composers in the execution of their intentions, and statements like the above are usually qualified by a stress on the need to adhere to the rules of harmony and to basic formal principles. Still, one finds Crotch acknowledging, in line with the conventional wisdom of the eighteenth century, that '[counterpoint's] rules are more useful in correcting blemishes than in conferring beauties, and that the ability of composing can only be acquired by practice and experience'.[116]

Crotch's stress on practical experience when rules prove inadequate is consistent with the teachings of Reynolds. This emphasis has an important bearing on the question of who should be the final arbiter on matters of artistic quality and, therefore, ultimately on the role of professionals in the management of artistic institutions. Reynolds's division of art into categories in which different rules apply was made necessary in the first place, as he relates in the last of his *Discourses* in 1790, because the theory of art he read and heard when he first set out to organize his

---

[113] Sir Joshua Reynolds, *Discourses on Art*, ed. Robert R. Wark (New Haven, CT, and London: Yale University Press, 1975), p. 130.

[114] Ibid., p. 71.

[115] *Lectures*, 11231/1.

[116] Ibid.

thoughts as a critic – a theory, created in most cases by literary men without practical experience, that was paid constant lip-service by wealthy connoisseurs – was inconsistent with his own practical experience.[117] In other words, no single set of rules could account for the empirical fact that a variety of different approaches succeeded in accomplishing what he thought was the ultimate purpose of art, 'to make an impression on the imagination and the feeling'.[118] His statement about artistic categories is made, moreover, in the context of other statements that exalt the professional as the only legitimate authority. There is sometimes more than a hint of frustration on this point, especially in Reynolds's final retrospective discourse in 1790. Here, Reynolds is reluctant to divert 'the Student from the practice of his Art to speculative theory, to make him a *mere* Connoisseur instead of a Painter' and insists that

> one short essay written by a Painter, will contribute more to advance the theory of our art, than a thousand volumes such as we sometimes see; the purpose of which appears to be rather to display the refinement of the Author's own conceptions of impossible practice, than to convey useful knowledge or instruction of any kind whatever.[119]

The primacy of the professional applies particularly to kinds of art that are based on a union of different kinds of excellence. It is the professional artist alone, Reynolds insists, who 'knows what is, and what is not, within the province of his art to perform' and who can avoid perplexing the student 'with an imaginary union of excellencies incompatible with each other'.[120] This statement echoes an earlier remark in which he complains about the 'many writers on our art, who, not being of the profession, and consequently not knowing what can or cannot be done' who 'praise excellencies that can hardly exist together'.[121] At the same time, Reynolds acknowledges in the earlier source, that 'the summit of excellence seems to be an assemblage of contrary qualities, but mixed, in such proportions, that no one part is found to counteract each other'. Again, he insists that 'how hard this is to be attained in every art, those only know, who have made the greatest progress in their respective professions'.[122]

Reynolds's notion of a highest class of art that is made up of a union of different kinds of excellence and is susceptible to evaluation only by

---

[117] Reynolds, *Discourses*, pp. 267–8.
[118] Ibid., p. 241.
[119] Ibid., pp. 269 and 267.
[120] Ibid, p. 267.
[121] Ibid., p. 78.
[122] Ibid., p. 79.

specialists is important for the present purposes because it was the model for Crotch's sublime style and therefore for the notion of classical music. From the beginning, Reynolds speaks of a highest style that, unlike lesser species of art, is based on qualities that only have their desired effect on the cultivated viewer.[123] In his first discussion of this style Reynolds contends 'it is not easy to define in what this great style consists; nor to describe, by words, the proper means of acquiring it, if the mind of the student should be at all capable of such an acquisition'. Both here and elsewhere he is as unsure about whether the most refined appreciation of his highest style can be acquired by anyone other than a practitioner of the art. Years later, in *Discourse* XIII, he suggests that refined taste 'is the consequence of education and habit' but adds an important specific recommendation: that 'A critick in the higher style of art, ought to possess the same refined taste, which directed the Artist in his work.'

Reynolds initially applied his notion of a higher style of art to the art of a particular time and place. But as the concept of a higher style unfolded in later discourses, his highest category became more like a fundamental dichotomy than a class in the sense of Reynolds's other, lesser species; the great style is a notion applied to all of Reynolds's other divisions and categories, and is specifically identified in other art forms including music.[124] The terminology varies, much as earlier eighteenth-century discussion of, for example, the musical sublime was slow to standardize its critical vocabulary. In different discourses Reynolds speaks of the 'grand style', the 'great style', and the 'great manner', which are related to if not identical with the '*gusto grande*', the '*beau ideal*', and the 'epick stile'. His lesser approach, similarly, is variously called the 'ornamental style', the 'sensual style', the 'splendid', and even the 'little style'. Although Reynolds commonly associates the great style with the high Renaissance, his later formulation of the idea makes it ahistorical, limits it to no particular subject-matter, and applies it to all genres of art from history painting to landscape.

There is a central principle underlying Reynolds's higher approach that translates unusually well into music, as Reynolds himself indicates. In an early version of *Discourse* XV, he observes that 'our art in its highest and most refined state has perhaps a little of what I apprehend Musick has much more', that is, the quality of 'depending on

---

[123] Ibid., p. 135.

[124] The idea that Reynolds's Great Style is not a simple category but rather a more fundamental kind of distinction is found in Walter John Hipple, jr, *The Beautiful, the Sublime, & the Picturesque in Eighteenth-Century British Aesthetic Theory* (Carbondale, IL: Southern Illinois University Press, 1957), pp. 147–8.

Convention, to understand which requires some habit study and attention'.[125] In the final version of this discourse he reminds his audience that 'as this great style itself is artificial in the highest degree, it presupposes in the spectator, a cultivated and prepared artificial state of mind', adding that 'it is an absurdity therefore to suppose that we are born with this taste, though we are with the seeds of it, which, by the heat and kindly influence of his genius, may be ripened in us'.[126]

A closely related idea is found at the beginning of *Discourse* IV and is quoted often by Crotch: 'The value and rank of every art is in proportion to the mental labour employed in it, or the mental pleasure produced by it.'[127] Crotch, however, usually shifts part of the burden of mental labour from the composer to the audience and emphasizes their need for patience more than their right to intellectual pleasure. His paraphrase of the above makes it, 'the value and rank of every style bears a correspondent proportion to the mental labour employed in its formation and the mental attention required for the enjoyment of its performance'.[128] In still another place Crotch says that 'the rank and value of each style are deduced from a consideration of the mental labour employed in their formation and the mental capacities required for the comprehension and enjoyment of them'.[129] Reynolds and Crotch would have agreed that the higher class does not appeal at first. 'It is the lowest style of the arts, whether of Painting, Poetry, or Musick', Reynolds writes, 'that may be said, in the vulgar sense, to be naturally pleasing. The higher efforts of those arts, we know by experience, do not affect minds wholly uncultivated.'[130] This is also an idea that Crotch quotes often, adding that 'The good composer must not, therefore, write for the majority of hearers; he must not be discouraged by the inattention or censures of the public.'[131]

Crotch's earliest Oxford lectures divide music into two categories modelled after Reynolds's great–lesser style dichotomy. These categories were modified around the time he began lecturing in London, after a more careful reading of Reynolds, Uvedale Price, Burke and others[132] that caused Crotch to extend Reynolds's ideas in a direction

---

[125] Frederick Whiley Hilles, *The Literary Career of Sir Joshua Reynolds* (Cambridge: Cambridge University Press, 1936), p. 246.

[126] Reynolds, *Discourses*, p. 277.

[127] Ibid., p. 57.

[128] *Lectures*, NRO, MS 11229/10.

[129] Crotch, *Substance*, p. 38.

[130] Reynolds, *Discourses*, p. 233.

[131] Crotch, *Substance*, pp. 19–20.

[132] *General Account*: 'I also made some alterations in the latter part of the introductory lecture, having become *somewhat* better acquainted with Sir Joshua Reynolds

Crotch contended was implicit in the *Discourses* from the start. To view this transformation from the beginning, it is necessary to look at Crotch's earlier Oxford lectures, where he lays out a version of Reynolds's original dichotomy:

> There are two styles of music. The one has for its object an endeavor to excite the most sublime affections – the most noble passions. It possesses uncommon richness and depth of contrivance in the harmony and modulation (or change of key) and a certain steadiness and sobriety of melody, which precludes all levity and is peculiarly suitable to sacred subjects. The other style has also for its object the excitement of the various affections of the mind but by neglecting harmony and depth of contrivance and by possessing great contrasts, novelty, variety, levity and abundance of ornament, seems peculiarly calculated to excite surprise and pleasure, and is less suitable to sacred subjects but very proper for the theatre.[133]

He concludes that 'the first of these styles is generally known by the name ancient music though compositions are still produced in the same style and it was at its highest pitch of perfection in the beginning of the 18th century'. He adds that 'the latter style is denominated modern music though its invention took place before the ancient style had arrived at perfection'.[134]

This linkage between ancient music and the higher style is not maintained after the earliest lectures, nor did Crotch continue to think in terms of a dichotomy. Instead, claiming that what he calls the 'beautiful' is actually a separable and lesser subspecies of Reynolds's sublime, much as Burke had contended in *A Philosophical Enquiry into the Origin of our Ideas of the Sublime and Beautiful*, Crotch describes three categories.[135]

As late as the introduction to the January 1805 series to which Burney objected so strongly, Crotch had not found a satisfactory name for his third and lowest style category. Its characteristics include,

> playfulness of melody, broken and varied measure, intricacy of harmony and modulation, and a perpetual endeavour to excite surprise in the mind of the auditor. This style which has not yet obtained a name is perfectly analogous to the picturesque in painting, and I shall distinguish it by the term ornamental, which however is not so appropriate as I would wish.[136]

Lectures, and Uvedale Price, Burke &c. and divided music into the sublime, the beautiful and a third style which I afterwards called the ornamental.'

[133] *Lectures*, NRO, MS 11064/7.
[134] Ibid.
[135] Hipple, *The Beautiful, the Sublime*, p. 95.
[136] *Lectures*, NRO, MS 11229/1.

At this point Crotch did not yet realize that Reynolds himself had sanctioned the use of 'ornamental' for this style.[137] Crotch's reluctance to use Uvedale Price's perfectly serviceable alternative term 'picturesque', on the other hand, no doubt had to do with a contemporary vogue for the picturesque that was inconsistent with the low rank Crotch intended.[138] It was essential for this style to be at the bottom of Crotch's hierarchy because it lacked intellectual substance and relied on the short-term expediency of surprise to hold the listener's attention. 'That which once pleased from its beauty will always please', Crotch contends, and 'that which was once sublime can never be mean.' But 'that which depends on mere novelty for its effect is the flower of a day and when it ceases to be new all its charms will wither and be forgotten'.[139]

Like Reynolds's great style, Crotch's sublime could be created by seemingly opposite means. Reynolds notes that 'Grandeur of effect', an essential component of his higher style, can be produced either by 'reducing the colours to little more than chiaro oscuro', or by 'making the colours very distinct and forcible, such as we see in those of Rome and Florence'.[140] In the same way, Crotch reports that the effect of the sublime can be produced in music not only 'when a few simple notes are performed in unison or octaves by a variety of instruments or voices, in the manner of the ancients' but, conversely, when there is 'a multitude of voices and instruments, performing different species of melody and rhythm at once, yet all conspiring in harmony'. Crotch speaks of a musical sublime 'when the harmony is clear and simple, but the melody and measure dignified and marked', but also, and again conversely, 'when the harmony and modulation are learned and mysterious, when the ear is unable to anticipate the transitions from chord to chord, and from key to key, if the melody and measure are grave'. As Samuel Wesley later summarized, describing the basic issues of Crotch's system better than Crotch himself (whom he quotes), the '*one* principal character of the *sublime* is simplicity' but there are in fact two ways in which the effect of simplicity can be accomplished in music. One is obvious, the use of a single melodic line as in chant. But there is also a '*complex* Species of Sublimity which may be produced without *injuring* or *weak-*

---

[137] In *Lectures*, NRO, MS 11229/1 Crotch observes 'The term "*Ornamental*", which I have bestowed on this third style in music, is perhaps not altogether so improper as I once imagined since Sir Joshua Reynolds in one of his works makes use of the words "*The Picturesque or Ornamental style*" and this he opposes to that higher walk which unites Sublimity and Beauty.'

[138] *Lectures*, NRO, MS 11231/1.

[139] *Lectures*, NRO, MS 11232/12.

[140] Reynolds, *Discourses*, p. 61.

ening that simplicity of general Effect which ought ever to *characterize devotional music'.*[141]

Reynolds was reluctant to allow that the great style could be mixed with lesser styles, notwithstanding his eventual acceptance that the mixed excellence is the highest form of art. In *Discourse* IV he speaks of a 'composite style', but he adds that it is a 'perilous' undertaking in which few have succeeded. Moreover, what few successes Reynolds could detail in painting involved the elevation of a lesser approach by the addition of elements of the great style; the latter, Reynolds argues, is always contaminated by the mixture of lesser approaches.[142] This position is considered further in his next address, which examines how and under what circumstances various excellencies can be united. But it was not until some 14 years later, in *Discourse* XIII, that Reynolds seems fully to have understood the implications of a great style that is a basic principle rather than a simple category. In *Discourse* XIII Reynolds purposefully steps back to take a broader view of the principles that guide his art by comparing them with other arts.

Crotch, in contrast with his intellectual model, was from the beginning more at home with the notion of a highest style that is abstract and made up of a union of different approaches. In a lecture from 1806, Crotch describes his three styles as basic principles whose origins antedate cultivated music itself. Speaking of their invention, he is forced to explain that he actually means

> merely the adoption of these styles into scientific music. Their original invention I must conceive to have taken place at a very remote period even far anterior to Christianity to have been preserved in national music to the present time and applied by composers to the music of the church, the madrigal, the cantata, the oratorio, and the opera according to the nature of the subject, and the gradual improvements made in the various kinds of musical instruments and in the elements of practical harmony.[143]

It may be worth noting, in the same vein, that Crotch conceives of the mythical music of the Greeks of antiquity as a varied corpus in which all three of his styles were represented. Indeed, he uses a progression in ancient Greek art from Dorian to Ionian to Corinthian (i.e., from most simple to most ornamental) as a model for the cyclical degeneration he thinks all arts continue to suffer. Crotch believes the arts must

---

[141] From a lecture concerning 'the sublime, the beautiful, and the ornamental in music' BM Add. Ms 35.014. On this lecture is written 'The Third Lecture/Bristol Institution/ Friday Jan. 15.1830'.

[142] Reynolds, *Discourses*, p. 72.

[143] *Lectures*, NRO, MS 11230/6.

degenerate in this way because of an inevitable periodic emphasis on, respectively, the sublime, then the beautiful and, finally, the ornamental.[144]

Crotch's conception of the mixed excellence as the highest style category in music comes from a passage in Reynolds's *Discourses* that Crotch may have given greater emphasis than Reynolds intended. In *Discourse* V, Reynolds contrasts the artists Raphael and Michelangelo as a way of demonstrating two very different routes to the highest style. Raphael, Reynolds says, was excellent in a larger number of different stylistic areas, but Michelangelo achieved a higher degree of excellence in the sublime in particular. Raphael is supposed to have had more 'Taste and Fancy', while Michelangelo had more 'Genius and Imagination'. Michelangelo's work is said to have been original and highly personal. Because of these qualities, it also demands more intense concentration and study on the part of the viewer. In Raphael, on the other hand, the 'materials are generally borrowed though the noble structure is his own', and this makes his work easier to grasp.[145] Crotch found this a useful parallel to extend to music because Raphael thus depicted bore an affinity to Handel, just as J. S. Bach was a natural candidate for music's Michelangelo.[146] Unlike Reynolds, Crotch did not hesitate to state a preference between the two approaches he outlines. Remarking that Handel 'excelled by uniting the styles and preserving their due subordination', Crotch notes that 'in our art Bird, Purcell, and Sebastian Bach were undoubtedly more sublime than Handel, but Handel seems to be our *Raffaelle*. We therefore deem him the greatest of all composers'.[147] In time, Crotch even found it possible to recognize Mozart as a legitimate master of the mixed excellence and, therefore, as a successor to Handel.

In the eighth lecture of his 1818 series, that on *Alexander's Feast* reprinted below, Crotch demonstrates an important benefit of his decision to overlook Reynolds's scepticism of the mixed excellence: Crotch's highest subspecies of his sublime style, which he calls the 'pure sublime', is identified with the original repertoire of ancient music, the *stile*

---

[144] *Lectures*, NRO, MS 11066/2.

[145] Reynolds, *Discourses*, p. 84. See also Crotch, *Substance*, p. 94: 'When Raffaelle borrowed from Masaccio, he improved upon his model; but when he copied from the antique (as for the sacrifice at Lystra), he took the whole, much as it stands in the original.' Crotch refers to a passage in *Discourse* XII, p. 216.

[146] In other lectures, however, especially *Lectures*, NRO, MS 11233/2 written in 1819, Crotch equates Palestrina, Bird, and Carissimi with the approach of Michelangelo.

[147] See Part Two in this volume, *Lectures*, NRO, MS 11232/8. But in an even later lecture, *Lectures*, NRO, MS 11066/5, probably written in 1829, Crotch refuses to state whether excellence in the sublime alone or in all three styles combined is greater, claiming that Reynolds himself had not taken a position on this question.

antico. Finding a way to venerate this old music while at the same time allowing an equally high place for the more impressive-sounding mature Baroque style, was a challenge for the ancient-music community late in the century. As Weber notes, in his capacity as musical director of the Concert of Ancient Music Joah Bates 'in effect redefined the term "ancient music"' by shifting the Ancient Concert's repertoire toward a more diverse and audience-pleasing formula that drew on a variety of earlier musical traditions but minimized the *stile antico* and relied most on the music of Handel.[148]

Pergolesi and the moderns

To some musicians who took sides in the ancient–modern conflict, the most remarkable aspect of Bates's redefinition of ancient music was not his substitution of Handel for Palestrina as the definitive composer of ancient music. Both men, from a certain point of view, already belonged in the same category of what William Mason calls 'professed harmonists'. Rather, it was Bates's programming of music by Pergolesi and related Italian composers as a major part of the Ancient Concert's repertoire that contemporary moderns viewed as an unexpected departure from the aesthetic of ancient music and, therefore, as still further evidence of the ancient-music community's bigotry and lack of solid critical principles.

Burney is particularly fond of charging that ancient-music lovers criticize, in his words, 'sans connoisance de cause' and therefore base their preferences on mere bigotry. He makes this charge whenever he finds seeming inconsistency in the ancient aesthetic, a case in point being the music of Gesualdo, whose harmony Burney thinks inconsistent with the ancient faction's value of classical accuracy.[149] Crotch, as can be noted shortly, is almost unique among ancient music's admirers in agreeing with this assessment of Gesualdo. Burney, however, knew little about Crotch's ideas or of the relative consistency of his aesthetic theory when he first took issue with the lectures in 1805. The older man is therefore quick to suggest in his letter to Crotch that his young colleague would not be able to back up his censure of Haydn with a reasoned and consistent explanation.

The moderns express surprise at the concept of Pergolesi as an ancient composer because Neapolitan opera composers were venerated by Mason, Burney and others of their circle as the legendary founders of

---

[148] Weber, *Rise of Musical Classics*, p. 169.
[149] Burney, *General History*, vol. 2, p. 179.

the modern style. As Burney wrote in the *General History*, Pergolesi began at the age of 14 'to perceive that taste and melody were sacrificed to the pedantry of learned counterpoint'.[150] After 'vanquishing the necessary difficulties in the study of harmony, fugue, and scientific texture of the parts' young Pergolesi 'intreated his friends to take him home, that he might indulge his own fancies, and write such Music as was most agreeable to his natural perceptions and feelings'.[151] It was somewhat later, however – as Burney observes in the *General History*, around 1756 – that

> *fugues* began to lose their favour, even in Germany, where their reign had been long and glorious; but Rousseau's *Lettre sur la Musique Françoise*, and the beautiful melody, taste, expression, and effects of theatrical compositions, so much cultivated in Italy and in all the German courts, brought about a general revolution in Music, which Vinci, Hasse, and Porpora began, and Pergolesi finished.[152]

The ancient faction's admission of Neapolitan opera into the genus ancient music was a particular problem for Crotch because of his tendency to view ancient and modern music as styles and because he too thought of Neapolitan homophony as the origin of modern music.[153] In one of his January 1805 lectures, Crotch reports that 'the modern style of instrumental full music which the Germans so successfully cultivated seems to have made its first appearance in the accompaniments of the Italian opera songs of Jomelli, Vinci, Hasse, and Pergolesi'.[154] Elsewhere he identifies the modern style with yet another story of musical revolution – presumably a different one from that

---

[150] Ibid., p. 920.

[151] Ibid., p. 919.

[152] Ibid., p. 948.

[153] For example, in *Lectures*, NRO, MS 11229/5, Crotch notes that 'the modern style of instrumental full music which the Germans so successfully cultivated seems to have made its first appearance in the accompaniments of the Italian opera songs of Jomelli, Vinci, Hasse and Pergolesi. In NRO, MS 11232/1 the modern style is the result of a musical revolution: 'the extraordinary genius of the elder Scarlatti seems to have been the unintentional occasion of this Revolution. He was not a composer of sacred music; he applied the ornamental style to the accompaniments of the cantata and the opera, but did not by these means attempt to *improve* (or more properly to destroy) the character of church music. But his great scholar Durante (who many called the father of the modern school since many of the greatest composers studied under him and copied his style) was the real root of the evil from his misapplying the novelties of his master to sacred subjects. Pergolesi imitated Durante and carried these defects still farther. In his sacred works he sometimes evinced his power of composing in the sublime style *already invented*, but he generally abounded with the most striking characteristics of the beautiful & ornamental styles which were comparatively new'.

[154] *Lectures*, NRO, MS 11229/5.

mentioned above which was 'attempted, but, happily, not effected' in 1778:

> The extraordinary genius of the elder Scarlatti seems to have been the unintentional occasion of this Revolution. He was not a composer of sacred music; he applied the ornamental style to the accompaniments of the cantata and the opera, but did not by these means attempt to *improve* (or more properly to destroy) the character of church music. But his great scholar Durante (who many called the father of the modern school since many of the greatest composers studied under him and copied his style) was the real root of the evil from his misapplying the novelties of his master to sacred subjects. Pergolesi imitated Durante and carried these defects still farther.[155]

Crotch admits that 'in his sacred works [Pergolesi] sometimes evinced his power of composing in the sublime style *already invented*',[156] but he stresses that even here Pergolesi 'generally abounded with the most striking characteristics of the beautiful & ornamental styles which were comparatively new'.[157]

Because Pergolesi was widely accepted as both an ancient and a modern, Crotch struggled to define his ancient and modern styles in the first of his January 1805 lectures in London. His sentence remarking that 'music is commonly divided into ancient and modern' even though 'compositions are still produced in the ancient style',[158] is followed in the manuscript by a revealing additional sentence which he later over-scored: 'and it is remarkable that at that admirable institution, the Concert of Ancient Music productions of either style are admitted if they are more than 30 [*sic*] years old'.[159]

Crotch presumably over-scored this sentence because of its misstatement of the Ancient Concert's statutory age requirement; in fact, as is well known, most kinds of music had to be only 20 years old. One often finds the Ancient Concert's policies exaggerated in contemporary references, though such exaggeration is usually by its detractors. In a letter to Burney, Thomas Twining confessed to having 'worked the *exclusionists*, & the *Handelomaniacs* a little' in an anonymous book review he wrote for the *Critical Review*. 'I cou'd not help it', Twining adds, '& I have lent the Ant. Concert a flick' because this institution 'admits no compositions younger than 40 years'.[160]

---

[155] *Lectures*, NRO, MS 11229/1.
[156] Ibid.
[157] Ibid.
[158] *Lectures*, NRO, MS 11232/1.
[159] Ibid.
[160] TT to CB 15 Feb. 1785 BM Add. Ms 39929, ff. 350–51.

The review Twining mentions was one he had earlier conspired with Burney to write of Burney's own *Account of the Musical Performances in Westminster-Abbey* (London, 1785).[161] In the course of his predictably favourable treatment of this slender volume, which memorializes the Handel commemoration concerts mentioned above, Twining enjoys the irony of Pergolesi as an ancient composer. It was natural for Twining, a good classical scholar, to be struck by what he calls the 'very young kind of antiquity' reflected in the Antient Concert's age limits and to substitute at every turn the word 'old' for what he views as the more positive 'ancient'.[162] 'The writer of this article remembers a time, not very distant', Twining observes, 'when *Pergolesi*, who is now adopted as an *Ancient*, and whose works are become of *age* to merit *preservation*, was regarded with a jealous eye by the *Handelomaniacs*, as one of the chief fountains of *modern* degeneracy and corruption.'[163]

As Twining mentions in the letter to Burney cited above, this last sentence refers to the fact that Bates, one of Twining's Cambridge classmates, objected to the music of Pergolesi on stylistic grounds when he was a musically active university student but later programmed the same music as Director of the Ancient Concert.[164] In fact, if one accepts Crotch's formulation of the genres of ancient and modern music as styles, dismissing chronology as a measure of ancientness and thereby placing Pergolesi in the latter category,[165] it could reasonably be argued that Bates's most important contribution to music programming was his mixture of the two species under the dignified cover of ancient

---

[161] Anonymous [Thomas Twining], Review of *An Account of the Musical Performances in Westminster Abbey ... in Commemoration of Handel*, by Charles Burney, *Critical Review*, 59 (1785), 130–38.

[162] Ibid., pp. 130–31: 'The compositions of Corelli, Geminiani, and Handel, say the partisans of what is called the *old* music, are admirable: *therefore*, those of Abel, Boccherini, and Haydn, being *different* from them, must be good for nothing ... ' Twining adds in a footnote, 'it seems decided, that to be denominated *ancient*, or *good*, (for the words are synonymous,) a composition must be at least *twenty years* old'.

[163] Ibid.

[164] TT to CB, 15 February 1785, BM Add. Ms 39929, ff. 350–51.

[165] Crotch was not alone in viewing Pergolesi as a modern on stylistic grounds. Vincenzo Manfredini does this in his 'Defense of Modern Music and Its Celebrated Performers', in Enrico Fubini, *Music and Culture in Eighteenth-Century Europe: a Source Book*, trans. W. Fries, L. Basbarrone and M. L. Leone, ed. B. J. Blackburn (Chicago and London: University of Chicago Press, 1994), pp. 351–7. In this work, originally published as *Difesa della musica moderna e de' suoi celebri esecutori* (Bologna, 1788), Manfredini compares contrapuntal ancient music to 'the music of fine modern composers (among whom, however, are also to be included Pergolesi, Leo Durante, Hasse, Galuppi, Jommelli, Traetta, and various others, who greatly helped to improve the art, and have left monumental works that will always be good and beautiful, although they were written many years ago)'.

music. On the other hand, one of the reasons Burney despised Bates – and was wary of Crotch, who seemed to be moving in the same direction – was no doubt the ease with which Bates could compromise what Burney sometimes called his 'musical principles' in return for the patronage of the old-music community.[166]

The central place Pergolesi occupied in the moderns' account of the development of their aesthetic ideology is well documented in the writing of Burney and Twining. Twining describes his own conversion from ancient worship in stages starting 'from a youthful interest in polyphonic music' to a later 'fondness for the *Cantata* style of [Alessandro] Scarlatti, Gasparini, Lotti &c &[a]'.[167] But it was the poet Thomas Gray and a circle of amateurs Twining knew at Cambridge, including William Mason, who had the most profound effect on his development. Twining continues that it was

> Mr Gray, principally, who made me first turn my back upon all this, by his enthusiastic love of *expressive & passionate* Music, which it was hardly possible for me to *hear & see* him *feel*, without catching something even of his *prejudices*. For Pergolesi was his darling: he had collected a great deal of him, & Leo, in Italy, & he lent me his books to copy what I pleased. This was the *bridge* over which (throwing bundles of old prejudices in favour of Corelli, Geminiani & Handel, into the river) I passed from *Antient* to *Modern* Music.[168]

Twining's confession prompted Burney, in turn, to recount the story of his own musical progress in a fascinating letter written a few days later.

Noting that 'Handel, Geminiani & Corelli were the sole Divinities of my Youth' Burney indicates that he was first 'drawn off from their exclusive worship before I was 20, by keeping company with travelled & heterodox gentlemen, who were partial to the Music of more modern composers whom they had heard in Italy'. These 'heterodox gentlemen'

---

[166] Weber, *Rise of Musical Classics*, pp. 151–5. Weber indicates (p. 153) that Burney's hatred of Bates was partly motivated by the latter's greater success at playing the social game. See also a letter from Twining to CB in Ribeiro, *Letters*, p. 430, n. 34, in response to Burney's letter of 31 July quoted above. Twining comments, 'I knew B[ates] well at Camb., & was glad to meet him as a *Musician*, but the *man* I never *took* to; & he is now *more* offensive to me by a sort of unmeaning *courtly palaver* that he has picked up of late years. Of humour he never had a glimpse; & in point of sense & abilities is quite a *common man*.'

[167] Ribeiro, *Letters*, p. 328, n 5.

[168] Thomas Twining, *Recreations and Studies of a Country Clergyman of the Eighteenth Century*, ed. Richard Twining (London, 1882), p. 106; TT to CB 8 December 1781, *Letters*, vol. 1, p. 328, n. 5; Ralph S. Walker, ed., *A Selection of Thomas Twining's Letters 1734–1804: the Record of a Tranquil Life*, 2 vols (Lewiston, Queenston, Lampeter: Edwin Mellen Press, 1991), vol. 2, p. 219.

included his patron Fulke Greville, at whose estate in Wiltshire Burney first learned to move gracefully in the company of the Great, and Burney's later intimate friend Samuel Crisp. Burney describes Crisp as 'a man of infinite taste in all the fine Arts, an excellent Scholar, & who having resided many years in Italy, & being possessed of a fine tenor voice, sung in as good taste as any professed opera singer with the same kind of voice, I ever heard'.[169] It was at Wilbury house, as Burney describes in his recently published fragmentary memoirs, that he had his first encounter between partisans supporting competing sets of 'musical principles'. In that instance the two sides consisted of Handel and the 'old Italian school' and '[Domenico] Scarlatti, & the [new?] Italian School'.[170] The latter, Burney says, were 'fanciful, capricious, wild, and full of new effects and passages'.[171] Handel's music, by contrast, is described as 'rich in regular harmony, masterly in design, original, and grand and new in the style of his youth, even in Italy'.[172]

Much later, Burney could recount the progress of his subsequent musical development in remarkable detail:

> for songs those of Hasse[,] Vinci, Pergolesi, Rinaldo di Capua, Leo, Feo, Selli[t]i, Buranello, with a few of Domenico Scarlatti, won my heart, & weaned me from the ancient worship. However, at all times in my life I honoured an elaborate & learned composition for the Church whatever its age & country, & at all spare hours I was scoring pieces of Bird, Morely, Luca Marenzio, Stradella; and studying Palestrina, Steffani's admirable Duets, with Cantatas by old Scarlatti, Gasparini, the Baron D'Astorga, & Marcello. Before I was 18 I scored Geminiani's 2 sets of Concertos, for improvement in Counterpoint, & I remember when he was about to print them in score, with new *readings*, he borrowed my MS which he never returned.
>
> As to Harpsichord music besides the study of Handel's *Lessons*, which in that elaborate style are admirable, I was early a great admirer of the original Fancy, boldness, delicacy, & Fire of Domenico Scarlatti, so different from all lessons before & since! – Then the Taste, refinement, & elegant *Chant* of Alberti, struck me as new in instrumental music; & tho' the easy monotony of his division Bases is so easy to imitate, yet none of those who have used the like expedient for supplying the short-lived tone of the Harpsichord by this kind of bustle, have equalled him in the taste & elegance of his treble part. From the time his pieces were first printed Composers of all kinds seem only to pour water on these *leaves* of others till the German Symphonies appeared by Stamitz,

[169] Slava Klima, Garry Bowers and Kerry S. Grant, eds, *Memoirs of Dr. Charles Burney 1726–1769* (Lincoln, NB: University of Nebraska Press, 1988), p. 70.
[170] Ibid., p. 71.
[171] Ibid.
[172] Ibid.

Filtz, Haultzbaur, Canabich, &c. The two Martinis indeed had original merit, the one on the old plan, & the other on the new; but the Sonatas of Zanetti & Campioni seemed models of grace & elegance till those of Schwindl & Abel appeared. After these, however, came Haydn, Vanhal & Boccherini for Bowed-instruments, & for vocal music after Pere[z], Jomelli, Piccini, Sacchini, Monza &c out skips me Paesiello, more original, bold, yet natural & pleasing, than any one of them. As to Harpsichord music you know my opinion of our friend Em. Bach. Schobert, Eichner, & now & then Echard, are *stock* composers for the P. F. with me, and since then I can recollect nothing like a new *genre* struck out.

'Here's my Profession de Foi musicale', he concludes, indulging in an implied characterization of the ancient faction he would only have used with a trusted intimate, '& if it deserves the Inquisition, I think you would equally deserve the danger of fire & faggot.'[173]

Surveying numerous other references to an old and a new school in the writing of Twining and Burney, the network of stereotypes that made up their musical principles – and, it would also be fair to assume, the musical principles of the modern partisans with whom they associated casually – might be summarized as follows: ancient music is invariably linked with qualities like uniformity, learning, correctness, judgement, reason, restraint, heaviness, manliness, contrivance, seriousness and timelessness. Above all, it is universally connected with the musical element of harmony – a word used in the common eighteenth-century sense that is roughly synonymous with 'counterpoint' – and with harmony's inevitable companion or surrogate, 'contrivance'. The modern style, by contrast, is identified with an alternate set of qualities that are as much related to its secular, operatic origins as the above characterization of ancient music is to the *stile antico*. These include not only the novelty, wildness, fancy, and capriciousness mentioned above but variety, elegance, licence, imagination, feeling, delicacy, expression and, above all, the musical element of melody.

Probably the most common impression of the two musical species in the writing of Burney and Twining is the old truism in which ancient music is a cold-blooded music for connoisseurs and professors. Modern music, by contrast, is depicted as a repertoire that avoids cerebral complications, flows from inspiration and passion and, because it speaks the universal language of the emotions, can be understood by anyone. There are a number of reasons for both of these sets of associations, especially stemming from the origins of ancient music in a learned musical tradition, from its partisans' high-minded rejection of popularity as a criterion for canonicity and from the deliberately restrained,

---

[173] CB to TT 14 December 1781, *Letters*, vol. 1, pp. 328–32.

undramatic, almost academic quality of its most conspicuous institutions. But an important and unappreciated contributing factor to the image of musical expertise claimed by the forces of old music has to do with different abilities and mental processes that were widely thought to be employed in the perception and understanding of melody and harmony.

Harmony is not learned merely because of the intellect required for its creation, but because its appreciation is supposed to require skill and experience from the listener. Melody – by which proponents did *not* mean the elaborate, highly ornamented style of some contemporary opera and concert music – is supposed to require no such special ability.[174] As Thomas Robertson noted in his *An Enquiry into the Fine Arts* (London, 1784), melody is to most listeners 'almost the whole of Music'. That is not because 'Harmony wants charms; for she has charms, and still more powerful than those of Melody; but study and pains are required to understand them. Harmony is the amusement of the learned and of the few: Melody, that voice which nations hear and obey.'[175] William Thomson describes stages in a student's progress toward the development of a good ear, the highest of which is the oratorios of Handel. This plateau must be approached only after extensive preparation, otherwise 'the exertions of the full band, and the chorusses, will appear to him only a *confusion of sounds*, in which he neither can distinguish the *parts*, nor relish the *whole*'.[176]

This melody-harmony formula obviously owes much to Rousseau and to ideological French writing of the mid-to-late eighteenth century that rejected counterpoint as unnatural and élitist. But the present focus on the abilities of the listener and the psychology of the perception experience goes back much earlier in British writing, to the late seventeenth century and the 'Battle of the Books' between William Wotton

---

[174] Several sources remark on a species of complex melody that they think shares the worst qualities of elaborate harmony. Alexander Molleson complains in 'Melody', the Soul of Music, in *Miscellanies in Prose and Verse* (Glasgow, 1806), pp. 69–70, of a 'scientific kind of melody' that is filled with 'rapid and difficult divisions, sudden transitions, singular passages very high in the scale, and affected and abrupt cadences ... '. In a similar vein, Burney remarks in *General History*, vol. 2, p. 931, 'this principle [that art should be easy to understand] is carried to such excess in Italy, that whatever gives the hearer of Music the least trouble to disentangle is Gothic, pedantic, and *scelerata*. As to difficulties of *execution*, in a *single part*, the composers and performers may spin their brains, and burst their blood-vessels, and welcome, provided the texture of the parts is clear and simple'.

[175] Thomas Robertson, *An Enquiry into the Fine Arts* (London, 1784; New York: Garland, 1971), p. 133.

[176] William Thomson, *Enquiry into the Elementary Principles of Beauty in the Works of Nature and Art* (London, 1798), p. 47.

and Sir William Temple. The former's *Reflections on Ancient and Modern Learning* (1694) can be considered further in Chapter 3. Here, Wotton uses the intellectual demands of counterpoint as an argument for the superiority of 'modern' contrapuntal music over the fabled music of the ancient Greeks. Similarly, Christopher Simpson complains of the decline of polyphonic fancies for viols because of 'the scarcity of Auditors that understand it: their Ears being better acquainted and more delighted with light and airy Musick'.[177]

The long history of the network of associations set forth briefly above, together with the fact that the stereotypes which develop from it are so often employed in the literature without clarification, suggest that almost any sophisticated listener of the late eighteenth century could be expected to be familiar with them. Crotch's cliché above pitting the 'trifling melodies of the opera' against the 'barbarous and mechanical structure of the fugue'[178] is used with an easy confidence so that his audience could recognize the two sides without further explanation. Burney had made a similar observation in the 'Essay on Criticism' that begins the third volume of the *General History* in 1789, although without actual use of the potentially dangerous terms 'ancients' and 'moderns'.[179] In the context of arguing that 'a critic should have none of the contractions and narrow partialities of such as can see but a small angle of the art', Burney speaks of those who are 'so bewildered in fugues and complicated contrivances that they can receive pleasure from nothing but canonical answers, imitations, inversions, and counter-subjects'.[180] On the other side are their opponents, who 'are equally partial to light, simple, frivolous melody, regarding every species of artificial composition as mere pedantry and jargon'.[181] 'A chorus of Handel and a graceful opera song should not preclude each other', Burney insists, since 'each has its peculiar merit'.[182]

---

[177] Christopher Simpson, *A Compendium: or, Introduction to Practical Music. In Five Parts*, (1671; 6th edn, London, 1714), p. 115.

[178] Crotch, *Substance*, p. 148. See also, *Lectures*, 11232/2.

[179] Burney's sensitivity for these terms can be found in some of his earliest published writing. In *The Present State of Music in Germany, the Netherlands and United Provinces*, 2 vols 2nd edn, (London, 1775, New York: Broude, 1969), vol. 1, p. 37, he uses the expression 'modern' to describe the organ playing of a M. Vanden Bosch in discussion of music at Antwerp. He quickly adds in footnote: 'When I use the epithets *old* and *new*, I mean neither as a term of reproach, or a stigma, but merely to tell the reader in which style a piece is conceived, or written; and he will suppose it to be better or worse, as he pleases.'

[180] Burney, *General History*, vol. 2, p. 8.

[181] Ibid.

[182] Ibid.

The surprise and confusion in the writing of the quarrel's militant partisans when these simplistic categories are violated is instructive. In a letter to Burney concerning the works of Josquin, Twining is astonished to find that 'there is even contrast too, which the moderns think they have all to themselves; for he throws in passages of beautiful simplicity and stable solemnity in the midst of all his art and complication'.[183] Burney's criticism inevitably anticipates a simplistic formula linking the music of Haydn, the musical element of melody, and the virtue of ease of communication and opposing these with ancient music, harmony and pedantry. As a result, his review of William Jackson's *Observations on the present State of Music, in London* in 1791 fails to recognize a growing voice in music criticism that rejected both composers for having abandoned the common man in an egocentric fascination with the vice of excessive complication. Burney complains that 'the invariable language of the enthusiastic admirers of Handel, and of every thing ancient in music, has long been, that the moderns *neglect harmony* for air'. At the same time, 'the whole tenor of Mr. Jackson's pamphlet is to prove, that "melody is best qualified to exist alone, and that modern music has *no air*"'. 'Mercy on us!' Burney concludes, 'have we then neither soul nor body?'[184]

This soul-versus-body opposition is itself of some interest. Despite writers like Jackson who objected to a movement towards greater complexity and sophistication in the modern style, the view persisted of Haydn as a naïve, melody-dominated composer for the masses who was guided more by intuition than formal learning. A 'Memoir of Haydn' in *The Harmonicon* in 1823 reports that

> Haydn was reputed, by his contemporaries, to have performed miracles; and he was once asked how he worked them? His reply is worthy of the attention of all composers, living or unborn: 'Let your *air*', said he 'be good, and your composition, whatever it be, will be so likewise, and will assuredly delight. It is the soul of music, – the life, the spirit, the essence of a composition: without it, Tartini may succeed in discovering and using the most singular and learned chords, but nothing is heard after all, but a laboured sound, which though it may not vex the ear, leaves the head empty, and the heart cold and unaffected by it.'[185]

---

[183] TT to CB 8 December 1781, Thomas Twining, *Recreations and Studies of a Country Clergyman of the Eighteenth Century*, ed. Richard Twining (London, 1882), p. 107.

[184] Anonymous [Charles Burney], review of *Observations on the present State of Music, in London*, by William Jackson of Exeter, in *Monthly Review*, 6 (October 1791), 196–7.

[185] Anonymous, 'Memoir of Haydn', *The Harmonicon*, 1 (1823), 17.

Accordingly, the writer notes, Haydn's 'productions were generally the creations of impulse, rather than of regular habits of study'. On a less positive note, Crotch observes of the first movement of Symphony No. 73 ('La Chasse'), that here 'we meet in the second part with that experimental kind of writing in which the composer seems to hesitate as uncertain how to proceed'.[186] Similarly, he holds up a small group of Haydn symphonies in another lecture as works in which 'the flights of fancy are less outrè than they generally are'.[187]

John Marsh on the quarrel

The consequences of a notion of ancient music that could, in popular usage, embrace either the contrapuntal style in particular or a body of stylistically diverse old music in general, are illustrated by John Marsh's 'A Comparison Between the Ancient and Modern Styles of Music'. Marsh's writing is important because it is by far the most extended treatment of the two musical species aside from Crotch's little-known and inaccessible early lectures. Marsh's essay has, accordingly, been the foundation for much of what has been written on the subject of ancient and modern music, and the reason many writers continue to envision the ancient–modern conflict as a matter of Baroque versus modern concert music rather than a more global phenomenon extending through all musical genres. The 'Comparison' is flawed, however, by Marsh's own inconsistency over the nature of the styles he is trying to compare and especially by his narrow perspective as an amateur instrumentalist.

In Marsh's scenario, the ancient–modern quarrel began at the time of yet another 'great revolution in instrumental music'.[188] In this case the revolution was 'chiefly occasioned by a more general knowledge of the powers and effects of wind instruments'.[189] Many of the qualities he stresses in the modern style, therefore, have to do with its greater emphasis on instrumental 'effect'. This is a quality he sets in opposition to the 'classical accuracy' of ancient music.[190] Towards the end of his essay, Marsh expands on his ancient–modern stylistic dichotomy by allowing as an afterthought that it might apply equally well to vocal music as it does to the concert works and chamber music he has

---

[186] *Lectures*, NRO, MS 11232/5.
[187] *Lectures*, NRO, MS 11064/13. Crotch's list of down-to-earth Haydn symphonies includes the 'Festino', vol. 1, p. 53 in D, and 'La Roxelane', vol. 1, p. 63 in C.
[188] [Marsh], 'Comparison', p. 984.
[189] Ibid.
[190] Ibid., p. 982.

considered at length. But when he describes his ancient vocal style, its qualities are close to the exact reverse of what he has presented in his discussion of instrumental ancient music.

It should be noted from the start that Marsh insists the expressions 'ancient' and 'modern' music denote styles and not particular repertoires as, indeed, the title of his essay indicates. He presents his ancient and modern styles, moreover, as living traditions susceptible to further development.[191] Accordingly, Marsh's complaint against the Concert of Ancient music has to do with its apparently self-destructive age requirements. If the managers of this organization have in mind a scheme to 'discountenance the *modern* style of composition, and to encourage the *ancient*', he remarks defensively, they 'entirely frustrate their own design',[192] since

> what composer, however, attached to, or capable of writing in the ancient style (of which there are doubtless many in the metropolis) can have the least encouragement to do so, whilst his works must necessarily be rejected at both the above mentioned concerts; at those of modern music, on account of its antique style, and at those of ancient music, because recently composed.[193]

The stated purpose of his essay is to argue for concerts featuring the mix of ancient and modern styles he finds lacking in the programmes of the Ancient Concert. He indicates that this format is unusual in London subscription concerts and attributes its lack to concert managers' unfortunate acquiescence to the prejudices of amateurs. Clearly, however, this statement has in mind the Ancient Concert – which he singles out for discussion – rather than the entrepreneurial efforts of Salomon and the moderns that are not named. When musicians are left to their own devices, as in benefit concerts, Marsh seems to be saying, they find it in their interests to blend the two styles in an effort to please a wider audience and make a larger profit. Presumably, Marsh thinks musicians would be doing the very same thing in subscription concerts if it were not for the bigotry of the ancient audience and its desire to isolate itself socially.[194]

If Marsh recognized the historical roots of the modern style in Neapolitan opera as Crotch and others did, he presumably would not have been able to direct his frustration so pointedly at the Ancient Concert.

---

[191] Marsh is said to have composed music in both styles himself. In 'Handel's Influence on English Music', *The Monthly Musical Record*, 90 (1960), 169, Temperley reports that Marsh's *Three Overtures in Several Parts* (*c.* 1800) were expressly 'composed after the manner of the Ancient Masters'.

[192] [Marsh], 'Comparison', p. 981.

[193] Ibid.

[194] Ibid.

In fact, as Marsh's discussion of the modern style's development unfolds, it becomes clear that while he accepts the basic harmony-versus-melody opposition of Rousseau's famous *Lettre*, he is unacquainted with the role of opera in the modern style's creation and actually knows little about vocal music. With regard to melody versus harmony, Marsh complains that ancient music composers 'appear to have frequently thought it sufficient that their works should possess good harmony and classical accuracy, and stand the test of theoretical examination'.[195] But this, he contends, is only 'negative praise' since 'the same merits might exist without melody being much attended to; melody being, indeed, of a mere arbitrary nature, cannot be subjected to those mechanical rules of criticism by which harmony is judged'.[196] Still, Marsh does allow that 'as too much attention is sometimes paid to harmony in the ancient music, to the neglect of melody and contrast, so in the modern too much attention is frequently paid to air and contrast, to the neglect of harmony, and *sometimes of modulation*'.[197]

The above is, of course, entirely consistent with the common stereotype of ancient music in which its excellence lies primarily in the area of harmony. Marsh, moreover, directly relates the qualities of harmony and contrivance to issues of musical longevity and substance. Despite his plea for musical simplicity presented above, Marsh acknowledges in the 'Comparison' that 'Single airs, solos, and music of few parts are apt to lose their effect and become insipid from too frequent repetition' and that 'music of a complicated kind has quite the contrary effect'.[198] He illustrates this point with an example from the works of Handel, claiming that those who hear the oratorios often grow tired of the airs but continue to enjoy the choruses. He explains that the choruses are 'apt to please less at first than after a few hearings; and they constantly improve in their effects on repetition, as the ear then frequently discovers new beauties or excellences that had before escaped it'.[199]

In both the 'Comparison' and the later *Hints to Young Composers* Marsh depicts a modern style in jeopardy. Its inventor in the symphony is supposed to have been Richter. Richter's works were 'more scientific than those of the generality of his immediate successors (the last strains of many of them being short fugues)' and consequently were 'more pleasing to *connoisseurs*'.[200] This defect (as Marsh views it here) was

---

[195] Ibid., p. 982.
[196] Ibid.
[197] Ibid., p. 983.
[198] Ibid., p. 985.
[199] Ibid.
[200] Ibid., p. 984.

remedied by Richter's successors, especially Stamitz, who made the symphony more generally appealing. In simplifying it, however, they also nearly destroyed it, for the new symphonic style, 'not having in general that body of harmony and laboured contrivance to support it that ancient music had', risked degenerating into a 'light, trivial and uniform character'.[201] The salvation of the symphony came at the hands of the great Haydn, who, 'by his wonderful contrivance, by the variety and eccentricity of his modulation, by his judicious dispersion of light and shade, and happy manner of blending simple and intelligible air with abstruse and complicated harmony' transformed the style into something more substantial.[202] Haydn's style offered two sources of mental exercise for the listener in that it blended intricate contrivance with the element of surprise. 'Instead of being able, as was before the case, to anticipate in great measure the second part of any movement, from its uniform relation to the foregoing', Marsh observes, 'it is on the contrary, in [Haydn's] works impossible to conceive what will follow, and a perpetual interest is kept up in much longer pieces than any of the same kind ever before composed.'[203]

One particular aspect of Marsh's writing that must have provoked a younger and more impetuous William Crotch to reply to Marsh's essay in the *Monthly Magazine* in 1800 and 1801 is actually more apparent in Marsh's later *Hints to Young Composers* than in the 'Comparison'. The William Crotch of 1800 – who, at the time, still spoke petulantly at Oxford of Haydn and Scarlatti as 'inferior geniuses who to the extravagant wildness of their ideas would add irregularity & incorrectness'[204] – cannot have been pleased by Marsh's claim that modern music possessed the defining qualities of ancient music, harmony and contrivance. Marsh further suggests in the essay that Haydn and Pleyel were not given the credit they deserve in this area because their works were too long to be published in full score, as Corelli's and Handel's were. If they were so published, he thinks 'perhaps quite as much ingenuity would be evinced, though in a style totally different'.[205] The *Hints to Young Composers* is a step in this direction, since Marsh offers it as both a

---

[201] John Marsh, *Hints to Young Composers of Instrumental Music, Illustrated with 2 Movements for a Grand Orchestra in Score* (Chichester, n.d.), p. 1.

[202] Ibid.

[203] Ibid. The present work was published, then, after 1797 but probably before Crotch's second essay for the *Monthly Magazine* in 1801, as described below.

[204] *Lectures*, NRO, MS 11064/12. NRO MS 11064 contains some very early lectures dating back as far as 1798. It is of interest that there are actually two nearly identical versions of the present lecture. The first is more strongly negative and uses Haydn's name in places it is omitted in the milder second version.

[205] [Marsh], 'Comparison', p. 985.

primer on orchestration and a kind of introduction to score-reading in the modern style.

Reading music from score was an ability the ancients often claimed as a mark of their musical sophistication. As William Jones had written,

> where there is Learning there will of course be more taste and better discernment: and when a person who is presented at a performance of Choral Music has skill enough to see the progress of it in a Score book at the same time, he hears it with as much effect as if he had more ears than Nature has given: and indeed so he has; for as Learning gives a *Second sight* to the mind of man, so doth Skill in Music improve the Hearing in the same degree.[206]

Jones argues that studying scores can be a valuable end in itself.

> As we amuse ourselves by reading a Tragedy without seeing it acted on the stage, so is it possible to be entertained by Music without hearing it: and at times, when I could neither hear Music nor play it, I have found satisfaction and improvement by casting my eye over the Score of some excellent composition.[207]

The more enlightened William Crotch of 1818 would presumably have applauded Marsh's effort to give the moderns this ability. Indeed, it now appears that for the most part Marsh's writing advocates precisely the point of view Crotch encourages in his 1818 lectures. One might say that the main difference between these individuals is not unlike the difference Samuel Johnson once found between Torys and Whigs in the famous definitions he gave Boswell. The two parties, Johnson says, are distinguishable not by their ultimate conclusions, which will necessarily be the same among reasonable people, but by their modes of thinking and their respective prejudices for establishment and innovation. As a practical matter, it is not more power that the Tory wants for Church and State but more respect.[208] In much the same way, Crotch's second rebuttal essay to Marsh's 'Comparison' does not object to Marsh's conclusions about the desirability of mixing the styles but rather to his reluctance to extend a deferential bow in the direction of old music before launching into praise of the moderns.

There is, however, a fundamental difference in the views of these individuals. That difference has to do with Crotch's more disciplined adherence to the idea that ancient and modern music are styles rather

---

[206] Jones, *Treatise*, p. ii.

[207] Quoted in Charles Burney, Review of *A Treatise on the Art of Music*, by William Jones, in *Monthly Review*, 75 (1786): 107.

[208] James Boswell, *The Life of Samuel Johnson* as quoted in Donald Greene, *The Politics of Samuel Johnson* (New Haven, CT: Yale University Press, 1960; Port Washington, NY: Kennikat Press, 1973), p. 14.

than repertoires. The emphasis on harmony that both men accept as a fundamental aspect of ancient music appears most often in Marsh's essay in reference to intrusive accompaniments in ancient music and in Handel in particular. One might expect, since Handel is Marsh's quintessential ancient-music composer, that Handel would surface in this context in the 'Comparison Between the Ancient and Modern Styles of Music' when the subject turns to vocal music. One might also expect that Marsh's conception of vocal ancient music would naturally share with his conception of ancient instrumental music the central failing Marsh identifies of noisy accompaniments and insufficient attention to melody. But when Marsh describes his ancient style as it relates to vocal music, it is the ancients not the moderns who 'depended almost wholly upon the voice for the effect, leaving little for the accompaniments besides the bass and the introductory, intermediate and concluding symphonies'. It is, curiously, the moderns whom Marsh claims 'may be said frequently to fall into the opposite extreme, by making the instrumental frequently the principal part of the composition, and the voice part little more than an accompaniment'.[209] Marsh's ancients, then, are presumably Neapolitan opera composers.

To describe Pergolesi as an ancient composer is not unreasonable since, again, both of the major eighteenth-century British concert organizations promoting old music did so. What is troublesome about Marsh's essay is his inability to maintain the critical principles with which he begins, a fault that parallels his vacillation on the role and value of complexity in music. In these respects, Marsh's essay brings Crotch's comparatively consistent approach into sharper relief. To repeat a point made above, however, it is not, in general, moderns like Marsh but, rather, ancient supporters like Hawkins who tend to receive the most frequent eighteenth-century complaints for criticism not securely grounded in principle and based, therefore, on mere prejudice.[210] Thus, in the *General History* Burney risks a public use of the term 'moderns' to refer to the musical party Crotch describes when he comments with respect to Elizabethan virginal music that:

> However the old masters may be celebrated for their simplicity and sobriety of style, and the moderns indiscriminately censured for multiplied notes, rapidity of performance, tricks, whip-syllabub,

---

[209] [Marsh], 'Comparison', p. 986.

[210] For example, in a manuscript volume of 'Materials Towards the History of German Music & Musicians' in YUL, Osborn that Burney wrote in preparation for *General History* he notes, comparing Handel and Hasse, that 'nothing can be more illiberal & unjust than to exalt the one at the Expence of the other, especially when it is done, as is frequently the Case, sans connoissance de Cause'.

froth, tumbling, and mere difficulties: it would not be very easy to find, among the most complicated pieces of modern times, difficulties equally insurmountable with those in which these old *Fancies* and variations abound.[211]

It is with an eagerness to expose an ancient-music movement motivated by bigotry that Burney's letter to Crotch in 1805 is quick to point out that 'the first concert of Anc^t. Music [i.e., the Academy of Vocal Music, a title later changed to 'Academy of Ancient Music'] established in this country in 1711 or 12 was set up *against Handel*' because of that composer's innovations.

In his response, Crotch is at pains to demonstrate the consistency of his critical principles and to show that he neither values 'music in proportion to its age' nor regards all inventions as improvements. Crotch also hopes to break down persistent stereotypes when he claims to admire the 'vocal melodies of Stradella' – thus acknowledging, as he knew Burney himself already had,[212] that an ancient composer could achieve excellence in the characteristic modern realm of melody – and to abjure 'the harmonies & modulations of ye Prince of Venoso [*sic*]'.[213]

Don Giovanni and the birth of classical music

Judgements based on principle that run against the grain of the ancient critical tradition are not uncommon in Crotch's writing. Crotch, in sharp contrast with other ancient apologists, thought Corelli was 'inferior in genius, science, and variety' to his contemporaries and complains that 'he was also a mannerist' and that 'manner is only upheld by its novelty; it ceases to charm when it is no longer new'.[214] He expands on this 'mannerist' theme in another lecture:

> the concertos of Corelli have been justly compared by a critic (whose name I must always mention with affectionate gratitude, the late Mr Malchair of Oxford,) to the landscapes of Claude Lorraine. Each was a perfect whole considered by itself and the

---

[211] Burney, *General History*, vol. 2, p. 98.

[212] In *General History*, vol. 2, p. 580 Burney finds in Stradella's music 'the germe [*sic*] of many favourite compositions produced after his death' and notes that in Stradella 'the natural and clear style of vocal melody appears, which was afterwards much improved by Hasse and Vinci'. Crotch was well acquainted with Burney's *General History*. In his *General Account* Crotch describes his first course of lectures, which 'consisted of extracts from Burney's history following the chronological order of the several compositions'. These early lectures, however, were never used.

[213] WC to CB, 4 March 1805.

[214] Crotch, *Substance*, pp. 102–3.

clearness & beauty of the harmony and the homogeneous character of the several movements must afford a tranquil pleasure to all
unprejudiced ears. But viewing them in succession, they were, like
Claude's subjects in the Liber Veritatis, deficient in variety, the
same objects being continually repeated.[215]

Even Handel does not escape Crotch's critical appraisal, and the nature
of his objections is instructive. In several relatively early lectures Crotch
indicates that he is ready to concede the 'inferior' domains of instrumental music and opera to the moderns.[216] And since he has decided to
allow that the moderns are superior in these areas, his letter to Burney
tries to be conciliatory by unreasonably taking Handel to task for not
writing both his instrumental music and his opera in the modern style.
Beautiful as Crotch allows Handel's instrumental chamber works to be,
the 'subjects are fitter for what he afterwards applied them to, – Oratorios and Choruses'. He adds that the organ fugues 'want ... light and
shade, contrast of passage, episodes, variety', each of these being traditional virtues of the modern style.[217] Elsewhere he admits that Handel's
'opera music' 'cannot be too highly praised if considered in the abstract', but adds that it is still 'too solid, too serious, too grand for
secular subjects and is certainly fitter for sacred words'.[218] The overtures of Handel's operas were 'less fit for secular than for sacred subjects
... the fugues were regular, classical, and dignified ... They were, I must
repeat, admirable productions considered as abstract music, but they
have not the brilliancy, the variety, the gaiety of the modern opera
overture'.[219]

Before Crotch's evolving point of view could recognize a genre that
closely resembles classical music he had to overcome his reluctance to
allow a 'lesser' sphere of composition like instrumental music or opera
to take on the values of ancient music and exhibit the sublime. The fifth
and sixth lectures of his 1818 series, which analyse *Don Giovanni* in
some detail, are an important step in this direction. There are two
related themes in Crotch's remarks about this work. The first is that
Don Giovanni stands out among Mozart's operas popular in England at

---

[215] *Lectures*, NRO, MS 11066/4.

[216] For example *Lectures*, NRO, MS 11230/1, where he notes that 'We will allow then
that the moderns excel in the opera as indeed they do also in instrumental music. But we
must maintain that the opera is inferior to the oratorio and instrumental to vocal music.'

[217] *Burney, General History*, vol. 2, pp. 1037–8.

[218] In somewhat the same vein, he charges in *Lectures*, NRO, MS 11229/10 that
'instances may not unfrequently be found in which ancient madrigals and even canzonets
would, in our opinion at least, have been better calculated for serious subjects than for
absurd love ditties'.

[219] *Lectures*, NRO, MS 11067/3.

the time – which Crotch identifies as *Die Zauberflöte, Così fan tutte, Le nozze di Figaro* and *La clemenza di Tito* – as a work intended for connoisseurs. As Crotch puts it repeatedly, *Don Giovanni* was supposedly written 'principally for the amusement of [Mozart] himself and *friends*, by which, of course, we are to understand his pupils, his professional brethren, his musical friends and admirers'. This is said to have been even more true of the still little-known *Idomeneo*, which 'is yet more abstruse & scientific, & not being comic or containing many graceful & intelligible arias is still less likely to be performed on the stage & be generally admired though it will form a rich repast for the private contemplation of the student of harmony'.[220]

Crotch indicates that the quality of being difficult or demanding explains the 30-year delay between *Don Giovanni*'s first performances in Prague in 1787 and its British première in 1817. First, Crotch explains, 'we may observe that Mozart's music in general did not reach us for many years after it was composed. I do not remember to have seen his operas till about the year 1800'.[221] But even after Mozart's belated English introduction, the choice of *which* Mozart operas were to be performed was in the hands of the Italians who controlled opera and who 'were not enthusiastic admirers of scientific harmony'.[222] Crotch explains that the 'exclusive predilection for melody' among Italians was by no means 'universally countenanced in this nation from the first'.[223] Italian tastes were, therefore, out of step with an important segment of the British concert audience, the lovers of ancient music. 'A division of the musical world into two distinct parties was as I have before shewn the unavoidable result', Crotch observes, reiterating a major theme of this entire lecture series.[224] In short, then, 'Don Giovanni seems rather to have been demanded by this nation rather than pressed upon us', and if it had only been 'performed here as soon as composed', Crotch is sure that it would 'have met with the same success and admiration which at present it so deservedly enjoys'.[225]

Crotch's second main point is that *Don Giovanni* makes extensive use of what he calls the 'ancient style'. He finds subjects in the overture that remind him of 'Handel, Leo, Corelli, and even earlier masters, whom it is clear our author held in one veneration'.[226] Statements such

---

[220] *Lectures*, NRO, MS 11232/7.
[221] Ibid.
[222] Ibid.
[223] Ibid.
[224] Ibid.
[225] Ibid.
[226] Ibid.

as this now seem far-fetched and may well have been unconvincing even to Crotch's contemporaries. He observes of Zerlina's second act aria 'Vendrai, carino' that 'its resemblance of style and even of whole passages to Handel is not, however, generally remarked, because Handel's opera music is so little known, and so unjustly depreciated by the lovers of modern music'.[227] Specifically, Crotch finds similarities between 'Vendrai, carino' and both 'Mirerò quel vago volto' in *Radamisto* and 'Charming Beauty' in the *Triumph of Time & Truth*. He also thinks Leporello's aria 'Ah pietà signori miei' 'contains a passage bearing a considerable resemblance to one in Handel's overture to *Parnasso in festa* afterwards prefixed to the oratorio of *Athalia*'.[228] The 'ancient style' is further identified in the sextet 'Sola, sola in bujo loco' in *Don Giovanni*, which exhibits the 'scientific treatment of the score for which our author is so justly celebrated'.[229] He notes that in the following 'spirited allegro "mille torbidi pensieri" the experienced ear will perceive transitions & harmonies of a similar description'.[230]

What stands out most in these examples is Crotch's greater interest here than in earlier lectures in demonstrating Mozart's ancient roots and Crotch's new and still inconsistent appreciation for contrivance in opera and in modern music in general. In the previous year's lectures on *La Clemenza di Tito* he had remarked that

> Mozart is never coarse or inelegant, incorrect or careless. Even in the airs for the inferior characters, where neither the words of the poet nor the capacity of the singer would admit of much beauty in melody or expression, the harmony is revised and finished with exactness. A richness of counterpoint, not met with in the generality of opera music is here also conspicuous. The alto viola seldom moves in octaves or unisons with the Bass but is one of the real parts of the score. The wind instruments produce a variety of effects. One which frequently recurs and never fails, is when the chords of the harmony are sustained in the manner of an organ. When to this is added the beauty and expression of the melody, which, though inferior to that of the Italian, is superior to that of every other school; and [in] the skilful and scientific treatment of the subjects we cannot but be astonished at such an accumulation of knowledge, genius and taste in an individual, and especially in one who died so young.[231]

In his lecture on *Don Giovanni* he praises similar qualities. A particular sequence near the end of Act I captures his attention:

---

[227] Ibid.
[228] Ibid.
[229] Ibid.
[230] Ibid.
[231] *Lectures*, NRO, MS 11230/1.

It is almost impossible to enumerate the several excellences of this long scene. One however is too curious to escape notice. A dance is heard at a distance played in common time and in this the principal characters agree to join. It is discontinued however and the drama proceeds. Soon after, a minuet is heard and Donna Anna, Donna Elvira, and Don Ottavio, who attended the feast in masks for the purpose of detecting and counteracting the designs of Don Giovanni, sing a beautiful slow trio accompanied only by wind instruments. At length the minuet is commenced by a complete orchestra on the stage and danced. While this is proceeding a second orchestra tunes and commences the former air in common time which is also danced while the minuet continues. Then a third orchestra tunes and a waltz is danced, and these three all continue together for some bars till interrupted by the rescue of Zerlina from Don Giovanni by the principal characters, who unmask and reproach him for his baseness and in the following spirited finale of the first act threaten him with the vengeance of heaven. He is at first confused and alarmed but his rash courage returns and he sets heaven and earth at defiance. All this is admirably expressed by the music which in the performance must produce a most terrific effect.[232]

Elsewhere, Crotch comments on a different kind of elaborate contrivance in the second act trio 'Ah taci, ingiusto core', in which 'the principal excellence lies in the admirable management of the accompaniments'.[233] In particular, Crotch approves of 'The Modulation from E major with four sharps to C major', which 'is striking and masterly'.[234] His uncertainty over the value of surprising modulation is apparent, however, in a lecture from only the year before on *Judas Maccabaeus*. Here, he complains about 'young, and especially modern, composers [who] endeavour to surprise us by strange and unaccountable transitions into remote and irrelative keys; and the effect on the mind frequently resembles that produced by the unmeaning changes of scene in a pantomime'.[235] The modulation he praises by comparison in *Judas Maccabaeus* is 'so perfectly natural and agreeable that it is called going into the relative key'.[236]

Conclusion

Crotch's abstract conception of 'ancient music' abandons age as a defining quality and bases the category instead on a composer's intentions,

---

[232] *Lectures*, NRO, MS 11232/6.

[233] *Lectures*, NRO, MS 11232/7.

[234] Ibid. Crotch apparently refers to a section in C major at mm. 35–48.

[235] *Lectures*, NRO, MS 11229/7.

[236] Ibid.

on the psychological effects music tries to produce in a receptive listener and on the intellectual faculties it is thought to engage. Crotch did not, however, use the word 'classical' in a similarly abstract manner to describe any music in which the sublime style predominates, since the word 'classical' still had too much the connotation of 'old' to be applied to recent music and to living composers. Still, when he uses classical to describe music, the word can carry so strong an emphasis on 'science' that it almost begins, like its near synonym 'ancient', to loose a connection with the past.[237] Crotch's full acceptance in 1818 of a mixed style that could both entertain and edify, a style in which sublime musical effects are extended legitimately to the 'lesser' musical genres of symphony and opera, and in which these sublime effects can be identified in music by comparatively recent and even living composers, marks a point at which, for the first time, a conception reasonably close to classical music began to be promoted widely among the British concert audience.

The ancient–modern quarrel Crotch describes becomes a more important feature of contemporary culture when the period 1780–1820 is viewed in the context of a struggle between perennial opposing forces leading to a synthesis in the new musical world of 1818. Crotch's abstract understanding is a useful way of approaching the extended and diffuse controversy that emerges from music criticism of the time, but it requires taking a broader view of ancient and modern music than has been true of studies that rely on John Marsh's limited perspective. If the ancient–modern quarrel is viewed as a matter extending into genres other than large-scale instrumental concert music Marsh describes, its time span should be adjusted backward from Marsh's beginning in the 1760s. Others have seized upon the 1760s as a pivotal point in the history of British taste because of an explosion of interest in the *galant* style in larger instrumental works from this period.[238] The modern style's prosperity in the period coinciding approximately with Handel's death in 1759 is consistent with the most reasonable-sounding explanation for the *galant* style's failure to penetrate further in the years from its first introduction in the 1740s: the idea that Handel's dominance somehow discouraged interest in the new style. If, however, the ancient–modern dichotomy is viewed as Crotch's fundamental opposition,

[237] Thus in *Lectures*, NRO, MS 1229/11, Crotch writes that Handel's 'fugues were so regular, classical and scientific, that when performed as voluntaries on an organ in the church service, they do not appear trifling or improper'.

[238] Roger Fisk, 'Concert Music II', in H. Diack Johnstone and Roger Fisk eds, *The Blackwell History of Music in Britain*, vol. 4, *The Eighteenth Century*, (Oxford: Blackwell, 1990), p. 205.

and if the quarrel therefore applies to categories like the keyboard music of Domenico Scarlatti, its traces should be visible in criticism much earlier than Marsh's 'Comparison' indicates. In particular, one might expect to find traces in Charles Avison's important *Essay on Musical Expression*.

Burney's writing suggests a need to explore further whether some aspect of the aesthetic embraced by the moderns might be inconsistent with the notion of musical longevity and classicism. Writers associated here with the modern side like William Mason often trivialize the very music they otherwise argue for by contrasting its 'feminine' qualities with the supposed 'manliness' of ancient music. There is also an unmistakable sense of embarrassment in the moderns' writing over what they are prepared to concede is a useless pastime. Poet Thomas Gray writes of Mason's future wife, 'I know, she sings a little, & twiddles on the harpsichord ... but these are only the virtues of a Maid'.[239] Similarly, in a letter to Mason from 1763, Gray dispatches piano sonatas by 'Carlo' (that is, C. P. E.) Bach that are 'charming, & in the best Italian style' as unworthy of careful practice. 'Mr. Nevile & the old Musicianers here do not like them', Gray observes, but to him they 'speak not only musick, but passion'. 'I can not play them', Gray concludes, 'tho' they are not hard: yet I make a smattering, that serves – *to deceive my solitary days*.'[240]

Along these same lines, Fanny Burney d'Arblay tells of how Crisp 'made himself something of a laughing stock at Wilbury House by preferring his "favourite pieces of Bach of Berlin, Handel, Scarlatti" to hunting'.[241] Fulke Greville is said to have been 'sometimes diverted, and sometimes nettled, by this double defection; for in whatever went forward, he loved to be lord of the ascendant: but Mr. Crisp, whose temper was as unruffled as his understanding was firm, only smiled at

---

[239] Paget Toynbee and Leonard Whibley, eds, *Correspondence of Thomas Gray*, with corrections and additions by H. W. Starr, 3 vols (Oxford: Clarendon Press, 1935). Gray to Mason, 8 October 1763 (vol. 2, pp. 821–2), on Mason's upcoming marriage: 'I rejoice. but has she common sense, is she a Gentlewoman? has she money? has she a nose? I know, she sings a little, & twiddles on the harpsichord, hammers at sentiment, & puts herself in an attitude, admires a cast in the eye, & can say Elfrida by heart: but these are only the virtues of a Maid.'

[240] *Correspondence of Thomas Gray*, vol. 2, p. 804. It is also enlightening to read a letter from Gray to West dated 25 March 1742, in which Gray, whose interest in Italian Opera is well documented, nevertheless expresses approval over Pope's merciless satire of the genre in the *Dunciad*. See, Duncan C. Tovey, ed., *The Letters of Thomas Gray*, 3 vols (London: G. Bell and Sons 1900–12), vol. 1, p. 95.

[241] Frances (Burney) d'Arblay, *Memoirs of Doctor Burney*, 3 vols, (London, 1832), vol. 1, pp. 48–55.

his friend's diversion; and from his pique looked away'. Mrs d'Arblay's expression 'double defection' refers both to the eclectic tastes Crisp exhibited and to the fact that he took music too seriously, even to the point of giving it a kind of classical status. As Fanny indicates, 'far from demanding, according to the present mode, every two or three seasons, new compositions and new composers', Crisp would hear the music mentioned above 'with the same reiteration of eagerness that he would again and again read, hear, or recite chosen passages from the works of his favourite bards, Shakespeare, Milton, or Pope'.[242]

Dr Burney's role in the ancient–modern quarrel is not entirely clear at this point. Although in the sources above he comes across as generally sympathetic to the moderns, there are indications of a more complex pattern of allegiances in his letter to Twining. In that document he does not seem an implacable enemy of polyphony, or even church polyphony, but rather a more balanced figure with extensive studies in the area and some level of appreciation for ancient music.

At the same time, previous studies have shown that the cornerstone of Burney's aesthetic is a notion that has much in common with the modern stereotype above that disparages musical complexity: the notion of *chiarezza* or clearness. This is an idea that Kerry Grant observes, 'in its variety of guises ... is fundamentally the same as Rousseau's "Unity of Melody"'.[243] One of Rousseau's discussions of unity of melody is the 'Lettre sur la musique française' that Burney continued even in his last writing to claim 'may be safely pronounced the best piece of musical criticism that has ever been produced in any modern language'.[244] In Burney's writing *chiarezza* is inevitably 'placed in opposition to the style of accompaniments, such as those of Handel, containing contrapuntal activity that detracts from the melody'.[245]

In his *Cyclopaedia* article '*Chiarezza*', Burney offers some insight into his musical value system when he remarks that,

> a musical idea, apart from all expression, is not an operation of the mind. It arises from a kind of instinct, or, if you please, from a sentiment which taste only directs; and just as it springs from the head of the musician, it is received by the audience, without the least obscurity. We speak here of simple melody. But if harmony is added to it, each part increases complication, obscures the principal idea, and it is then that clearness is wanted.

---

[242] Ibid., vol. 1, pp. 51–2.

[243] Kerry S. Grant, *Dr. Burney as Critic and Historian of Music* (Ann Arbor, MI: UMI Research Press), p. 35.

[244] Abraham Rees, ed., The Cyclopaedia; or, Universal Dictionary of Arts, Sciences, and Literature, 39 vols (London, 1802–19), s.v., 'Rousseau'.

[245] Grant, *Dr. Burney as Critic*, p. 35.

When he claims that music *per se* is merely a kind of instinct while at the same time leaving the door open to the possibility that the emotional content it expresses may be an operation of the mind, he seems to offer a view of music itself as a merely sensual art that is entirely consistent with the moderns' stress on expression and musical content and with their general reluctance to assign it a higher place among the arts.

In the same *Cyclopaedia* article, Burney offers a brief explanation for why *chiarezza* should not be as important a concern in sacred music as it is in other genres:

> in productions for the church, where tranquillity and profound attention are supposed to reign, learning and complication are more likely to be understood than in a theatre, where the interest of the drama, the beauty of the poetry, the gestures of the actors, and the pomp of the representation, all conspire to attract the attention of the audience from the labours of the musical composer. These considerations not only furnish an apology for a thin score in opera songs, but render it an object of praise. Clearness in dramatic music is so much more necessary than in that of the church or even chamber, as the objects that distract the attention of the audience are more numerous.

When other writings are examined, however, his thinking on the value of clearness and musical simplicity is by no means as straightforward as these very late quotations seem to make it. Aside from direct attacks on clearness elsewhere in his writing, it will become evident that Burney is by no means certain that music by itself cannot be an operation of the mind.

CHAPTER TWO

Charles Burney, the ancients and the moderns

Burney and musical Toryism

Charles Burney continues to be discussed in recent scholarly literature as both a progressive and a champion of Haydn and the modern style and 'a professed Handelian who had publicly maintained that the master's works "were so long the models of perfection in this country, that they may be said to have formed our national taste"'.[1] This second 'professed Handelian' interpretation relies on Burney's *Account of the Musical Performances in Westminster-Abbey*, a source that with good reason has come to be viewed with suspicion. The sincerity of Burney's public remarks on Handel and ancient music began to be called into question some time ago, when Kerry Grant first brought to light the conflicting private opinions Burney expressed in his notebooks and other sources. Grant's view of Burney as a covert modern, forced for practical reasons to disguise his allegiances to retain the patronage of the ancient faction, is supported by candid correspondence with like-minded individuals such as Thomas Twining and, of course, by Burney's 1805 encounter with Crotch.

But at the same time, Burney's public veneration of old music including that of Handel cannot have been entirely a pretence. His backward-looking obsession where opera was concerned – the reason Weber associates him with the movement for ancient music – is certainly genuine. The situation of Neapolitan opera in the present quarrel is problematic by Crotch's understanding of the dispute, but it is not at all difficult to find sincere if subdued appreciations even of contrapuntal music in Burney's private papers and the published *Cyclopaedia* articles from the end of his career. The latter were written at a point at which Burney was drafting memoirs he claimed would be 'drawn up with too much sincerity and integrity to appear during the Author's life',[2] and probably represent his

---

[1] Richard Luckett, '"Or Rather Our Musical Shakspeare": Charles Burney's Purcell', in Charles Cudworth, Christopher Hogwood and Richard Luckett, eds, *Music in Eighteenth-Century England* (New York: Cambridge University Press, 1983), p. 71.

[2] Slava Klima, Garry Bowers and Gerry S. Grant, eds, *Memoirs of Dr. Charles Burney 1726–1769* (Lincoln, NB: University of Nebraska Press, 1988), p. xxxii.

most candid thoughts. Finally, Burney's correspondence and diaries show that when he had a choice of how he spent his time in the years of his maturity, he chose old music more often than any other. Burney had a pass guaranteeing free admission for life to the Ancient Concert, and is usually portrayed as an 'old friend' of its founder John Montagu. In fact, he can be found conspicuously more often at Ancient Concerts than at the Italian opera, a genre he thought on the decline from its earlier golden age.[3]

Dr Burney's letters to his daughter Fanny, moreover, reveal his almost simpering pleasure from occasional encounters with royalty at the Ancient Concerts.[4] This calls to mind Weber's view of a connection between Tory politics and old music, for despite occasional public lapses into Republican rhetoric that Weber points out, Burney's correspondence clearly shows him to have been a high-church Tory and a stalwart defender of the aristocracy. Biographers depict him as an 'unshakeable … conservative and monarchist' whose solid principles are contrasted with those of William Mason and Burney's second wife's brother-in-law, Arthur Young. The latter, as Roger Lonsdale observes, did not share 'the simple clarity of [Dr Burney's] own attitude' with regard to the revolution in France.[5]

The coexistence of ancient and modern sympathies in this individual can serve to undermine the perception of a pervasive ancient–modern quarrel. There were others who found it possible to embrace both the music of Handel and J. C. Bach, such as Salisbury Member of Parliament and writer on aesthetics James Harris.[6] But Harris was a man of

---

[3] In Frances (Burney) d'Arblay, *Memoirs of Doctor Burney*, 3 vols (London, 1832), vol. 3, p. 350 Fanny writes with regard to Dr Burney's diaries from 1805 that they show 'he rarely missed the Concert of Ancient-music'. In a letter to Fanny dated 8 April 1799 (British Library (BL), Barrett Collection (hereafter Barrett) Eg. 3690, ff. 98–9), Dr Burney describes his recent activities: 'Evenings M[rs] M. Montagu 2 days when I can go. L[y] Polly friday Even[g] Anc[t] Music – L[y] Rothes, M[r] Pepys, & S[r] Jos. Banks Sunday Evenings – opera I have been at but once, & once at D. L. [Drury Lane] since X[mas].'

[4] D'Arblay, *Memoirs*. Dr Burney writes to Fanny, 'I must tell you that your dear Royal Mistress never fails finding me out at the Concert of Anc[t] Music' and notes that after the last time he was there 'L[y] Harrington told me that she had seen me at the Concert, but that it was the Queen who shewed her where I sat. – is not this gracious & flattering?'

[5] Roger Lonsdale, *Dr. Charles Burney: a Literary Biography* (Oxford: Clarendon Press 1965), pp. 347–8.

[6] In his article 'Harris, James' in Abraham Rees, ed., *The Cyclopaedia; or, Universal Dictionary of Arts, Sciences, and Literature*, 39 vols (London, 1802–19) Burney tries to explain Harris's eclecticism. He notes that in his *Discourse on Music, Painting, and Poetry* (London, 1765) Harris 'illustrates his precepts and reflexions almost exclusively from Handel' but adds that later, 'keeping pace with the times in the refinement of melody, without injuring harmony, Jomelli and Sacchini became [Harris's] favourite composers: the first for rich harmony and grand new effects; the second for grace,

letters and an amateur. If Burney, the most important figure in music criticism of the later eighteenth century, could have been at once a Handel enthusiast and a passionate admirer of Haydn and the moderns, it is an easy step to the conclusion that the clash of these ideologies must not have had the significance even among specialists that it is given in Crotch's account of bitter ancient–modern rivalry. This, in turn, can make Burney's encounter with Crotch in 1805 easy to misunderstand.

C. B. Oldman was the first modern scholar to examine the 1805 exchange between Crotch and Burney. Oldman was aware of Burney's reaction to the Royal Institution lectures mentioned above and knew of the correspondence cited in Chapter 1 between Burney and both Crotch and Latrobe when he discovered Crotch's original manuscript lecture notes some years ago in the Norfolk Record Office.[7] He could find nothing in the NRO lectures that seemed capable of eliciting Burney's vigorously defensive response, however. Indeed, Crotch's rather mild criticisms in these lectures are likely to be viewed as provocative only if they are seen in the context of a larger dispute in which Burney was a partisan for the moderns. Oldman did not interpret the lectures in such a context and, therefore, concluded that Burney must have been offended by still earlier and more inflammatory lectures not held in the NRO. The NRO lectures, he assumed, must represent a weaker anti-modern rhetoric to which Crotch was compelled to revert after his January 1805 series generated a more hostile response than he expected outside the confines of Oxford.

A closer look at the manuscripts preserved in Norwich, however, shows that the 1805 lectures are indeed there, though many have been edited for later reuse and this has the effect of disguising their origins.[8]

---

pathos, and delicacy'. Burney must have known of Harris's alleged conversion from personal contact at the blue stocking parties of Hester Thrale at Streatham, since there is no indication of any such change in Harris's published writing. In fact, Burney's portrait of Harris as a reformed ancient sympathizer, belatedly converted to the aesthetic principles of modernism, cannot be completely accurate for, as director of the annual Salisbury music festival, Harris had already discovered the Italian works that were supposed to have been the foundation of the modern style long before the *Discourse* was written. See, Douglas J. Reid and Brian Pritchard, 'Some Festival Programmes of the Eighteenth and Nineteenth Centuries: 1. Salisbury and Winchester' *R. M. A. Research Chronicle*, 5 (1965), 51–79, and Betty Matthews, 'Addenda and corrigenda to Brian Pritchard and Douglas Reid, "Some Festival Programmes of the Eighteenth and Nineteenth Centuries: 1. Salisbury and Winchester"', *R. M. A. Research Chronicle*, 8 (1970), 23–33.

[7] C. B. Oldman, 'Dr. Burney and Mozart: Addenda and Corrigenda', *Mozart Jahrbuch 1964*, (Kassel: Internationale Stiftung Mozarteum Salzburg, 1964), p. 110.

[8] See Howard Irving, 'William Crotch on "The Creation"', *Music and Letters*, 75 (1994), 548–60.

In many cases the original content can be pieced together reasonably well despite latter additions and obliterations, but the result does not shed much light on the dispute. There are certainly places in which Crotch modified his tone when the first lectures he gave at Oxford in 1798 are compared with more cautious talks in London from 1805 onward, but few major changes can be detected between the 1805 lectures that offended Burney and those that followed immediately thereafter in 1806–07. The rhetoric of Crotch's much later book is indeed noticeably softer, as Oldman noted,[9] but this can be attributed to the passing of time and to Crotch's new understanding of 1818. In short, then, mild as they now may seem, the NRO lectures include the most severe criticisms of Haydn that the London audience ever heard. Further, the most substantive changes in Crotch's critical outlook pre-date Burney's proposed intervention and were actually prompted, as Crotch explains in his *General Account of all the Courses of Lectures*, by a more careful reading and rereading of the authorities on which the lectures were based.

Understanding what the ancient–modern quarrel meant to Burney requires surveying a discourse that began to appear in British letters near the beginning of his literary career with the publication of physician and naturalist Benjamin Stillingfleet's translation of Tartini's *Trattato di Musica* in 1771. A similar point of view but with a more partisan character appeared in print in the spring of 1782 with the publication of a brief essay by William Mason that was prefaced to an obscure anthem word book. A revised version of this essay was reissued as the second of Mason's *Essays historical and critical on English Church Music* in 1795.[10] Unlike Stillingfleet, who does not express an appreciation for cultivated music much beyond the level of the *Beggar's Opera*, Mason's sympathies are expressly with a group of recent composers including Haydn and Pleyel, whom he calls 'our modern masters' and contrasts with a moribund contrapuntal school of Handel and other 'professed Harmonists'.

---

[9] C. B. Oldman, 'Dr. Burney and Mozart', *Mozart Jahrbuch* 1962–1963, (Kassel: Internationale Stiftung Mozarteum Salzburg, 1964), 80.

[10] Benjamin Stillingfleet's translation was published in London in 1771 under the title *Principles and Power of Harmony*. Stillingfleet adds comments of his own in a preface, and introduction, and an appendix, as well as commentary included among the extracts translated from Tartini's book. John Mason's *Essays, Historical and Critical on English Church Music* (York, 1795; London, 1811) is composed of four essays: 'On Instrumental Church Music', 'On Cathedral Music', 'On Parochial Psalmody' and 'On the Causes of the present imperfect Alliance between Music and Poetry'. In a footnote to the second essay, Mason writes 'This Essay was originally prefixed to a Collection of the Words of Anthems, &c. in the year 1782; it is here reprinted with some additions'.

Mason's earliest essay was written with the stated purpose of 'abating an ill-grounded deference to antiquity, merely because it is antiquity'.[11] It was therefore something of a direct public challenge to the forces of ancient music during roughly the same period of time the Ancient Concert was founded and Jones published his *Treatise*, with its declaration of war against the moderns.[12] Still, Mason and related writers including Stillingfleet have a significant area of common ground with the likes of Hawkins and Jones, and this may help to explain their non-appearance in the literature as antagonists of old music. The ancient faction and this second group, at least some of whom could fairly be called moderns, both consistently couch their arguments in moral terms and both conceive of music at its best as a force for moral renewal. The most extreme form of the ideas associated here with the moderns advocates a musical primitivism that can resemble the ideology of ancient music in its yearning for a lost golden age and in the severe moral tone of its rejection of modern luxury and degeneracy. Both of the ideologies considered here also support their positions with the same familiar aesthetic theory, so that the same well-worn ideas and critical rhetoric can appear on both sides of the debate. In some cases this is a result of the casual use of clichés by authors who make no pretence at rigour, but along with reflexive invocations of catch-phrases there are instances in which the underlying critical principles themselves are interpreted in interesting and radically different ways.

The most detailed recent study to discuss Burney's critical writing in detail in the context of an ancient–modern quarrel is Kerry Grant's above mentioned view of Burney as a 'Critic in Conflict'.[13] This view has much in common with the present understanding, but there are important differences. Grant's study shows Burney trying to steer a neutral course in public between parties whose good he will need to maintain. The music historian's motives are conceived as largely pragmatic and his actions, to see them in the most favourable light, reflect the precarious existence of an eighteenth-century musician dependent on the patronage of what Burney sometimes called 'the Great'. There is

---

[11] Mason, *Essays*, p. 358.

[12] William Jones (of Nayland), *A Treatise, on the Art of Music, in which the Elements of HARMONY and AIR are Practically Considered* ... (Colchester, 1784), p. iii. After claiming that 'we are now divided into Parties for the Old and New in Music', Jones remarks: 'It is easy for a man to affect liberality of sentiment, and disclaim all prejudice: but where there is variety of Judgment, we are apt to offend one another by opposition, and then it is hard to be perfectly clear of prejudice. I confess very freely, that my feelings give their testimony to the Style which is now called ancient.'

[13] Kerry S. Grant, *Dr. Burney as a Critic and Historian of Music* (Ann Arbor, MI: UMI Research Press, 1983), ch. 1.

also the undeniable fact that Burney often demonstrates a powerful need to remain on good terms with all sides of a conflict.

In Grant's view, then, Burney's own values are reasonably consistent, much as they are conceived in the earlier works of Scholes and Lonsdale, and inconsistencies in his critical writing might be said to stem from the accommodation of outside forces and from deliberate and, perhaps, necessary misdirection on his part. The present study, by contrast, stresses more of an internal conflict in which this complex personality could, depending on the context, argue sincerely for either side of the ancient–modern dispute. Burney was not alone in his ability to see issues simultaneously from multiple points of view or in his tendency to take an opposite line from extreme positions in an instinctive search for equilibrium. Both traits have contributed to charges of inconsistency against the major commentators of the period and to seemingly inexplicable reversals of position. A case in point is Burney's acquaintance Edmund Burke.[14]

Another important difference between the present view and Grant's rests on a different understanding of the issues of the quarrel itself, in which the dispute was shaped by two complex musical ideologies that cannot be reduced to a simple formula of reactionaries struggling with progressives. It is on this last basis, however, with Burney as a straightforward progressive, that Percy Scholes first introduced elements of the ancient–modern quarrel into Burney scholarship. Scholes used Burney's modern sympathies to put a better face on an unflattering chapter of the historian's life, his rivalry with Sir John Hawkins.[15] At the same time, however, he did not interpret this clash of orientations as a factor in Burney's relations with other prominent figures in the movement for old music, such as Sandwich, or indeed as a part of a pattern of bias that dominated his professional life. This may be a result of his not having had access to Burney's notebooks and other papers or to an important part of his correspondence with Twining that shows his opinion of Sandwich to have been less than it might appear from other sources. One indication of Burney's thinking Scholes did know about can be found in the remarkably candid articles in the *Cyclopaedia* Burney wrote very late in his career.

---

[14] See, for example, Tom Furniss, *Edmund Burke's Aesthetic Ideology: Language, Gender, and Political Economy in Revolution* (Cambridge: Cambridge University Press, 1993).

[15] Percy A. Scholes, *The Great Dr. Burney*, 2 vols (Oxford: Clarendon Press, 1948), vol. 1, p. 298.

Burney and the ancients

In an article in the *Cyclopaedia* that is based on material he had used in the earlier *General History*, Burney defines the word 'SOLO' in music by restating a familiar modernist stereotype. This stereotype contrasts the clarity of expressive melody and unintrusive harmony with the noisiness and confusion that are supposed to characterize the ancient style. At the same time, Burney enjoys a parting shot at his supposed old friend, the now deceased Sandwich. Easily shifting the terms of the quarrel from its origins in vocal music to its adopted home in instrumental, Burney begins by noting that a solo is 'a composition for a single instrument, with a quiet and subdued accompaniment, to display the talents of a great performer'. He follows this with a reference to Sandwich's habit of playing the timpani in public that tries to be humorous but instead introduces an unmistakable element of contempt and bitterness.

One of Burney's characteristic ways of dealing with uncomfortable subjects involved humour. In the *General History* years earlier he had tried to shrug off the Concert of Ancient Music's rejection of musical principles close to his heart by offering a relatively impersonal joke that risked only mild offence from the sober directors of that organization. 'The penalty for the crime of playing a solo at the Concert of Ancient Music', he claimed,

> is five guineas; but at this time [the sixteenth century], if instead of that sum being forfeited, five hundred had been offered to the individual who could perform such a feat, fewer candidates would have entered the lists than if the like premium had been offered for flying from Salisbury steeple over Old Sarum, without a balloon.[16]

By the time he wrote his *Cyclopaedia* article, Burney had received support for his opinions in a conversation with George III himself, in which the monarch had agreed 'ab^r Ld Sandwich's fondness for drums, & noisy music'.[17] Accordingly, the older and more outspoken Burney was moved to note in the later source that,

> SOLOS, which used to afford the most exquisite delight to persons of refined taste, when composed and performed by great masters, are now wholly laid aside; and whoever attempts to perform one, is subjected to a penalty instead of a reward; a law instituted at the concert of ancient music, where a composition was never thought complete by the late earl of Sandwich, without a kettle-drum, nor with, unless he beat it himself.

---

[16] Charles Burney, *A General History of Music*, with critical and historical notes by Frank Mercer, 2 vols (London, 1935; New York: Dover, 1957), vol. 2, p. 123.

[17] CB to FB, 8 January 1787, YUL, Osborn. Dr Burney produces a list of a dozen topics on which he and the King were in agreement.

'At the Commemoration of Handel', he adds, 'the double drums, double curtals, tromboni, &c. augmented his lordship's pleasure, in proportion to the din and stentorophonic screams of these truly savage instruments.'[18]

This is indeed a rare public mood for Burney. His writing often employs images drawn from law and politics, but such references are usually of a very different character from the ironic example above. Most, in fact, celebrate the right of the 'enlightened public' to legislate in the arts or, as Weber points out, take the form of Republican phrases about the 'common good'.[19] Burney observes in one of his later book reviews that,

> Our House of Lords, which is the highest court of judicature in Great Britain, and from which there is no appeal, is supposed to be out of the reach of individual influence; and the enlightened public, in every kingdom, is the supreme judge of such productions of art as are exhibited for its amusement.[20]

There are exceptions to this pattern that will need to be considered in due course, but he is in general far less inclined than writers in the ancient tradition to restrict the right to make judgements in the arts to a cultivated élite. Burney might, accordingly, be expected to bridle at the policies of a closed and authoritarian society like the Concert of Ancient Music, but the vehemence of this exaggeration of the Ancient Concert's rules may be unique in his published writing.

It may be easy to see from his description how the numerous provincial spin-offs of the Westminster Abbey concerts earned, by virtue of both volume and politics, one of the more colourful epithets of the late eighteenth century by being dubbed 'Rory Torys'.[21] It is also worth noting as an indication of Burney's conflicted thinking about the issues raised here that in most of his writing he seems genuinely awed by the fullness of sound made by the commemoration concerts' unprecedented orchestra and chorus of more than 500 performers.[22]

---

[18] Rees, *Cyclopaedia*, s.v., 'SOLO'.

[19] William Weber, *The Rise of Musical Classics in Eighteenth-Century England: a Study of Canon, Ritual, and Ideology* (Oxford: Clarendon Press, 1992), p. 217.

[20] Charles Burney, review of *Observations on the present State of Music, in London*, by William Jackson of Exeter, in *Monthly Review*, 6 (October 1791), 196.

[21] See, *The Torrington Diaries; Containing the Tours Through England and Wales of the Hon. John Byng (Later Fifth Viscount Torrington)* ed. C. Bruyn Andrews, 4 vols. (London: Eyre and Spottiswoode, 1935; New York: Barnes and Noble, Inc., 1970) vol. 2, p. 26 on the use of this expression. Scholes draws attention to this expression in Scholes, *The Great Dr. Burney*, vol. 2, p. 75.

[22] For example, in a letter to Sir Robert Murray Keith, British Envoy Extraordinary and Plenipotentiary to the Imperial Court at Vienna in Alvaro S. J. Ribeiro, ed., *The*

A source Scholes did not know but Lonsdale did are the remaining fragments of Dr Burney's memoirs.[23] Fanny d'Arblay suppressed many candid references to controversial issues when she examined her father's papers with an eye toward their eventual publication. Still, she edited the memoirs between 1817 and 1820, by which point Crotch's pacification between ancients and moderns had presumably taken place. It may be an indication of this *détente* that an incident Dr Burney related from 1805 which might then have been viewed as a serious *faux pas* on his part could be viewed later by Mrs d'Arblay as merely a humorous incident. Thus, Fanny did not obliterate a remarkable account of a heated dispute over ancient and modern music at the home of the Duke of Portland, and even included part of it almost verbatim in her own edition of the *Memoirs*.[24] Burney's argument with Crotch had taken place earlier that same year and the issues of that exchange might still have been on his mind, a possibility reinforced by the existence of still another letter to Crotch on this subject that autumn. In any case, this second controversy over old music in 1805 was, as Burney himself observed (though Fanny deleted this part), a matter that 'had I known my monde, I certainly w^d have avoided'.[25]

Dr Burney relates that he was dressing when the Duke's only other guests, the Lord and Lady Darnley, arrived at Bulstrode Park and he was therefore not introduced. Since he did not know the Lord and Lady and was unaware of their tastes, he let slip a reference to 'modern refinements' in music without a thought to the potential consequences of this loaded expression. Immediately thereafter, 'my Lord and Lady wth the most consummate contempt – repeated: "Modern refinem^{ts} indeed" – We'll call it modern changes of style and taste'. Showing

---

Letters of Dr Charles Burney, vol. 1, *1751–1784* (Oxford: Clarendon Press), p. 446 Burney writes, 'the followers of Handel are very numerous in England: indeed the belief in his infalibility & *supremacy* forms a part of our national musical creed. But even those who being accustomed to more modern, and, as they contend, more graceful, elegant and fanciful music; & who call his style of composition Gothic, inelegant & clumsy, readily allowed that the effects in performance by a band of voices & instruments in Westminster-Abbey, amounting to 525, were such as they had never experienced, & excited sensations of delight for which they were wholly unable to account'.

[23] Much of the material Dr Burney compiled for his memoirs was destroyed by his daughter Fanny. Detailed discussions of Mrs d'Arblay's treatment of Dr Burney's memoirs and of the present state of the existing manuscripts can be found in *Frag.Mem.*, pp. xxiii–xxxiv. See also, Grant, *Dr. Burney as Critic*, pp. 2–6.

[24] D'Arblay, *Memoirs*, vol. 3, p. 359.

[25] YUL, Osborn. In *Memoirs*, vol. 3, pp. 358–60, Mrs d'Arblay inserts instead a remark that 'unacquainted, therefore, with the bigoted devotion to the exclusive merit of Handel that I had to encounter, I got into a hot dispute that I should else, at the Duke's house, have certainly avoided'.

much less caution than he would have 20 years earlier, Burney reports 'we then went to it ding dong'. He continues in the breathless style his private writing can take on, in which he finds no need to amplify on ideas that are widely held in the world of fashion:

> I made use of the same arguments wch I have so often used in my musical writings: that ingenious men during a century cannot have been idle; and the language of sound is never stationary any more than that of conversation an[d] books. New modes of expression, new ideas from new discoveries and inventions required new language, and in the cultivation of instruments and the voice emulation us^d produce novelty, wch above all things is wanted in music. and to say that the symphonies of Haydn, [and] compositions of Mozart & Beethoven have no merit because they are not like Corelli Geminiani and Handel, or that the singing of [a] Pacchierotti, a Marchesi and a Rubinelli, a Banti, and a Billington, in their several styles is not superior to the composition and singers in the time of Handel, puts a stop to all argument, as the *exclusive* admiration and *patronage* of Handel's music (excellent, as some of it is, and ever will be thought by candid and competent judges) has checked the progress of the art so much, that we are at least 50 years behind the rest of Europe in its cultivation, taste, and variety.[26]

Mrs d'Arblay chose to omit Dr Burney's last complaint on the backwardness of English music. It may also be worth noting, Dr Burney's claim notwithstanding, that it would be difficult to find a convenient place in his writing in which all or most of the arguments in this paragraph appear in a forthright manner. In any case, from this point in the account the only surviving documentation includes a heavily obliterated page of the manuscript and Mrs d'Arblay's sanitized version of the resolution of the dispute. In the latter, the Duke of Portland is said to have intervened in the nick of time, whispering 'you are upon *tender ground*, Dr. Burney!'[27]

The uncharacteristic bitterness of Burney's *Cyclopaedia* article seems entirely in character with Burney as a militant modern when viewed in the light of the Bulstrode incident. This facet of Burney's personality actually surfaced much earlier in correspondence with Twining that dates from shortly after the Handel commemoration concerts. If it is not seen in the context of an ancient–modern quarrel, one remarkable letter in particular that Burney wrote to Twining in July 1784 is indeed difficult to square with the picture offered by Mrs d'Arblay, Lonsdale and Scholes, in which Dr Burney is an intimate of Sandwich. This letter

---

[26] YUL, Osborn.
[27] D'Arblay, *Memoirs*, vol. 3, p. 359. In Dr Burney's fragmentary Memoirs, an entire page is heavily obliterated at this point.

to Twining also emphasizes the need to approach even Burney's private writing cautiously, since it demonstrates by its very uniqueness how unusual it was for him to speak frankly on this subject even with his soul mate.

As Burney tells the story, a chance remark to Sandwich resulted in the music historian agreeing to write a book memorializing the Handel commemoration concerts. It was a decision he soon came to regret for a number of reasons. Not the least of these was the fact that his *Account of the Musical Performances in Westminster-Abbey* turned out to be a much bigger project than he anticipated and took time he desperately needed for the remaining long overdue volumes of his *General History*. Equally serious problems were the fact that he was thrust into the constant company of supporters of ancient music and the fact that he had to deal in a very public forum with issues he might otherwise have wanted to side-step gracefully. Both circumstances forced him to confront his feelings about this music and its partisans in a way he had not previously been required to do.

His original enthusiasm for writing the *Account* seems to have been made up not only of desire to curry the Royal favour but also of a genuine interest, motivated by his own unexpectedly positive experience at the Commemoration, to praise 'honestly & heartily what I felt deserving – & to be silent as to the rest'.[28] He soon found himself in a situation in which he did not have the freedom of expression to which he had become accustomed. 'The instant a sheet is written', he complains, 'it is given to be transcribed on gilt Paper for the Royal Eye.' The King and Sandwich's humourless minion Joah Bates edited Burney's work in first draft, carefully expunging passages that did not meet with their approval and particularly passages in which Burney tried to use his characteristic device of humour. But in addition – in Burney's mind at least – a bias in Handel's direction was expected.[29] 'If I was to act *politically & wisely*', he wrote to Twining, 'I sh^d openly abuse all other Music, Musicians, & lovers of Music in all parts of the world, but Handel & his insatiable & exclusive admirers ... I see that I am in great danger of doing myself more harm than good by this Business, – however circumspectly I may act.'[30]

This letter also includes a rare instance of Burney letting down his guard and openly giving in to bitterness. The passage in question is important, for while Burney's remarks here are ostensibly directed toward Bates and Jones of Nayland, it seems clear in context that his

---

[28] CB to TT 31 July 1784, Ribeiro, *Letters*, vol. 1, p. 427.
[29] Ibid., p. 425.
[30] Ibid., p. 424.

resentment took in the ancient faction as a group and that it must have included Sandwich and his fellow directors of the Ancient Concert. Repeatedly Burney touches on aspects of his intense preoccupation with the ancient-music movement, its ideology, humourlessness, prejudice, conservatism and illiberality. If his brain could be microscopically examined, Burney wrote to Twining, 'Handel and Commemoration w^d be seen clinging to every fibre'.[31] Hawkins's name comes up in the course of his grumbling for no apparent reason other than a perceived similarity of ideology. The same is true of Jones, whose Treatise, as Twining knew well before its publication, was to appear that same year.

In a letter a year earlier, in fact, Twining had conspired to have Burney savage Jones's forthcoming book in an anonymous review. Twining justifies treachery against his college friend Jones by complaining that the latter's 'absurd prejudices, & obstinate immobility of opinion, are provoking'.

> I know if his brain cou'd be laid open & inspected, the first thing one shou'd see wou'd be a number of great iron [picture of large twin S shapes], such as one sees upon houses, cramping down all his opinions, in religion, Politics, Music &c &c. To be sure there is no necessity for a man's ideas to be always whirling about like a weather-cock – but here, for a man as soon as ever he gets an opinion into his head, to go for to drive a great bolt in it, & make it as fast as the mainmast of a Ship – why, if so be I may be so bold to say so, its quite what you may call a *disagreeable* thing.[32]

Even though Burney repeatedly denied to Twining any interest in following through with his request – reluctant, perhaps, to let even his intimate friend and co-conspirator see this side of his personality – he did indeed take on this book in the Critical Review a few years later.[33]

In his letter to Twining Burney complains of his having been ignored during dinner meetings at which the commemoration concerts were planned, so that 'all I had to do was stuff – drink – & be a witness to their importance & blunders'.[34] He speaks of his having become 'a slave to other peoples opinions and prejudices' (the word 'slave'

---

[31] Ribeiro, Letters, vol. 1, p. 423.

[32] TT to CB 5–6 July 1783 in Ribeiro, Letters, vol. 1, p. 379, n. 36.

[33] See CB to TT 31 July 1784, in Ribeiro, Letters, vol. 1, pp. 429–30: 'I had wholly forgotten y^r Fr^d Jones & his book, till you put me in mind of it – Why it died still-born – I never heard it cry – or be cried-up – What is become of it – sh^d it be allowed X^{tian} burial, with so much unchristian spirit in it against modern Music – Peace to its ashes, if they burned sufficiently to produce any ... I have other Game to pursue – & therefore shall not make game of him.' Ribeiro notes, however that Burney's review of Jones's Treatise on the Art of Music, is indeed in Monthly Review, 75 (1786), 105–12, 174–81.

[34] Ribeiro, Letters, vol. 1, p. 431.

appears more than once in this letter) and of his being reduced to the status of 'a hireling ministerial Scribbler without the Pay'.[35] This is a reference to his having been pressured into giving to charity the profits from the sale of his *Account*. He complains, along the same lines, of having to sacrifice his 'youngest babe to please his M——y & their Lord^ps and Baronetships'.[36] Burney further refers to Directors of the Ancient Concert in contemptuous terms that make Welsh baronet Sir Watkin Williams Wynn into 'Sr W. Sea-calf ... the *true* Prince of Wales'.[37] It is in this context, then, that Burney writes,

> Yes, yes, he [Bates] has made up his mind [about ancient music], *avec une vengeance* – my God! – what contraction, & childish prejudices – how deaf, as well as how blind are both [Bates and Jones of Nayland] to real Genius! – These people in fastening on Handel & Clinging so closely to him, are sure of being right sometimes – & if they were to let go their hold, what w^d become of 'em? – They will be too insolent now. Les grands Hommes! qu'ils sont![38]

Still, he was determined to preserve his critical independence. Elsewhere in the letter, Burney insists that he 'will not write like an Apostate'.

> I will not deny my liberal principles – I will not abuse the lovers of the best Music of Italy & Germany, & say that they are only admired *through fashion*, & want of good taste & judgment. – I will ransack the language for terms of praise, in speaking of his best works – & the Manner in wch they have been lately performed; but cannot, will not say that there is no other Music fit to be heard, or as well performed.[39]

This does not mean that all of the resulting *Account* is necessarily insincere and unreliable, only that it must be read with a sensitivity for what is tactfully left unsaid and with a constant awareness of Burney's exact choice of words.

The ideologies of ancient and modern music

The quotations above show Burney at odds with Jones and the old-music faction in a moment of anger and frustration, but was this the real Burney? Or should one instead point to the Tory, Charles Burney, the one who invariably speaks for the government in political correspondence

---

[35] Ibid., p. 428.
[36] Ibid.
[37] Ibid., p. 430.
[38] Ibid.
[39] Ibid., p. 425.

and who, for all his seeming impatience with the proponents of old music, continued whenever he could to surround himself with them. It is easier to see occasional outbursts like those detailed above as a matter of conflicting personalities rather than conflicting ideologies, focusing instead on Burney's public persona as an unbiased historian at ease with the high-born world of ancient music, if he is regarded as the 'church and King man' Scholes wrote about, a figure who, as Lonsdale put it, 'undoubtedly felt an almost religious reverence for royalty'.[40]

Weber's study is the first to see the movement for old music in ideological terms and the first to place Burney's work in the context of an ideology of ancient music. As noted in Chapter 1, the essence of the ancient ideology as Weber defines it is that ancient music 'was beneficial to society, a means of moral regeneration'.[41] In addition, however, all of the writers cited in his chapter on 'The Ideology of Ancient Music', with the very noteworthy exception of Burney, specifically recommend old music for its ability to counter the less salutary effects of the fashionable modern music with which it is inevitably put into direct opposition. Weber quotes Jones of Nayland's *Treatise*, where Jones pointedly charges the 'modern Style' with 'degenerate Harmony, wildness of Air, effeminacy, tautology and affected difficulties, inconsistent with the powers and beauties of Expression'.[42] Another of Weber's sources, Jones of Nayland's colleague Bishop George Horne, inveighs against 'the light movements of the theatre'[43] and the 'effeminate and frittered music of modern Italy', both of which are contrasted with 'our English Classics in this sacred science'.[44] Weber cites a complaint by Hawkins over the 'exuberant fancy which distinguishes, or rather disgraces, the instrumental performance of this day', and observes that in such statements Hawkins 'used these moral themes to justify musical classics with a new kind of dogmatism'.[45]

To those accustomed to seeing the late eighteenth century in terms of an ancient–modern polarization, Burney seems out of place in the ancient camp alongside his bitter enemies Jones and Hawkins. Weber allows that Burney was 'his own sort of musical ideologist'[46] and

---

[40] Lonsdale, *Dr. Charles Burney*, p. 324.

[41] Weber, *Rise of Musical Classics*, p. 198.

[42] Jones, *Treatise*, Introduction, p. iv.

[43] George Horne, *The Antiquity, Use, and Excellence of Church Music, A Sermon Preached at the Opening of a New Organ in the Cathedral Church of Christ, Canterbury, on Thursday, July 8, 1784* (Oxford, 1784), cited in Weber, *Rise of Musical Classics*, p. 204.

[44] Ibid., p. 205.

[45] Ibid., pp. 209–10.

[46] Ibid., p. 214.

acknowledges a number of ways in which he seems very different from other ancient apologists. He notes that Burney was not 'a musical moralist' and points out that Burney and his arch-rival Hawkins 'grew out of separate traditions within eighteenth-century English musical thinking'. Burney is described as a 'musical anti-cleric', antagonistic to the high-church tradition of sacred music that was so central to many definitions of ancient music.[47] At the same time, Weber does not identify Burney with the central issue of the ancient ideology, the matter of music's capacity to promote moral regeneration.

There are, however, important ways in which he shares common ground with Hawkins in particular. Weber shows that Burney 'struggled to come to grips with many of the same issues in musical thinking as Hawkins, with not entirely different results'.[48] In particular, in order for music to merit classics – a goal Burney and Hawkins are supposed to have pursued in common – it needed to be promoted as an art worthy to stand alongside its sister arts. The main areas of common ground between Burney and Hawkins, accordingly, have to do with music's status and rank among the arts and its place in British intellectual life. Weber notes that both men exhibited a 'desire to free music history from over-reverence of antiquity, to establish authority over musical taste upon true learning, and to bring due recognition to great composers from the past'.[49]

There is certainly an important element of truth here, for in both Hawkins's writing and one strain of Burney's there is an insistence that music should be judged on its own terms by competent judges. But Burney's writing also contains so many contradictory statements on the points Weber makes that this interpretation of the historian's purposes is likely to be unsatisfying without further explanation. It will be possible in Chapter 3 to consider in greater detail Burney's inconsistent position with regard to music's relationship with the sister arts and his troubled associations with the prestigious men of letters who formed an important part of his social circle. These issues are related in a complex way to his interest in 'freeing music history from over-reference on antiquity'. It is, however, the last of Weber's three points of similarity, Burney's interest in bringing 'due recognition to great composers from the past', that is the most essential aspect of his similarity with Hawkins and the ancient faction. Burney deserves to be labelled a friend of ancient music and a promoter of the idea of classical music only to the extent that he could put composers on a level with literary figures and

---

[47] Ibid., p. 206.
[48] Ibid.
[49] Ibid., p. 214.

allow masterpieces of music to have a moral authority that makes them worthy of preservation and classical status.

As Chapter 3 shows, however, Burney very often sides with the men of letters he otherwise opposes, and when he is in this frame of mind tends to dismiss music as a justly ephemeral art. This strain of Burney's thinking accordingly places a greater value on the words or content music can convey than on the integrity of its construction, treating music *per se* as an amusement and, at best, a sensuous vehicle for poetry. This assessment is incorporated in his most familiar definition of music, in which the art has no moral purpose at all but is merely 'an innocent luxury, unnecessary, indeed, to our existence, but a great improvement and gratification of the sense of hearing'.[50]

Weber contends that to write a history of music at all is necessarily 'to invoke the intellectual significance of the art, and to vest an authority in its past'.[51] He may be correct in this, and Burney's monumental effort by a middle-aged and severely overworked piano teacher may indeed be the sincerest possible statement of his actual convictions. But it is difficult to take Burney seriously as a crusader for musical classics when one reads in the Will he prepared in 1807, literally his final word on this subject, that while he wanted his collection of valuable books about music to be preserved in the British Museum, he was content to have his 'Collection of Music, printed and manuscript' be sold at auction. With a few words his Will dismisses as inconsequential the music of '[Alessandro] Scarlatti, Durante, Jomelli, Perez, Galuppi and Sacchini' as well as '[Domenico] Scarlatti, Sebastian and Emanuel Bach, Schobert', and even 'nearly all the works of Haydn, Mozart and Beethoven'. The best he can say for the present value of this sheet music is that 'it was most of it good in its day, [though] now some of it is out of fashion'.[52]

This belief that music, once out of fashion, has the value of a commodity while words deserve to be enshrined forever in the British Library points to the most important omission in Weber's discussion, the question of Burney's thinking on music's moral rank and purpose. What Burney had to say on this subject changed substantially over the course of his literary career. The 'innocent luxury' definition of the *General History*'s first volume in 1776 contrasts sharply with one he wrote only five or six years earlier in the introduction to his first major publication, which is now known as *The Present State of Music in*

---

[50] Burney, *General History*, vol. 1, p. 21.

[51] Weber, *Rise of Musical Classics*, p. 206.

[52] *A Catalogue of the Valuable and Very Fine Collection of Music, Printed and MS, of the late Charles Burney* (London, 1814; Amsterdam: Frits Knuf, 1973), p. viii. This sale catalogue was based on Burney's will, which was written in 1807.

France and Italy. In the earlier source, dating from a point before the founding of Sandwich's Concert of Ancient Music and well before the most heated skirmishes of the ancient–modern quarrel, Burney sounds very much like a later disciple of ancient music. He complains that 'perhaps the grave and wise may regard music as a frivolous and ener-vating luxury; but, in its defense, Montesquieu has said that "it is the only one of the arts which does not corrupt"'.[53]

This statement, which credits music with not corrupting by denying it any moral stature at all, is followed by several defences of the art against its most common contemporary objections. These effectively conflict with Montesquieu's assessment by assuming a higher role for the art. On utilitarian grounds, Burney contrasts music as an idle amuse-ment with a different possibility, comparing it to the once seemingly useless curiosity of electricity and citing Benjamin Franklin's dramatic invention of the lightning rod.[54] The lightning rod, it should be remem-bered, was both an early instance of the scientific method being applied successfully to a practical need and an invention that saved lives and property. With music placed on a level with this life-saving develop-ment, Burney proceeds to list among the art's beneficial uses the possibility that it can actually cure disease. Referring to the annual performances of Handel's *Messiah* at the Foundling Hospital, he seems ready to give his art the quasi-magical powers that men of letters still sometimes assigned the music of antiquity when he observes that 'the pangs of child-birth are softened and rendered less dangerous and dreadful by the effects of its power' and that it 'helps, perhaps to stop the ravages of a disease which attacks the very source of life'.[55] 'Music has indeed ever been the delight of accomplished princes', Burney concludes, 'and the most elegant amusement of polite courts: but at present it is so com-bined with things sacred and important, as well as with our pleasures, that it seems necessary to our existence.'[56] If, many years later, Burney thought of literary works on the fine arts as 'the *entrements* of our literary repasts: with which, after the more solid food, we are glad to amuse ourselves',[57] the present introduction to his own first contribu-tion hopes for a very different reception.

---

[53] *The Present State of Music in France and Italy: or the Journal of a Tour through those Countries, undertaken to collect Materials for a General History of Music*, 2nd edn (London, 1773; New York: AMS Press, 1976), p. 3.
[54] Ibid., p. 4.
[55] Ibid., p. 5.
[56] Ibid., p. 6.
[57] Charles Burney, review of Thomas Robertson, *An Inquiry into the Fine Arts*, *Monthly Review*, 74 (1786), 191–8.

Was Burney really a Tory?

Since Burney's 'innocent luxury' definition of music is directly contrary to the ideals of musical Toryism, and since he so often endorses innovation and even embraces the rhetoric of Republicanism, it is not unreasonable to ask whether Burney was actually a sincere Tory at all. This approach offers the simplest possible explanation for his inconsistencies: by one reading, the 'Church and King' Burney was an act; he was simply in need of the patronage of the Great and prepared to resort to insincerity, even to the point of adopting political protective coloration, to accommodate the notoriously Handelophilic George III and the aristocrats who controlled the world of ancient music late in the century. Accordingly, he may have wanted to present music in his first major publication as an art deserving of the support of those who thought so highly of it, including Lord Sandwich, Burney's benefactor and patron.[58] In any event, since one of the two views of music above must be unreliable, should not the one be disregarded that makes it into a force so compelling it can cure disease? Besides, the 'innocent luxury' view is reinforced repeatedly in Burney's later writing, but this earlier attempt to give music a status approaching the art of the ancient Greeks is unique.

Suppose, then, Burney's own words are examined as the best possible evidence of his political ideology. His letters speak often of how 'unguarded an aristocrate' he is and condemn the 'furious democrates' and 'the levellers [who] are now bent on a republican form of Governm''.[59] His correspondence with Frances Crewe, daughter of his patron Fulke Greville and wife of John Crewe, prominent Whig and sometime supporter of Charles James Fox, is filled with Tory rhetoric. Much of this centres on his apprehension over a possible breakdown of the social order. Burney constantly fears for the constitution and worries about restlessness that will be spurred by the movement for reform in

---

[58] On the support Burney is said to have enjoyed from Sandwich see Scholes, *The Great Dr. Burney*, vol. 1, p. 151. In the introduction to *The Present State of Music in Germany, the Netherlands and United Provinces*, 2nd edn, 2 vols (London, 1775: New York: Broude, 1969), Burney notes: 'I am principally indebted to the patronage of the Earl of Sandwich, who, to assist me in calling the attention of the public to the history of his favourite art … was pleased to honour me with recommendatory letters, in his own hand, to every English nobleman and gentleman who resided in a public character in the several cities through which I passed; the influence of which was so powerful as to gain me easy access to those who were not only the most able, but whom I was so fortunate as to find the most willing to forward my undertaking.'

[59] CB to FB 9 June 1795, New York Public Library (hereafter NYPL) Berg Collection (hereafter Berg).

Parliament. He sounds most like a Tory during the period of hostilities
in France, when he indulges in flag-waving about the 'true principles of
our mild & gentle government, So justly poised between Tyranny &
Anarchy'[60] and complains that 'to *agitate the people*, & flatter them
with notions of right to power and property, as well as legal protection,
is wicked, profligate, and subversive of all liberty, Law, and happiness'.[61] Burney could not understand how his friend in later life the
Duke of Portland, a prominent Whig and also sometime supporter of
Fox, '& his worthy independent friends of property & principle' could
'abet or wish for anarchy, degradation, beggary, & atheism!'[62] Give the
people a taste of liberty and they can be expected to want more, just as
'men corrupted & voluptuous, like savages in innocence & ignorance',
could scarcely be expected to 'submit to eat acorns after corn is found'.[63]

But even as Burney wrote to Fanny in all seriousness of 'how open &
unguarded an aristocrate' he was, he did so in a self-congratulatory
context that stresses his ability to maintain the 'good word of so many
furious democrates'.[64] In the same letter he lists with pride the radicals
who had either offered him kind words in print or had cited his work in
their own. He points out that

> *Godwin*, the Editor of the new Annual Register, has abridged my
> acc^t of the state of Music in Engl. during the reign of Qu. Eliz. with
> *maint Eloge* – Sr Wm Jones, always a decided republican – Mason,
> formerly a naughty boy – Hayley of his faction against Johnson, &
> much more a democrat, now – then what do you say to the douceurs
> of Ld Lansdowne, last summer? & those of Erskine?[65]

This, in turn, prompted Fanny to tease him in response that 'the Demo-
crats court you so violently, that Monsr d'Arblay insists they have *found
you out!* & that your Aristocracy is a feint'.[66]

At the risk of an unfair guilt by association, one has to wonder how
close this was to the truth, so often does Burney's name surface cheerfully in the company of the other side. Many of his book reviews appear
in the newly formed and decidedly liberal *Monthly Magazine*, a publication that also published contributions by Godwin and Peter Pindar.
Burney also published in the *Monthly Review*, edited by the self-styled

---

[60] Charles Burney to Frances Crewe 19 September 1792, YUL, Osborn.

[61] Ibid.

[62] CB to Frances Crewe, 13 February 1793, YUL, Osborn.

[63] CB to Frances Crewe 8 October 1792 YUL, Osborn.

[64] CB to FB 9 June 1795, NYPL, Berg.

[65] Ibid.

[66] Fanny Burney, *The Journals and Letters of Fanny Burney*, eds, Joyce Hemlow,
Patricia Boutilier and Althea Douglas, 8 vols (Oxford: Clarendon Press, 1973), vol. 3,
p. 113.

'Old Whig and Consistent Protestant' Ralph Griffiths, whose writers, Samuel Johnson is said to have remarked, 'were Christians with as little Christianity as possible, inclined to pull down all establishments'.[67]

It is helpful in assessing the depth of Burney's commitment to Tory principles to look at a single element of his politics, his thinking about the movement for reform in Parliament. His position on this issue can be as variable and self-contradictory as his treatment of contrapuntal style. In the same letter to Fanny in which he writes of being an 'unguarded aristocrate', he tells of a luncheon at Mrs Crewe's at which he was pulled aside by radical barrister Thomas Erskine to talk about the latter's plan for parliamentary reform. One can sense from his letter that Burney seems to have been most concerned about the external appearance of this display before a crowd of his aristocratic friends, since he complains to Fanny that all the while 'he had hold of my arm, – & people stared at our intimacy – [and] that rogue Mrs Crewe, & the Marchioness of Buckingham, were upstairs sitting at a window wondering & laughing at our conjoberation!'[68]

But at the same time, he was less than sanguine about Erskine's plan and its possible effects on the maintenance of the social order. Two years earlier he had written to Mrs Crewe that 'as to a *reform* of P.[,] remember the effect of doubling the Tiers-Etat, in France'. 'Abolish Nobility & where will the constitution be? – pull down the Bishops & Church, & what becomes of learning & the Clergy?'[69] This is an almost constant refrain in his correspondence during the 1790s. But in an article on William Mason he wrote for the *Cyclopaedia* shortly afterwards, Burney praises Mason's liberalism and cites his stand on the very issue of parliamentary reform.[70] He eulogizes Mason as a man 'warmly attached to the

[67] Walter Graham, *English Literary Periodicals* (New York: Octagon Books, 1966), pp. 188–9 and 211.

[68] CB to FB 9 June 1795, NYPL, Berg.

[69] CB to Frances Crewe 1 January 1793, YUL, Osborn.

[70] It can be difficult to determine the authorship of the Rees *Cyclopaedia* articles. The present attribution to Burney of the article 'Mason, William' is based on the author's comments on Mason's publications on church music: 'we did not, however, agree with him in his reforming schemes of church music. He had been himself a good performer on the harpsichord; had some knowledge of composition, a refined taste, and was a very good judge of modern music; but his ideas of reforming cathedral music would reduce it to Cavinistical psalmody. He wished for nothing but plain counterpoint in the services and full anthems, and dull and dry harmony in the voluntaries, without melody, accent or measure; and he preferred the mechanical execution of a barrel organ in church music, to the most judicious accompaniment of a consummate organist'. These ideas may be compared with those voiced in the review of Mason's *Essays, Historical and Critical on English Church Music*, Burney wrote for the *Monthly Review*, 20 (1796), 398–408.

principles of liberty'[71] and remarks that 'during the contest with America, he strongly expressed his disapprobation of the hostilities carrying on against the transatlantic part of the community'.[72] Beyond this, Mason 'was a zealous member of the Yorkshire Association for procuring a reform in parliament, which, notwithstanding the exertions of the wisest patriots, and most virtuous of our countrymen, is still, apparently, at great distance'.[73] Burney makes Mason's love of liberty a theme of his article, referring to his preaching against the slave trade, 'which animated declamation against the inhumanity of that traffic'[74] and finally to his commemoration of the centennial of the Glorious Revolution. This centennial 'called forth a new exertion of his lyric powers in a "Secular Ode", which breathed the spirit of his must of freedom'.[75] Burney's only concession to the earlier 'naughty boy' Mason – the Mason who wrote satires of the government, who 'took pride in being neither a Demagogue nor an Aristocrat', and who, as Mrs d'Arblay points out, was 'singularly for *The Sovereign, The Government*, yet palpably not for George the third, nor William Pit'[76] – is to point out that Mason 'lived to witness the French revolution, the horrors of which wrought a complete change in his political principles'.[77]

Presumably this latter-day conversion made it possible for Burney to claim in a letter to Mason in 1795, that 'I believe we are in perfect unison as to religion & politics, the two main pillars of a state; and indeed of a friendly & cordial intercourse between man & man'.[78] In her edition of the *Memoirs*, Fanny tries to put greater distance between her father and Mason. Dr Burney had written to her in June 1794 of a warming of his almost lifelong relationship with Mason, which may have been strained not only by Mason's apparent sympathy for the Republican cause but just as importantly by their differences on church music. Burney notes in his letter that 'Mr Mason has been here twice, & I have visited him in town 2 or 3 times', adding that Mason, 'from being long a seeming republican & attached to the Rockingham's Wyvill's &c is now become as much an allarmist as my self, & holds Anarchists & Jacobins in equal horror'.[79]

---

[71] Ibid.
[72] Ibid.
[73] Ibid.
[74] Ibid.
[75] Ibid.
[76] FB to CB 29 November 1796 in Burney *The Journals and Letters of Fanny Burney*, vol. 3, p. 244.
[77] Rees, *Cyclopaedia*, s.v., 'Mason, William'.
[78] CB to WM 8 June 1795, NYPL, Berg.
[79] CB to FB 10 June 1794, BL, Barrett, Eg. 3690, f. 77.

Fanny, however, describes this new turn in their relationship in 1794 in the *Memoirs* as a 'formation of intimacy, rather than renewal of acquaintance' and adds that

> while always admiring the talents, and esteeming the private character of that charming poet, he never lost either his regret or his blame for the truly unclerical use made of his powers of wit and humour, by the insidious, yet biting sarcasms, levelled against his virtuous Sovereign in the poetical epistle to Sir William Chambers.[80]

That Burney was in fact renewing an old acquaintance with Mason is evident from their substantial and friendly correspondence, evincing an ongoing relationship that may have begun as early as 1748.[81] Burney certainly had his differences with Mason and could be provoked to anger by the latter's opinions, especially on Samuel Johnson.[82] But Lonsdale's contention that there is 'a rather hypocritical air to the remaining years of Burney's apparent friendship with Mason' on account of this review does not recognize that the conflicts between these men were there almost from the start and may have only required the (perhaps illusory) secure platform offered by the anonymous review process for their expression.[83]

---

[80] D'Arblay, *Memoirs*, vol. 3, pp. 191–2.

[81] In Ribeiro, *Letters*, p. 39, Ribeiro indicates that Burney probably met Mason at the house of Robert D'Arcy, fourth Earl of Holderness in 1748. In a letter from 20 April 1764 to Elizabeth (Mrs Stephen) Allen, who would become his second wife, Burney notes, 'I must tell you that I have lately been so happy as to renew an old Acquaintance wth that Charming Poet Mr Mason. He has been at my House to Tea & to hear Hetty &c – he is I must tell you nearly as good a Musician & Painter as Poet – plays very well the Harp^d & knows the thing thoroughly.'

[82] See Roger Lonsdale, 'Dr. Burney and the *Monthly Review*', *Review of English Studies*, 14 (1963), 357, where Lonsdale remarks on the complex nature of Burney's relationship with Mason. He cites Burney's scathing review of *Poems by William Whitehead Esq. ... to which are prefixed, Memoirs of his Life and Writings, by W. Mason, M.A.* in *Monthly Review*, 78 (1788), 177–82, where Burney complains (p. 177) that 'Mr. Mason seems to have made his friend's Life a vehicle for the abuse of Dr. Johnson'.

[83] The security of the anonymous review may, however, have been illusory. In his review of the *Essays Historical and Critical on English Church Music*, by William Mason, *Monthly Review*, 20 (1796), 398–408, Burney plainly tries to disguise his identity, commenting (402) 'The taste of Mr. M. and of his friend Mr. Gray in *Poetry*, now that Dr. Johnson is no more, few will dispute: but in *Music*, as mere *dilettanti*, like themselves, we may venture to have an opinion of our own, though it should be a little different from that which they hold.' Still, it is improbable that Mason would have failed to detect Burney's thinking.

Politics and the moderns

If the above suggests that Burney had a soft spot in his heart for some elements of liberal thinking, a plausible connection can be traced between radicalism and the modern style in the last quarter of the eighteenth century. This, of course, is not to say that all radicals were admirers of Haydn any more than all Torys were lovers of Handel. It is significant, however, even if it is hardly proof of any such connection, that some of the most public voices speaking against the movement for old music after 1780 were connected with the political opposition, and that some of these same individuals were to some extent supporters of the musical moderns. Mason, as noted above, was an outspoken advocate of Haydn and Pleyel. Even satirist Peter Pindar (that is, Dr John Wolcot), who is wary of the élitism of cultivated music in general, can be found occasionally on the modern side.

Because he does not recognize an intellectual position for the moderns made up of both ideological and aesthetic components, Weber tends to see Wolcot's work in straightforward political terms. He comments, accordingly, on the satirist's treatment of the pretensions of the leadership of the movement for old music but not on Pindar's occasional identifications of support for an alternate repertoire of modern music.[84] In the context of the quarrel, however, one can see that Pindar is not only an enemy of ancient sympathizers in his satire *Ode upon Ode or a Peep at St. James* but a friend of moderns such as 'Sacchini, Haydn, [J. C.] Bach, and Gluck,/and twenty more who never had the luck/To please the nicer ears of *some* Crowned Folk'.[85] It is yet more evidence of guilt by association that Burney himself received support from Pindar in a passage in the same satire that comments on his having been passed over for the position of Master of the King's Band upon the death of John Stanley in 1786.[86]

Mason not only approved of the music of the moderns in the concert hall but in church. The *Essays* advocate the use of slow movements from Haydn's symphonies as voluntaries, and in 1794 Mason adapted airs by Pleyel for the Morning and Evening Prayer services. In the end, he was unable to use his Pleyel adaptations because of an early instance of copyright protection and Burney himself wrote music in their place.[87]

---

[84] Weber, *Rise of Musical Classics*, pp. 240–42.

[85] John Wolcott, *The Works of Peter Pindar, esq.*, 5 vols (London, 1812), vol. 1, p. 414.

[86] Lonsdale, *Dr. Charles Burney*, p. 321.

[87] William Mason, *Essays Historical and Critical, on English Church Music* (York, 1795; London, 1811), p. 316. Burney comments unfavourably on Mason's suggestion on the sacred uses of the modern style in his review (p. 401). In a letter to Fanny from 10 June 1794 (BL, Barrett, Eg. 3690, f. 77), however, he is more positive about Mason's plan. In

Much to Burney's disapproval, Mason also promoted congregational psalmody in his *Essays, Historical and Critical on English Church Music* as a simple music for the common man.

A focus on the common man is something Mason shared with Wolcot. Weber notes that Pindar's satires 'attacked Anglicanism by bowing toward Dissent, citing its psalm tunes as a kind of popular religion possessed of a spirituality deeper than the overeducated music of the established church'.[88] The impetus that prompted Wolcot's rejection of learned church music can be found in a broad spectrum of religious and musical opinion, however, including writing by John Wesley,[89] Mason – whose *Essays* are pointedly addressed to the Church of England,[90] and even a few cathedral organists like Wolcot's friend William Jackson of Exeter. Jackson, Mason and Wolcot were all educated in the liberal arts, they each wrote for the stage and, perhaps not coincidentally, each advocated a simpler style of sacred music with roots in the modern style.[91]

There may even be a suggestion of sacred uses of the modern style in *Ode upon Ode*. Pindar observes of 'Mistress Walsingham' – that is, author Mary Robinson[92] – that

---

this letter, Dr Burney notes that Mason 'has consulted me ab^t 2 Charming Hymns (& given your mother a copy) wch he has written to a slow air of Pleyel for his own Parish'. Noting that Pleyel's air could not be used, Burney remarks, 'I have therefore set these 2 Hymns for my fr^d of 46 years & am going this Morning to play & sing them at Mr Stonhewer's'.

[88] William Weber, 'The 1784 Handel Commemoration as Political Ritual', *Journal of British Studies*, 28 (1989), p. 68.

[89] On Wesley's ideology, J. C. D. Clark quotes a letter to Lord North in *English Society 1688–1832: Ideology, Social Structure, and Political Practice During the Ancien Regime* (Cambridge: Cambridge University Press, 1985), p. 236: 'all my prejudices are against the Americans; for I am an High Churchman, the son of an High Churchman, bred up from my childhood in the highest notions of passive obedience and non-resistance'. Wesley's opinions on music are discussed below with regard to his 1779 essay entitled 'Thoughts on the Power of Music', in *The Works of the Rev. John Wesley, A. M.*, 3rd edn, 7 vols (New York, n. d.), vol. 7, pp. 455–7.

[90] Mason, *Essays*, p. 295.

[91] Jackson was organist and choirmaster at Exeter Cathedral. The facts of his biography, including some information on his classical education, are given in somewhat greater detail in Jamie Croy Kassler, *The Science of Music in Britain 1714–1830: a Catalogue of Writings, Lectures, and Inventions*, 2 vols (New York: Garland, 1979), vol. 1, p. 575 than in other accessible sources. His literary pretensions and association with Wolcot are mentioned in DNB. Ronald R. Kidd's article in *New Grove*, 439–40 provides a useful summary of Jackson's stage works, commenting on both their continuing popularity in the nineteenth century and their greater impact than his church music. The former include *Lycidas*, an afterpiece from 1767 to which music is no longer extant, a comic opera entitled *The Lord of the Manor* from 1780, and *The Metamorphosis*, a comic opera on a libretto by Jackson himself, from 1783.

[92] Robinson, author of 'Walsingham; or the Pupil of Nature', is best known as an actress and mistress of the Prince of Wales.

when fiddle, hautboy, clarionet, bassoon,
On Sunday (deemed by *us* good Christians, *odd*),
Unite their clang, and pour their merry tune
In *jiggish* gratitude to God:
Lo! if a witless Member should desire,
Instead of Handel, strains perchance of Haydn,
A fierce Semiramis she flames with fire,
This Amazonian crotchet-loving Maiden.[93]

Pindar's remarks are reminiscent of a passage in Mason's *Essays* complaining that 'since the rage for Oratorios has spread from the Capital to every Market Town in the Kingdom', anyone who thinks he can sing at sight

> can by no means be satisfied unless they introduce Chaunts, Services, and Anthems, into their Parish Churches, and accompany them with, what an old Author calls, *scolding Fiddles*, squalling Hautboys, false-stopped Violoncellos, buzzing Bassoons; all ill-tuned and worse played upon, in place of an Organ, which, if they had one, they would probably wish to improve by such instrumental assistance.[94]

Arguing that 'no Instrument should have been admitted into the Church, the tone of which was naturally calculated to produce merriment and festivity' Mason would like to restrict instrumental music in church to the organ.[95]

Mason may seem to undermine his own proscription against levity when he recommends slow movements from Haydn symphonies as organ voluntaries in the first essay of his collected edition. This is considered further below; for the present, it is more useful to reflect on the commonality of Mason and Wolcot's thinking, and the differences between both men and Burney. Burney had no desire to involve the common man in sacred music as anything other than a spectator and objected neither to orchestrally accompanied church works nor to accepting Handel's oratorios as a legitimate species of sacred music.[96] He

[93] Wolcot, *Peter Pindar*, vol. 1, 417.
[94] Mason, *Essays*, p. 388.
[95] Ibid., p. 319.
[96] Burney's thoughts on congregational singing are made abundantly clear in his chapter 'Music in England During the XVI Century' (Burney, *General History*, vol. 2, pp. 13–127). He argues (vol. 1, pp. 59–60), 'But why is the *whole* congregation to *sing* any more than preach, or read prayers? Indeed it seems to have been the wish of illiterate and and furious reformers, that all religious offices should be performed by *Field-preachers* and *Street-singers*; but it is well known by all who read the Scriptures, or hear them read, that both *singing-men* and *singing-women* were appointed to perform distinct parts of religious rites among the ancient Hebrews as well as Christians ... *Singing* implies not only a tuneable *voice*, but *skill* in Music: for Music either is, or is not an *Art*.'

was, however, quick to brand Mason's advocacy of the modern style in church inappropriate in his review of Mason's *Essays*, since 'the popular composers, whom he mentions, would instantly carry the minds of many hearers from the church to the opera, concerts, and playhouses'.[97] In this review, Burney actually makes a better case for the ancient contrapuntal style than did contemporary ancient-music supporters.

Two views on moral music

Burney's consistent position after the Italian tour that music could have no moral purpose or effect is decidedly out of step with individuals like Mason whose ideas and conversation must have done much to form his view of the modernist ideology. Before looking at the modern side of a quiet debate on the moral applications of music, it is necessary first to take a closer look at the connection between music and morality in the context of Weber's ideology of ancient music.

The critical ideas and rhetoric that were taken up at the century's end in the case for musical Toryism had, first, been in the air since the century's beginning. At that point they were used in an attack on Italian opera that had no specific intent to establish a canon of old music. John Dennis is just as concerned about music's integrity and moral rank as Jones, however, when he inveighs against 'Opera's after the Italian Manner' in 1706, and he has the same fears as Jones does about music's effects on morality when he adds his 'Reflections on the Damage Which They May Bring to the Public'.[98] Dennis regards Italian opera as an 'effeminate Trifle' that has 'emasculated the Minds of Men, and corrupted their Manners' by being a 'Promotor of wanton and sensual Thoughts than ever the drama was pretended to be'.[99]

Dennis does not try to explain what aspect of opera has this undesirable effect other than to voice a standard complaint that '*Sense upon the Stage seems to have given place to Sound*'[100] and to protest that

---

[97] [Charles Burney], review of *Essays*, 401.

[98] John Dennis, *Essay on the Operas after the Italian Manner, Which Are about to be Establish'd on the English Stage: with Some Reflections on the Damage Which They May Bring to the Public* (London, 1706).

[99] John Dennis, 'The Stage Defended, from Scripture, Reason, Experience, and the Common Sense of Man', in Edward Niles Hooker, ed., *The Critical Works of John Dennis*, 2 vols (Baltimore, MD: Johns Hopkins University Press, 1939–43), vol. 2, p. 301.

[100] Dennis's thoughts on sound and sense come from the preface to his *Essay on the Operas after the Italian Manner* as quoted in Siegmund A. E. Betz, 'The Operatic Criticism of the *Tatler*, and *Spectator*', *Musical Quarterly*, 31 (1945), 325.

operas have 'nothing of that good Sense and Reason, and that artful Contrivance which are essential to the Drama'.[101] Other writers had already expressed a more precise critique of opera, however, and their understanding of music's weaknesses has affinities with much later figures like Hawkins. In his Preface to *Albion and Albanius*, John Dryden – acknowledging his debt to Dutch scholar Isaac Vossius – draws a distinction between 'the recitative part of the *Opera*' which 'requires a more masculine Beauty of expression and sound'[102] and other aspects to which he specifically objects. The latter include that 'which (for want of a proper *English* Word) I might call *The Songish Part*', in which music 'must abound in the softness and variety of Numbers: its principal Intention, being to please the Hearing, rather than to gratify the understanding'.[103] Dryden's remarks are not the same kind of comment on musical values that Hawkins later expressed in a contemptuous comparison of 'the feeble efforts of simple melody' with 'the irresistible charms of elegant modulation and well-studied harmony'.[104] But even though music's intellectual integrity comes from different places in these two quotations, each man is at least able to pinpoint the source of its intellectual weakness in sensuous, effeminate melody.

At the centre of complaints by Dennis and Jones is the need for rule and order. Dennis contends that the great design of the arts should be, 'to restore the Decays that happen'd to human nature by the Fall, by destroying Order'.[105] Accordingly, he asks 'but how should these arts re-establish Order, unless they themselves were regular?'[106] He does not mention melody in particular, but such remarks call to mind Marsh's later observation about 'melody being, indeed, of a mere arbitrary nature, [it] cannot be subjected to those mechanical rules of criticism by which harmony is judged'.[107] Jones, unlike others in the critical

---

[101] Ibid. On opera's lack of artful contrivance, see Ion Paul Eustace Zottos, 'The Completest Concert or Augustan Critics of Opera: a Documentary and Critical Study in English Aesthetics' (PhD, University of Pennsylvania, 1977), p. 120.

[102] H. T. Swendenberg jr, ed., *The Works of John Dryden*, 20 vols (Berkeley and Los Angeles: University of California Press, 1976), vol. 15, p. 4.

[103] Ibid.

[104] [Sir John Hawkins], *An Account of the Institution and Progress of the Academy of Ancient Music with a Comparative View of the Music of the Past and Present Times by a Member* (London, 1770), p. 12.

[105] John Dennis, 'The Grounds of Criticism in Poetry', in *The Critical Works of John Dennis*, vol. 1, p. 336.

[106] Ibid.

[107] [John Marsh], 'A Comparison Between the Ancient and Modern Styles of Music in Which the Merits and Demerits of Each are Respectively Pointed Out', *Monthly Magazine*, supplement to vol. 2 (1796), p. 982.

tradition of ancient music, denied that melody was in fact arbitrary.[108] Still, he might have agreed with Dennis not only on the need for order in the arts but also that the right kind of music, if apprehended under appropriate circumstances by a fit audience, *could* engage both the senses and the reason. Both men, in addition, thought music did this at least in part by serving as an abstract model of order rather than by virtue of any content it conveyed. 'Those Arts that make the Sense instrumental to the Pleasure of the Mind, as Painting and Musick', Dennis claims, 'do it by a great deal of Rule and Order.'[109]

Jones is concerned about a particular kind of disorderliness in modern music. He cites the style's discursive quality, noting that 'instead of being properly connected, and melting into one another', the harmonies of the modern style 'are chopped into pieces'.[110] Disorderliness tends to be equated with what ancients sometimes call 'connexion', that is, with the relationship of musical events in succession. Jones does not try to explain on the simplest level *how* this kind of disorder in music might be related to disorder in society, or, for that matter, how music can be a moral influence at all. His closest approach to this second question appears in his earlier *Physiological Disquisitions*, where Jones quotes James Beattie's 'An Essay On Poetry and Music, as They Affect the Mind' on the latter's charge that 'a great part of our fashionable music seems intended rather to tickle and astonish the hearers, than to inspire them with any permanent emotions'.[111]

Beattie's remarks here have the spirit and vocabulary of writing sympathetic to ancient music, especially the use of the loaded word 'fashionable'. This aspect of the Beattie's *Essay* together with its

---

[108] Jones, *Treatise*, p. 41: 'But as Air is the production of the fancy or imagination, some have falsely supposed that it may be left, like the Nightengale, to the wildness of Nature; and that all rules can only serve to fetter and restrain it. Air, it is true, is an effusion of the fancy; and indifferent artists, of original Genius, it will have a different turn and character, like the air of the face: yet there is no Science, nor any one part of a Science, in which Nature will not derive much assistance from Art and Experience. The Extempore Performer, When his fancy is inspirited, does not forget his rules; but utters the fruits of his knowledge and experience; without which he would have nothing to produce, it being impossible to reap what was never sown ... I am very sensible I have a difficult subject before me, and that the attempt to reconcile Air with Reason, will appear like that of giving Laws to the Wind, *which bloweth where it listeth*; but when the matter is properly considered, it will appear in a different light.'

[109] Dennis, 'The Grounds of Criticism in Poetry', p. 336.

[110] Jones, *Treatise*, p. 43.

[111] William Jones (of Nayland), *Physiological Disquisitions; or Discourses on the Natural Philosophy of the Elements* (London, 1781), p. 351. Jones quotes James Beattie, in 'An Essay On Poetry and Music, as They Affect the Mind', *Essays* (Edinburgh, 1771; New York, 1971), p. 461.

moralizing tone may have lured Jones into quoting the *Essay* without considering more carefully its content, for once Beattie's reflexive nods in the direction of established doctrine are discounted, it appears he and Jones had very different notions of how music can be a moral force. This is crucial to identifying the ideology of the moderns. The disciples of ancient music might have argued that while *they* regarded music as having a higher moral purpose, the moderns treated it as a mere amusement. In fact, however, some advocates of the modern position have the same kinds of pious objections to music as an amusement as the most sober ancient advocates, and the best writers on the modern side offer a consistent argument in support of music as a means of promoting morality. This argument resembles closely the view of Beattie and differs sharply from the most common view in the tradition of ancient music.

One of Beattie's main points is to advocate a simpler musical style in contrast to music that ' ... may give a little exercise to the mind of the hearer ... but, without engaging the affections ... can never yield that permanent, useful, and heart-felt gratification, which legislators, civil, military, and ecclesiastical, have expected from it'.[112] The word 'simple' can mean many things when applied to eighteenth-century music, but Beattie's reference to mental exercise suggests a complaint one often finds directed against ancient music by moderns like Mason. In this common usage, a simple style is one that avoids contrapuntal textures that are supposed to render texts unintelligible. This was certainly the inference Burney drew from Beattie's use of this code word in the 'Essay', and Burney had the advantage of being able to converse with Beattie directly through their common association at Hester Thrale's bluestocking parties. Burney's irritation at Beattie's remarks, in fact, led him to complain (notwithstanding the music historian's own pleas for a musical simplicity along similar lines) that 'though we respect [Beattie's] good taste in poetry, morality, and theology, yet, when he writes on the subject of music with little knowledge or experience in refined, polished, or learned compositions ... we cannot but regard his musical decisions as narrow and contracted'.[113] Significantly, Burney does not say Beattie's position is wrong, only that Beattie himself is bigoted. As he notes elsewhere, 'Beattie's ear is not physically defective, but prejudiced in favour of old ditties with which it has been fed'.[114]

---

[112] Beattie, 'An Essay On Poetry and Music', p. 461.

[113] [Anonymous] Charles Burney, review of *Melody the Soul of Music: an Essay towards the improvement of the Musical Art*, by Alexander Molleson, in *Monthly Review*, 27 (1798), 190.

[114] Ibid.

It is not clear that Beattie refers exclusively to vocal music in the quotation above, although the 'Essay' does adhere to eighteenth-century orthodoxy by conceding the superiority of vocal music to instrumental. Beattie says this more than once, but there is a reflexive quality to his insistence on the primacy of vocal music that becomes increasingly apparent as he draws most of his specific examples from the realm of instrumental music.[115] Besides, the 'Essay''s main argument, based on the ideas of Rousseau, is that music functions as a moral force by virtue of its emotional content in a manner that would not necessarily be limited to texted music.

Beattie clarifies music's moral role by applying to it a standard formula of eighteenth-century aesthetics that is rarely applied to instrumental music except by ancient music's ardent supporters. Music's purpose, Beattie claims, is 'to instruct as well as to please (one is necessary to the other)'. To this he adds that

> by instruction I do not here understand merely the communication of moral and physical truth. Whatever tends to raise those human affections that are favourable to truth and virtue, or to repress the opposite passions, will always gratify or improve our moral and intellectual powers, and may properly enough be called *instructive*.[116]

If this means that words are not necessary to moral instruction through music, Beattie's remarks have the effect of elevating music *per se* from the status assigned it by other literary men as a merely sensuous vehicle for poetry to a role as a moral force on its own.

Jones, as shown above, took issue with music that seemed 'inconsistent with the powers and beauties of Expression'. This is a position that seems to focus on the capacity of the art to convey content, but, much like Beattie's remarks above, this statement has the feel of a critical cliché more than a position that is consistent with the bulk of the *Treatise on the Art of Music*. More often, Jones bases his appreciation for the moral dimensions of music on an abstract beauty and order in the contrapuntal style that has nothing to do with expression or with words and might be said to be moral in a different sense from what Beattie has in mind. The hallmark of the ancient position on moral music has to do with the ability of counterpoint to appeal to the reason

---

[115] Instrumental music is the medium Beattie chooses when he wants to illustrate that music needs to be studied in order to be appreciated. In the 'Essay', Beattie comments (p. 461) that 'a regular concerto, well executed, will yield [the student of music] high entertainment, even though its regularity be its principal recommendation. The pleasure which an untutored hearer derives from it is far inferior'.

[116] Beattie, 'An Essay On Poetry and Music', p. 353.

and to exercise the mind during the act of perception. A common view in the ancient community is that this abstract moral dimension is apparent only to an elect few who possess the skill to appreciate it. Hawkins claimed the ability to comprehend complex music was a gift of nature possessed by barely a tenth of the population. An important difference between Beattie and the disciples of ancient music, then, is that while Beattie imagines music as a way to make regular people moral, Jones and others only offer a test to determine who already is.

Canons and fugues are 'the most perfect kinds of composition', Jones claims, because this style is 'consistent and rational' and best demonstrates the artistic principle of *'variety with uniformity'*.[117] The principle usually known as 'unity within variety' is another basic element of seventeenth- and eighteenth-century aesthetics that continued to be cited as the foundation of some kinds of beauty as late as the sources upon which Crotch relied at the end of the century. In recalling this principle, Jones revives a critical thread that runs through the writing of Shaftesbury and his follower Francis Hutcheson.[118] It should be noted as a general observation that Shaftesbury's point of view is inherently élitist and therefore offered an obvious attraction to one of Jones's basic orientation.

Shaftesbury argues that the appreciation of the arts depends on a special innate faculty called a critical sense that closely resembles what he calls a moral sense; both have in common an association with the quality of 'Good-breeding'.[119] The philosophical starting-point for the Shaftesbury–Hutcheson point of view tends, therefore, to equate the moral with the beautiful. To the extent that it is self-consistent, it also prefers to judge beauty by absolute, formal considerations such as unity within variety as opposed to the vagaries of content. Hutcheson has been cited for his pioneering if less than completely satisfying use of unity amidst variety in connection with the species of beauty found in mathematical elegance.[120] In a section of his *An Inquiry into the Original of Our Ideas of Beauty and Virtue* that he calls 'Of the Beauty of Theorems', Hutcheson stresses the quality of mental exercise, observing that *'easy* or *obvious* Propositions, even where the Unity is sufficiently distinct, and determinate, do not please us so much as those, which being less *obvious*, give us some *Surprize* in the

---

[117] Jones, *Disquisitions*, p. 328.

[118] See, Peter Kivy, *The Seventh Sense: a Study of Francis Hutcheson's Aesthetics and Its Influence in Eighteenth Century Britain* (New York: Burt Franklin, 1976), especially pp. 12–21.

[119] Ibid., p. 17.

[120] Ibid., pp. 97–8.

Discovery'.[121] It is significant, however, that Hutcheson had his own problems reconciling theories of the beautiful that rely on form and content respectively, and that the *Inquiry* has been found least satisfactory in its discussion of music in particular.[122]

Hawkins likewise stresses the abstract or formal qualities of music. He, in fact, discounts far more than Jones the ability of music to express or convey content. Hawkins specifically rejects music's appeal to the imagination, the mental faculty he associates with imitation in the most common sense that word is understood in connection with the sister arts, and stresses instead its appeal to abstract reason. 'If we investigate the principles of harmony', he notes in the Preliminary Discourse to his *History*, 'we learn that they are general and universal',

> and of harmony itself, that the proportions in which it consists are to be found in those material forms, which are beheld with the greatest pleasure, the sphere, the cube, and the cone, for instance, and constitute what we call symmetry, beauty, and regularity; but the imagination receives no additional delight; our reason is exercised in the operation, and that faculty alone is thereby gratified.[123]

Hawkins revels in the beauty of canons. They are a kind of music 'in which perhaps, substance, that is to say, fine air and melody is made to give place to form; just as we see in those fanciful poetical conceits, acrostics, anagrams, chronograms, &c. where the sense and spirit of the composition is ever subservient to its form'.[124]

He adds to the last sentence above – possibly as an answer to Joseph Addison's strident criticism of acrostics, anagrams, and chronograms in the *Spectator*[125] – that 'the comparison does not hold throughout, for the musical compositions above spoken of derive an advantage of a peculiar kind from those restraints to which they are subjected'.[126] That is because

> in the first place the harmony is thereby rendered more close, compact, and full; nor does this harmony arise merely from the concordance of sounds in the several parts, but each distinct part

---

[121] Francis Hutcheson, *An Inquiry into the Original of Our Ideas of Beauty and Virtue* (London, 1726; New York: Garland, 1971), p. 32, in a section entitled 'Of the Beauty of Theorems'.

[122] Kivy, *The Seventh Sense*, especially pp. 97–108.

[123] Sir John Hawkins, *A General History of the Science and Practice of Music*, ed. Othmar Wessely, 2 vols (London, 1776; London, 1875; Graz: Akademische Druck- u. Vertagsanstalt, 1969), vol. 1, p. xx.

[124] Ibid., p. 303.

[125] Joseph Addison, *The Spectator*, ed. Donald F. Bond, 5 vols (Oxford: Oxford University Press, 1975), vol. 1, p. 265

[126] Hawkins, vol. 1, p. 303.

produces a succession of harmony in itself, the laws of fugue or canon being such as generally to exclude those dissonant intervals which take away from the sweetness or melody of the point. In the next place the ear is gratified by the successive repetition of the point of a fugue through all its parts; and the mind receives the same pleasure in tracing the exact resemblance of the several parts each to the other, as it does in comparing a picture or statue with its archetype.[127]

'The truth of this observation', he concludes, 'must be apparent to those who are aware of the scholastic distinction of beauty into absolute and relative.'[128]

It might be noted in passing that Hawkins and Burney express very different views on the nature of canon. In the quotation above, melody benefits from its subjugation to the discipline of harmony, much as, one might think, an otherwise unruly citizenry prospers under the ruling hand of a benevolent government. Burney contends to the contrary that 'imagination is so manacled during composition of these perpetual fugues, that elegant melody is always precluded, and, in general, harmony is rendered so meagre and imperfect, that in a canon of three or four parts, it is often reduced to a unison, octave, or insipid fourth'.[129] And a fugue, he argues, 'differs from a *canon* only in being less rigid in its laws'.[130]

It is because of Hawkins's understanding of the reason as an abstract and non-verbal faculty that he can describe his purpose in the *History* as 'to assert [music's] dignity, as a science worthy the exercise of our rational as well as audible faculties'. To do this, he seeks to 'investigate its principles, as founded in general and invariable laws'. He notes that the principles of music 'are founded in geometrical truth, and seem to result from some general and universal law of nature, so its excellence is intrinsic, absolute, and inherent, and, in short, resolvable only into His will, who has ordered all things in number, weight, and measure'.[131]

Jones is somewhat more inclined to claim words as the means by which music can reach the intellect and consequently to make vocal music superior to instrumental. This is consistent with an overall strategy of his *Treatise* that tries to elevate the status of music not so much by Hawkins's scheme of associating it with lingering Pythagorean ideas as by staking out a place for it within the liberal arts in order to put it on a level with the written word and make it worthy of its own classical

---

[127] Ibid.
[128] Ibid.
[129] Burney, *General History*, vol. 2, p. 414.
[130] Burney, *The Present State of Music in France and Italy*, p. vi.
[131] Ibid.

tradition. This approach is evident not only when Jones claims to 'quote *Corelli, Purcell, Geminiani,* and *Handel,* as naturally, and I hope as reasonably, as writers on Poetry and Oratory fetch their examples from *Virgil, Horace,* and *Cicero,* or as Aristotle exemplifies his precepts from *Homer* and *Sophocles*' but also when he tries to rationalize the musical element of melody by drawing a parallel with the figures of rhetoric.[132]

Along similar lines, Jones invokes an old cliché often found in the writing of literary men and complains that 'ever since Instrumental Music has been made independent of Vocal, we have been in danger of falling under the dominion of sound without sense'.[133] It is fair, however, to question what he means by this and even to doubt how seriously this statement should be taken. First, Jones lays this charge of sound without sense at the feet of the moderns without explaining why the purely instrumental music of Corelli or Geminiani for which he contends should not be subject to the same complaint. In general, his intention in this part of the *Treatise* is to comment unfavourably on the reliance of recent music on brilliant instrumental effects and to recommend the 'organ test' as a means of determining musical excellence. Immediately after his invocation of the 'sound without sense' cliché he continues,

> and I think it an unanswerable objection against the modern Style, which must have its weight with all lovers of Harmony, that if you try its effect upon an Organ, you discover its emptiness and insignificance. It is like that Painting which depends for its effect on a grace of colouring, to strike the eyes of the ignorant, rather than upon correctness of drawing, justness of design, and greatness of manner.

In context, then, Jones seems to be arguing that music *can* have some kind of intellectual appeal without the benefit of a text but that modern composers have set aside the musical qualities that make this possible in their headlong rush to promote the mere sensuality of orchestral colour.

Mason's *Essays*

Mason's partisan rhetoric in his *Essays Historical and Critical, on English Church Music* does not stop with his objection to the 'ill-grounded deference to antiquity, merely because it is antiquity' quoted above. The same essay casts an occasional barb at Hawkins, presenting him not as a

---

[132] Jones, *Treatise,* p. iii.
[133] Ibid., iv.

legitimate critical writer at all but merely as 'this laborious Compiler'.[134] Mason, moreover, clearly anticipates his remarks will provoke an enemy camp. When he attacks a 'defect of intelligibility' that occasioned his writing the anthem book to which his preface was attached, he acknowledges being 'well aware that many profound Harmonists may be disgusted at what I have already advanced, and think their craft in danger, when I seem to attack the very citadel of Music'.[135] By 1795, Mason's identification of the other side had shifted slightly, for in his later essays the enemy is not profound harmonists but specifically 'those, who patronize and admire exclusively what they call Ancient Music'.[136]

Mason's second essay in the published collection of 1795 speaks against polyphonic cathedral music, complaining that at the time it was written 'abstruse harmonical Proportions, which had neither common sense, nor, in this case a better judge, the approbation of the common ear, for their Support, were universally and diligently studied'.[137] From this abuse 'arose a multifarious contexture of parts, a total disregard for simple Melody, and in consequence, a neglect even of syllabic distinction'.[138] As a result, words were interchangeable and inexpressive of the sentiment 'causing confusion in the audience, and rendering the very language it was meant to express unintelligible'.[139]

This defect gives rise to several arguments that suggest a connection between music and morality. Mason attacks ancient music on utilitarian grounds, focusing his criticism on composers like Christopher Tye who 'had all the learning of their profession, without knowing or aiming to make it useful'.[140] Noting that 'the primary use of Music, is to please the ear, and of vocal to convey the words it is joined to in pleasing and intelligent strain',[141] Mason adds that 'the secondary, yet much more essential use, is to convey sentiment, and to affect the passions'.[142] Accordingly, he speaks of 'the powers which Vocal Music might have upon the mind, when so managed, that sound might be subservient or rather assistant, to sense'.[143] Mason adds that 'this can never be the case, but where melody, and consequently appropriated air are principally attended to'.[144]

---

[134] Mason, *Essays*, p. 335.
[135] Ibid., p. 334.
[136] Ibid., p. 294.
[137] Ibid., p. 327.
[138] Ibid.
[139] Ibid.
[140] Ibid., p. 338.
[141] Ibid.
[142] Ibid.
[143] Ibid., p. 347.
[144] Ibid.

In this second essay, Mason turns the tables on the ancient faction and accuses their music of the same faults he knew ancient-music enthusiasts like Hawkins – whom he had obviously read – assigned to the modern style. It is passionless counterpoint that Mason represents as a merely sensual art form, incapable of engaging the emotions through which Mason believes music can effect moral regeneration. By ancient music, 'we may be entertained and soothed, but seldom moved or affected', Mason claims.[145] But if, at the same time, 'Rhythm, Pause and Accent are peculiarly attended to by the composer, his productions will have an immediate and striking effect [and the hearer] will comprehend the spirit of the air at its very first opening; every succeeding passage will render it more generally intelligible'.[146] This last sentence does not mean that the ancient style can in fact convey musical content clearly if only the requisites Mason mentions are carefully supplied. Indeed, Burney's review of the *Essays* disagrees with Mason on just this point. Burney readily admits that 'fugue, though a very ingenious contrivance, and the delight of musicians and lovers of music of the old school, is very unfavourable to poetry, and indeed to the intelligence of prose, by the several performers having different words to pronounce at the same time'.[147] But he insists that 'if the words were never to be transposed, repeated, nor frittered by divisions till they had first been heard plain and well accented, by a single part, or by many parts in plain counterpoint', the problem could be resolved.[148] Mason, however, is adamant, claiming that 'fugue is indeed come into disrepute with modern Masters' since no matter who writes in the style, 'it does neither so easily and generally admit, nor so variously introduce those accentual inflections'.[149]

One quality shared by much of the writing identified here with the modernist ideology is its reference to a recent revolution in which forces supporting musical form and content contended with far-reaching consequences. In the first essay of Mason's 1795 collection 'On Instrumental Church Music', the revolution occurred, presumably, around mid-century. Its architect was Rousseau, whom Mason praises as an individual

---

[145] Ibid., p. 292.

[146] Ibid.

[147] Burney, review of *Essays*, p. 403.

[148] Ibid. Burney is effectively in agreement with Hawkins on this point. In his second essay from 1782 (p. 335), however, Mason takes issue with Hawkins for saying that the obscurity counterpoint produces 'is either the case or not, as the point is managed' (Hawkins, *General History*, vol. 2, p. 795). Mason answers, 'But as this laborious Compiler has not taught us how to manage the point, I shall be apt to think Dr. Tudway in the right.' He refers to a statement by Hawkins himself acknowledging that Tudway objected to fugue in vocal music on the grounds that it 'obscured the sense'.

[149] Mason, *Essays*, pp. 311–12.

with an 'uncommon force of genius'. Rousseau's genius allowed him to 'gain a complete victory over the Partizans of French Music' and to begin a 'musical revolution' that 'spread as speedily through the nation, as that political one, which, with sanguinary fury, is now hurrying to its crisis'.[150]

The first essay in the collected edition has a decidedly more polemic tone than the earlier contribution from 1782. By 1795, Mason was ready to take on Handel and Corelli directly, noting that music 'both vocal and instrumental by the composers in the early part of this century' is 'less accentual and rhythmical, than that of their later successors'.[151] He also comments gratuitously on the relative youth of musical classics, noting on his first use of the expression 'ancient music' that 'some of it, and perhaps the best, did not exist beyond the period of the last sixty years'.[152] The first several pages of this essay, moreover, set forth general principles that are broadly conceived and in fact have the character of a general statement of the modernist aesthetic.

Mason's 1782 essay had likewise spoken of musical revolution. In this case, the conflict concerned musical form versus content and was expressly between forces supporting harmony and melody. Two other qualities of this earlier revolution account are typical. First, Mason notes that 'this revolution, as it may be called, in Vocal Music, though attended with much additional pleasure to the hearer, induced also a new defect in point of simplicity, which, as the old one of complex harmony was not removed kept the art from achieving its perfection'.[153] It will be recalled that Marsh's modern revolution also soon led to the introduction of new impediments to intelligibility, and this is true of many of Burney's revolution accounts as well. Burney often presents an idealized earlier art resembling the fabled music of antiquity in both the ease with which it could be understood and in its eventual corruption by misguided attempts at progress. Another standard feature of moderns' revolution accounts is the presence of a defensive other side opposing all innovation and seeking absolute dominance. Mason reports that the emergence of a new melody-oriented style caused 'Dr. Boyce and other professed Harmonists to think, that by the addition of too much Air, by which these Masters deprived Harmony of its absolute supremacy, they robbed Church Music of its ancient solemnity'.[154]

---

[150] Ibid., p. 289. Mason indicates that this essay was written several years earlier but was being revised as the French Revolution reached its climax.

[151] Ibid., p. 292.

[152] Ibid., p. 294.

[153] Ibid., p. 349.

[154] Ibid., p. 347.

Despite these several points of similarity between Mason's earliest *Essay* and other writing of the moderns, the 1782 essay can only be viewed as a contribution to music's ancient–modern quarrel if the terms of that conflict are interpreted less rigidly than is typical of recent writing. When Mason refers to 'these Masters ... who deprived Harmony of its absolute supremacy'[155] he is not speaking of J. C. Bach or Haydn or Pleyel but rather of 'the pleasing Melodies of Wise, the pathetic Airs of Clarke, the majestic Movements of Blow, and the sublime Strains of Purcell'.[156] In other words, the revolutionary composers of Mason's new style are all figures who might otherwise be regarded as composers of ancient music. It is, in fact, certain music of some of these very composers that ancient-music sympathizer Bishop George Horne insists should be viewed 'as our English classics in this sacred science'.[157] At the same time, Mason's transplantation of the moderns' revolution myth to a new time almost a century before Marsh's putative revolution presents no problem within Crotch's abstract and non-historical understanding of the terms of the ancient–modern quarrel.

Admittedly, ideas like Mason's can appear in a less ideological context. John Wesley speaks against polyphony in his 'Thoughts on the Power of Music', asking, 'what has counterpoint to do with the passions? It is applied to a quite different faculty of the mind; not to our joy, or hope, or fear; but merely to the ear, to the imagination, or internal sense'.[158] Wesley does not try to make the same kind of direct challenge to English cathedral music that Mason later did, but with a similar interest in the common man and a confidence in the moral applications of intelligible music he rehearses a myth that is ubiquitous among the moderns and rare in criticism of ancient music. In this myth a simple and rational music of antiquity is corrupted by Gothic barbarians in the Middle Ages. This, the first of all myths of a vanished musical golden age, is an important component of Burney's writing and yet another indication of his intellectual common ground with Mason and the moderns. A perennial question associated with music's corruption myth concerns the inability of present-day music to produce the fantastic effects attributed to the pre-downfall music of the ancients. Wesley answered this by claiming that when music is 'extremely simple

---

[155] Ibid.

[156] Ibid.

[157] George Horne, *The Works of the Right Reverend George Horne, D. D.*, 2 vols (New York, 1848), vol. 2, p. 370. Horne's complete list includes 'Tallis and Bird, Gibbons and King, Purcel and Blow, Croft and Clark, Wise and Weldon, Green and Handel'.

[158] John Wesley, *The Works of the Rev. John Wesley, A. M.*, 3rd edn, 7 vols, New York, n. d. 456. This essay is dated 9 June 1779.

and inartificial' – that is, when composers have 'attended to melody, not harmony' and when 'the sound has been an echo to the sense' – modern musicians not only *could* produce the effects of Timotheus and Orpheus but in fact had actually done so.[159]

Unlike Mason, Wesley does not limit his attack to polyphonic cathedral music. He objects as well to 'those modern overtures, voluntaries, or concertos, which consist altogether of artificial sounds, without any words at all'.[160] While such ideas are most common in the last quarter of the century in the writing of men of letters with little or no practical musical ability,[161] there is not always a clear intellectual dividing line between modern music's advocates and the more extreme position of those whose objections to musical complexity are not limited to the contrapuntal style. The same myths and ideas, especially valuing melody over harmony and musical content over abstract orderliness, animate the thinking of writers who oppose all cultivated music, writers who celebrate the modern style but find its later examples incomprehensible, and writers who embrace Haydn and Pleyel as modern antidotes to the élitism of ancient-music. All three hold up the aesthetic principle of classical simplicity as an ideal, all three promote the notion of general intelligibility in a context sympathetic to the needs of the common man and the non-specialist, and all three quote with reverence the writing of Tartini and Rousseau.

To return, now, to Mason's *Essays*, an explanation is required for the seeming inconsistency of, on the one hand, his insistence on solemnity in church and his high value on words and content, and, on the other, his advocacy of 'Largo and Adagio movements of Haydn and Pleyel' as organ voluntaries. One reason he can accept these milder products of the modern style is related to his statement on the uses of music, in which the first purpose of the art is merely to 'please the ear'. He makes this clear from the outset of his collected edition, where he sets forth the framework in which he wants his criticism to be understood. Mason stresses, as do many others including Crotch, that music should be

---

[159] Ibid.

[160] Ibid.

[161] Lonsdale, 'Dr. Burney and the *Monthly Review*', 33. Lonsdale refers to the 'combination of primitivism and nationalistic antiquarianism' he finds in a particular subset of writers who promoted what Crotch later called 'national music', especially the folk music of Scotland and Ireland. Lonsdale contends that Burney became increasingly antagonistic to calls for musical simplicity by this faction after 1785, as can be seen in his reviews of Edward Jones's, *Musical and Poetical Relics of the Welsh Bards*, *Monthly Review*, 74 (1786) 49–63, J. C. Walker's, *Historical Memoirs of the Irish Bards*, *Monthly Review*, 77, (1787), 425–39, and Charlotte Brooke's *Reliques of Irish Poetry*, *Monthly Review*, Series II, 4 (1791), 37–46.

divided into categories that aspire to different purposes and in which different expectations ought to apply.[162] His statement on symphonic slow movements comes in a discussion of service music in which he argues that within this particular category it is legitimate for music not to engage either the emotions, or the intellect, or even the complete attention of the listener. Such music should 'flow on with that equable and easy modulation, which, while it gratifies the ear, should not too strongly affect the intellect'. 'We in some sort listen to such Music', Mason observes, 'as we do the pleasing murmur of a neighbouring brook, the whisper of the passing breeze; or the distant warblings of the lark or nightingale.'[163] He also indicates that when 'the Organist preludes an Anthem of praise or thanksgiving a spirited movement is certainly in its place, if kept within the limits which dignified exultation would prescribe'.[164]

As in the categories that Mason's friend Joshua Reynolds stresses in his *Discourses*, the intellectual faculties Mason identifies with a particular species of music define for him its relative significance. It is on this account that Mason begins his first essay in the 1795 collection by observing that 'music, as an imitative art, ranks so much below Poetry and Painting that in my opinion, which I have found confirmed by many late writers of the best judgment, it can hardly be so termed with propriety'.[165] It is only when music exhibits 'certain qualities, so analogous to those which constitute Metre or Versification, such as Accent, Rhythm, Pause, and Cadence', that Mason believes 'it thereby becomes, equally with Poetry, an object of criticism'.[166]

Burney and primitivism

Eighteenth-century primitivism, as the idea-complex has been described at some length,[167] combines aspects of an ideology and an aesthetic value-system. Its most familiar quality is the belief that the earliest condition of man was the best condition and that civilization has corrupted both society and art from its ideal state of nature. The backward-looking posture of primitivism together with its characteristic

---

[162] Mason, *Essays*, pp. 287–94.

[163] Ibid., p. 312.

[164] Ibid., p. 313.

[165] Ibid., p. 287.

[166] Ibid.

[167] Lois Whitney, *Primitivism and the Idea of Progress in English Popular Literature of the Eighteenth Century* (Baltimore: The Johns Hopkins Press, 1934; New York: Octagon Books, 1973).

rejection of artifice, fashion and luxury in favour of the 'simple' and 'natural', appear to be at odds with the values of innovation and elegance that are an important aspect of the moderns' critical value system. Indeed, attacks on recent cultivated music by those who support various earlier musics as a simpler alternative are constant from about 1770, and primitivists themselves are, accordingly, a natural target for advocates of cultivated music like Burney.

It has been shown, however, that the primitivist aesthetic ideology is remarkably adaptable. It is rooted in a complex set of interconnected ideas that stem from contradictory ideals. Individual components of the idea-complex are, therefore, both separable and susceptible to being taken up by different individuals for different reasons. Even the central myth of primitivism appears in a variety of guises that result in several possible models of social and artistic degeneration. Primitivism can be characterized by a progressive state of degeneration that has supposedly been at work since antiquity or by a cyclic pattern relieved by occasional periods of progress, or by a steady state of mediocrity that has persisted since mankind's initial fall.[168] Lois Whitney has shown that despite its intellectual starting-point, primitivism can even appear in close association with notions of inevitable progress and perfectibility, especially when a perfect future can be cast in the mould of the ideal past.[169] In the context of the present quarrel, finally, any faults of degenerate artificiality and complexity to which the modern style is susceptible have to be measured against a still greater prevalence of such vices in the Baroque style to which modern music is by definition placed into opposition.

Burney's first public encounter with musical primitivism came in connection with a translation of Tartini's *Trattato di Musica* published by Benjamin Stillingfleet as *Principles and Power of Harmony*. Like so many others associated in some way with the aesthetic issues at hand, Stillingfleet chose to try to avoid the controversy that he knew his writing would generate by publishing anonymously. He remarks in his Preface that,

> I doubt not but the greatest part of my Readers will be offended with some of Tartini's strict notions, particularly those contained in the 5th chapter, as being so very opposite to every thing they have been taught to admire: but before they condemn, I desire they will calmly weigh and consider them – that they will reflect that fashion is never the test of truth, though they may sometimes

---

[168] This point is made by Arthur Lovejoy in his Foreword to Whitney, *Primitivism*, pp. xii–xiii.

[169] Ibid., p. xiii.

happen to coincide – and that these strict notions do not come from a dull plodding artist ... but from one who ... led the way in the flowery regions of harmony.[170]

This fifth chapter is an 'investigation of the musical modes by means of which and by means of poetical oration, the ancient Greeks excited and calmed, as they desired, the passions of the human spirit'.[171] In it, Tartini calls polyphony a distraction to the listener and insists that only through a simpler approach can music express, as it should, a single passion. So important is the principle of simplicity to his purpose that Stillingfleet recommends this particular chapter as a contribution that 'contains the judgment of the greatest of all modern masters, on a subject that very much divides the musical world'.[172]

Burney read *Principles and Power* without recognizing Stillingfleet as the author even though both had lived for a time in Burney's adopted home of King's Lynn.[173] He was able to insert a footnote praising this book in the second edition of his Italian Tour two years after the publication of Stillingfleet's book.[174] Stillingfleet had earned Burney's confidence by speaking out against 'the old church music, where the parts were worked with great judgment and labor' but also by advocating a position Burney then viewed as moderate on the subject of the music of antiquity. In a review of *Principles and Power* in the *Critical Review* – only recently identified definitely as Burney's work[175] – the music historian remarks that 'as our author is less an enthusiast for the ancients, so his arguments are more reasonable, and urged with more strength than those of his predecessors'.[176]

Even so, Stillingfleet expresses opinions with which Burney's later writing consistently disagrees. Even as early as his *Critical Review* article of 1771, Burney could not resist a long digression that seeks

---

[170] [Benjamin Stillingfleet], *Principles and Power of Harmony* (London, 1771), p. vi.

[171] Fredric Johnson, *Tartini's Trattato di Musica Seconda la Vera Scienza dell'Armonia: an Annotated Translation with Commentary* (Ph.D. diss., Indiana University, 1985), p. 341.

[172] Stillingfleet, *Principles and Power of Harmony*, p. 18.

[173] Scholes speculates (Scholes, *The Great Dr. Burney*, vol. 2, p. 81) that the Burney's were personally acquainted with Stillingfleet.

[174] Burney, *The Present State of Music in France and Italy*, pp. 132–3: 'Since this Journal was prepared for the press, a book has been published under the title of *Principles and Power of Harmony*; from which I have received the highest pleasure that an elegant, clear, and masterly performance can give. Who the author is I know not, but he seems perfectly to understand Tartini's principles, and to have done justice to his genius, without being partial to his defects.'

[175] This review is identified by Ribeiro in *Letters*, p. 90, n. 13.

[176] Burney's review of *Principles and Power of Harmony*, by Benjamin Stillingfleet, *Critical Review*, 32 (1771), 23.

> to stem the torrent of popular complaint for the want of simplicity, which we did not expect to find abetted by so able and enlarged a writer as the author of the Principles and Power of Harmony; for, in fact, there seems to have been more true pathos in some plain and simple airs sung by Manzoli, Guarducci, and Guadagni, in our late operas, than can be found in any of those of ancient times, when melody was either rude, or overloaded with harmony.[177]

It is significant that in this case Burney's construction of the ancient faction includes both the ancients of antiquity – whose melody was, we may assume, 'rude' – and the more recent contrapuntal ones whose melody was 'overloaded with harmony'. This is the beginning of Burney's identification of an enemy camp that included anyone, whether they stood on the side of melody or harmony, who objected to the values of his particular brand of cultivated music and therefore, in his mind, anyone who opposed innovation itself.

In the later *General History* Burney notes that 'the *croaker* family is very ancient: Plato 2000 years ago complained of the degeneracy in the Music of *his* time, as much as the greatest enemies of innovation can do at present'. By the time of the still-later *Cyclopaedia* articles, Burney had come to view primitivists as obstructionists who stood in the way of progress. In his article 'Simplicity' he observes that

> there is much cant about simplicity in music, among the exclusive admirers of old things, and lamentation for the loss of our old melodies to the songs of Chaucer, Gower, Lydgate, and others of which the words are still extant. But if we may judge by what has escaped the ravages of time, the loss of our musical compositions of this period may be supported without much affliction, We may perhaps heighten that affliction considerably by censuring modern refinements, and extolling the charms of ancient simplicity; but simplicity in melody, beyond a certain limit, is unworthy of the name that is bestowed on it, and encroaches so much upon the rude and savage boundaries of uncouthness and rusticity, as to be wholly separated from proportion and grace, which should alone characterize the truly simple in all the arts: for though they may be ennobled by the concealment of labour and pedantry, they are always degraded by our aliance with coarse and barbarous nature.

By the time of his *Cyclopaedia* article 'Stillingfleet', Burney's opinions on both this particular individual and the consequences of offending the 'enemies of innovation' had changed. His later version of sentence quoted above, accordingly, reads 'the moderns, and modern music, are always to be abused; it was so in Plato's time; the custom has been continued by every writer on the subject; and every musician, who, like Timotheus, adds a new string to his lyre, will be said to endanger the state'.

---

[177] Ibid., p. 21.

In a lengthy review essay on *Principles and Power* for the *Monthly Review* Burney agrees with Stillingfleet that there is 'truth' in Tartini's 'appeal ... to the Vox Populi'.[178] Still, he is concerned about a section of the book entitled 'Greek music vindicated', where Stillingfleet indicates he is prepared to believe that some of the fantastic ancient stories on the power of music 'are most undoubtedly founded on truth'. Burney thought these stories ridiculous and said so a few years later in the first volume of the *General History*.[179] Stillingfleet, adding insult to injury, adds that he is more inclined to believe accounts of miracles when given by eyewitnesses such as the 'Plato, who was himself a practical musician'.[180]

Burney could overlook remarks like the above because alongside Stillingfleet's several objectionable expressions there is a short account of an Italian opera at Ancona in 1714 that was exactly what the music historian needed to hear. This account effectively made the kind of opera Burney loved into an art resembling the legendary music of antiquity, but did so in a credible setting that divested music of any supernatural powers. In this story, Stillingfleet relates how 'a passage of recitative, unaccompanied by any other instrument but the base' nevertheless managed to raise 'both in the professors and in the rest of the audience, such and so great a commotion of mind, that we could not help staring at one another, on account of the visible change of color that was caused in every one's countenance'. Burney was so struck by this story that he repeated it in his *Account of the Musical Performances in Westminster-Abbey* many years later.[181]

Stillingfleet's account may have made Burney more receptive to similar tales in which music is touted as an art able to bring about the near miraculous effects of antiquity working only through the emotions of the average listener. Thus, in the *General History* Burney repeats the

---

[178] Anonymous [Charles Burney], review of *Principles and Power of Harmony,* by Benjamin Stillingfleet in *Monthly Review*, 45 (1771), 482.

[179] In his 'Dissertation on the Music of the Ancients' Burney calls the ancient stories of music's supernatural powers 'too puerile and trivial to merit attention, unless among *stories to be laughed at*'. He does just this in a joke at the expense of Martianus Capella. Capella had written 'that Asclepiades cured deafness by the sound of the trumpet'. 'Wonderful, indeed!' Burney writes, 'that the same noise that would occasion deafness in some, should be a specific for it in others! it is making the viper cure her own bite. But perhaps Asclepiades was the inventor of the *Acousticon*, or ear-trumpet ... .' Burney, *General History*, vol. 1, pp. 159 and 156. Crotch uses Burney's *bon mot* about the ear trumpet repeatedly, especially in *Lectures*, 11229/1 and 11064/7.

[180] Stillingfleet, p. 134.

[181] Ibid., p. 62; Burney, *An Account of the Musical Performances in Westminster-Abbey* London, 1785; New York: Da Capo Press, 1979), p. 62. Burney's footnote credits the original source for this story, Tartini's *Trattato di Musica*.

familiar story of Stradella's deliverance from assassins when his would-be murderers heard his *Te Deum* performed at the church of St John Lateran and were so moved they found it impossible to kill him. Such events, Burney observes, evince 'an instance of the *miraculous powers of modern* Music, superior, perhaps, to any that could be well authenticated of the *ancient*'.[182]

Stillingfleet had been moved to write his book in the first place because of a remark by d'Alembert calling for 'some man of letters equally practised in Music and skilled in writing' to 'develop those ideas which [Tartini] himself has not unfolded with sufficient perspicuity'.[183] Burney had recently set out to remake himself into precisely such a writer, and needed a model for the kind of criticism he hoped to practice. Accordingly, he begins his review of Stillingfleet's book by examining the present state of music criticism itself. He notes that 'there is no science, perhaps, furnished with so few well-written books' and suggests that this is so because,

> those who treat music merely as a science, without possessing the practical part, are naturally contracted in their ideas, and useless to professors: and, on the contrary, mere practical musicians, who have seldom had either education or leisure, to qualify themselves on the side of learning, produce nothing but crude and indigested reveries, which a man of taste in literature disdains to read.[184]

He is particularly hard on musicians in this paragraph, depicting them (with Pepusch of the earlier Academy of Ancient-music as an obvious model) as men who 'have the ambition of passing for men of science' but who 'speak of Greek writers without Greek [which Burney himself did not have either] of arithmetical proportions, without the figures; of ratios without geometry, and equations without algebra'.[185] By contrast, he cites the then unknown author of the *Principles and Power of Harmony* as a kind of ideal.

Aside from Burney's early experience with Stillingfleet, it is mainly in book reviews written 20 years later that Burney can be found reacting strongly to musical primitivism. By then the situation in France had turned him into an allarmist who was ready to interpret primitivism in any form as evidence of radicalism and to react to any statement that

---

[182] Burney, *General History*, vol. 2, pp. 575–6. The Stradella incident is also found in Pierre Bonnet-Bourdelot's *Histoire de la Musique et de ses effets* (Paris, 1715).

[183] In William Coxe, *Literary Life and Select Works of Benjamin Stillingfleet* (London, 1811), p. 207, this request by d'Alembert is cited as Stillingfleet's reason for undertaking the book.

[184] Burney's review of *Principles and Power of Harmony*, in *Critical Review*, p. 458.

[185] Ibid.

seemed to suggest the perfectibility of mankind. Lonsdale finds Burney most severe as a reviewer when such ideas are applied to music, but Burney's objections are in fact based on ideology as much as aesthetics and can appear even when music is not in question at all. In his review of Robert Anderson's *Poems on various Subjects* (1798) in the *Monthly Review*, Burney complains that

> In every page, the author is perpetually extolling the innocence and felicity of a peasant's life. His shepherds, and even his clowns, are Arcadian. He never omits to censure the Great, (of whom, we should suppose, he can know but little,) as *miserable* tools of a court – slaves of a high degree – rapacious rulers of the blood stained earth – plagued with the noise of the town – with pride, – ambition, – dependence on a monarch's smiles, &c. &c.[186]

In this case, Burney already knew where Anderson stood politically from an earlier encounter and did not need his new sensitivity for traces of offending ideology.[187] His treatment of another primitivist, Jackson of Exeter, is perhaps less reasonable since Jackson's thinking on many points – even in connection with politics – was actually very close to Burney's own.

Jackson is the author not only of the previously mentioned *Observations* but of a later collection of essays called *The Four Ages; Together with Essays on Various Subjects* (London, 1798) that Burney also reviewed. In the former, Jackson denies partisan interests, insisting that '*things*, not *persons*' are his aim and '*Music*, not *Musicians*' is his subject. Still, the *Observations* provoked a stronger response in Burney's review than one might expect, even taking into account Burney's earlier encounters with Jackson over the latter's review of the *General History*.[188] Burney, in fact, found it necessary to apologize for his 'uncivil' treatment of the *Observations* when he later reviewed *The Four Ages*.[189] Significantly, most of what the *Observations* has to say is actually

---

[186] Anonymous [Charles Burney] review of R. Anderson's, *Poems on various Subjects* (1798) in *Monthly Review*, Series II, 29 (1799), 104–5.

[187] Burney had already reviewed Anderson's *The Life of Samuel Johnson, L.L.D.* (1795) in *Monthly Review*, Series II, 20 (1995). In that review he observes (p. 23): 'The only occasion, on which our candid and judicious author abandons [Johnson] to unqualified censure, is in speaking of him as a *political writer*. Johnson would never allow a Whig to be right on any occasion, and the Whigs were even with him. Moderation and candour, however, are seldom to be expected to extend to politics, however inherent in the writer on other occasions; and many readers, who are partial to Johnson's writings on other subjects, have no mercy on his *Toryism*.'

[188] Lonsdale, *Dr. Charles Burney*, pp. 344–6.

[189] Anonymous [Charles Burney], review of *Four Ages*, William Jackson, *Monthly Review*, Series II, 26 (1798), 191. Burney stresses that he wants to 'continue with [Jackson] on friendly terms'.

supportive of the modern position. Speaking of the symphony, Jackson had remarked that 'when Richter introduced among us this style of Music, it was justly admired, being the first instance of attention to the different character of Instruments, a nicety unknown to Handel, or to any of his predecessors'. He adds that 'Richter was very successfully followed by Abel, and many others'.[190] At the same time, Jackson echoes Marsh's concern about attempts to establish 'an exclusive taste for Handel's Music only' and brands the Handel commemoration concerts and their sequels 'illiberal, and unworthy of the age or country in which we live'.[191] Even some of Jackson's censures of the modern style resemble Burney's own, especially when he objects, as Burney did, to 'the perpetual running up and down the keys on the piano forte in *semitones*'.[192]

Burney was troubled, however, by Jackson's attacks on Haydn. Mentioning no individual by name, Jackson strikes out at 'later composers', who 'to be grand and original, have poured in such floods of nonsense, under the sublime idea of *being inspired*, that the present SYMPHONY bears the same relation to good music, as the ravings of a bedlamite do to sober sense'.[193] Worse, he accuses composers of trying to make up for a deficiency in air by complex modulations in which 'sometimes the Key is perfectly lost, by wandering so far from it, that there is no road to return'. Recent symphonies are 'perplexed by arbitrary divisions of Notes' and by Discords that 'get so entangled, that it is past the art of man to untie the knot'.[194] Burney was quick to interpret this as a specific attack on Haydn, noting that musical readers 'can no more help thinking of HAYDN, when *symphonies* are mentioned, than of HANDEL, when *oratorio choruses* are in question'.[195]

Burney's review of the *Observations* shows his sensitivity to the quarrel's stereotypes and common targets, but his treatment of Jackson's *The Four Ages* is a more revealing ideological statement. In this review, Burney correctly interprets Jackson's position as an aesthetic ideology connecting musical primitivism with moderately liberal politics and a

---

[190] William Jackson of Exeter, *Observations on the Present State of Music in London* (Dublin, 1791), p. 16.

[191] Ibid., p. 30.

[192] A few years later, Burney wrote in Rees, *Cyclopaedia*, s.v. 'Accelerando' about the 'daring imitators of the bold modulation of Haydn, and of the rapid running up and down the keys in half notes, as Mozart did in his Juvenile days'. These abuses, he thinks, 'have deformed melody and corrupted harmony'.

[193] Jackson, *Observations*, p. 16.

[194] Ibid., p. 17.

[195] Burney, review of *Observations on the present State of Music, in London*, by William Jackson of Exeter, *Monthly Review*, 6 (October 1791), p. 196.

progressive social philosophy. It is a militantly Tory Charles Burney who responds to the above combination, objecting to Jackson's vision of social progress and a utopian future. He piously accuses Jackson of the 'ridicule of religious ceremonies' and complains unreasonably of his failure to censure Edward Gibbon for 'trying throughout his work to degrade and destroy all reverence for the religion of his native land'. 'Mr. Jackson imagines that mankind are in the high road to the millennium of philosophy, when mind is to reign over body, and wars to cease', Burney notes.

> Are revolutions to accomplish this? without religion, or established principles of morality, or safety of person or property, can any thinking man be so totally unacquainted with human nature, its appetites and selfishness, as to wish to be at the mercy of sensual and rapacious beings, who can never be totally free and equal but in a state of nature?

'In society there must be hewers of wood and drawers of water', Burney concludes, returning to a theme that is common in his political correspondence, and 'inequality of mind will naturally occasion inequality of fortune and importance; and good laws and government must protect the feeble from the tyranny of physical strength and intellects'.[196]

Here, as in the *Observations*, Burney's often stated positions with respect both to politics and music are, in fact, little different from Jackson's. Jackson's support for limited monarchy as the best of all political systems resembles Burney's own thinking closely, as does Jackson's stated fear of Republicanism.[197] Jackson's opinions even with regard to music itself differ from Burney's mainly in specifics. Compare, for example, Jackson's comments on musical progress with Burney's own remarks above in connection with the Bullstrode park incident in 1805. 'Excellent performance', Jackson writes,

> naturally produces music which is to keep pace with it – for no artist can shew his superiority over his predecessors, were his powers to be limited by the old music; and though the desire of improvement may lead us beyond the mark, yet by degrees, we are brought back again within the bounds of good sense; and upon the whole, advance nearer to perfection.[198]

---

[196] Ibid., p. 193.

[197] In his essay 'The Venetian, French Captain, and Priest' in *The Four Ages; Together with Essays on Various Subjects* (London, 1798; New York: Garland, 1970), pp. 199–215, Jackson examines the virtues of monarchy, limited monarchy, Republicanism and aristocracy. He concludes (as Burney would have) that limited monarchy is the best possibility and rejects Republicanism as the tyranny of the majority.

[198] Of course, Burney's remarks were written later and may in fact unwittingly echo Jackson's.

'In the Silver-Age then', – that is, the present, the golden age having not yet arrived – Jackson claims that 'melody has been united with harmony, and both have been adorned by grace, taste, and expression'. He means that the best elements of earlier music are finally combined in a proper relationship.[199] Burney had said all of this himself many times. Probably Jackson's most objectionable specific reference to music in the essays was his contemptuous remark – significantly, in an essay entitled 'The middle way not always best'[200] – that 'for one musician who can make a simple tune like [Harry] Carey [the supposed composer of 'God Save Great George our King'] there are five hundred who can compose a noisy symphony like Stamitz'.[201]

Around the time he reviewed Jackson's *Four Ages*, Burney also had occasion to review Alexander Molleson's slender volume *Melody the Soul of Music: an Essay towards the improvement of the Musical Art* (Glasgow, 1798; reprint, 1806) for the *Monthly Review*. Molleson's pamphlet was perceived at the time as a continuation of the primitivist argument by writers who were obviously following this now three-decade long thread in music criticism.[202] An unidentified reviewer for the *Critical Review* recalls that Molleson's position had in fact been more satisfactorily presented in Jackson's *Observations* seven years earlier.[203] That this reviewer could recognize a core similarity given the two writers' rather significant differences on specific musical issues demonstrates the extent of music criticism's fixation on over-complexity. There is, however, a more important difference between Jackson and Molleson that the reviewer fails to notice. Jackson's *Observations* is addressed to those 'who have an *ear* and *taste*' and pursues no moral agenda. Molleson, however, makes his high-minded purpose clear from the start.[204] He objects to Burney's statement that music is a 'mere amusement', remarking, with a contempt for fashion at least equalling the disciples of ancient-music, that Burney 'certainly refers only to the greatest part of what is composed, in the present fashionable stile. For he will not, surely, apply this remark to that music, for instance, which is used for the purpose of devotion'.[205]

---

[199] Jackson, *Four Ages*, p. 76.

[200] Ibid., pp. 107–112.

[201] Ibid., p. 112.

[202] See reviews of this book in *European Magazine*, 34 (1798), 111, and in *Critical Review*, 25 (1799), 237–8.

[203] *Critical Review*, 25 (1799), 237.

[204] When Burney refers to music as an amusement, Molleson remarks, 'he certainly refers only to the greatest part of what is composed, in the present fashionable stile. For he will not, surely, apply this remark to that music, for instance, which is used for the purpose of devotion. Molleson, 'Melody, the Soul of Music', in *Miscellanies in Prose and Verse* (Glasgow, 1806), pp. 68–9.

[205] Ibid.

Molleson has much to say about 'those symphonies and concertos' which 'gratify a depraved taste for variety'. Such works serve only to 'display the science of the composer, and the talents of the performers' in contrast with 'genuine expressions of good music which affects the heart'. But Molleson is still more averse to the contrapuntal style. He acknowledges that 'harmony seems, from its nature, to be chiefly useful and entertaining to those who are fond of studying the science, and who are improving themselves in the performance of music' and that it is, in fact, merely 'what a seminary of education is to real life'. 'The parade of art, without genius, which [modern harmony] has introduced and the facility with which the defects of insipid melody are hid in the maze of concordant parts', has, Molleson complains, 'not a little contributed to confound the different kinds of expression'.[206]

Although Molleson assumes throughout his pamphlet the familiar melody–harmony dichotomy and invariably sides with melody when-ever it appears in this binary opposition, his support for melody is not absolute. He complains about a 'scientific kind of melody' that is filled with 'rapid and difficult divisions, sudden transitions, singular passages very high in the scale, and affected and abrupt cadences ... '. Such melodies merely tantalize the hearer's feelings since

> no sooner has the composer, perhaps, attuned your mind to a mournful sympathizing state, than he requires you to be bold and daring, to hurry along, and admire the surprizing flights of fancy and execution. Are you expecting and desiring a cadence on the key? He must lead you an intricate dance, before you arrive at it; or perhaps withholds it altogether. You are conducted into a laby-rinth, where you see many pleasant arbours, in which you wish to repose, and enjoy, for some time, the delights of the place; but no sooner have you reached them, than you are hurried away to dark passages and long winding alleys, and after being whirled round and fatigued, are abruptly left to find your own way out.[207]

He notes that some melody 'imparts some degree of pleasure to the ear; but, with regard to intellectual gratification, and real use, there is a material difference' between this and melody that can make a beneficial impression on the mind operating through the passions.

In his review of Molleson's pamphlet, Burney reverts once again to the stereotypes of the ancient–modern quarrel in an attempt to demon-strate the extremes of the melody–harmony debate. He refers to, on the one hand, the 'patrons of the antient school of composition' who speak of modern music as 'thin, flimsy stuff; whipt-sillabub, without

---

[206] Ibid., p. 77.
[207] Ibid., p. 70.

contrivance, and unsupported by harmony'. On the other hand there is Rousseau – here viewed with suspicion as one who suspects 'this harmony, with which we are so charmed to be a barbarous Gothic invention which we should never have wanted, if we had been gifted with more sensibility for the beauties of the art, for *melody*, and for music truly natural'. Burney contrasts his own centrist philosophy to both poles, claiming that 'to gain a little applause – or at least toleration – from both parties, what can a musician do, but court their favour alternately, by the contrasts of pathetic and cheerful, hard and easy, full harmony and solo, complication and simplicity?'[208] Besides, Burney remarks, harmony is not a sign of Gothic degeneration but rather a mark of legitimate progress. 'A composer who ceases to avail himself of the powers of harmony, since its laws have been settled', Burney concludes, 'would act as absurdly as an astronomer who determined never to observe the heavenly bodies with a telescope.'[209]

Conclusion: British music criticism at the end of the eighteenth century

Among the perceived shortcomings of eighteenth-century critical and aesthetic writing to which different commentators have called attention is an ostensible lack of dialogue between writers themselves.[210] Especially in regard to the multiplicity of later minor writers, British authors often appear blindly to produce elementary texts for a general readership, avoiding more sophisticated discourse. In fact, not only do writers seem unwilling to engage in critical dialogue, they also appear largely unaware of each other's work. Jones of Nayland, for example, was proud to announce in the introduction of his *Treatise* that he had consulted no music dictionary before undertaking his book.[211] He might have included a much broader range of literature in his list of unnecessary references – something which Burney comments on in his review of the *Treatise*.[212] Often writing of this period also gives the impression of being based more on casual conversation than on considered reading and scholarly reflection. Burney observes this phenomenon in his review of Thomas

---

[208] [Anonymous] Charles Burney, review of *Melody*, 191–2.

[209] Ibid.

[210] On this last point in particular, see William Weber, review of John Neubauer, *The Emancipation of Music from Language: Departure from Mimesis in Eighteenth-Century Aesthetics*, *Eighteenth Century Studies*, 21 (1987), p. 243.

[211] Jones, *Treatise*, p. vi.

[212] Anonymous [Charles Burney] review of Jones, *Treatise*, 105–112 and 174–81. Burney comments (108) that 'unluckily, Mr. Jones's musical reading has not only been scanty and superficial, but during paroxysms of inveterate prejudices'.

Robertson's *Inquiry into the Fine Arts* when he chides the author for 'much common-place, and superficial reasoning which passes off in conversation' but is inappropriate for 'books, which are purchased at an expense of money, and perused at a further expence of time'.[213] When, however, Burney himself tries to reason more deeply about music in the context of its sister arts (as can be examined further in Chapter 3), the critical pedigree of his ideas is often just as questionable.

Nevertheless, the writing examined up to this point demonstrates that, despite some notable exceptions, the level of sustained critical debate during the 40-year period which Crotch surveys in his 1818 introductory lecture was remarkably high. With the exception of Burney's anonymous book reviews, the debate rarely comprised direct dialogue amongst writers, even though mutuality is often apparent. Most often, when critical exchange does occur, it concerns the aforementioned melody-versus-harmony opposition. In the works of several individuals cited above – especially, Mason, Stillingfleet, Molleson and, above all, Burney – the words 'melody' and 'harmony' often function as polar symbols of familiar oppositions in the history of ideas. In particular, melody and harmony are often found paralleled with other polarities such as genius-versus-reason, freedom-versus-authority and nature-versus-art.

Although binary oppositions such as these are of general interest, in the present context it is the role of the melody–harmony opposition in relation to the purposes of art and the dangers of excessive complication that is most important. When, for example, Burney reverts to the stereotypes of music's protracted ancient–modern quarrel to show that Molleson's primitivist polemic in support of melody is merely a radical form of the modernist impulse, he provides a revealing glimpse into his conception of modernism and, more broadly, into what he thinks music's ancient–modern quarrel was about. More than a decade earlier, in his review of Jones of Nayland's *Treatise*, he had tried to show that the ancient faction's attachment to harmony represented the opposite pole. Objecting that Jones thinks '*unity of melody* ... which Rousseau has so well described and recommended ... is the greatest vice in composition', Burney cannot resist adding shortly afterward that 'it is hardly possible to read this book, without entering a little into the spirit of musical *party*'.

The extreme and possibly rhetorical positions of Beattie, Wesley and Molleson should not be mistaken for a more moderate point of view that would have been more typical of thoughtful enthusiasts of the

---

[213] Review of Thomas Robertson, *An Inquiry into the Fine Arts*, in *Monthly Review* 74 (1786), 192.

modern style. In another review of Molleson's book in the *Analytical Review*, the unidentified writer acknowledges, as John Marsh had before him, that he has 'felt the force of our author's objection against [modern symphonies and concertos]', namely 'the solicitous display of the composer's science, and the performer's talents'.[214] But this writer insists the concerns over musical complexity should focus on the movement for old music and not on the music of recent composers in the modern style. He observes that

> on many occasions, we have thought the air less shrouded, the melody less lost in accompaniments [in modern symphonies and concertos], than in pieces of the old school. We particularly refer to the modern compositions of Haydn and Pleyel, who, by the frequent use of semitones, and the judicious introductions of those delicate *lights* and *shades* of music, if the expression be allowable, the pianos and the fortes have produced some of the most touching melodies imaginable; at the same time we agree with our author, that the symphonies of Haydn and Pleyel are by no means invariably exempt from those false refinements, which he so severely censures.

'Surely [Molleson's] love of simplicity carries him too far', the writer concludes, remarking that 'simple melody however pathetic, must, in time, become insipid'.[215]

Burney's frequent self-contradictions, combined with his attacks on both extremes of the melody–harmony debate, should not obscure his legitimate status as a consistent champion of modern music and the aesthetic values it represents. In his review of Molleson's pamphlet, Burney acknowledges his own apparent inconsistencies, observing that '[Molleson] has frequently quoted Dr. Burney, and sometimes against himself'.[216] Indeed, Molleson more than any of the other writers mentioned above found it possible to justify his opinions through selective quotation from the *General History*. Burney observes in his own defence that he is 'as great an enemy of the abuse of complication and execution as [Molleson] can be' but that he also finds passages in the *General History* in which he 'distinguishes very properly ... between simplicity and rusticity'.[217] This is a reminder of how Burney would like

---

[214] A. N., review of Molleson's *Melody* in *Analytical Review*, 28 (1798), 396. In his review ('A Retrospect of the State of Music in Great Britain, since the Year 1789', *Quarterly Musical Register*, I [1812], 6–28) August Kollman identifies the reviewer for the *Analytical Review* during this period as Thomas Busby. Anonymous [Thomas Busby?] review of *Melody the Soul of Music* in *Analytical Review*, 28 (1798), 395–7.

[215] Ibid.

[216] Burney, review of *Melody*, 190.

[217] Ibid.

his work to be read, for it is not through selective quotations that the author's real message can be identified but through a careful reading of the totality of his argument that does not try to extract individual reactions from context.

Nevertheless, it must be allowed that Burney's criticism suffers from a more serious form of inconsistency than that which results from his reflexive tendency to argue the other side in response to positions he views as extreme. A particular instance in which he is shown to have been deeply conflicted over the purposes of his art can be found in his *Cyclopaedia* article 'Opera'. Here, he summarizes a lifetime of arguments on both sides of an issue that dominated his critical writing and tries for one last time, without success, to reach a satisfactory conclusion. This fascinating document has a significance for both the ancient and modern styles because it has to do with basic questions of the relationship between content and music, and because it specifically takes in both opera and oratorio.[218]

Burney begins by dividing music into two species, 'natural' and 'imitative', much as both Rousseau and Mason had done.[219] In the first and obviously lesser category – which, curiously, includes church music as well as 'the airs for dancing and for common songs' – music is a sensual art limited to 'the pleasure which results from melody, harmony, and rhythm'.[220] Combined with words in the 'lyric representation', by contrast, it can be imitative and thereby 'becomes one of the fine arts capable of painting every picture, exciting every sentiment, contending with poetry, giving it new force, embellishing it with new charms, and triumphing over it by enriching it with new beauties and new allurements'.[221]

Burney argues that 'the union of [words and music] is certainly best; as the words, *if they could be understood* [my emphasis], might not only please but convey instruction'.[222] But throughout this article he cannot seem to make up his mind whether it is possible for words to be understood. After the encouraging beginning quoted above, he relates the central problem he wants to revisit: That there is 'a jealousy

---

[218] Rees, *Cyclopaedia*, s.v. 'Opera'. Despite the title of this article, Burney indicates that his interests are broader when he notes at one point in his brief history of the 'lyric scene' that 'no music dramas, similar to those that were afterwards known by the names of operas and oratorios, had existence in Italy before the beginning of the 17th century'.

[219] Mason modified Rousseau's terms slightly in his first essay in the 1795 collected edition (Mason, *Essays*, p. 307), making the two categories 'simple' and 'impassioned' music.

[220] Rees, *Cyclopaedia*, s.v. 'Opera'.

[221] Ibid.

[222] Ibid.

between the two sisters, Music and Poetry, which prevents them not only from being good relations, but good neighbors'.[223] He then tries to find a way around this problem, noting that 'modern masters' have 'learned how to chuse and respect good poetry, in setting which they relinquish all the pedantry of canons, fugues, and other Gothic inventions'.[224] In some of his earlier writing on the 'feuding sisters' problem, this simple reform had worked satisfactorily.[225] He no longer thinks abandoning musical complication is a sufficient remedy, however, for Burney now has reservations over the value of lyric poetry itself. He had once entertained the highest regard for this poetry whose 'short effusions of passion or sentiment, in various measures ... best exercised the powers of musical expression'.[226] Now, he contemplates verses of a higher kind: those which are 'full of philosophy and ethics, strong reasoning bold metaphors, or epigrammatic wit'.[227] No matter how they are treated by the composer, this superior poetry must necessarily be 'enfeebled by music, which conveys them slowly to the mind'.[228] It is only verses that aspire merely to 'passion, sentiment, graceful and pleasing images and descriptions' that are 'embellished by [music]'.[229]

'People are dissatisfied', Burney remarks, 'if an opera does not read in the closet as well as a tragedy or comedy.'[230] That is why an obvious solution to the problem of words-versus-music that both he and Twining had suggested before – providing audiences with word books – is not acceptable.[231] 'Operas in general are not to be read or spoken, but

---

[223] Ibid.

[224] Ibid.

[225] For example, Burney, *General History*, vol. 1, pp. 528 and 722.

[226] Rees, *Cyclopaedia*, s.v. 'Opera'.

[227] Ibid.

[228] Ibid.

[229] Ibid.

[230] Ibid.

[231] TT to CB 27 March 1786 in Thomas Twining *Recreations and Studies of a Country Clergyman of the Eighteenth Century*, ed. Richard Twining (London, 1882), p. 132. Twining attacks the proposition 'that vocal music and vocal performance are good for nothing if the words are not perfectly intelligible to the hearer without the assistance of his eyes and memory. Won't you join with me in absolutely denying this? It seems to me much nearer the truth to say that when the words are perfectly distinct, as in reading, it must be proof that the music or the singer, or both, are bad ... All this is unmusical criticism, and goes upon the false notion of the words, or poetry, being principal. From the very nature of music, as a high sensible pleasure (for sensual is ambiguous), it always will and must be principal in the union with words, whatever may be determined as to the separate claims of poetry and music to superiority. But do we not carry prayer books to church to read even while the minister is reading? Are there not anthem books in all cathedrals? Who can understand even the common Psalms, when sung or chanted to the simplest music, without the assistance of a book?'

to be sung', Burney concludes.[232] In the appropriate setting of the theatre, the only possible way to reconcile words and music would amount to 'degrading poetry to elevate music'.[233] This, he acknowledges, 'would be acting in a hostile manner to our own pleasures'.[234] With the only options available to him being the choice of lesser poetry or lesser music, Burney can only concede, 'let poetry be regarded as an intellectual pleasure, if you please; and music be ranked, like painting, as an innocent gratification of sense'.[235] 'Sublime poetry', he adds in resignation, 'leaves the musician nothing to do.'[236]

---

[232] Rees, *Cyclopaedia*, s.v. 'Opera'.
[233] Ibid.
[234] Ibid.
[235] Ibid.
[236] Ibid.

CHAPTER THREE

Musicians and men of letters

Crotch and the liberal arts

Charles Burney's unprecedented success as a professional musician in the republic of letters made him a model for a generation of rising talents who were encouraged to follow his lead and aspire to the moral and intellectual rank conferred by study of the liberal arts. The very mention of Burney's name was sufficient to prompt the Reverend A. C. Schomberg, young Crotch's mentor during his student days, to launch into what must have become a tiresome diatribe on the subject of 'mere musicians'.[1] This is a constant refrain in their correspondence. Encouraging Crotch to cultivate his relationship with 'that worthy man', Schomberg asks rhetorically why Burney commands a level of respect other musicians do not. Because, Schomberg says, he is 'a scholar and a gentleman, respected by all and welcome where and whenever he appears', while most musicians are 'ignorant of all letters except the seven in the gamut, awkward, and therefore [indecipherable] to genteel company as soon as their instruments are put up in their cases'.[2]

Schomberg's attempts to push his young charge into a more respectable profession failed completely. Once he accepted Crotch's career choice, he urged a balanced educational programme combining music with the liberal arts. 'Dr. Burney can do both', Schomberg argued, 'Jackson of Exeter can do both, Jones of Nayland can do both – Avison, Rameau, and I dare say many others could do both – Pray then why may not Wm Crotch do both?'[3] But despite Schomberg's best efforts, Crotch developed no enthusiasm for the scholarly life and – in sharp contrast with Burney – no apparent need to be accepted by the wider intellectual community as anything but a remarkably talented musician. 'Though a gentleman and a scholar be a musician, it cannot be necessary that a musician should be a scholar', Crotch observes in his unpublished *Memoirs*, adding 'I never learnt anything from Phoebus, Caesar, Horace or Virgil that I might not have done without as a Christian musician.'[4]

---

[1] *Memoirs*, p. 45.
[2] Ibid.
[3] Ibid., p. 58.
[4] Ibid., p. 61.

Crotch's disinclination to venerate the classics, combined with his patient and ultimately successful insistence that music and musicians be accepted on their own terms, points to one of the most significant differences between his criticism and Burney's, and to a quality of his lectures that helped him avoid many of the sources of contradiction that plagued his older contemporary. Burney often objects to 'philosophers, mathematicians, and men of letters, absorbed in mere speculation', who 'condemn in their closets, unheard and unseen, the productions and performance of practical musicians'.[5] He also speaks scornfully in private of the music of antiquity, the subject of much of this speculation, claiming that his say on the subject in the *General History* would 'be more to Laugh at what others have written, perhaps, than to offer anything of my own Concerning them'.[6] But the fact still remains that Burney's first publications as an aspiring writer in the early 1760s, long before even the Italian tour, were by his own choice a series of articles on the music of antiquity contributed to a periodical called *The Monthly Magazine: or Monthly Orpheus*.[7] And for that matter, Burney's first act when he decided a decade later to begin work on a history of music was to correspond on this subject with William Mason, a man of letters who could fairly be charged with the objections Burney raises above.[8] What Burney wrote to Mason in this letter, which calls music 'a Chaos to which God knows whether I shall have Life, leisure, or abilities to give order',[9] could not be further from Crotch's comparatively insular view.

Burney faced the chaos he mentions because he laboured to find an organizing rationale for his *General History* but also because he conceived of music as 'connected with Religion, Philosophy, History, Poetry, Painting, Sculpture, public Exhibitions & private life', and felt a need to explain the connection.[10] No such ambition is apparent in the work of Crotch. Crotch's manuscript lecture notes accept in general terms that

---

[5] Charles Burney, *A General History of Music*, with critical and historical notes by Frank Mercer, 2 vols (London, 1935; New York: Dover, 1957), vol. 1, p. 107.

[6] CB to TT, 28 April 1773 in Alvaro Ribeiro, *The Letters of Dr Charles Burney*, vol. 1, *1751–1784* (Oxford, Clarendon Press), p. 126.

[7] Leanne Langley 'Burney and Hawkins: New Light on an Old Rivalry', paper delivered at fifty-fifth Annual Meeting of the American Musicological Society, Austin, Texas, 27 October 1990. On the basis of stylistic evidence and Burney's manuscript notes in YUL, Osborn, Langley makes a compelling case for Burney as the author of a series called 'An Historical Account of the Rise and Progress of Music' that ran in *The Monthly Magazine: or Monthly Orpheus* beginning in February of 1760 and continuing for some ten issues.

[8] CB to WM, 27 May 1770 in Ribeiro, *Letters*, p. 54.

[9] Ibid.

[10] Ibid.

the basic principles of aestheticians of the previous generation are applicable to music and freely employ some of the standard terminology. But they do not go into more than superficial detail about what these terms might mean in their new connection with music, nor do they explore implications of the theory that informs even relatively recent and therefore potentially easily misunderstood ideas.

Crotch, Burney and the musical picturesque

A good illustration might be found in Crotch and Burney's uses of the late eighteenth-century catchword 'picturesque'. As shown in Chapter 1, Crotch adopted this word as a musical term from his earliest lectures even though one of his primary authorities and the individual most connected in British letters with the picturesque, Uvedale Price, had not yet done so himself at the time. The closest Crotch comes to explaining what the musical and painterly picturesque might have in common is a statement drawn from Price's *Essay of the Picturesque as Compared with the Sublime and the Beautiful* (London, 1794) to the effect that 'as in painting & architecture the Picturesque style is the result of roughness of playful intricacy ... so in music whatever by its eccentric passages, varied rhythm & bold melody & violent contrasts is perpetually exciting surprise in the mind of the auditor may be included under the term ornamental'.[11]

Another quality that the musical picturesque was thought to share with the sister arts was one Reynolds had held up as an evidence of its inferiority. The excellence of the picturesque was supposed to lie in the nebulous realm of 'taste' as opposed to the concrete domain of rule.[12] After identifying Domenico Scarlatti as 'the father of that style which we have denominated the ornamental or picturesque'[13] and Haydn as a follower, Crotch recounts yet again the story of Scarlatti's calculated violation of textbook rules. When he composed for the opera, Scarlatti

---

[11] *Lectures*, Col/7/43.

[12] In a letter to William Gilpin from 1791 that is reprinted in the latter's *Three Essays: On Beauty; On Picturesque Travel; and on Sketching Landscape: To Which is Added a Poem on Landscape Painting*, 2nd edn (London, 1794), pp. 34–6, Reynolds wonders 'whether the epithet *picturesque* is not applicable to the excellences of the inferior schools, rather than the higher'. Reynolds notes (p. 35) that 'perhaps *picturesque* is somewhat synonymous to the word *taste*; which we should think improperly applied to Homer, or Milton, but very well to Pope, or Prior. I suspect that the application of these words are to excellences of an inferior order; and which are incompatible with the grand style'.

[13] *Lectures*, NRO, MS 11229/5.

did so 'in a beautiful and correct style', but later, when he turned to harpsichord music, 'he willfully broke through the established rules of composition and boldly appealed to the ear for his justification'.[14] This is a story Crotch took from Burney, who, in turn, attributed it to a certain 'M. L'Augier' in Vienna.[15] Starting around 1806, Crotch's lectures begin to tell the story somewhat differently. Scarlatti is said to have found it 'impossible to supersede the productions for the harpsichord of his rival Handel'.[16] He therefore 'struck out that more ornamental, humorous, or witty style, which gave birth to most of the eccentricities and novelties of modern piano forte music'.[17] 'To insure originality', he deliberately 'set the rules of composition (which he never violated in his vocal productions) at defiance.'[18]

In a revised edition of his *Essay* published five years after Crotch began lecturing in London, Price tacitly accepts some elements of Crotch's formulation of the musical picturesque and cites the same composers.[19] He does so, however, with reservations that may have something to do with a musical readership that was steeped in ancient music and more at home with a borrowed critical vocabulary long associated with that tradition. 'We no more scruple to call one of Handel's choruses sublime, than Corelli's famous pastorale beautiful',[20] Price observes.

> But should any person simply, and without any qualifying expressions, call a capricious movement of Scarlatti or Haydn picturesque, he would, with great reason, be laughed at, for it is not a term applied to sounds; yet such a movement, from its sudden, unexpected, and abrupt transitions, – from a certain playful wildness of character and appearance of irregularity, is no less analogous to similar scenery in nature, than the concerto or chorus, to what is grand or beautiful to the eye.[21]

Price's reservations about following Crotch's lead may be related to his reluctance to speak of the picturesque as a creation of actual (as opposed to merely apparent) irregularity, as Crotch had, but also may have to do with a general reluctance on his part to base aesthetic

---

[14] *Lectures*, NRO, MS 11064/10.

[15] Charles Burney, *The Present State of Music in Germany, the Netherlands and United Provinces*, 2nd edn, 2 vols (London, 1775), vol. 1, p. 253.

[16] William Crotch, *Substance of Several Courses of Lectures on Music* (London, 1831; Clarabricken, Co. Kilkenny, Ireland: Boethius Press, 1986), pp. 129–30. This story first appears in *Lectures*, NRO, MS 11230/4.

[17] Ibid.

[18] Ibid.

[19] Sir Uvedale Price, *Essays on the Picturesque, as Compared with the Sublime and the Beautiful ...*, 3 vols (London, 1810; London: Gregg International, 1971).

[20] Price, *Essays*, p. 45.

[21] Ibid., pp. 45–6.

categories on subjective psychological effects. A sentence added to the 1810 edition of his *Essay* stresses that Price intends to focus on the English word picturesque and not the Italian word 'Pittoresco', which 'is derived, not like picturesque, from the thing painted, but from the painter' and particularly from 'the turn of mind common to painters'.[22]

It is useful to compare the Crotch–Price conception of the musical picturesque with Burney's. Burney, first of all, invariably interprets the word picturesque literally to refer to the ability of music to represent or depict, to make a musical picture. In other words, where Crotch tries to explain picturesque by showing audiences what they should listen for in music, using his own personal experience and perceptions as a guide, Burney's strategy is to try instead to explain music's intellectual connection with the sister arts through their common reliance on imitation in the eighteenth-century sense of that term. In this respect, he views music more as a literary man and a non-musician might. Unfortunately, placing music in this context invites a comparison with the sister arts in an area in which, as most thinkers at the time including his friend Twining had already concluded, music was patently inferior. The inability of music to imitate soon draws Burney into one of his many long digressions on the relative significance of music among the sister arts, a detour that is entirely unnecessary for his stated historical purposes and eventually results in his associating the musical picturesque with qualities that are the near opposite of the picturesque as it is usually understood.

This digression appears in connection with Burney's first use of the word 'picturesque' in the *General History*, at a point in his narrative in which he identifies the first musical system for the notation of rhythm. When music made this great leap, he argues, it was finally able to liberate itself from the tyranny of poetic metre, on which earlier music was necessarily forced to rely for its rhythmic structure. Commenting on this emancipation prompts him to offer a few words on a subject that is never far beneath the surface of his writing, the familiar eighteenth-century question of whether music should be viewed as a rational or a merely sensual art form and, in the former case, how this rationality is manifested. 'I know that many of the learned think the liberty music acquired at this memorable revolution has often been abused by her sons, who are frequently *enfans gatés*, riotous, capricious, ignorant, licentious, and enthusiastic', he begins.[23] He also concedes early on that

---

[22] Sir Uvedale Price, *An Essay of the Picturesque as Compared with the Sublime and the Beautiful; and, on the Use of Studying Pictures, for the Purpose of Improving Real Landscape* (London, 1794), p. 36.
[23] Burney, *General History*, vol. 1, p. 526.

'whenever poetry is at their mercy [musicians] are more in want of instruction and restraint than the most wild and ignorant school-boys'.[24]

This said, however, he insists that music 'considered abstractedly, without the assistance, or rather the shackles of speech, and abandoned to its own powers, is now [because of its notational advances] become a rich, expressive, and picturesque language in itself; having its forms, proportions, contrasts, punctuations, members, phrases, and periods'.[25] Thus, while Crotch and to some extent even Burney himself stresses the unruliness of the musical picturesque, speaking of its wantonness and irrationality or its wildness of character and appearance of irregularity, Burney has somehow also connected it with notions of meaningfulness, order and syntax.

Burney does not always connect the picturesque with order, but one thing that is constant in his writing is the appearance of this term in a context that stresses the eternal tension between the desire for artistic freedom of expression and the need to control the excesses of the imagination. It is significant that poetry is not, in his writing, the only restraint on the imagination with which music must negotiate a balance in its bid to be a meaningful art form on its own terms. Elsewhere in the *General History* Burney alludes to the famous Artusi–Monteverdi controversy centuries earlier. He sides with the latter, whom he calls 'one of the principal legislators of the musical drama'.[26] He notes, however, that even though

> in the new *musica rappresentativa*, [Monteverdi] was to emancipate himself from the trammels of canon, fugue, and other restraints which had been thought necessary in composing *à capella*, and was now to have a poetical and picturesque Music, more varied and impassioned than that of the church or chamber; yet there were certain fundamental rules and prohibitions, totally independent of taste, which to violate, would offend cultivated ears.[27]

These mechanical rules include, 'the common precept of avoiding two fifths or two eights, particularly in two parts', which Burney says Monteverdi 'frequently and wantonly neglected, without the least necessity or pretence of producing new and agreeable effects by such a licence'.[28]

---

[24] Ibid.
[25] Ibid., pp. 526–7.
[26] Ibid., vol. 2, p. 516.
[27] Ibid., p. 517.
[28] Ibid.

Burney and the men of letters

In view of the many complications that stem from trying to explain music in the context of the sister arts, one might well wonder why Burney should have chosen this approach. Even his friend and to some extent his model Joshua Reynolds succeeded, as he describes in his final discourse, because he was able to side-step the 'conceptions of impossible practice' set down by literary men and focus instead on art as it is experienced by practicing artists.[29] One explanation for Burney's chosen critical point of view has to do with his well-established need to be accepted as an intellectual and a man of letters. But at the same time, one should not overlook the effects of his modest stature within his own profession, which was not on a level comparable to that which Crotch and Reynolds enjoyed.

It was Burney's ingratiating personality and elegant turn of phrase that ultimately won him the role of elder statesman for his art, not his performance or composition. Especially at the beginning of his career, he did not have the prestige as a musician to expect a sceptical public to allow him to set his own critical agenda. Burney recognized his own limitations as a musician, especially by comparison with the impressive talents of the next generation. As he indicated in a letter to the Reverend Samuel Hook, 'I began music late; my eldest daughter was a better player at 7 y^{rs} old than I was at 17; but early players were then Phenomena.'[30] Crotch, by contrast, was granted the privilege of speaking for his art largely because his early reputation as a brilliant young talent enabled him to capture and hold the public imagination. In fact, his early reputation was such that he could maintain his status as a musical phenomenon without actually performing regularly as an adult.[31] His lectures succeeded because he told audiences they should try to understand and experience music the way he did and they found him credible enough to accept his direction. Burney's comparatively modest professional stature, by contrast, was rubbed in his face repeatedly during his lifetime as he was passed over for significant posts. One final

---

[29] Sir Joshua Reynolds, *Discourses on Art*, ed. Robert R. Wark (New Haven, CT, and London: Yale University Press, 1975), p. 267.

[30] CB to the Reverend Samuel Hook, 23 October 1804, YUL, Osborn.

[31] Anonymous, 'Memoir of William Crotch, Mus. Doc', *The Harmonicon*, 9 (1831), 4–6, notes that 'Dr. Crotch's talent as an organist or piano-forte player, which are of the highest order, has, with the exception of his performance at his Lectures, been chiefly confined to the circle of his private friends ... To the musical world in general, he has for the last thirty years been chiefly known as a composer, and as an elementary writer on the science, to the cultivation and advancement of which his public life has been devoted.'

insult was delivered unintentionally by Crotch himself, when Burney lost the Heather Professorship at Oxford to his less experienced protégé.[32]

Still another important contributing factor in Burney's choice to play the game of music criticism by the rules of men of letters is that compared with Crotch, Burney had a more lively curiosity about how music ought to fit into the aesthetic systems of the eighteenth century. His correspondence reveals an impressive familiarity with a much wider array of writers, both foreign and domestic, than Crotch or probably even Reynolds knew, and an inclination to debate their meaning with competent if unambitious thinkers like Twining and Mason. He had read *The Spectator* on wit and judgement, for example, and for all his criticism of Addison as a man of letters who was 'ignorant of Music and impenetrable to its powers'[33] he implicitly accepts this dichotomy as a fact of nature whose implications ought to be reflected in music criticism. Burney wanted very much to believe that the unified theory of the arts which better thinkers than he had sought unsuccessfully where music was concerned actually existed. His 'chaos' letter recognizes a connection between music and the sister arts, and desperately seeks a common denominator that in practice he never found. Ironically, his colleague and collaborator Twining, relying on ideas he clarified in correspondence and conversation with Burney, actually *did* make a significant contribution toward explaining music in the aesthetic language of late eighteenth-century pre-romanticism.[34]

Then, too, Burney's writing reveals an instinctive sensitivity for and curiosity about the phenomenology of perception. Crotch's writing typically assumes without saying so one point of view: that of the highly trained professional musician consulting the one unimpeachable final

---

[32] In *Memoirs*, p. 84 Crotch describes the process by which he was awarded the professorship in 1797: 'The electors for the professorship thus vacated were the Vice Chancellor for the time being, and the heads of the four chairs, Ch.Ch., New Coll. Magd., & St. Johns, two of them, the Dean of Ch.Ch. and Dr. Marlow prov^t by St Johns were my patrons and the vice ch Dr. Breadmore has [ ] of Merton [ ] was well known to the Dean of Ch.Ch. who put me to him. These three being secured the thing *was done*.' Crotch adds, 'afterwards learned from D. Burney that he had long thought of standing for the Professorship but of that I was quite ignorant'. On the same page, concerning the events of August 1797, Crotch writes that he 'called on Dr. Burney at Chelsea'. On Burney's interest in this position see Roger Lonsdale, *Dr. Charles Burney: a Literary Biography*, (Oxford: Clarendon Press, 1965), p. 387 and Fanny Burney, *The Journals and Letters of Fanny Burney*, eds Joyce Hemlow, Patricia Boutilier and Althea Douglas, 8 vols (Oxford: Clarendon Press, 1973), vol. 3, p. 301.

[33] Burney, *General History*, vol. 2, p. 535.

[34] Thomas Twining, *Aristotle's Treatise on Poetry Translated with Notes on the Translation, and on the Original; and Two Dissertations, on Poetical, and Musical, Imitation* (London, 1789; Garland, 1971).

authority – the musical score itself – in the acoustically perfect imaginary world of his own mind. His personal scores are littered with
pencilled-in comments in the margins pronouncing passages by J. S.
Bach or Domenico Scarlatti 'Astonishing' or 'ingenious'.[35] Much of his
criticism, also, is obviously based on reading the score rather than on
the experience of live performance. Burney often 'heard' music as Crotch
did. His correspondence with Twining, whose ability to read musical
scores was not on the same level, occasionally explores this mode of
perception.[36] Burney's published writing often deliberately contrasts the
ideal world of the trained musician studying scores with the more
complex practical situation of the unskilled listener hearing difficult
and unfamiliar music in the confusing acoustical setting of the cathedral. An important difference between Burney and Crotch, however, is
that while Crotch was practising what he himself might well have called
pedagogy, and in that context could explicitly offer the specialist's point
of view as the *only* acceptable point of view, Burney was less sure about
the critic's purpose.

An early reviewer of the *General History*'s first two volumes imagined that Burney had written them with the goal of 'regulating and
correcting the public taste in music, as sir Joshua Reynolds has done in
a sister art'.[37] Burney certainly recognized the need for someone to do
this. In a fascinating letter written shortly after one of the earliest
London performances of Haydn's *The Creation* (quoted below) and
based largely on an entry in his diary made that very night, he speaks of
sitting at this concert with Frances Anne Crewe and her husband, who
'wished me to tell them how to hear Haydn's music, wch the public in
general want to be told ... '.[38] In this particular case, he made a special

---

[35] A particularly interesting example of this phenomenon is found in Crotch's copy of
the *Art of Fugue*, which is held by the NRO as MS 11256.

[36] See CB to TT, 14 December 1781 in Ribeiro, *Letters*, vol. 1, p. 327. Burney
acknowledges having heard old music mostly in his imagination: 'I have scored them all,
& transcribed them for you without trial of effect, except in my *minds ear*; but, as you
very comically say, by long habit & experience one's *Ear* gets up into one's *Eye*. – My P.
F. is always so loaded with books, & so out of tune, that I have neither industry nor
inclination to unload & put it in order for a momentary use. In the summer, however, I
did try the effects of Old Okenheem's Conundrum [i.e., the three voice canon 'Prenez sur
moi'] after I had decyphered it, & found it quite as nasty as you have done.'

[37] Quoted in *Critical Review*, 55 (1783), 118.

[38] Salomon's performance of this work on 21 April was not, as he had planned, the
first London performance of the work. That distinction belongs to John Ashley, who
premiered *The Creation* at the Covent Garden Oratorio on 28 March. See Nicholas
Temperley, *Haydn: The Creation* (Cambridge: Cambridge University Press, 1991), p. 39.
There are several references to Burney's letter on *The Creation* in his papers. In a diary
entry for 16–21 January 1800 (NYPL, Berg, 198788B, folder 7, item 11), Burney notes

effort to collect and analyse his thoughts and set them down in manuscript, possibly as a prelude for discussing *The Creation* in the face-to-face social encounters in which he probably engaged in most of his criticism of recent music. Burney did not, however, publish these remarks, nor did he claim consistently in print the authority to guide the public taste. But given the evolving state of music criticism itself at the time and the fact that a piece of music can be perceived in radically different ways depending on the circumstances in which it is heard and the capacities of the listener, it was unclear what point of view the critic *should* adopt. Often Burney's writing, like that of professionals before him who shared a sense of curiosity on these points, like Avison, can shift its perspective radically within the same sentence.

There is one final way in which Burney's writing takes on a burden that Crotch's does not. Although Crotch, like Reynolds, enjoys repeating pithy statements of aesthetic truth that sprang from age-old stories all eighteenth-century writers on the arts knew, he does not try to translate aesthetic mythology into musical terms. For whatever reasons, Burney does attempt this, and the result is a fascinating array of contradictions in which familiar myths are stretched and manipulated to make them apply to an art for which they were not conceived and to which they do not easily conform. But along with the confusion this produces there is an opportunity. In the course of Burney's reinterpretation of artistic platitudes there are distortions that say something not only about music's interface with the sister arts but about the contradictions inherent in the myths themselves.

The music of antiquity

Since the aesthetic mythology of interest here concerned the fabled music of antiquity, it is appropriate to begin by considering briefly what the late eighteenth century knew and thought about this music. For the present purposes what matters is the thinking of Burney's immediate circle, since it is their approval and acceptance he is supposed to have sought in a lifelong quest to be respected as a man of letters. The

---

for Monday 21 April 'Haydn's Oratorio of the *Creation* was performed at the Opera-house Concert Room, under the direction of Salomon, who took great pains to have it well executed.' He adds, 'see a paper written immediately on my return home, after hearing it: describing its effect on myself'. This paper is held in YUL, Osborn, under the title 'On Haydn's Creation. Performed in London Apr. 21. 1800'. Burney also wrote a letter to C. I. Latrobe with essentially the same text that is dated in YUL, Osborn, *c.*22–25 April 1800.

literary men of Burney's circle had no direct knowledge about the music of the Greeks and did not think they needed to know anything in order to have an opinion on the subject. In fact, with the exception of Twining, who was scholar enough to have something new to say about Aristotle and musical imitation, the classicism of British writers after John Brown's *Dissertation on the Rise, Union, and Power, the Progressions, Separations, and Corruptions, of Poetry and Music* (London, 1764) usually does not even focus on the actual texts of ancient writers.[39]

Much of Burney's 'Dissertation on the Music of the Ancients' is not about the ancient music itself as much as it is later commentary on it. He devotes so much space to carefully dissecting the great arguments of earlier times and lining up and counting off the writers on different sides of relevant controversies because he knew that this was what interested parties of his generation knew best and cared most about.[40] Brown, on the other hand, not only quoted the ancients directly at every turn but struggled to understand them in the face of an unfortunate imprecision on their part. He complains of their 'promiscuous Use of the Word Mode, signifying either *Pitch*, *Measure*, or *Species* of *Diapason*', noting that because of this 'it has come to pass, that some time the Signification of the Word is *clear*, at others it is only *probable*, and often it is *obscure* and *doubtful*'.[41] By the 1770s, literary criticism of music more often relied on standard interpretations and rarely quibbled any more over the translation of key words and phrases.[42]

---

[39] A good discussion of earlier British writing on this subject can be found in D. T. Mace, 'Musical Humanism, the Doctrine of Rhythmus, and the Saint Cecilia Odes of Dryden', *Journal of the Warburg and Courtauld Institute*, 27 (1964), 271–92.

[40] A good example is the question of whether the ancients had counterpoint. Burney carefully tabulates the score in *General History*, vol. 1, p. 106. Arguing in favour of ancient counterpoint were 'Gaffurio, Zarlino, Gio Battista Doni, Issac Vossius, Zaccharia Tevo, the abbé Fraguier, and Mr. Stillingfleet, author of *Principles and Power of Harmony*'. On the other side were 'Glareanus, Salinas, Bottrigari, Artusi, Cerone, Kepler, Mersennus, Kircher, Claude Perrault, Wallis, Bontempi, Burette, the fathers Bougeant and Cerceau, Padre Martini, M. Marpurg, and M. Rousseau'.

[41] In his *A Dissertation on the Rise, Union, and Power, the Progressions, Separations, and Corruptions, of Poetry and Music* (London, 1763; New York, Garland, 1971), p. 66, Brown complains of the ancients' 'promiscuous Use of the Word Mode, signifying either *Pitch*, *Measure*, or *Species* of *Diapason*', noting that because of this 'it has come to pass, that some time the Signification of the Word is *clear*, at others it is only *probable*, and often it is *obscure* and *doubtful*'.

[42] Burney comments in *General History*, vol. 1, p. 33 on a long-running argument over whether 'the terms *high* and *low*, had different acceptations among the ancients, from those in which they are understood by the moderns'. Significantly, Brown's name is the last on a list of writers asserting this point that includes Galilei, Zarlino, Bontempi, Tevo and Rousseau.

The earliest of Mason's *Essays Historical and Critical, on English Church Music* illustrates this tendency. The purpose of this essay, as Walpole encouraged Mason in correspondence, was to 'show all the blunders and faults of the old masters [i.e., sixteenth- and seventeenth-century church composers], and prove that there can be no music, but by exploding prejudices [i.e., against the modern homophonic style], and by restoring ancient [i.e., simple] harmony'.[43] In the essay, Mason claims no knowledge about the 'ancient harmony' except for a confident assertion that the 'concurrent voice of all antiquity' believed it 'highly assisted the sense, and marked the measure so precisely, that without its aid the higher kinds of Poetry were found defective'.[44] So pervasive were legends about the music of antiquity in 1782 that he did not need to quote a single ancient writer to buttress his claim; readers had all heard this before. Nor did he have to go into detail on what aspect of Greek music earned it universal commendation. His audience already knew that, unlike the modern-day music that Mason claims 'constantly perplexes the common ear',[45] the music of antiquity was characterized by an elegant simplicity that made it capable of remarkable, if somewhat exaggerated, effects.

Mason looks back no further than Erasmus in his argument for the reform of church music. He follows this powerful name by noting that he could have cited 'many of the most learned and judicious Persons, who flourished at the dawn of the Reformation' who 'reprobated very strongly that complicated Harmony, which accompanied the Church Service'.[46] Beginning with Erasmus's familiar complaint that counterpoint obscures the text and therefore 'the tinkle of the words is all that strikes the ears, and soothes them with a transient and slightly pleasurable sensation',[47] Mason finds support for valuing words over music through a variety of Renaissance and more recent scholars, including Benedetto Marcello and Count Algarotti. He even stops along the way to show that an individual firmly associated with ancient music in the later, eighteenth-century sense of the expression, Thomas Tudway, agreed with him.[48]

Mason, then, views himself, his educated predecessors, and his like-minded contemporaries as participants in a centuries-long debate within

---

[43] Walpole to Mason 22 January 1780 in Horace Walpole, *The Yale Edition of Horace Walpole's Correspondence*, ed. W. S. Lewis (New Haven, CT: Yale University Press, 1937–83), vol. 29, p. 7.

[44] William Mason, *Essays Historical and Critical, on English Church Music* (York, 1795; London, 1811), p. 332.

[45] Ibid.

[46] Ibid., p. 363.

[47] Ibid., p. 339.

[48] Ibid., p. 335.

music criticism over fundamental values. It is with his own status as a legitimate critical writer in mind that Mason pronounces Brown's *Dissertation* 'a masterly piece of Musical criticism', and claims immodestly that an essay he himself had written in his 'very early youth' on the music of antiquity 'cut the Gordian knot, which it has not been in the power of the profoundest Musical Critics to unravel'.[49] Burney, of course, had a different opinion about the credentials needed for valid music criticism. The Preface to the *General History* is one of several places in which he considers what music criticism should be and who ought to practise it. He is less candid here than in the 'Essay on Musical Criticism' published 13 years later in the third volume of the *General History*, where he insists that professional credentials are required for anyone who would claim the right to speak on certain aspects of music.[50] Still, the milder Preface dispatches men of letters like Addison, Pope, and Swift, along with Apuleius, Pausanias and Athenaeus among the ancients, as men who were ill-equipped to judge.[51] Even ancient writers, it seems, needed to be practising musicians for their remarks to be taken seriously.

Two reasons might be added to those that are usually offered for Burney's decision to devote an entire volume of his four-volume history to the music of antiquity even though he basically agreed with Twining that this was a subject about which 'there is so little to be known it is rather unlucky that there should be so much to be said'.[52] First, while Burney acknowledges his own uncertainty over the nature of ancient music in his Preface to the *General History*, he is still confident that 'it was something with which mankind was extremely delighted: for not

---

[49] His comments on Brown's essay are in ibid., p. 307 n. Mason's early essay was reprinted 'with a little variation' as the fourth of his *Essays*. Charles Avison uses Mason's essay in the second edition of *An Essay on Musical Expression* (London, 1753; New York: Broude, 1967), p. 72.

[50] Burney, *General History*, vol. 2, pp. 7–11.

[51] Ibid., vol. 1, p. 17. 'Indeed, I have long since found it necessary to read with caution the splendid assertions of writers concerning music, till I was convinced of their knowledge of the subject; for I have frequently detected ancients as well as moderns, whose fame sets them almost above censure, of utter ignorance in this particular, while they have thought it necessary to *talk about it*.' Burney also notes his regret over not having been able to locate the writings of Dionysius Halicarnassensis. 'Of all the ancient musical writers', he observes, 'the name of no one is come down to us, of whose work I was in greater want.' That was because Dionysius wrote a *History of Musicians* in which he 'celebrated not only the great performers on the Flute and Cithara, but those who had risen to eminence by every species of poetry'.

[52] TT to CB 7 April 1773 in Ralph S. Walker, ed., *A Selection of Thomas Twining's Letters 1734–1804: the Record of a Tranquil Life*, 2 vols (Leviston, Queenston, Lampeter: Edwin Mellor Press, 1991), vol. 1, p. 75.

only the poets, but the historians and philosophers of the best ages of Greece and Rome, are as diffuse in its praises, as of those arts concerning which sufficient remains are come down to us, to evince the truth of their panegyrics'.[53] This comes just two paragraphs after the first of Burney's many statements to the effect that the public is the only authority in music that counts. If ancient music really did please the Greek audience, Burney needed no further evidence of its value.

But another reason for his attention to this music and, more importantly, to three centuries of commentary about it does not emerge until well into his 'Dissertation on the Music of the Ancients' when he considers the question of 'The Effects Attributed to the Music of the Ancients'.[54] In the Preface Burney had complained that 'the study of ancient music is now become the business of an Antiquary more than of a Musician'.[55] He is ready to make it the business of musicians here because he charges there has been a conspiracy on the part of men of letters. Many 'bigoted admirers of antiquity' have not really 'given way to credulity so far as to believe' in the exaggerated powers of ancient music; they only 'pretend to believe in these fabulous accounts, in order to play them off against modern music'.[56] Their goal is to put modern music 'in a state far inferior to the ancient, till it can operate all the effects that have been attributed to the music of Orpheus, Amphion, and such wonder-working bards'.[57]

A perennial question of literary men underlies Burney's concerns. As John Wallis put it in 1698, that question might be phrased, 'whence it is that these great effects which are reported of *Musick* in *Former Times* (of *Orpheus, Amphion,* &c.) are not as well found to follow upon the *Musick* of *Later Ages*'.[58] Wallis, who thought very much as Burney did about many aspects of music, had expressed his own frustration with this question in the famous letter he wrote to the Royal Society. In that letter,

---

[53] Burney, *General History*, vol. 1, p. 15.

[54] Ibid., pp. 149–163.

[55] Ibid., p. 16

[56] Ibid., p. 163.

[57] Ibid.

[58] John Wallis, 'A Letter of Dr. John Wallis, to Mr. Andrew Fletcher; concerning the strange Effects reported of *Musick* in *Former Times*; beyond what is to be found in Later Ages', *Philosophical Transactions of the Royal Society*, 20 (1698), 297. Wallis complains, 'the Question you lately proposed to me (by a Friend of yours) concerning *Musick*; was not, Whence it comes to pass that *Musick* hath so great an Influence or Efficacy on our Affections, Passions, Motions, &c'. – a question he would have liked to answer – 'But whence it is that these great effects which are reported of *Musick* in *Former Times* (of *Orpheus, Amphion,* &c.) are not as well found to follow upon the Musick of *Later Ages*.'

Wallis is as sceptical about the ancient stories as Burney, noting that these accounts are 'highly *Hyperbolical*, and next door to *Fabulous*'.[59]

Wallis handles the basic question posed above by claiming that even the species of modern music he thinks weakest and least effective – that is, complex, contrapuntal works which 'aim only at pleasing the Ear, by a sweet Consort', as opposed to music that is 'adjusted so as to excite particular Passion, Affections, or Temper or Mind'[60] – really *could* do for a susceptible listener all that the ancient music ever did. And with the greater attention to certain requisites he advises, all of which exactly parallel those of the moderns of the late eighteenth century, music could do still more.[61] In particular Wallis, like Mason, would like to see 'good Measures and Affectionate Language', that are 'set to a Musical Tune, and sung by a decent Voice, and accompanied but with soft Musick (instrumental) if any, so as not to drown or obscure the emphatick Expressions'.[62]

The question Wallis answered so well in 1698 continued to be asked more than a century later. Mason's 'Gordian knot' essay answered it by setting up different kinds of excellence. The Greeks were superior at melody and 'pushed the musical Art as far as it would go, when considered as an adjunct to Poetry'.[63] At the same time, 'Melody united with Harmony is the perfection of Music as a single science', and in that respect, modern instrumental music has the edge.[64] The moral of Mason's essay, then, is that if music is to have a significance that can extend beyond the esoteric interests of a single discipline and its specialists, its only hope is to sacrifice an important part of its capabilities and forego unnecessary complication.

Even Crotch was not immune early in his career to a variation on the literary man's question, which by then was no longer 'how could the ancient music work miracles that modern music can't', but rather, 'how can we find a way to make the ancient music into an art worthy of the praise given it in classical sources'. In the essay Crotch wrote in response to John Marsh's *Monthly Magazine* article, the young academic claims to offer an hypothesis by which 'we may be induced to entertain a higher opinion of the excellence of ancient music, than can be derived from any arguments I have hitherto seen on the subject'.[65] This hypothesis

---

[59] Ibid., p. 298.

[60] Ibid., pp. 302–3.

[61] Ibid.

[62] Ibid., pp. 299–300.

[63] Mason, *Essays*, p. 396.

[64] Ibid.

[65] 'W. C.' [William Crotch], 'Remarks on the present State of Music', *Monthly Magazine*, 10 (1800–1801), 125.

turns out to be much like Mason's, though Crotch adds to Mason's formula the possibility that a degenerate remnant of the ancient music lived on in the form of 'national' melodies. This was nothing new; the late eighteenth-century primitivists had attempted to recast the myth of ancient music by substituting Welsh or Irish melodies for the unknown music of antiquity and thereby giving it powers only slightly less remarkable than the music of Orpheus and Amphion.[66] In addition, the story had long circulated that Gregorian chant was itself a degenerate relic of ancient Greek music.[67]

Some of Crotch's later lectures openly dismiss the legends of ancient music as absurd.[68] Others employ a different and possibly inconsistent strategy, claiming that

> the universally powerful effects produced by ancient music, far from proving its excellence, demonstrate the direct contrary; for it is not the most ingenious harmony, refined melody or expressive performance, but the most simple and intelligible tunes performed by a simple voice or instrument that please the majority of mankind.[69]

Crotch had conceded early on in his *Monthly Magazine* essay that we may 'very reasonably infer, that the music of the ancients was more pure, expressive, and simple than our's; which on the other hand, possesses excellencies unknown to the ancients – harmony, fugue, and imitation; excellencies which it is folly to depreciate'.[70]

Crotch's second approach to dealing with ancient music in the quotation above resembles reasoning used late in the previous century by

---

[66] See, for example, Burney's review of Joseph Walker's, *Historical Memoirs of the Irish Bards* in *Monthly Review*, 77 (1787), 425–39. There Burney notes ironically: 'Here music and poetry are still united, and form, as in high antiquity, a kind of Androgyne, Dr. Browne, when he complained of their separation, and Fontenelle, when he supposed that music would never be restored to its former miraculous powers till re-united in a single individual were ignorant of the beauty and even existence of these extemporaneous compositions.'

[67] In Burney's letter to Mason from 27 May 1771 (Ribeiro, *Letters*, p. 56) this idea is attributed to Rousseau in the *Dictionnaire de musique* (Geneva, 1767; Paris, 1768) s.v. 'plain-chant'.

[68] *Lectures*, NRO, MS 11064. In this 'occasional lecture on Haydn's Oratorio of the Creation', Crotch remarks that 'Indeed the hyperbolical accounts of the supernatural powers of ancient music are for the most part not only too improbable for belief, but too ridiculous to be treated seriously'.

[69] *Lectures*, NRO, MS 11064/7. This lecture bears the dates 1798, 1800, and 1801. It appears, then, to be a very early production, apparently from the first of Crotch's lectures at Oxford.

[70] 'W. C.', 'Remarks on the present State of Music', *Monthly Magazine*, 10 (1800), p. 125.

Wallis and by William Wotton in his famous Battle of the Books controversy with William Temple. Wallis's letter recognizes that the perception
of music is dependent on the listener's capacities and charges that the
Greeks, whom he calls 'Rusticks', probably lacked the sophistication to
appreciate 'compounded Musick'.[71] Wotton, along similar lines, notes
that:

> To [the ancients], many of our Modern Compositions, where sev-
> eral Parts are sung or played at the same time, would seem confused,
> intricate and unpleasant: Though in those cases, the greater this
> seeming confusion is, the more Pleasure does the skillful hearer
> take in unravelling every several part, and in observing how artfully
> those seemingly disagreeing Tones join, like true-cut Tallies, one
> within another, to make up that united Concord, which very often
> gives little Satisfaction to common Ears; though in such sort of
> Compositions it is, that the Excellency of Modern *Music* chiefly
> consists.[72]

In other words, the claims of both Wallis and Wotton in support of
modern progress do not stop with the possibility that fundamental
improvements had been made in music since antiquity; listeners have
improved in proportion.

Although Wallis and Wotton were in one sense on the same side as
advocates of music that was 'modern' by comparison with the music of
antiquity, they should be placed on opposite sides of the later quarrel
over musical form versus musical content that is the subject of this
book. Just as Wallis's position supporting musical content resembles
closely that of the later moderns including Mason, Wotton's remarks
valuing abstract musical qualities are exactly in line with later disciples
of ancient music like Jones of Nayland and Hawkins. Wotton contends,
much as Hawkins did, that '*Music* is a *Physico-Mathematical* Science,
built upon fixed Rules, and stated Proportions'.[73] And since these rules
had been the same, Wotton believed, since Pythagoras, music was an
area in which the moderns could be said to have bettered the ancients
on a level playing field.

Wotton's thinking also resembles the ideology identified here with the
later proponents of a different kind of ancient (i.e., contrapuntal) music
in his more conspicuously élitist approach than Wallis. Wallis's self-
conscious musical sophistication may give the impression that he too
was something of an élitist, but it is nevertheless significant that the
musical approach he advocates as an ideal is specifically calculated to

---

[71] Wallis, 'A Letter of Dr. John Wallis', pp. 298–9.

[72] William Wotton, *Reflections on Ancient and Modern Learning*, 2nd edn (London,
1697), p. 331.

[73] Ibid., p. 329.

appeal to relatively uncultivated listeners. The melody-dominated style Wallis advocates does not 'obscure the emphatick Expressions (like what we call *Recitative-Musick*)' and therefore 'will work strangely upon the Ear'.[74] He thinks such music 'must needs operate strongly on the Fancies and Affections of ordinary People', even those 'unacquainted with such kind of Treatments'.[75]

Wotton, by contrast, is more inclined to stress an intellectual appreciation of music based on abstract qualities.[76] Modern listeners, Wotton believes, employ the 'Understanding' in the perception of art, whereas the ancients had had to depend on an ultimately less satisfying appeal to the 'passions'.[77] Sounding much like a later disciple of ancient music, Wotton notes that

> in making a judgment of *Music*, it is much the same thing as it is in making a judgment of *Pictures*. A great judge in *Painting* does not gaze upon an exquisite Piece, so much to raise his passions, as to inform his *Judgment*, as to approve, or to find fault: His Eye runs over every Part, to find out every Excellency; and his pleasure lies in the Reflex Act of his Mind, when he knows he can judiciously tell where every Beauty lies, or where the defects are discernible: Which an ordinary Spectator would never find out.[78]

As for less informed judges of painting (or, as might be added in this case, music), Wotton notes that 'the chiefest thing which this Man minds, is the Story; and if that is lively represented, if the Figures do not laugh when they should weep, or weep when they should appear pleased, he is satisfied, if there are no obvious Faults committed any where else'.[79] Thus, even though Wotton concedes, as Crotch later did, that 'the great end of *Music*, which is to please the Audience, was Anciently, perhaps, better answered than now', he does not view satisfying a mass audience as the highest purpose music can have.[80]

Classic and Gothic

One of the most ubiquitous myths of eighteenth-century art is the story of how the idealized art of the ancients was corrupted in the Dark Ages

---

[74] Wallis, 'A Letter of Dr. John Wallis', p. 300.

[75] Ibid.

[76] John Locke, *An Essay Concerning Human Understanding*, ed. Peter H. Niddeth (Oxford: Clarendon Press, 1975), p. 156.

[77] Ibid.

[78] Wotton, *Reflections*, p. 331.

[79] Ibid., p. 332.

[80] Ibid., p. 333.

at the hands of Gothic barbarians.[81] One part of this myth is visible in the writing of Wesley, Stillingfleet and Molleson. In the context of their writing and with the individuals quoted briefly above in mind, it appears that Burney was right: the literary man's continuing, credulous acceptance of the fantastic accounts of the music of antiquity was no remnant of a dying classical tradition, but rather a weapon that men of letters with a particular moral fervour could take up in a struggle with ill-educated professionals and élitists who were taking music and music criticism in directions they could not follow.

The musical judgements of Wallis and Wotton above show none of the defensiveness one finds a century later in the writing of men of letters who are less confident about their right to make judgements on music. Shortly before Burney reviewed Stillingfleet's *Principles and Power of Harmony*, a divine named William Hughes complained in a pamphlet on church music that Thomas Tallis had 'sacrificed the whole Sense and meaning of the Te Deum for the Sake of his Favorite Counter-Point'.[82] Like Stillingfleet and Mason, Hughes expects professional men to object:

> If I was to own that I could not be pleas'd at a Discourse I did not understand, my Confession would have nothing singular in it. But, was I to say the same thing of a Piece of Musick, a Musician might ask me if I thought my self a Connoisseur enough to enter into the Merits of a Piece of Musick that has been work'd up with the greatest Care? And I would venture to reply Yes; for the Business of Musick is to move.[83]

'The Literati in Harmonicks are of an Opinion (as I have often heard)', he opines contemptuously, 'that Mr. Tallis's Harmony is an excellent

---

[81] The concept 'Gothic', especially as contrasted with its inevitable opposite 'Classic' has been the subject of several important studies, especially Arthur O. Lovejoy, 'The First Gothic Revival and the Return to Nature', *Modern Language Notes*, 27 (1932), 414–46, reprinted in Lovejoy, *Essays in the History of Ideas* (Baltimore, MD: Johns Hopkins Press, 1948), pp. 135–65; Lawrence Lipking, *The Ordering of the Arts* (Princeton, NJ: Princeton University Press, 1970) pp. 146–55; Wayne Dynes, 'Gothic, Concept of', in Philip P. Wiener, ed., *Dictionary of the History of Ideas*, 5 vols (New York: Scribner, 1973–4) vol. II, pp. 366–74; Sherard Vines, *The Course of English Classicism from the Tudor to the Victorian Age* (New York: Harcourt, Brace, and Co., 1930; reprinted New York: Phaeton Press, 1968); Kenneth Clark, *The Gothic Revival: an Essay in the History of Taste* (New York: Humanities Press, 1970), and Paul Frankl, *The Gothic: Literary Sources and Interpretations through Eight Centuries* (Princeton, NJ: Princeton University Press, 1960).

[82] William Hughes, *Remarks Upon Church Musick, to which are added Several Observations upon some of Mr. Handel's Oratorios and other Parts of his Works*, 2nd edn (Worchester, 1763), p. 26.

[83] Ibid., p. 37.

Piece of *Counter-Point*, nay the very best Piece of *Counter-Point* that ever was compos'd'.[84] This, however, is not what Hughes believes music should be about. 'Let us have a little Life, a little Spirit, a little Invention', he insists, outlining a position with which the later moderns would have agreed.[85] Moderns like Mason would also have agreed with his quotation from Addison in *The Spectator* to the effect that 'Musick is not design'd to please only chromatick Ears, but all that are capable of distinguishing harsh and disagreeable Notes. A man of ordinary Capacity is a Judge whether a Passion is expressed in proper Sounds, and whether the Melody of those Sounds be more or less pleasing'.[86]

The literary man's answer to attacks on his fitness as a critic was to resurrect a version of the story of a simple and rational classical art that could fulfil the eighteenth century's most illusive aesthetic fantasies in a way that no real music ever could. This Greek music of the imagination not only exhibited properties far superior to music of the present but was still somehow capable of being understood by everyone on first hearing. Tragically, as the story goes, the fantastic art of antiquity was lost when Gothic barbarians, in a misguided attempt at progress, contributed the only improvement of which they were capable: they loaded it with meaningless ornaments, just as the fabled young painter, unable to render Helen more beautiful, is said to have arrayed her in gaudy apparel.[87] Though it is usually applied to old music by individuals who see themselves as progressives, the ubiquitous pejorative adjective 'Gothic' is informed by a myth that serves as a cautionary tale on the dangers of artistic progress.

Gothic, in the sense the word is of interest here, describes a principle rather than a specific kind of art or a period in history. Addison called it a 'Gothick manner' and identified it in a variety of artistic media, including a few passing references to music. Most literary men left music out of their discussions altogether, possibly because the concept was a difficult

---

[83] Ibid., p. 37.

[84] Ibid., p. 25.

[85] Ibid., p. 27.

[86] Ibid., p. 27 n. See *The Spectator* for 3 April 1711: 'Musick, Architecture and Painting, as well as Poetry and Oratory, are to deduce their Laws and Rules from the general Sense and Taste of Mankind, and not from the Principles of those Arts themselves; or in other Words the Taste is not to conform to the Art, but the Art to the Taste. Musick is not design'd to please only Chromatick Ears, but all that are capable of distinguishing harsh from disagreeable Notes.' Quoted in John Neubauer, *The Emancipation of Music From Language: Departure from Mimesis in Eighteenth-Century Aesthetics* (New Haven, CT, and London: Yale University Press, 1986), p. 60.

[87] Crotch gives his own version of this story of the young painter in *Lectures*, NRO, MS 11229/7.

one to apply to music but also because few before the publication of the rival music histories in 1776 were in a position to understand what the ancient music was like or what the Middle Ages could have done to corrupt it. It was, therefore, the earliest critic from the ranks of professional musicians, Charles Avison – with the questionable behind-the-scenes assistance of William Mason – who first described an approach to music that might be analogous to Addison's 'Gothick manner'.[88]

Avison and Burney both offer confused and inconsistent interpretations of what the concept Gothic means as it might be applied to music. Before considering their unorthodox formulations, it will be useful to look more carefully at more typical qualities of this principle as it was known at the time. First, much like the notion 'modern music', which reveals itself fully only by contrast with an ancient-music opposite, the notion Gothic is illuminated by opposition with its often implicit companion, Classic. Thomas Warton's *Verses on Sir Joshua Reynolds's Painted Window at New College, Oxford*, published the year Burney's second volume of the *General History* appeared in 1782, offers a succinct presentation of this opposition. Acting under the influence of a recent conversion to the principles of Reynolds's neo-classicism, Warton's poem repents an earlier appreciation of Gothic architecture. 'Thy powerful hand', Warton writes, has 'broke the Gothic chain/And brought my bosom back to truth again;/ To truth, by no peculiar taste confin'd,/Whose universal pattern strikes mankind'.[89] Warton's Gothic is seductive and unruly; it is 'By no Vitruvian symmetry subdu'd',[90] especially by comparison with the simple truth of rational, disciplined neo-classicism. This truth is a restraining force on the imagination, a force whose 'bold and unresisted aim/Checks frail caprice, and fashion's fickle claim'.[91] It is truth 'whose charms deception's magic quell,/and bind coy Fancy in a stronger spell'.[92] The Gothic cathedral, on the other hand, is a place 'Where elfin sculptors, with fantastic clew,/O'er the long roof their wild embroidery drew;/Where SUPERSTITION with capricious hand/In many a maze the wreathed window plann'd'.[93]

---

[88] For Dryden's treatment of the Gothic in drama and painting see 'A Parallel of Poetry and Painting', in George Watson, ed., *John Dryden: of Dramatic Poesy and other Critical Essays*, 2 vols (London: J. M. Dent, 1962), vol. 2, p. 202. In essays in *The Spectator* Addison applies this idea to various arts, including Italian opera in *The Spectator*, no. 63. *The Spectator*, ed. Donald F. Bond, 5 vols (Oxford: Oxford University Press, 1965), vol. 1, p. 271.

[89] *The Poetical Works of the Late Thomas Warton*, 5th edn 2 vols (Oxford, 1802), vol. 1, pp. 63–4.

[90] Ibid., p. 28.

[91] Ibid., pp. 67–8.

[92] Ibid., pp. 69–70.

[93] Ibid., pp. 21–4.

This conception of the Gothic as a product of unbridled imagination is consistent with another writer who was much closer intellectually to Burney than Warton, Horace Walpole. Walpole's *Anecdotes of Painting* contrasts the 'rational beauties of regular architecture' with the 'unrestrained licentiousness of that which is called Gothic'.[94] 'One must have taste to be sensible of the beauties of Grecian architecture', but 'one only wants passions to feel Gothic'.[95] 'Gothic churches infuse superstition', Walpole writes, 'Grecian, admiration'.[96] Likewise, the French encyclopaedists whose aesthetic is very often visible in Burney's writing defined 'Gothique' in painting as 'a manner which does not recognize any rules, is not directed by any study of the ancients, and in which one can only perceive a caprice which has nothing noble in it'.[97]

Since music had no tradition of the use of this word it had to invent the concept anew in the eighteenth century, drawing from contemporary and in some cases noticeably ideological speech. In common usage as an epithet, Gothic meant something like tasteless or crude. Burney, accordingly, writes of those 'who call [Handel's] style of composition Gothic, inelegant & clumsy'.[98] Gothic in this epithetic sense is a comment on taste and fashion and, therefore, is usually applied to ancient music rather than modern and to audiences more often than to music itself. Thus, Handel's critic Robert Price[99] calls the British public 'abominable Goths' who 'cannot bear anything but Handel, Courelli, and Geminiani, which they are eternally playing ever and ever again at all their concerts'[100] and John Lockman says he 'would not be thought so much a *Goth*, as not to have any Taste for *Italian* Operas in general'.[101]

---

[94] Horace Walpole, *Anecdotes of Painting in England*, 4 vols (London: printed for J. Dodsley, 1782), vol. 1, p. 120.

[95] Ibid., p. 119.

[96] Ibid.

[97] Denis Diderot, Jean le Rond d'Alembert and Pierre Mouchon, *Encyclopédie ou Dictionnaire raisonné des sciences, des arts et des métiers, 1751–1772*, 35 vols (Paris, 1751–80; Stuttgart-Bad Cannstatt: Frommann, 1966) s.v. 'Gothic': 'une maniere qui ne reconnoît aucune regle, qui n'est dirigée par aucune étude de l'antique, & dans laquelle on n'apperçoit qu'un caprice qui n' rein de noble'.

[98] CB to Sir Robert Murray Keith, 9 November 1784 in Ribeiro, *Letters*, p. 446.

[99] In *Handel: a Documentary Biography* (New York: W. W. Norton, 1955), p. 529, Otto Deutsch identifies Price as the author of the critical section (i.e., pp. 165 to the end) of John Mainwaring's *Memoirs of the Life of the Late George Frederic Handel* (London, 1760; New York: Da Capo Press,1980).

[100] From a letter to Thomas, Earl of Haddington, dated 19 December 1741 in Deutsch, *Handel*, p. 528.

[101] John Lockman, preface to *Rosalinda, a Musical Drama. To which is prefixed, An Enquiry into the Rise and Progress of OPERAS and ORATORIOS, with some Reflections on LYRIC POETRY and MUSIC* (London, 1740).

The ancient-music associations of this concept of the Gothic together with the familiar, often unmerited, stereotype of ancient music as noisy and unrefined, recall a connotation of the word Gothic suggesting dullness and insensitivity.[102] Burney remarks that viols appeared in Elizabethan times only in smaller, chamber-music settings because they 'were too feeble for the obtuse organs of our Gothic ancestors'.[103] One is reminded of the writing of opposition figures like Mason, who remarks, 'Let Handel's music vibrate on the tough drum of royal ears; I am for none of it.'[104]

A musical use of the notion Gothic that better resembles Warton's thoughtful formulation connects the idea with fashionable opera rather than inelegant ancient music and does so, in fact, not only because it views opera as over-refined and decadent but because the form's popularity suggests a transient appeal. In *The Spectator* No. 63, Addison relates his dream of 'a Monstrous Fabrick built after the *Gothick* manner' that turns out to be 'a kind of Heathen Temple consecrated to the God of *Dullness*'.[105] In it, he finds the 'Deity of the Place dressed in the Habit of a Monk', upon whose 'right hand was *Industry* ... and on his left *Caprice*'.[106] Gothic music appears in a 'region of false Wit' alongside anagrams, acrosticks, chronograms and rebuses. There, amid 'Trees blossom'd in Leaf-Gold' Addison says 'The Fountains bubbled in an Opera Tune'.[107] Elsewhere, Addison stresses, again, the need for an enduring, universal art when he extols the virtues of 'an ordinary Song or Ballad that is the Delight of the common People' because it 'cannot fail to please all such Readers as are not unqualified for the Entertainment by their Affectation or Ignorance'.[108] Had the old ballad Chevy Chase 'been written in the *Gothic* Manner' Addison observes, 'which is

---

[102] Price's treatment of Handel in Mainwaring's biography make the music simultaneously into a music of unrefined, common people and connoisseurs. He remarks (*Memoirs of the Life of the Late George Frederic Handel* [London, 1760; New York: Da Capo Press, 1980], pp. 191–2) that 'there are indeed but few persons sufficiently versed in Music, to perceive either the particular propriety and justness, or the general union and consent, of all the parts in these complicated pieces. However, it is very remarkable that some persons, on whom the finest modulations would have little or no effect, have been greatly struck with HANDEL's chorusses. This is probably owing to that grandeur of conception, which predominates in them; and which, as coming purely from Nature, is the more strongly, and the more generally felt'.

[103] Burney, *General History*, vol. 2, p. 123.

[104] John Draper, *William Mason: a Study in Eighteenth-Century Culture* (New York: New York University Press, 1924), p. 301.

[105] *The Spectator*, vol. 1, p. 271.

[106] Ibid.

[107] Ibid.

[108] Ibid., p. 321.

the Delight of all our little Wits, whether Writers or Readers, it would not have hit the Taste of so many Ages, and have pleased the Readers of all Ranks and Conditions'.[109]

The most significant difference between the Gothic of the earlier eighteenth century and the concept at Burney's time is the latter's greater stress on the Gothic as a fickle creation of the imagination and, therefore, on the qualities of capriciousness, sensuality and intellectual weakness. The epithets above notwithstanding, it is, one might think, the modern style that would be more susceptible to this later eighteenth-century interpretation of the Gothic than ancient music. Aside from the common association of the modern style with the imagination, Gothic is often viewed – much as the modern style is viewed even by its friends – as a seductive trifle to which ordinarily sober people are lured out of boredom with the plain, predictable reason. 'When genuine elegance in furniture or architecture has been long the fashion', Alexander Gerard writes, 'men sometimes grow weary of it, and imitate the Chinese, or revive the Gothic taste, merely for the pleasure they receive from what is unlike to those things which they have been accustomed to see. The pleasure of novelty is, in this case, preferred to that which results from real beauty'.[110]

It is important at this juncture to examine once again the melody–harmony opposition that has figured so prominently in virtually all the criticism considered to this point. By long tradition, the musical domains of harmony and melody were linked with separate operations of the mind based on familiar categories of eighteenth-century British psychology. As mathematician and music theorist Alexander Malcolm put it in his *Treatise of Music Speculative, Practical, and Historical* (Edinburgh, 1721),

> *Melody* is chiefly the Business of the Imagination; so that the Rules of *Melody* serve only to prescribe certain Limits to it, beyond which the Imagination, in searching out the Variety and Beauty of Air, ought not to carry us: But *Harmony* is the Work of Judgment; so that its Rules are more certain, extensive, and in Practice more difficult. In the Variety and Elegancy of the *Melody*, the Invention labours a great deal more than the Judgment; but in *Harmony* the Invention has nothing to do, for by an exact Observation of the Rules of *Harmony* it may be produced without that Assistance from the Imagination.[111]

---

[109] Ibid.

[110] Alexander Gerard, *An Essay on Taste* (Edinburgh, 1764; facsimile reprint New York, Garland, 1970), p. 7.

[111] Alexander Malcolm, *A Treatise of Music Speculative, Practical, and Historical* (Edinburgh, 1721; New York: Da Capo Press, 1970), p. 420.

For some, melody was a symbol of the grace that lies beyond the reach of art and a positive quality. Francis Bacon writes that 'a painter may make a better face than ever was, but he must do it by a kind of felicity (as a musician that maketh an excellent air in music), and not by rule'.[112] Musicians, however, were often frustrated by this same quality. Roger North, for whom 'ayre' (or 'air') meant something more complex and less distinct from harmony than Avison, wrote that 'it seems odd to give descriptions and caracters to a thing so litle understood as musicall ayre is – a meer *je ne scay quoy*',[113] but he still tried to rationalize it on several occasions. In the end, he was forced to conclude that air 'is no more to be taught than witt, or a good style in wrighting' because 'in the first place it seems that Air is in great measure derived from the accidentall flights of fancy in some masters'.[114]

That air cannot be reconciled with reason became a truism of eighteenth-century criticism. It is an idea, North complains, that 'from Musick ... hath bin translated to the vulgar, who call *air* every singular disposition not literally expressible, as the air of a man's face, and the like'.[115] In Burney's case, the impossibility of reducing melody to rules was a primary cause of the mutability of styles that rely primarily on melody as a means of expression. In one of his many digressions on music's ephemeral nature, he justifies his art's continual obsolescence, which in this case he accepts cheerfully as a matter of course, by observing that 'melody ... being a child of Fancy and Imagination, will submit to no theory or laws of Reason and Philosophy; and therefore, like Love, will always continue in childhood'.[116] Elsewhere, he explains why music cannot have the classical status of the literary arts by observing that 'poetry does not lose so much by age as Melody, which is a mere child of fancy'.[117] As an example, he cites the fact that 'the poetry of Milton, Dryden, and Pope, is now in as high estimation as ever' but 'the melodies of Henry Lawes, Dr. Blow, and Dr. Green, the favourites of their day are become uncouth and vulgar'.[118]

At one point in the *General History* Burney seems temporarily to entertain the idea that this deficiency might also apply to harmony. He

---

[112] Francis Bacon, *Essays, Advancement of Learning, New Atlantis, and other Pieces*, ed. R. F. Jones (New York, P. F. Collier, *c.* 1937), p. 125.

[113] Roger North, *Roger North on Music: Being a Selection from his Essays Written during the Years c. 1695–1728*, (London: Novello, 1959), pp. 67–8.

[114] Ibid., p. 68.

[115] Ibid., p. 73.

[116] Burney, *General History*, vol. 2, p. 150.

[117] Charles Burney, Review of *Melody the Soul of Music: an Essay towards the improvement of the Musical Art*, by Alexander Molleson, *Monthly Review*, 27(1798), p. 191.

[118] Ibid.

notes in the course of his study of early music that the preferred intervals upon which music is based have changed over the centuries. This
prompts the observation that, 'a few tonal and fundamental laws ex-
cepted, [melody] is abandoned to all the caprice and vagaries of
imagination. But that the immutable laws of harmony should be subject
to the vicissitudes of fashion, is wonderful'.[119] Since there has been 'a
mode and *fashion* to Harmony, as well as Melody', he concludes, 'little
hope can remain to the artist that his productions, like those of the
poet, painter, or architect, can be blest with longevity!'[120]

By the time the third and fourth volumes of the *General History* were
published some years later, he seems to have reached an understanding
that these fashions of harmony were simply stages in a development
process and that, once it achieved its mature form, harmony became the
relatively changeless component he assumes it to be in other places.[121]
His concerns about music's mutability mostly appear after this point in
the *General History* and should be seen as applicable to musical species
in which the quality of melody is predominant – i.e., homophonic
secular music and particularly the theatre style – and not to the art as a
whole. This is clarified in a discussion of the lesser composers of
Palestrina's orbit, in which Burney praises the sacred contrapuntal writing of Antonio Cifra but is less impressed by his homophonic secular
productions. He attributes this disparity to the fact that 'harmony and
fugue are long-lived; but no powers of invention can give longevity to
divisions and embellishments, which are either written for particular
talents, or the gratification of caprice and fashion'.[122]

It is interesting, in view of this background, that Burney never applies
the word Gothic to the modern style and rarely uses it in connection
with melody.[123] Instead, it is invariably in discussions of harmony and
ancient music that his most elaborate treatments of the concept are

---

[119] Burney, *General History*, vol. 1, p. 557.

[120] Ibid.

[121] Later in the second volume there is an acknowledgement that melody and harmony
are different, though in this case the longevity of Harmony is relative. He observes
(Burney, *General History*, vol. 1, p. 713) that 'with respect to melody, its flights will ever
be so wild and capricious, as to elude all laws, or require a new code every year; it is as
subject to change, as the surface of the sea, or the fluctuating images of an active mind.
But harmony is somewhat more permanent; however, *that* cannot be long fixed by
immutable laws'.

[122] Ibid., vol. 2, p. 165.

[123] When he does use 'Gothic' in connection with melody, the word has more the
character of an historical term or an epithet rather than an abstract, non-historical
principle of musical style. 'At the revival of letters', Burney remarks in *General History*,
vol. 1, p. 528, 'when poetry began again to flourish', melody 'was so Gothic and devoid
of grace, that good poets disdained its company or assistance'.

found. The Gothic's greater definition and substance in this setting – especially by comparison with the casual epithets applied to ancient music and its partisans above – is accompanied, however, by two completely different understandings of what the Gothic is. Alexander Molleson quotes a good example of one of these formulations in his pamphlet 'Melody the Soul of Music' in order to show Burney's supposed primitivist sympathies. This version of music's corruption myth originally appeared in the *General History* in connection with invention of recitative. It begins at a point at which music has already received its fatal wound and is in need of a renaissance. Before recitative was invented and a rational music with a new relationship to its sister art of poetry was reborn, musicians are said to have been 'chiefly employed in gratifying the ear with "the concord of sweet sounds," without respect to poetry, or aspiring at energy, passion, intellectual pleasure, or much variety of effect'.[124] This corrupt, intricate and sensual music was characterized by a rage for 'fugue, elaborate contrivance and the laboured complication of different parts', that rendered texts unintelligible.[125] Happily, however, music was saved by 'lovers of poetry' who were already 'meditating the means of rescuing her from musical pedants, who, with a true Gothic spirit, had loaded her with cumbrous ornaments, in order, as was pretended, to render her more fine, beautiful, and pleasing'.[126]

This construction of the Gothic is, of course, all very conventional. By contrast, in Burney's discussion of the sacred music of the High Renaissance, he writes that as the sixteenth century opened, 'Melody, itself the child of fancy, was still held in Gothic chains' which were appropriate because 'to check imagination's wild vagaries, and restrain her wanton flights' is 'not only required by propriety, but duty' in sacred music.[127] This second understanding of the Gothic, then, exactly reverses the idea as it is usually understood, giving it the qualities of order, discipline and restraint over the excesses of the imagination that are more typical of its opposite, Classic. Further, although Burney's first and relatively conventional understanding of the Gothic is the more common, his second formulation is given support in other places, including what is effectively his last word on this subject. His article 'Gothic' for Rees's *Cyclopaedia* begins by clearly associating the word as a critical term in music with the contrapuntal style of ancient music. Fugues and canons are not condemned in this case as 'unmeaning' or

---

124 Ibid., vol. 2, p. 506.
125 Ibid.
126 Ibid., p. 508.
127 Ibid., p. 128.

'Barb'rous Jargon', however, they are praised instead as music for 'inteligent hearers' that 'can never become vulgar or obsolete', at least in their proper domain of sacred music.[128] He even attempts to transform the word 'Gothic' itself from a term of derision to a neutral term of description when he claims that Spanish theorist Antonio Eximeno's reference to fugues and canons as 'Gothic compositions' does not 'disgrace their structure any more than he would our cathedrals, by calling them Gothic buildings'.[129]

The quality of restraint that is typically a part of Burney's conception of the Gothic is a familiar element of the literary Gothic as well. Fanny Burney's description of Walpole's Gothic villa Strawberry Hill, based on her father's brief visit there in 1786, captures the gloomy essence of it:

> And Strawberry Hill itself, with all its chequered and interesting varieties of detail, had something in its whole of monotony, that cast, insensibly, over its visitors, an indefinable species of secret constraint; and made cheerfulness rather the effect of effort than the spring of pleasure; by keeping more within bounds than belongs to their bouyant love of liberty, those light, airy, darting, bursts of unsought gaiety, yclept animal spirits.[130]

But Dr Burney's restraint is not the stuff of Walpole's *Castle of Otrano: a Gothic story*, it is a usage with profoundly ideological overtones that resembles an application of the word Gothic described by A. O. Lovejoy. This connotation, which Lovejoy associates with progressive characterizations of Tories, includes the general sense of 'old fashioned' but also carries a suggestion of illiberality and stemming from an implied linkage with feudalism. Lovejoy cites yet another use of the 'Gothic chain' image, in an *Ode* by Mark Akenside that eulogizes the Restoration as a point at which 'England spurns her Gothic Chain,/and equal laws and social science reign'.[131]

When Gothic takes on the meaning of pedantic or is associated with unjust and arbitrary laws it is important to note who is subject to repression. Burney constantly inveighs against the 'trammels of canon, fugue, and other restraints'[132] in which music was held for much of its history as he knew it, and in each case he refers to restrictions that would be both visited upon and evident to musicians rather than audiences of non-specialists. The same is true when he calls figured bass a

---

[128] Abraham Rees, ed., *The cyclopaedia; or, Universal Dictionary of Arts, Sciences, and Literature*, 39 vols (London, 1802–19), s.v. 'Gothic'.

[129] Ibid.

[130] Frances (Burney) d'Arblay, *Memoirs of Doctor Burney*, 3 vols (London, 1832), vol. 2, p. 69.

[131] Lovejoy, 'The First Gothic Revival', p. 136.

[132] Burney, *General History*, vol. 2, p. 517.

'Gothic restraint',[133] that is, a restraint on the imagination of the composer. It may seem odd for Burney to have seized upon this particular aspect of the Gothic since Gothic as a critical term usually describes art from the perspective of the audience, not the artist; cathedrals are Gothic, after all, not because of any arbitrary restrictions to which their anonymous builders were subjected but rather because they confuse the eye with a flood of images that forces the mind to suspend rational analysis. This difference of perspectives is, admittedly, less an issue in some arts than in music, where the perceptions of musician and audience are conditioned by radically different levels of skill and training.

The fact that music can be heard completely differently depending on the skill and preparation of the hearer helps to explain the dual nature of counterpoint as both highly ordered and in some sense disorderly in Burney's various formulations of the Gothic. A distinction – found almost exclusively in professional music criticism – that is relevant to this difference in critical perspectives is often made between the perceptions of the ear and the eye. Burney writes of the thirteenth-century rota *Sumer is icumen in* that 'its defects may not be discovered by every *Ear* during the performance, [but] it is hardly clean and pure enough to satisfy the *Eye*, in score: as many liquors may be tolerably palatable, and yet not bear a glass'.[134] He is usually reluctant to allow that music can be appreciated as an intellectual art at all by listeners unless they have the aid of the score. He observes elsewhere, with respect to the counterpoint of the High Renaissance, that 'the ears of the congregation seem to have been less consulted than the eye of the performer, who was to solve canonical mysteries, and discover latent beauties of ingenuity and contrivance, about which the hearers were indifferent, provided the general harmony was pleasing'.[135] To this he contrasts the musician's point of view, adding that 'the performer's attention was kept on the stretch, and perhaps he gained, in mental amusement, what was wanting in sensual'.[136]

Recasting the corruption myth

Confusion often results when professional musicians shift from one perspective to another – that is, from the ear to the eye – without recognizing the potential for contradiction. Sometimes this occurs when

---

[133] Ibid., p. 352 n.
[134] Ibid., vol. 1, p. 682.
[135] Ibid., vol. 2, pp. 738–9.
[136] Ibid.

they try to accommodate the mythology handed them by men of letters who served as their unacknowledged consultants. Such an alternation of perspectives can be found in the work of Charles Avison. When Avison introduces music's corruption myth in his *Essay on Musical Expression*, his initial focus is on the effect of counterpoint on the listener. Music began to degenerate when counterpoint was invented during the middle ages. The 'plodding Geniusses of those Times (and since, their rigid Followers)' discovered new laws of harmony, which they used to corrupt the 'true Simplicity' of the music of antiquity by introducing a '*Confusion of Parts*'. This '*Confusion of Parts*, like the numerous and trifling Ornaments in the *Gothic Architecture*', was 'productive of no other Pleasure, than that of wondering at the Patience and Minuteness of the Artist'.[137]

Avison's Gothic, like Addison's before him, is characterized by useless and confusing ornaments, the intricateness of which was supposed to destroy the effect of unity needed for great art. As it applies to writing, Addison's Gothick manner also employs 'False wit', a shortcoming that has affinities with the musical Gothic in that the false wit of anagrams and rebuses requires industry of its creator rather than 'solid sense and elegant expression'.[138] It is a waste of effort both for the artist and the reader who must struggle to understand it, only to find that it has nothing to say. False wit can also be based on inappropriate similarities, as in 'Puns and Quibbles' that give the impression of being reasonable but only to what Addison identifies as the lowest class of reader.[139]

The first indication of trouble in Avison's *Essay* appears in the first of his chapters on musical style, which has to do with the fault of '*too close Attachment to* AIR, *and the Neglect of* HARMONY'. It is not harmony but melody, that Avison associates with the lowest class of listener. He indicates that music in which 'Harmony and Fugues' are neglected in favour of the questionable pleasure of a '*tedious solo*', is in fact 'apt, above all others, at first hearing, to strike an unskilful ear'.[140] More serious inconsistencies appear in the following chapter, 'On the too close Attachment to HARMONY, and Neglect of AIR'. There, in the brief statement of the corruption myth quoted above, Avison shifts perspectives from the confusion of the listener trying to comprehend a meaningless babble of contrapuntal lines to the pleasure of the musician 'wondering at the Patience and Minuteness of the Artist'. The latter betrays more admiration for the musical Gothic than Addison ever had

---

[137] Avison, *Essay*, pp. 46–7.
[138] Bond, *The Spectator*, vol. 1, pp. 268–9.
[139] Ibid.
[140] Avison, *Essay*, p. 34.

for its literary equivalent in his *Spectator* essays, where 'anagrams, chronograms and acrosticks', could produce no legitimate pleasure however intricately crafted they might be.

To complicate matters, Avison observes only a few pages after the 'plodding Geniusses' passage above that some composers, by 'the Force of their Genius and the wonderful Construction of their Fugues and Harmony, hath excited the Admiration of all succeeding Ages', extending to contrapuntal music the timelessness of Classical art.[141] It is also of interest that Avison's Gothic was created in the first place when the Middle Ages invented new laws of harmony. An essential element of Gothic as a critical concept is that it was a creation of medieval ignorance. As Paul Frankl puts it, the early eighteenth century 'acted as though the mediaeval architects really *should* have and *would* have built Greek temples had it not been that they were unfortunately *unable* to do so before Vitruvius was rediscovered'.[142] In music, on the other hand, critics had to explain how music could have been corrupted by harmonic innovations that were commonly viewed as legitimate progress, since it was widely though not universally accepted that harmony in all its forms was a modern invention, unknown to the ancient Greeks. Even those who saw elaborate counterpoint as a regrettable stage in musical development would mostly have agreed that harmony itself was a significant advance.

Avison's solution to this problem was to suggest that the music of the Greeks did not consist of only a single melodic line after all but may have been accompanied by 'plain unperplexed harmony'.[143] Counterpoint could then be recognized as a degenerate medieval application of a pre-existing harmonic practice. This had the virtue of making the music of antiquity seem less primitive while at the same time conferring classical sanction to the 'modern' homophonic style, to which ancient Greek music now bore a striking resemblance.

Burney may have been too honest or knowledgeable a historian to use this strategy, but he was also unconvinced that artless simplicity in music was a virtue. Since he did not accept that the Greeks had harmony in any form, he thought of their music as monophonic and simply primitive. The invention of counterpoint therefore actually *was* an improvement in his mind, though in some of his scenarios it was carried to an unfortunate excess by later figures. His several attempts to apply the Classic–Gothic opposition to music consequently tend to avoid the subject of the music of antiquity and focus on ways in which counter-

---

[141] Ibid., p. 49.
[142] Frankl, *The Gothic*, p. 366.
[143] Avison, *Essay*, p. 46.

point can be both an improvement in some sense *and* a product of corruption. One way to do this involved transplanting the corruption myth to a new point in time, the beginning of the seventeenth century. This rearrangement puts the onset of corruption conveniently after the invention of harmony and coincident with the earliest operas. In fact, Burney usually treats counterpoint as a product of corruption only in secular music, which he imagines effectively to have begun with opera. Because of this transplantation of the myth he was also able to accomplish a separation that is implied but often not directly stated in the criticism of other arts, between Gothic as a timeless principle in art and Gothic as a racial or historical designation.

The most essential element of the corruption myth as it has surfaced repeatedly in this book – a simple earlier music that everyone could understand and appreciate that was corrupted by misguided attempts at progress – remains in Burney's transplanted version, but in place of the ancient Greeks he substitutes early opera composers. 'The airs of the first operas were few and simple', Burney writes, expressing almost as unrealistic a view of early opera as literary men had for the music of antiquity they had never heard,[144] 'but as singing improved, and orchestras became more crouded, the voice-parts were more laboured, and the accompaniments more complicated.' This corruption came about because of the

> pedantry of musicians, who forgetting that the true characteristic of dramatic music is clearness; and that sound being the vehicle of poetry and colouring of passion, the instant the business of the drama is forgotten, and the words are unintelligible, music is so totally separated from poetry, that it becomes merely instrumental.[145]

In this instance, the musical renaissance was begun by Leonardo Vinci, who, 'without degrading his art, rendered it the friend, though not the slave to poetry'.[146] He did this, by 'simplifying and polishing melody, and calling the attention of the audience chiefly to the voice-part, by disentangling it from fugue, complication, and laboured contrivance'.[147]

The capacity of music's corruption myth to bear transplantation to almost any time period can be seen as well in Crotch's lectures. Crotch

---

[144] Burney actually had access to very little in the way of early seventeenth-century opera, as Kerry S. Grant reports, *Dr. Burney as Critic and Historian of Music* Ann Arbor, MI: UMI Research Press, 1983), p. 226. In *General History*, vol. 2, p. 546 (as cited by Grant), Burney calls the arias of Cavalli's *Erismena* 'psalmodic, monotonous, and dull' and is amused to see 'how contented, and even charmed, the public is at one period with what appears contemptible at another'.

[145] Rees, *Cyclopaedia*, s.v. 'Vinci'.

[146] Ibid.

[147] Ibid.

uses it, predictably, to explain the birth of the ornamental style, which
in this case was not invented by Domenico Scarlatti or even Pergolesi
but a group of late seventeenth-century composers:

> The composers, at the period of which we are treating, finding that
> it was difficult if not impossible to rival the simple grandeur and
> chaste beauty of their predecessors in church music, madrigals, and
> songs, attended more to instrumental music, adopted a more la-
> boured and intricate harmony, a more chromatic and capricious
> melody, and in short cultivated the ornamental style. But as this
> was an addition to what was already invented and as the sublime
> and the beautiful were not yet superseded, we must consider music
> as still improving in proportion as its boundaries were enlarged.[148]

Crotch relates this pattern directly to architecture, noting that 'in our
national architecture the massive strangeness and plainness of the Saxon
and Norman buildings were productive of the sublime' while 'the taper
shaft and springing arch of those of a later period were eminently
beautiful'.[149] It was only 'when grandeur and elegance were obscured
by profuse decoration', that 'the Gothic architecture soon fell and ex-
pired'. Accordingly, Crotch remarks that 'even from church music (which
ought ever to be the pattern of what is sober, dignified and solemn) the
ornamental style has not been entirely excluded'. This is acceptable to
him as long as the ornamental does not take on undue prominence. He
specifically objects, however, to 'the organ voluntary where extempore
performers giving the reigns to their fancy and impressed with the
passages which they have heard in concerts or operas too frequently
divert the attention of the congregation from grave subjects of fix it on
such as are most unworthy and improper'.[150]

The organ voluntary has an interesting role to play in the present
summary of critical thinking about the need for a balance between
imagination and reason or freedom and discipline. Burney's central
difficulty as a critic and the cause of much of his inconsistency might be
attributed to the fact that music can appeal to the higher intellectual
faculties in two completely different ways: by virtue of its content or by
virtue of its contrapuntal structure. These two approaches to what
might be called rational music are, however, not merely different but
mutually antithetic. In order for music to appeal to the intellect by
virtue of a clear transmission of content, its structure must be simplified
to the point that the connoisseur can no longer take pleasure in the

---

[148] *Lectures*, NRO, MS 11232/13. This lecture concerns Blow, Creighton, Aldrich,
Durante, and Purcell.
[149] Ibid.
[150] Ibid.

ingenuity of its contrivance. With one main exception, it is only in the ideal setting of the mind that a dense contrapuntal texture can be fathomable *and* its associated content can be understood completely in unfamiliar music. That exception is the organ voluntary. Burney, quoting Rousseau, insists that it is 'principally, during such a prelude, that great Musicians, then exempted from that extreme subservience to rules, which the critical eye requires them to attend to on Paper, produce those brilliant and skilful transitions, which enrapture the Ears of an Audience'.[151] Accordingly, the one aspect of Handel's music about which both Burney and Mason can speak with undiluted praise is his ability as an 'improviser'.[152]

Crotch on the moderns

Crotch also suffers – though much less than Burney – from inconsistencies that stem from his accommodation of the ideas and critical commonplaces of literary men. In particular, Crotch's earliest lectures tend to defer to the opinions of the musical men of letters who preceded him in the criticism of ancient music, especially Jones of Nayland. Jones, in turn, often tries to criticize music in the language of the liberal arts. In the process he incorporates ideas from the sister arts that are superficially understood at best and in some cases well out of date as critical concepts in their original settings. Crotch's inconsistency is most noticeable in connection with the modern style, where his ideology occasionally interferes with objectivity. Tracing his thinking about the moderns and, more generally, his early development as a critic, requires dating the available lectures. This is not always possible with absolute precision, but with the aid of his *General Account of all the Courses of Lectures*, his correspondence, unpublished memoirs, pencilled-in marginalia and text that he over-scored in later versions of the lectures that can still be read at least partially, it is possible to piece together in

---

[151] Charles Burney, Review of *Essays, Historical and Critical on English Church Music*, by William Mason, *Monthly Review*, 20 (1796), pp. 399–400.

[152] Crotch, who did not know Handel as a living composer but as an idealized classical figure, had a different opinion. In *Lectures*, NRO, MS 11230/5, he remarks 'doubtless, many of these extempore productions are mere rhapsodies and the best are probably less correct and methodical than might be expected; but the merits of the pieces and their respective claims to preservation and immortal fame might be deliberately weighed after notation, and various alterations, corrections and improvements might be made by the authors themselves; and some of the more original and wild ideas which characterize these movements might be turned to good account in the way of expression on other occasions'.

some detail the pattern of his thinking about the moderns in the critical period from his early Oxford days to his mature lectures of 1818.

Crotch tells in the *General Account of all the Courses of Lectures* of how he prepared for his academic career by putting together 'extracts from Burney's History following the chronological order of the several compositions'.[153] Though he never used these materials in this form, the method by which he collected and organized Burney's thoughts is of some interest. First, Crotch's reference to structuring his lectures around 'the several compositions' as selected from those discussed in the *General History* reveals not only his unfortunate lack of confidence as a critic but his intention from the start to focus his presentations on a small body of paradigmatic works.[154] This is consistent with the lecture-performance approach for which Crotch later became known, and it is not surprising also to find indications in his earliest surviving notes that selected examples were performed. Since many of the examples he used are preserved in the *Specimens*, it is even possible in some cases to estimate the percentage of time – typically half or more of most presentations – he devoted to performance. This can also be estimated from the fact that Crotch often indicates the lectures were to last an hour, but the written text usually consists of somewhere between 2 000 and 3 000 words – at most, perhaps 20 minutes reading time at a moderate pace.[155]

Crotch soon abandoned the chronological organization of the *General History* in favour of dividing the Burney extracts into a course of 13 lectures based on the five 'styles' of church, oratorio, opera, concert and chamber. This attraction to categories that are based on style and are not strictly chronological is consistent with later organizational schemes. It should be noted, however, that the 'styles' described above, if discussed in the order in which Crotch lists them, approximate a

---

[153] *General Account*.

[154] With regard to Crotch's diffidence, his first Oxford lecture from 1798, now included in *Lectures*, NRO, MS 11064/7, begins by remarking that the lecturer feels unequal to the task of lecturing 'but encouraged by the honor of having been elected to the office, which he should otherwise have deemed himself unworthy to fill, (an honor ever to be remembered with the most lively gratitude) he will constantly endeavour in some degree to deserve the opinion formed of his capacity'.

[155] Crotch's delivery may also not have been at a moderate pace. In a letter the Reverend Dr Jowett dated 24 January 1805 in *Correspondence*, Crotch accepts constructive criticism over what must have been his first Royal Institution lectures: I never had any idea that my lectures had so few defects as they seem to have. To your objection to my opening the piano forte I most readily acquiesce. The task was very unpleasant and I will endeavour to read slower – knowing my lectures [are] to be corrected will give me more confidence – I know so little of Belles Lettres that the term *diffuse style* is not quite clear. My style was not quite Diffuse enough – not explanatory enough? or were the sentences *too short*?

chronological sequence, since Crotch identifies the highest points of excellence in each category in roughly this same order beginning with church music of the sixteenth and seventeenth centuries. Crotch recognized the chronological implications of his stylistic division and tells in the *General Account* of his growing dissatisfaction with an organizational scheme in which the students' last impressions were of what he regarded as the weakest music. Beginning in 1817 he experimented with a reversed order that started with *La clemenza di Tito* and worked its way through Haydn's *Seven Last Words* and *The Creation* to end with his notion of the golden age and *Judas Maccabaeus*.

Crotch provides an exceptionally detailed syllabus of his 13 Burney lectures. It shows that from the beginning of his career he had already gravitated towards the issues and positions that appear in most of his later lectures. The primary difference between these and his more mature series is that the latter tend to be more devoted to practical music. The introduction to his Oxford lectures by contrast, – much like his first contribution to the *Monthly Magazine* around the same time – is largely occupied with the standard topics of literary men. These include 'the powers of the music of the Ancients – showing that it had not counterpoint' and a brief treatment of acoustics he calls 'Discoveries concerning Sound'. Other topics are reminiscent of Reynolds's *Discourses*, especially 'Manner', 'Plagiarism', and a section 'on Genius and on Taste'. Crotch's main real-world interests in this lecture show the possible influence of Jones of Nayland, especially 'On the Ancient and Modern Styles of Music' and a section 'On Design'.[156]

The second lecture in the series includes still more on 'the Music of the Ancients and on the Theory of Sound', and the third and fourth lectures are entirely concerned with different kinds of 'National music'. If Crotch's lectures were read at the rate of one per week, then, it would not be until the fifth week, nearly a third of the way through the class, that his students could finally leave behind the concerns of eighteenth-century men of letters and enter permanently into the realm of 'scientific' music with a lecture 'On Church Music'. Oratorios and Handel occupy the sixth through eighth lectures of his series. It is only in the ninth lecture that his audience is introduced to the earliest kind of 'modern' music in the form of Italian opera – if, that is, one accepts the style-centred aesthetic system Crotch presents in his opening lecture, in which early Italian opera was the beginning of the modern style.[157]

---

[156] *General Account.*

[157] Crotch explains further in the first of his lectures on the oratorio in this series, *Lectures*, NRO, MS 11064/17, that Pergolesi was simultaneously one of the last composers of the ancient style and one of the first of the modern.

With opera as a bridge between ancient and modern, the lectures continue by dealing in order with concert music, vocal chamber music, and finally instrumental chamber music. The concluding lecture 'On Composition' is a return to more general principles in the manner of a summary, but it also has the character of a pronouncement of a verdict or final judgement. The preceding instalments of the series assume the ancient–modern dichotomy of Crotch's introduction but are not overtly polemical. One can see as the series draws to a close, however, that the principles Crotch has patiently established over the preceding weeks are being brought to bear in a case for the superiority of ancient music.

Crotch's early rhetoric can be reminiscent of William Jones, not only in its fervour but in its stress on grammatical correctness, its innate suspicion of imagination and taste, and especially its high-minded rejection of popularity as the most important measure of music. Though Crotch does not connect his musical remarks with Jones's social ideology, he hints at a similar sensibility when he stresses instances of the deliberate flouting of rules by self-conscious revolutionaries intent on undermining a musical system for their own purposes. The famous Preface from Domenico Scarlatti's first London edition of 30 *Essercizi* in 1738 provides him with a case in point:

> The rules of composition have been frequently regarded as fetters to genius and bars to invention – and as the celebrated harpsichord lessons of Domenico Scarlatti were written expressly with an intention of breaking through some of the most rigid rules, the author appealing to the ear in defense of such violations ... many flimsy composers have consequently added to the wildness and extravagancy of their ideas a shameful irregularity and incorrectness. But it may be answered that in the same manner as the rules of grammar were formed from the works of the greatest classical authors, so the rules of composition were formed from the chaste productions of Carissimi, Cesti, Stradella and the elder Scarlatti.[158]

This lecture, significantly, appears in two nearly identical versions, the second of which is far more militant concerning the moderns than its milder companion. In the former, Crotch includes Haydn in a list of authorities similar to the conclusion of the above but follows this with the observation that

> no composition has indulged in more daring flights of fancy, has produced more extraordinary effects or has been a greater favorite of the public than Haydn whom we have just mentioned in the list of respectable authors who have strictly observed the rules of composition. But what can we expect from inferior geniuses who

---

[158] *Lectures*, NRO, MS 11064/11.

to the extravagant wildness of their ideas would add irregularity and incorrectness?[159]

In order to understand this strange dual status for Haydn as both an authority and a wilful revolutionary it will be necessary to examine further a critical concept that is at the centre of Crotch's objections.

Crotch on 'design'

To his 13 Burney lectures, Crotch's *General Account* describes the addition of a group of four presentations not based on Burney. These directly compare Handel and Haydn by examining in detail *Israel in Egypt* and *The Creation*.[160] Crotch's additional lectures conclude with a new lecture on what he calls 'design' that might have been conceived as the conclusion of an expanded 17-lecture series. If so, Crotch's plans must have changed, since he indicates at the end of the manuscript of the *Creation* lecture that it was read only once, in November 1800.[161] Crotch's design lecture is related in an important way to his criticism of Haydn. Like his earlier presentation on composition mentioned above, the present lecture seeks to make a point about incoherence in modern music and does so in the context of a line of that argument Jones of Nayland and other ancient sympathizers had begun decades earlier and Crotch himself had introduced in the opening lecture of this series. It is in the study of design, Crotch observes, that music can be viewed 'rather as a science than an art'.[162] Crotch accepts Haydn as a capable and in some respects even a learned composer. He even remarks occasionally that Haydn 'cannot in general be called a daring violator of the grammatical rules of composition'.[163] Still, it was possible in Crotch's

---

[159] This lecture exists in two nearly identical versions, the present *Lectures*, NRO, MS 11064/12 and 11064/11. The former, a noticeably more militant presentation, pointedly uses the name Haydn in several places it is tactfully omitted in the milder 11064/11.

[160] The two *Israel in Egypt* lectures Crotch describes are not included among the NRO materials. This is most unfortunate since, as Crotch observes in *Lectures*, NRO, MS 11228/8, he regarded *Israel in Egypt* as Handel's second greatest oratorio, inferior only to *Messiah*. The *Creation* lecture, *Lectures*, NRO, MS 11064/8, is transcribed in full in Howard Irving, 'William Crotch on *The Creation*', *Music and Letters*, 75 (1994), 548–60.

[161] An anonymous article on Crotch's lectures in *The Director* 1 (1807), 60–62, describes a course of 13 lectures by Crotch that include the *Israel in Egypt* lecture but not its companion on *The Creation*. Instead, an entire lecture – unfortunately not included among the NRO materials – is devoted to the Mozart *Requiem*.

[162] *Lectures*, NRO, MS 11064/16. At the end of this manuscript Crotch indicates: 'written February 12 1802. Read March 29'.

[163] *Lectures*, NRO, MS 11065/6.

mind for a composer to exhibit correctness in these and other respects while at the same time being deficient in an area that Crotch – acting under the influence of Jones and others in the tradition of ancient music – regarded as more important.[164]

'Design' in this case refers to aspects of structure but does not concern musical form in the modern sense of a particular formal stereotype. Instead, Crotch examines what he calls the 'logic' of events in sequence. It is through a logical arrangement that music is supposed to reveal its depth and character and through an ability to comprehend and appreciate an orderly arrangement that the listener becomes more than a casual spectator engaged in an elegant pastime. As Crotch observes,

> to be a sound critic – to understand the intention of the composer to unriddle his seeming obscurities and fathom the depth of his learning – is more than a mere amusement. The critic when listening with rapture to those strains which do not affect the generality of auditors may be truly said to be 'untwisting all the chains that tye/the hidden soul of harmony'.

After playing the chorus 'O Lord in thee have I trusted' from the *Dettingen Te Deum* to illustrate his point, Crotch urges again that there are more subtle aspects of design than the relatively gross elements of structure he cites in Handel:

> Other beauties in design may be discovered, not indeed immediately, but by a deliberate examination. Such are the disposition of the passages and the arrangement of the ideas. Let the student try the effect of a change in the order; let him place the final passages at the beginning, and those which constitute the commencement in the middle of the movement, the episodes before the principal subjects and the elaborate parts of the fugue before the simpler combinations. When he finds, as he very soon will, that he has mangled and dislocated the whole frame, its former beauty will only be the more obvious. He will then be led to admit, that a fine composition does not merely consist of a collection of thoughts committed to paper in the order in which they presented themselves to the mind, but he will perceive that every suite of ideas must have one preferable arrangement, the discovery of which is the test of a composer's experience, taste, and abilities ...

He concludes that

> the want of this excellent arrangement of ideas is the most striking feature of juvenile and inferior productions, which frequently abound with fine and original but unconnected and coherent thoughts – while the compositions of the greatest masters constructed on simple and even disagreeable subjects are rendered interesting by their excellent treatment.

---

[164] Ibid.

There is a faint echo in this lecture of much earlier ideas that are recycled here in the service of changing conceptions of musical orderliness. Crotch's reference above to a 'hidden soul of harmony' – a quotation from Milton's *L'Allegro*[165] – and his description of a mysterious, hermetic musical order that only initiates have the skill to unravel and appreciate brings to mind a set of ideas Milton and the seventeenth century knew by the Latin oxymoron *concordia discors*, the concord of discords. The literary tradition of *concordia discors* relishes the surprising appearance of orderly relationships among seemingly disparate elements, much as William Wotton speaks of the skilful modern listener deriving a pleasure that his ancient counterpart could not have from the ability to make sense of the confusing events of the moment in a polyphonic texture.

After the middle of the eighteenth century, the most common point of view on the *concordia discors* no longer had confidence that, as Pope once expressed it, 'All Nature is but Art, unknown to thee;/All Chance, Direction, which thou canst not see'.[166] To the contemporary thinkers Burney most respected, the characteristic strange associations of the tradition were not a reflection of a subtle underlying order, they were unnatural and far-fetched. Samuel Johnson speaks of wit as 'a kind of *discordia concors*; a combination of dissimilar images, or discovery of occult resemblances in things apparently unlike'. Among the metaphysical poets, 'the most heterogeneous ideas are yoked together; nature and art are ransacked for illustrations, comparisons, and allusions; their learning instructs, and their subtlety surprises; but the reader commonly thinks his improvement dearly bought, and though he sometimes admires, is seldom pleased'. Worse, they were 'not successful in representing or moving the affections'.[167]

Writers connected with the ancient-music tradition, especially Hawkins, continued later than their literary counterparts to draw on the images and language of the *concordia discors* and related Pythagorean ideas. They did so, however, with little apparent awareness of the literary traditions that preceded them and with a tendency to pick and choose among aspects of the tradition they wished to emphasize. Often this distorts the original conception.[168]

---

[165] Crotch's reference is to *L'Allegro* lines 143–4.

[166] Quoted in Martin Battestin, *The Providence of Wit: Aspects of Form in Augustan Literature and the Arts* (Oxford: Clarendon Press, 1974), pp. 141–2.

[167] Samuel Johnson, *Lives of the English Poets*, ed. George Birkbeck Hill (New York: Octagon Books, 1967), '[Abraham] Cowley' [1618–67], p. 20.

[168] Though Hawkins does not speak of the joys of finding unsuspected relationships in music, his writing does resemble the tradition of *concordia discors* in its value of abstract musical relationships over the transmission of musical content. See Neubauer, *The Emancipation of Music from Language*, especially p. 172.

One common aspect of musical references to the *concordia discors* is its natural association with the musical element of harmony, especially harmony in the explicit sense of counterpoint. The process by which the mind creates or perceives contrapuntal lines is typically linked to the most central of all images of the literary tradition of *concordia discors*, the act of Divine creation. Just as the Deity look upon primordial chaos and found order among its discordant elements, the human mind is supposed to contemplate the contending voices of counterpoint and find order in its seeming nonsense. Thus, Alexander Malcolm writes that

> the Mind is ravished with the Agreement of Things seemingly contrary to one another. We have here a Kind of Imitation of the Works of Nature, where different Things are wonderfully joyned in one harmonious Unity: and as some Things appear at first View the farthest removed from Symmetry and Order, which from the Course of Things we learn to be absolutely necessary for the Perfection and Beauty of the Whole; so *Discords* being artfully mixed with *Concords*, make a more perfect Composition, which surprises us with Delight.[169]

Hawkins did not compare musical composition with Divine creation but he did not hesitate to call ancient music a reflection of Divine order and to insist that this order did not come from extra-musical content but from the music's structure.[170] Others invoke Handel and the Deity in the same breath. An anonymous poet notes that 'When HANDEL deigns to strike the sense,/'Tis as when heaven, with hands divine,/Struck out the globe (a work immense!)/Where harmony meets with design'. Handel's lesser contemporaries, on the other hand, are dismissed with the charge that 'When you attempt the mighty strain/Consistency is quite destroy'd;/Great order is dissolv'd again,/Chaos returns, and all is void'.[171]

When a writer like Jones of Nayland wonders at 'the method of setting together Several parts, moving different ways at the same time, yet so as to agree in one design, and constitute one entire harmony' it is probable that he does so with an awareness, however superficial, of the critical

---

[169] Malcolm, *Treatise*, p. 597.

[170] See in particular the Preliminary Discourse to the first volume of Sir John Hawkins *A General History of the Science and Practice of Music*, ed. Othmar Wessely, 2 vols (London, 1776; London, 1875; Graz: Akademische Druck-u. Verlagsanstalt, 1969). Hawkins's emphasis on musical structure over content is discussed in Neubauer, *The Emancipation of Music from Language*, pp. 172–8.

[171] Deutsch, *Handel*, p. 389. Deutsch takes this from the 'Grub-Street Journal', 8 May 1735. The poem, by 'a Philharmonick', is entitled *On Mr. Handel's performance on the Organ, and his opera of Alcina*.

traditions that preceded him. For Jones, however, just as for Crotch still later, such ideas appear as a kind of automatic invocation of a literary commonplace. The writing of both the former and sometimes the latter as well often takes from earlier traditions the quality or order and regularity that is supposed to characterize the post-creation orderly universe while rejecting the aspect of disparateness that the seventeenth century expected in the individual elements of its chaotic system. It was, of course, not merely harmony that characterized the *concordia discors*, but a harmony that arose from conflict. And since, without conflict, there can be no surprise in the order that is eventually born from chaos, the tradition of ancient music as Crotch knew it had come to expect only predictability and correctness. Jones speaks of 'variety with uniformity' as the characteristic excellence of fugue and insists that 'the principle may be extended almost to every thing' – meaning that it should be a governing principle in other aspects of music than harmony, in other arts than music and, possibly, in other areas of life than the arts. But his order is a highly regulated order. He insists that to be 'consistent and rational' there must be 'an harmony in the *measures* as well as in the *sounds*'. Thus fugues and canons, 'where the melodies are more strictly commensurate, are the most perfect kinds of composition'.[172]

In most of his early introductory lectures, Crotch stresses predictability of design. His 'design' lecture naturally summons the most common image of *concordia discors*, the metaphysical argument from design. In this early presentation, Crotch views a musical composition as an entity in which, much like Jones of Nayland's rigid social order, each individual component has its fixed place and rank:

> Although it would be highly improper to compare the feeble and imperfect works of man with those of divine origin, I may be permitted to remark that one of the most striking characteristics of the creation is regularity of design. The parts are subservient to the whole, many of the phenomena appearing useless or at least mysterious when considered individually, but of the highest and most unquestionable importance if regarded with reference to the great and faultless whole. In poetry, painting, and all the fine arts, the necessity of a good design is acknowledged. In music it is equally essential.[173]

This particular version of Crotch's introductory message comes from 1806, the year after his unfortunate confrontation with Burney. It is

---

[172] William Jones (of Nayland), *Physiological Disquisitions; or Discourses on the Natural Philosophy of the Elements* (London, 1781), p. 328.

[173] *Lectures*, NRO, MS 11231/1. This lecture, which Crotch indicates was first read at the Royal Institution in November of 1806, is quite similar to the introduction of Crotch's 1805 series.

different from his earliest Oxford presentations mainly in the choice of musical examples: instead of the *Dettingen Te Deum*, Crotch placates an angry modern-music faction by making the finale of Mozart's 'Jupiter' symphony an exemplar of design.[174]

In other places, it is clear that, when he could think for himself, Crotch's opinions about Haydn and intricate musical relationships were not as simplistic as some of his earliest lectures suggest. This is particularly noticeable in his remarks on tonal organization, which can follow the ancient-music stereotype of requiring predictability and order but at other times show a remarkable tolerance for quite surprising relationships. Crotch's openness to the exploitation of such relationships often conflicts, however, with his reflexive and unexamined reiterations of the complaints of less gifted predecessors. The result is a series of contradictory messages that alternatively affirm harmonic ingenuity and reject it.

'Modulation', a word typically used in the clear sense of key-change, is a term that often appears alongside 'design' in Crotch's writing because both can relate to the orderly sequence of events. Crotch complains, following Jones, that 'young, and especially modern, composers, endeavour to surprize us by strange and unaccountable transitions into remote and irrelative keys; and the effect on the mind frequently resembles that produced by the unmeaning changes of scene in a pantomime'. By way of contrast, Crotch praises a modulation in *Judas Maccabaeus* that he says 'is so perfectly natural and agreeable that it is called going into the relative key'.[175] In a lecture on modulation from 1806, however, Crotch first indicates that modulations which are 'unconnected and irrelative' might be 'far from improper when used for the sake of expression and effect'. He cites as an example Handel's modulation from F minor to D minor in Handel's chorus 'For Sion Lamentation make' in *Judas Maccabaeus*, where he thinks the requirements of the text justify harmonic boldness.[176]

In still another lecture on Handel, Crotch reinforces his emphasis on the acceptability of unusual procedures as a means of transmitting content. He finds fault with a double chorus from *Solomon* in which there are 'some enharmonic transitions already used by our author in

---

[174] *Lectures*, NRO, MS 11231/1: 'The specimen which I have chosen to exemplify this beautiful order is perhaps the finest symphony that Mozart ever composed, and one of the most laboured productions of the modern school. Each of the movements [ ] excellent in this respect, but particularly the last, which is a fugue on four subjects, all springing naturally out of each other and when combined a perfect whole which is indeed a most extraordinary effusion of genius and learning.'

[175] *Lectures*, NRO, MS 11229/7.

[176] *Lectures*, NRO, MS 11231/2.

his well known chorus "as from the power of sacred lays" to express the horror and dismay at the approach of the great day of retribution but here adapted with less propriety to the words "with pious hearts and holy tongue/resound your maker's praise"'. Crotch adds, to soften his criticism, that

> the error before us is not peculiar to the ancient style, and is one which the lover of modern music would be apt to overlook. His ear is so inured to discords and extraneous transitions with which the music of the present day is overloaded that if he should bestow due commendation on the harmony he would probably disregard the false expression of the sentiment conveyed by the poetry.[177]

Elsewhere, however, Crotch contends that enharmonic modulations are appropriate not only for the sake of content but for simple contrast. He indicates that 'a succession of similar modulations soon tire the ear; in this, as in every other branch of the art, the ear should always fancy it can anticipate what follows, and should always find itself agreeable disappointed'.[178] On the same basis he approves of interesting key relationships between movements in the cycle. In Pergolesi and the Italian school he objects that 'the transitions from the key note of one movement to that of another, are so strictly related, as never to excite any degree of surprise in the mind' and recommends instead the music of Handel 'in which he has given additional force and beauty to several movements, by the use of modulation, and by the situation of their respective key notes; the neglect of which excellence is one of the greatest errors of the modern school'.[179] In still another lecture he praises Mozart's shift from 'E major with four sharps to C major' in the second act Trio 'Ah taci, ingiusto core' in *Don Giovanni*, which he thinks is 'striking and masterly'.[180]

It is in this context, then, that Crotch approves of Haydn's use of enharmonic key relationships in his piano trios, citing in particular a work he identifies as a Sonata Op. 75. In context, it appears that his reference is to a passage in the development section of the third movement of the trio Hob. XV:28, which was published, along with Hob. XV:27 and 29, as Op. 75 by Longman and Broderip in 1795.[181] In this case, Haydn modulates from C sharp major (i.e., = D flat) to A flat major. Crotch comments that enharmonic modulation

---

177 *Lectures*, NRO, MS 11063/4.
178 *Lectures*, NRO, MS 11231/2.
179 Ibid.
180 *Lectures*, NRO, MS 11232/7.
181 This example is reprinted in Howard Irving, 'Haydn and Laurence Sterne: Similarities in Eighteenth Century Literary and Musical Wit', *Current Musicology*, 40 (1985), 39.

by substituting one note for another which gives nearly the same
sound, excite[s] surprise in the mind. One instance of this has been
given from Haydn [the Sonata Op.75 mentioned above]; and the
student is referred for examples to the latter part of the song
'Return O God of Hosts' and the recitative 'My genial spirits
droop' both in Samson, 'Thy rebuke hath broken his heart' in the
Messiah, and 'Alma del gran Pompeo' in Julius Caesar, in all of
which movements the sorrow is rendered wild by this kind of
modulation. The conclusion of Haydn's chorus from his oratorio
of the Creation, 'The heavens are telling the glory of God' is a fine
instance of the use of this kind of transition. The whole turns upon
the note B flat, which is used as if it were A sharp, and the discord
resolved accordingly and afterwards A sharp is used as B flat.[182]

Curiously, he follows this with an unnecessary and possibly contradictory parting shot at the moderns:

I shall conclude this lecture with recommending the young composer to avoid absurd fashion of the modern school, which renders
one movement of a piece wholly independent of the others by
putting it in a key that has no connection with them. Many excellent Judges, possessed of nice ears, cannot bear, in a concert, the
succession of pieces in keys wholly independent of each other; and
if the ear cannot bear this change in pieces which profess to be
distinct, how can it bear it in the various movements of an oratorio
or an opera, which form a connected whole.[183]

Crotch undoubtedly makes this charge with a passage from A. F. C.
Kollmann's recently-published *Essay on Practical Musical Composition*
(London, 1799) in mind.[184] In that work, Kollmann unreasonably takes
Haydn to task for what are viewed as inappropriate key relationships
between the movements of Hob. XV:27, another of the three works
published in the same Op. 75 Crotch praises above.

The three movements of Hob. XV:27 are in C major, A major, and C
major. Kollmann's *Essay* actually approves of the shift from C to A
between the first and second movements because it is 'allowable, according to the rules of abrupt modulation by omission' in that 'C is the
key, and the triad of A the leading chord to a related key'.[185] The return

[182] *Lectures*, NRO, MS 11231/6.
[183] Ibid.
[184] A. F. C. Kollmann, *Essay on Practical Musical Composition* (London, 1799), p. 10.
[185] In other words, the dominant triad in A major happens also to be the dominant
triad to a legitimate (i.e., closely related) tonal destination, the key of a minor. As long as
one initially sets out in a direction that is 'legal', it is acceptable in Kollmann's system,
once the E major triad is reached, to 'omit' the last stage in the process and proceed to A
major instead. Kollmann refers to a rule he gives in his earlier *Essay on Musical
Harmony* (London, 1796), which seems to have been adapted from C. P. E. Bach's
Versuch über die wahre Art das Clavier zu spielen. The original Bach treatment of this

from A to C between second movement and finale cannot be rational-
ized by Kollmann's rule, however, since the elaborate trail of reasoning
he uses to legitimize the first key change will not work in reverse.
Kollmann accordingly brands this 'too great a skip in harmony' which
'ought not to be imitated by young composers'.[186] At the same time,
however, he specifically approves of the much stranger key scheme of
Hob. XV:29, in which the three movements are in E flat, B major (i.e., =
C flat), and E flat.[187]

Along with the youthful William Crotch's eagerness to pass along
unreasonable criticisms of Haydn, one often detects in these early lectures a much harsher treatment of Haydn in comparison with several
lesser contemporaries and still more noticeably, with Mozart. Especially
at the beginning of his career, it is clear that Crotch thought Mozart
vulgar. With the popular cult of Neapolitan opera in mind as an ideal
that could never be equalled in modern times, Crotch cites Mozart for
the 'deficiency of elegant and clear melody' and faults his modulations,
as he does Haydn's, for being 'ingenious but outrè and carried through
keys wholly foreign to the original key'.[188] But at no point is Mozart
ever admonished for what Crotch views as Haydn's most grievous
shortcoming, a weakness of the guiding intellect that produces lucid
order. Crotch does not approve of all that Mozart does, but he at least
accepts it as deliberate. In the lectures to which Burney most vigorously
objected in Crotch's 1805 series, on the other hand, Haydn is presented
as an anti-intellectual dominated by impulse and unwilling to impose a
ruling order on his undisciplined imagination; Crotch says Haydn was
'not nice in his selection from the innumerable thoughts which crouded
on his imagination' in that 'he seemed to reject none that presented
themselves but for the sake of novelty adopted what his predecessors
had shunned'.[189]

---

subject is discussed in detail in Richard Cramer, 'The New Modulation of the 1770's: C.
P. E. Bach in Theory, Criticism, and Practice', *Journal of the American Musicological
Society*, 38 (1985), 551–92. Kollmann and Bach's rationale is also examined in Howard
Irving and H. Lee Riggins, 'Advanced Uses of Mode Mixture in Haydn's Late Instrumen-
tal Works', *Canadian University Music Review*, 9 (1988), 104–35, and in Irving, 'Haydn
and Laurence Sterne', 34–49.

[186] Kollmann, *Essay on Practical Musical Composition*, p. 10.

[187] Ibid. Having earlier cited four cases of unusual key change in Op. 75, Kollmann
writes with regard to XV:29 that 'The third and fourth case is in Sonata III, where the
first movement is in E-flat major, the second in B (or C-flat) major, and the third in E-flat
major again. Both of these changes are very good, according to the rules mentioned just
now.' His rules for 'abrupt modulation by omission', however, would obviously not be
applicable here.

[188] *Lectures*, NRO, MS 11064/10.

[189] *Lectures*, NRO, MS 11228/12.

This view of Haydn as a natural genius guided by an unruly and whimsical fancy persisted, to some extent, through Crotch's lectures in 1831. Crotch's view of Haydn is sometimes transferred from the composer to the genre for which he was best known, the symphony. Noting that 'ere Handel died Haydn [indecipherable] 25 years of age must I conceive have invented the instrumental sinfonia for the concert and carried it almost at once to perfection'. In a sentence he later overscored, Crotch notes that this species of music 'sprung up to maturity at once' without any period of development. Haydn thus resembles the moderns' semi-mythical vision of Pergolesi, whom Burney presents as a 'child of taste and elegance, and nurstling of the Graces'.[190] Pergolesi's mature style was supposed to have been achieved with minimal study and without the need for a lengthy period of apprenticeship.

Crotch's 1805 Royal Institution lecture does not openly explore a natural genius characterization of Haydn but it succeeds in damning him with faint praise by underestimating at every possible turn his 'science' and by repeatedly stressing Haydn's excellence in areas that call for originality more than learning. Crotch thinks that Haydn's piano trios are 'amongst the finest productions of the age', but what he praises in them is the fact that they 'abound with a variety of invention and ingenuity found in no other composer'. The quartets are still greater because 'the importance of each part, the striking modulations and the management of the subjects which are in themselves original and fanciful all conspire to produce the most masterly and novel effects'. In the symphonies it is Haydn's 'novelty and brilliancy of effect, gaiety of style, and disposition of the score' in which he 'leave[s] all similar productions far behind'. But when Crotch talks about Haydn's scientific music he can find little that pleases him. In what he regards as the best of Haydn's oratorios, the *Stabat Mater*, he complains that 'The fugues of Haydn's choruses are frequently on obvious and easy subjects and are not remarkably well sustained nor satisfactorily concluded.' This sentence is followed by one which, in its original form, would barely have acknowledged Haydn to have employed counterpoint at all. Crotch notes that 'the modulations and learned passages [the word 'fragments' is over-scored] of counterpoint are truly masterly'. This lecture concludes by restating Crotch's position that Haydn is 'the most original, ingenious, and extraordinary composer of the present age. Crotch adds, in a sentence whose past tense indicates it was added after Haydn's death in 1809, that although he is 'compelled to admit that as a vocal composer [Haydn] was inferior to many, yet, unquestionably he was the greatest of all instrumental composers that ever existed'.

---

[190] Burney, *General History*, vol. 2, p. 919.

Crotch on *The Creation*

In a lecture Crotch delivered in 1800 on Haydn's then new work *The Creation*, young Crotch betrays persistent uncertainty over what critical frame of reference should be employed in the evaluation of Haydn's challenging creative effort.[191] Should *The Creation* be judged according to the very different standards of the oratorio, the opera or the symphony? It bore a certain resemblance to each category but fit completely into none. It is appropriate to conclude this look at Crotch's development as a critic with a brief look at two later treatments of *The Creation*. The first is from Crotch's lecture on Haydn from the January 1805 series, the series to which Burney objected so strongly. The second, Crotch's last treatment of *The Creation*, comes from a collection of eight new lectures written in 1817 for presentation at the Surrey Institution. Especially in the 1817 lecture, Crotch is more sure of himself and more definite about what expectations ought to apply to Haydn's work.

The Creation's elevation to the status of a musical classic can be traced through Crotch's several lectures. His 1800 lecture identifies it as 'a work which at present attracts the attention of the whole musical world'. By 1805, Crotch thought it was a work 'which at first attracted the attention of the whole musical world and excited a variety of contradictory opinions [but] is now however less generously admired than when it first appeared'.[192] This is followed in the manuscript by an over-scored phrase predicting *The Creation* 'will not probably in future ages be regarded as one of his superior productions'.[193] This statement must have been over-scored before 5 June 1809, the last date on which this lecture is known to have been read. By 1817 there was no need for Crotch to offer a prediction on *The Creation*'s fate. Despite the place in the repertoire Haydn's work had earned, however, Crotch's tone is at least as negative in 1817 as before, although for somewhat different reasons.

He knew *The Creation* much better by 1817. His first talk in 1800 is based, like much of his criticism of modern music, almost entirely on an examination of the score; all he had actually heard was a single chorus performed in the Music Room at Oxford. By 1817 he had heard *The Creation* 'performed on various occasions, and sometimes under the most favourable circumstances, and by the finest principal singers and the most complete orchestras'.[194] Still, for his last presentation Crotch

---

[191] See, Irving, 'William Crotch on *The Creation*', 548–60.

[192] *Lectures*, NRO, MS 11228/12.

[193] Ibid.

[194] *Lectures*, NRO, MS 11230/10.

returned to the score for a fresh perspective 'in order to soften down any prejudices, and correct any erroneous opinions which I might too hastily have formed of a production abounding with novel and extraneous effects'.[195] 'Such a precaution', Crotch remarks, 'becomes the duty of a lecturer when he presumes to bestow less praise and more censure than is usually met with on a work of such notoriety, and the production of so great a master'.[196]

In the years between his 1805 and 1817 lectures Crotch had come to accept the uniqueness of Haydn's music, and – although he continued to display a preoccupation with categories – no longer objected when Haydn's sacred works did not fit easily into simplistic divisions. In an earlier lecture from the 1817 series, on Haydn's *The Seven Last Words*, Crotch observes that

> A comparison of this work [indecipherable] must not be made with that of Mozart [*La Clemenza di Tito*] considered in the two first Lectures. That is a secular composition – this is sacred and meant to be performed in a church. That is an opera, and its melodies are therefore generally more flowing and elegant than those of the piece before us, which is wholly instrumental. Rich and harmonious as Mozart's opera undoubtedly is compared with similar pieces, the work before us is as might be expected, yet more elaborate and scientific. Considered as a modern instrumental piece, it is unusually serious and sublime. The lover of ancient music must not indeed expect to hear much of canons and fugues or passages in the true ecclesiastical style and he may perhaps complain of a deficiency of pathos and learning. Let him remember that this is the production of Haydn *in his own peculiar* style, and intended, not for voices, or an organ (which are peculiarly suitable to the church music) but for a full orchestra with no voices and in which the organ would scarcely be touched. Others again may think it heavy and monotonous and too scientific. Let them remember the nature of the sacred subject.[197]

Crotch concludes by recommending this piece 'to every lover of Haydn's music, of instrumental, of serious, [and] of modern sacred music'.[198]

Crotch had a much clearer sense in 1817 that *The Creation* should be evaluated as sacred music. His 1800 lecture describes the work as an oratorio but criticizes it for faults that he would ordinarily have applied to secular music, especially a perceived lack of unoriginality and melody that did not seem appropriately operatic. He specifically refers to *The Creation* as sacred music only twice in the early lecture but such

---

[195] Ibid.
[196] Ibid.
[197] *Lectures*, NRO, MS 11230/7.
[198] Ibid.

references are constant in the 1817 treatment: *The Creation* 'differs widely from that of any sacred music with which we were before acquainted'; The air 'The marv'lous work' is 'void of pure sublimity and sacred expression' as is the following chorus;[199] The soprano air 'With verdure clad' 'abounds with unaccented cadences which are light and pretty but neither vocal nor sacred';[200] The conclusion of the chorus 'Awake the Lyre [*sic*]' 'is abrupt and ill adapted to a sacred subject'; the first act in general exhibits 'the want of sacred character and the absence of that science and skill in the treatment of a fugue which strike us so forcibly in the works of all the great composers of the ancient style of music', and so on.[201]

The most significant departure in 1817 from his earlier lectures is a new set of faults Crotch identifies in *The Creation* that show his very different frame of reference. The earlier lecture includes a few passages in which Crotch objects to Haydn's attempts to depict or represent. He complains, for example, that 'musical expression is carried to an unwarrantable length – or rather – attempts are made beyond the very limited bounds of musical imitation'.[202] This, however, appears in a brief paragraph in the 1800 lecture and is softened by an observation that 'Haydn is indeed by no means the only composer who has committed these errors'.[203] By the 1805 lecture, this general complaint – about which Crotch supplies greater detail later in the lecture – is offered near the lecture's beginning and is more specific and more confrontational:

> Haydn did not regard the bounds which good taste has long prescribed to musical imitation. The sun and moon are heard to rise, the flight of the eagle, the unwieldiness of great whales, the roaring of the Lion, the boundings of the tiger and the paces of the stag and the horse, *storms of wind*, thunder, and lightning, showers of rain, hail and snow are in this work all indicated by music.[204]

Several of these specific instances of imitation also appear briefly in 1800, but in that lecture more of Crotch's censures have to do with purely musical issues such as the commonness of Haydn's fugue subjects or the overuse of instrumental effects. The earlier lecture is much less concerned with Haydn's success at conveying his sacred message; in particular, there is no reference in it to any shortcomings in the English text.

---

[199] Ibid.
[200] Ibid.
[201] Ibid.
[202] Ibid.
[203] *Lectures*, NRO, MS 11064/8.
[204] *Lectures*, NRO, MS 11228/12.

In the 1817 lecture, by contrast, Crotch focuses on *The Creation*'s weaknesses as what Burney had once called the 'first of all sacred *melodramas*'.[205] In a letter to C. I. Latrobe written shortly after he heard *The Creation* for the first time, Burney had objected that

> The Handelians, who are most of them utterly unable to judge of Handel's real merit and all jealous of that of others – as well as pert and flippant *soi-disant* connoisseurs, have handed it ab^t as a *bon mot*, that the opening of the *Creation* is so confused, that 'Chaos is come again'. – and what sh^d be come again, but *chaos*, when chaos is to be described? are sounds to be arranged in harmonic and symmetric order, before order was born?[206]

Accordingly, in his angry letter to Crotch in 1805, Burney – who had not actually heard what Crotch had to say but relied instead on second-hand reports – anticipated that Crotch would object to this passage and was prepared to do battle over it. As has been shown elsewhere, however, Crotch did not respond as the ancient-music bigot Burney expected him to and actually offered cautious praise for the depiction of chaos as a strange unmusical passage that was entirely appropriate under the circumstances.[207]

In the 1817 lecture he is somewhat more critical, but again in a different way from what Burney might have expected. Crotch is much more interested in what this curious passage is supposed to express and less inclined to evaluate it in abstract musical terms. 'The introductory Symphony which serves for an overture is meant to represent Chaos – that state of creation before the Almighty separated light from darkness or land from water',[208] Crotch begins. Unlike his earlier lectures, this last effort examines carefully the sources of Haydn's text, noting that 'the inventive fancy of Milton has described this as far from being a motionless and uniform mass'.[209] He suggests that this quality of motion should be represented in the music. Crotch quotes directly from Milton, who describes creation as a state

> Where eldest night
> and Chaos, ancestors of Nature, hold
> Eternal anarchy, amidst the noise
> of Endless wars, and by confusion stand.
> For hot, cold moist and dry, four champions fierce
> strive here for mast'ry to battel bring
> Their embryon atoms –[210]

---

[205] CB to C. I. Latrobe, no date, YUL, Osborn.
[206] Ibid.
[207] Irving, 'William Crotch on *The Creation*', p. 550.
[208] *Lectures*, NRO, MS 11230/10.
[209] Ibid.
[210] Ibid.

Afterwards, Crotch indicates, 'the Poet speaks of "the strong rebuff of some tumultuous cloud, Instinct with fire and nitre" as "hurrying the arch-fiend Satan many miles aloft" when he traversed this boundless ocean'.[211]

Crotch recognizes that 'Haydn seems to intend something like this. Here are passages of various kinds – harmonies quite new, discords never before heard, and the stringed instruments play with mutes on, ("Con sordine"), which adds much to the mysterious effect.'[212] While Crotch agrees that 'all the passages which consist of long holding notes and of interrupted and uncertain phrases are admirably expressive', he objects that some passages of Haydn's Chaos, 'particularly those in the major key, appear to me to be too regular and symmetrical. And I have always felt sorry that this movement is brought to a full close before the Recitative commences – Chaos should have been terminated only by the creation of Light'.[213] Crotch's earliest lecture had praised Haydn's famous setting of the creation of light and compared it to a similar passage in *Samson*. Here, however, he remarks that the

> little abrupt symphony intended to represent the Creation of light seems rather like the explosion of a mine in the night or the glare of a transient meteor for it ceases almost immediately. Hence I greatly prefer an attempt of the same kind by Handel in his oratorio of Samson in the chorus 'O first created beam' where the words 'Light was over-all' are forcibly expressed by the ceaseless and rapid motion of the Instruments.[214]

In the Handel work, Crotch remarks, underlining a point he makes in all of his *Creation* lectures, 'the aid of Drums, Trumpets, Clarionets, and Trombones was not thought necessary to heighten the contrast'.[215]

Crotch's new stress on musical expression resembles Burney's thinking about *The Creation*. As noted above, Burney had set down his thinking about this work immediately after hearing it for the first time on the night of Monday, 21 April 1800. He is not known to have published his impressions in any setting to which Crotch might have had access, however, and any shift in Crotch's thinking that is owed to Burney must have resulted either from some face-to-face encounter or the network of dinner-party conversation that seems to have been a mainstay of British aesthetic discourse. Since Burney's interesting remarks are at present available to the scholarly readership only in

---

211 Ibid.
212 Ibid.
213 Ibid.
214 Ibid.
215 Ibid.

manuscripts at the New York Public Library and the Osborn Collection, it may be useful to reprint them in full for comparison with
Crotch's remarks above:

> On Haydn's Creation. Performed in London Apr. 21. 1800

> If I had leisure, I could write a folio dissertation on the beauty of
> that divine music, and the intelligence, the mind, and conceptions,
> of the matchless composer! The Handelians, who are most of them
> utterly unable to judge of Handel's real merit, are all as jealous of
> that of others, as if they themselves had composed Handel's works.
> and pert, as well as flippant *soi-disant* connoisseurs, have handed it
> about as a *bon mot*, that the opening of the *Creation* is so con-
> fused, that 'Chaos is come again'.[216] And what should be come
> again (may be asked) but *chaos*, when chaos is to be described?
> Were sounds to be arranged in harmonic & symmetric order before
> order was born? It struck me as the most sublime idea in Haydn's
> work, his describing the birth of order by dissonance & broken
> phrases – a whisper here – an effort there – a groan – an agonizing
> cry – personifying nature, – & supposing her in labour, how admi-
> rably has he expressed her throes! not by pure harmony & graceful
> melody, but by appropriate sounds, wch applied to any other pur-
> pose w^d be down right jargon; but here, *in loco*, are sublimely
> beautiful! Yet if the hearer does help the composer, musical imita-
> tion is so feeble, that his designs and conceptions will never be
> understood. But if this is not picturesque music, it is in vain ever to
> be attempted. When dissonance is tuned, when order arises, and
> chaos is no more, what pleasing, ingenious and graceful melody &
> harmony ensue! What a new & powerful effect had the encored
> choruses on the feeling part of the audience! who unable to stay till
> it was finished to express their rapture, broke in upon the perform-
> ers with impassioned applause, both times, before the movement
> was ended; and what a flash of harmony on the last word of the
> sublime text of genuine Scripture – 'God said let there be light, &
> there was *LIGHT*!'[217]

Below this in the manuscript, Burney offers a sentence that may help
explain Crotch's remarks in 1805 predicting *The Creation*'s eventual
failure: 'though professors and a few other real judges of composition,
and new effects are enthusiastic admirers of this Oratorio, the public in
the cant of the modern language, is *not up to it*, and must *learn to hear
it*, as will professors to perform it'.[218]

Crotch's criticism of the depiction of chaos is followed by a number
of other observations that have a similar emphasis. Crotch believes that
'much of the uncouth effect which this oratorio produces is to be
attributed to the incorrectness of the translation of the words, though

---

[216] William Shakespeare, *Othello* III. iii.
[217] YUL, Osborn.
[218] YUL, Osborn.

some of it is owing to incorrect accentuation'. Where Haydn's attempted imitations of nature are concerned, Crotch has a specific
objection: that the things depicted appear in the music before the words
describing them appear in the text. Thus he notes:

> Haydn has, by an unwarrantable deviation from the usual custom,
> rendered the expression unintelligible, by placing the symphonies
> intended to imitate storms, thunder, snow and other meteoric phe-
> nomena, before the words which describe them are heard. Nothing
> could more decisively prove the utter incapability of music to
> define particular objects. It is impossible to pronounce what these
> symphonies when heard alive are intended to represent. It has
> therefore been suggested as an improvement of this Recitative and
> was adapted by the late Mr Barthelemon that the definitive words
> should precede instead of follow the imitative symphonies and then
> all becomes clear and intelligible. When storms are mentioned, the
> turbulent symphony is immediately understood. When thunder is
> spoken of, the rolling drum is known to be meant as its imitation –
> and so of the others.[219]

He notes also that 'a better translation has also been made and occasionally but I fear not generally used, or published'.[220]

Crotch seems to recognize the unusual text centredness of his criticism.
In the second of his two-lecture series on *The Creation* in 1817, he tries
to shift away from a text-centred approach, perhaps to avoid any shifting
of responsibility for weakness in *The Creation* from composer to translator. Concerning the soprano air 'On mighty pens uplifted' he remarks:

> It must be remembered that the question now is not, 'what could
> Haydn have done better with *these* or with *such* words' but 'is this
> song interesting, beautiful, and pathetic, or not?' It must be owned
> that the subject which our author had to set was throughout ill
> calculated for musical expression. All imitations are improper, and
> a narrative which does not excite pain or pleasure in an eminent
> degree in the mind, is not likely to receive much effect or additional
> interest from the cooperating aid of music.[221]

Crotch then summarizes his main problem with *The Creation*: 'Awe,
Astonishment, veneration, adoration are the feelings excited by reading
the description of the Creation and these are by no means the most easy
to express.'[222] 'They require', Crotch claims, 'a predominance of the
Sublime style, and this could not be expected from a composer of the
present age.'[223]

---

[219] *Lectures*, NRO, MS 11230/10.
[220] Ibid.
[221] *Lectures*, NRO, MS 11230/11.
[222] Ibid.
[223] Ibid.

Conclusion: Crotch as critic

The tension between content and form that is a constant backdrop in the writing considered above is not resolved in Crotch's criticism so much as it is simply ignored. Accordingly, the lectures reprinted in Part Two of the present volume betray only occasional hints of the issues discussed above. The first of the 1818 lectures, for example, invokes the quarrel's perennial melody–harmony opposition when Crotch caricatures the two sides as those who think fugues are 'Gothic and barbarous' and those who think Italian airs are 'senseless and childish'. Similarly, Crotch speaks of 'directing the attention to rich and ingenious contrivances rather than to the charms of melody alone'. But at no point does he ever take up in detail the underlying questions that so preoccupied Burney and Mason, of how musical contrivance and musical expression can coexist and which should take precedence when the two conflict. That is partly because in the ideal world of the mind in which Crotch's score-oriented criticism takes place the practical realities of the average listener are not important and a complex design is not necessarily an impediment to musical expression or to the intelligible transmission of a text.

Still, Crotch's lectures suffer in their own way from the competing demands of two ways in which music can be a meaningful art form. Crotch is most successful as a critic – and at the same time, most tolerant of the modern style – when he can appreciate music in self-referential terms as an abstract design in sound. In this critical mode he deals in only the most general way with what he thinks music is trying to express and can evaluate unconventional musical practices as interesting contrivances that need not be meaningful in an expressive way. Often his criticism of Haydn in particular makes a distinction along these lines between two frames of reference from which music might be judged. His earliest lecture on *The Creation* suggests one such critical starting-point when Crotch concludes with the most positive language he could find for a work he never learned to appreciate: 'considered therefore as anything but a vocal composition it is highly deserving of the study of every lover of modern music'. Similarly, in the second of his 1817 lectures on *The Creation*, Crotch's generally negative assessment is punctuated by his observation that 'some of the passages, indeed, considered abstractly as music are very pleasing'; it is only in an expressive framework that he finds them inappropriate.

It is presumably on the former basis that he can praise an enharmonic modulation in the aria 'In Native Worth', which 'passes from E minor with one sharp into A♭ with four flats', as 'ingenious original and masterly'. His only observation on musical 'meaning' in the aria is a brief comment that Haydn's 'attempt is not unsuccessfully made to contrast the bolder qualities of man with the softer attractions of woman by a correspondent character in the melody'. It is perhaps fortunate in view of his frequent objections to Haydn's levity that Crotch does not consider what significance if any the composer might have intended by separating the parts of the aria that deal, respectively, with man and woman by so remarkable and deceptive a modulation.[224]

When Crotch contends that 'to understand the intention of the composer' and 'to unriddle his seeming obscurities and fathom the depth of his learning' is to appreciate music as something more than a mere amusement, he places himself on the side of those who value elaborate contrivance over readily accessible musical content. Accordingly, and keeping in mind that his most common approach to musical content in earlier lectures takes the form of brief, almost ritual objections to specific acts of attempted imitation, Crotch's extended objections to Haydn's expression in later lectures on both *The Creation* and *The Seven Last Words* seem forced and out of character. They create the impression that Crotch – stung, perhaps, by complaints from moderns like Burney that his earlier lectures had misunderstood Haydn's intent – has deliberately set out to demonstrate the composer's weakness in the area that the moderns claimed as his greatest strength.

---

[224] Crotch is not alone in finding no expressive purpose for Haydn's enharmonic modulation. Nicholas Temperley observes of this passage in *Haydn: The Creation*, p. 77, that 'No amount of rehearing of this amazing passage [mm. 33–43] can make it sound ordinary. But I can think of no reason for it arising out of the text ("the breath and image of his God"), and I must conclude that it is simply an example of Haydn's well-known love of tricking his audience.'

CHAPTER FOUR

Conclusion:
Crotch and classical music

The musical values Crotch advocates in his lectures that follow in Part Two show a great many points of similarity with the ancient-music tradition and with the tradition of classical music that developed from it. First, Crotch's new musical world of 1818 was shaped fundamentally by interests and values that were only later taken up on the Continent as a result of the posthumous influence of Mozart. Just as William Weber finds the origins of musical classicism in the movement for ancient music, so Crotch views his new concert culture of 1818 as an extension of the habits and preferences of the English old-music community.

The old-music movement took pride in its resistance to fashion and self-conscious cultivation of the esoteric. Accordingly, the Ancient Concert sometimes dealt with popular composers of old music by choosing from their lesser known works, especially programming obscure selections from Handel oratorios. Such choices served to underline the learning of the Ancient Concert's leadership but also to remind its audience that the most valuable music is not necessarily the most familiar or the most superficially appealing. In the same spirit, Crotch selects for criticism two Haydn symphonies in the fourth of the lectures reprinted in Part Two (NRO, MS 11232/5) that he claims are well off the beaten track. These include Symphonies No. 73 ('La chasse') and 85 ('La reine'). The former, Crotch stresses, is 'scarcely known' while the latter had only just become widely available for study in an edition prepared by Crotch himself. In both cases Crotch deliberately compares Haydn's earlier works with popular favourites from the London symphonies. While the London Symphonies are cited for 'continually striking out novel effects',[1] there is no such reference in his commentary on the earlier works. Likewise, neither Symphony No. 73 nor 85 employ the larger orchestral resources of the later works (Symphonies 99, 103 and 104) to which they are compared. Instead of glamour and impressive-sounding effects, Crotch suggests, Haydn's earlier symphonies have 'treasures [that] lie somewhat beneath the surface and only seem to increase by being sought'.[2] Although Symphony No. 73, 'may please the

---

[1] *Lectures*, NRO, MS 11232/5.
[2] Ibid.

first time of hearing', it will nevertheless 'require much repetition to discern all its excellence'.[3]

Crotch also constantly demonstrates his respect for great composers, much as Weber has shown is true of earlier ancient-music culture. He is encouraged that 'pieces are listened to with deep attention and high approbation, which but a few years since were only known by the musical antiquarian'[4] and also that recent composers have intentionally studied and imitated the ancient style. At the same time, Crotch is troubled that Haydn's Quartet Op. 76 No. 6 has been inaccurately represented in an English adaptation as the work of Joseph Gelinek.[5] He is eager to set the record straight and to give the original composer due recognition. He insists on the faithful transmission of music and lashes out at 'the wanton, capricious, unnecessary alteration of passages'[6] in adaptations. That great music has been wilfully mutilated and disfigured is, he believes, a travesty that cannot be condemned with sufficient force.

Above all, in Crotch's brave new world of 1818, much as in the earlier culture of ancient music, the art is appreciated not only with the senses and the emotions, but also with the mind. It appeals to the mind, moreover, in two distinct ways that are consistent with earlier ancient-music criticism. Music began its slow ascent from a nadir in the 1770s, Crotch argues, when music by Haydn, Clementi, Boccherini and Kozeluch began to cultivate both 'harmony and imitation', that is, both contrivance and content.[7] Accordingly, while Crotch thinks vocal music adds sense to sound and 'calls in the attention of the mind as well as of the ears',[8] he also acknowledges that purely instrumental music can delight 'the mind, as well as the ear, not only of the experienced connoisseur but every lover of music'.[9] The music Crotch values most wears its 'science' conspicuously; it tries to 'elevate [the listener's] mind and fill it with serious admiration'.[10] He regrets that too much instrumental music still offers 'so little for the mind to dwell upon, so little that we desire to have repeated or protracted'.[11] Crotch's most sophisticated listeners 'delight and improve their minds by examining, analyzing, and dwelling upon [music in their] retirement'.[12] Because listeners can now

---

[3] Ibid.
[4] *Lectures*, NRO, MS 11232/2.
[5] Ibid.
[6] *Lectures*, NRO, MS 11232/3.
[7] *Lectures*, NRO, MS 11232/2.
[8] *Lectures*, NRO, MS 11232/6.
[9] *Lectures*, NRO, MS 11232/3.
[10] Ibid.
[11] Ibid.
[12] *Lectures*, NRO, MS 11232/4.

study the music in score – something Crotch, as much as anyone, helped to make possible – even humble piano exercises 'now prepare the hand, the eye, and the mind for score'[13] rather than merely drilling the fingers for vapid display. Levity, of course, has no place in Crotch's serious musical environment, any more than it did in the Academy of Ancient Music that Hawkins knew. Crotch's best music seeks not merely to entertain but to inspire awe, wonder and veneration.

If all the statements above are consistent with values expressed in nearly a century of earlier ancient-music criticism, there are, however, fundamental differences between the ancient-music culture that Weber describes and the concert culture of Crotch's 1818 lectures. In each case, Crotch's departures from the positions of his predecessors put him much closer in spirit to the values of classical music than any of the several distinct ancient-music traditions that preceded him. Weber's old music movement – at least in one of its most important and influential manifestations, the Ancient Concert – maintained a close connection with political interests and the concerns of a particular social strata. Crotch, however, describes a musical world under the control of professionals who pursue no moral or political agenda. He worries about the degeneration of the art but not, at least openly, about the maintenance of social order.

Crotch is most adamant that good judgement in music is unrelated to social class in a paragraph he later rejected from the first lecture series he wrote after his removal as lecturer at the Royal Institution in 1807. In this paragraph, Crotch argues that

> concerts indeed are not attended by [indecipherable] a mixture of different orders of society – the company consist of the elegant and the accomplished. Yet these perhaps are no better judges of music than the lower orders are of the inferior walks of painting. Music not being a mimetic art, to have a right judgment of its lower styles is therefore at least as difficult if not more so than for those who attend an exhibition to judge of the merits of some styles of painting which are founded on nature.[14]

This lecture series reveals Crotch's sensitivity to criticism in the period immediately following his difficulties at the Royal Institution, for these lectures, unlike the bulk of his writing, were obviously submitted in advance to some respected critic whose comments may be read in the margins of the manuscript. The objections of this reader, in fact, apparently prompted Crotch to reject the passage quoted above.[15]

---

[13] *Lectures*, NRO, MS 11232/2.

[14] *Lectures*, Col/7/43. Crotch indicates that this lecture was 'written in Oct & Nov. 1807'.

[15] It is also of some interest that Crotch originally titled his 1807 lecture series (i.e., Col/7/43–53), 'A Course of Lectures on Ancient Music', but later changed this title –

It is significant that while Weber's ancient tradition was defensive and largely driven by its fear of a decadent new musical style, Crotch could still find considerable merit in this very music in the lectures below. He regrets that for so long its many positive qualities were overlooked and looks forward to a new era of co-operation among musicians specializing in different styles. His concert world has a place, albeit a lower one, for music that seeks to amuse and entertain as well as to edify.

Finally, and most importantly, Crotch's lectures acknowledge, at least in theory, the possibility of the contemporary master-work. They acknowledge, in other words, that Crotch's highest musical style can be created by musical means that transcend any particular style or type. Admittedly, this recognition came reluctantly. As late as 1805 Crotch still could not bring himself to apply the concept of the sublime to the music of Haydn. The first paragraph of his Royal Institution lecture on Haydn in that year concludes by noting that Haydn's 'style embraces in their turns the grand, the beautiful and the ornamental'.[16] The word 'grand' – a lesser stand-in for the word 'sublime' that Crotch would have used in any other context – was added later, however, perhaps for an 1809 revival of this lecture at the Hanover Square Rooms. By 1818, Crotch had reconsidered the modern style and acknowledged that it – like Handel's music – could combine the best of different approaches. The first movement of the Mozart Quartet K. 387, a work some 36 years old at the time and scarcely new music, might be a kind of paradigm of Crotch's conception of classical music. This quartet 'arrests and commands the attention but does not surprise by difficulties of execution or excite a smile by its levity and eccentricity'.[17] Crotch is impressed that its 'subjects are treated with profound skill' and that 'many passages are in strict canon, and the modulation, though perfectly natural, is interesting and masterly'.[18] This praise admittedly stops short of Crotch's validation of a living composer's music, but there is some indication of his more contemporary preferences in his personal copy of the *Substance*, now held in the Norfolk Record Office. This volume concludes with Crotch's handwritten sentence pronouncing 'the 3 books of songs without words by Mendelssohn' as 'the finest productions for the Piano Forte of the present age'.[19]

---

consistent with the possibility that he had received complaints over his perceived partiality to ancient music – to 'A Course of Lectures on the Rise & Improvement of Music'.

[16] NRO, MS 11228/12.

[17] *Lectures*, NRO, MS 11232/4.

[18] Ibid.

[19] NRO, MS 11074.

PART TWO
Crotch's 1818 Lectures

Editorial introduction

NRO, MS 11232 is a bound volume containing 12 lectures as assembled by A. H. Mann. Several of these lectures have original titles by Crotch that indicate they were part of an 1818 lecture series. According to Crotch's *General Account of all the Courses of Lectures*, a group of eight new lectures was read at the Surrey Institution that year. The lectures are described as follows (Crotch's exact spelling and organization are preserved):

Surry Institution 1818. 8 New Lectures

Lecture	
I Feby 13.	Introductory. Gradus ad Parnassum Clementi Dulce & Utile. Cramer.
II Feby 20.	Dulce & Utile Continued – Haydn's Quartetts adapted, Gelinek's Haydn Nehrlich
III [Feb.] 27th	More Haydn's Quartetts adapted – Mozart Dr Kreutzer's Rondo
IV March 6th	La Chasse & N° 10 Haydn Sinfonias
V [March] 13th	1st & 2nd Acts of Don Giovanni Mozart. (20th Good Friday)
VI [March] 27th	3rd Act of D————
VII April 3rd	Alexander's Feast – Handel
VIII [April] 10th	Dettingen Te Deum D°

The *General Account* shows that Crotch used some or all of these lectures on several other occasions after 1818. Beginning on 28 April 1820, he read a course of seven lectures at the Royal Institution, his return to that venue after many years of lecturing elsewhere. For that occasion, he substituted an introductory lecture from 1808 for the provocative 1818 lecture reprinted here and eliminated his lecture on the *Dettingen Te Deum*. The revised lecture series, then, would have been very heavily weighted in the direction of modern music. This new direction might be consistent with the possibility that Crotch was removed as Royal Institution lecturer several years earlier for his strong ancient-music bias. Crotch's later use of this series also accounts for the present conclusion of NRO, MS 11232/8, which he must have altered in accordance with that lecture's new role as the conclusion of the series. NRO, MSS 11232/5 and 11232/8 reappeared still later in 1822 at the Surrey Institution, and several lectures from the 1818 series (NRO, MSS 11232/2–5) were repeated there as well in 1823. Crotch did not use the entire 1818 series – especially the important introductory lecture – again, however, until 1827, in a series at the London

Institution. After that lecture series, the only lecture from 1818 to be used again was Crotch's lecture on Haydn's symphonies (NRO, MS 11232/5), which, as the *General Account* reports, required significant alterations. This lecture's final appearance was in Crotch's last documented public lecture series at the London Literary and Scientific Institution in 1830.

The entire contents of NRO, MS 11232, are described below in the order in which they appear in Mann's bound volume. Crotch's original titles are given in italics. They are followed by the numbers by which the lectures are cited in the present study together with brief descriptions of the contents of each lecture where necessary.

Lecture 10th NRO, MS 11232/1. Early eighteenth-century composers including Croft, Steffani, Leo, A. Scarlatti and Pergolesi.

Introductory Lecture 1818 NRO, MS 11232/2. The improvement of modern music; ancient versus modern music since 1778; Clementi's *Gradus ad Parnassum* and Clementi's *Dulce et Utile*.

Lecture II 1818 NRO, MS 11232/3. Continuation of NRO, MS 11232/ 2 on Clementi and Cramer.

Lecture. III 1818 NRO, MS 11232/4. Mozart, Quartets in G, K. 387 and D minor, K. 421; Haydn, Quartets in G, Op. 76 No. 1, D minor, Op. 76 No. 2, and B flat major, Op. 76 No. 4; Kreutzer\Cramer.

Lecture IV. 1818. Sinfonias NRO, MS 11232/5. Haydn symphonies Nos 73, 85, 99, 103, 104.

Lecture V.1ˢᵗ Act of Don Giovanni NRO, MS 11232/6.

2ⁿᵈ Act of Don Giovanni NRO, MS 11232/7.

Lecture VII Alexander's Feast. Handel. 1818 NRO, MS 11232/8.

Lecture 12th NRO, MS 11232/9. The music of Handel; musical styles: the sublime, the beautiful, and the ornamental; mixture of styles.

Lecture XI.ᵗʰ NRO, MS 11232/10. Early to mid-eighteenth century composers other than Handel: J. S. Bach, Caldara, Green, Galliard\Cooke, Marcello, Graun, D'Astorga, Keiser, Lotti, Hasse.

Lecture 8ᵗʰ or 20ᵗʰ NRO, MS 11232/11. Chamber and keyboard music: Vanhal; on the character of different keys; Edelmann, Eichner, Staes, Sterkel, Schroeter, Schobert, Boccherini, Kozeluch.

Lecture 9ᵗʰ NRO, MS 11232/12 The late seventeenth century: Blow, Creighton, Aldrich, Durante, Locke, Keiser, Lotti, Colonna, Gasparini, Clarke, Goldwin, Purcell.

The coincidental appearance of consecutive numbering, together with the fact that many of Crotch's lecture series contain 12 or more lectures, may have prompted Mann to bind these lectures together. In fact, however, there is no evidence that NRO, MSS 11232/1, 9, 10, 11 and

12 were ever used in the same series as the original eight lectures of the 1818 series. The only lecture from the original 1818 series that is not now included in NRO, MS 11232, is Crotch's lecture on Handel's *Dettingen Te Deum*. This lecture appears as the ninth item in NRO, MS 11229.

Editorial conventions

The following editorial conventions are observed: In the body of Crotch's text, abbreviations such as 'w^ch' or 'w^d' or 'accomp^ts' have been expanded and Crotch's inevitable 'y^e' is replaced throughout with 'the'. Crotch's spelling and punctuation have both been modernized. Variant readings significant enough to merit being included are placed in notes. In notes, the following conventions are observed: braces { } indicate over-scored text and text presented +thus+ was added with a caret. Conjectural readings and indecipherable text are indicated by angle brackets < >, and editorial insertions are placed in square brackets [ ]. Unless otherwise indicated, text that was added after the first draft is presented in italics. Such insertions appear in the manuscript either on the reverse of a facing page or on new leaves attached to the original manuscript. Indications of musical examples in the lectures are given at exactly the points in the text where Crotch put them, with his own notations of the volumes and page numbers from which they are drawn. The examples themselves are not provided and this omission calls for some explanation. In many cases, especially where minor figures are concerned, it is simply not possible to identify with confidence the work in question from the very limited information Crotch provides. Most such examples were not taken from Crotch's *Specimens of Various Styles of Music Referred to in a Course of Lectures read at Oxford and London*, which survives, but rather from various other score collections and published editions that have not been located. By providing the reader with Crotch's own descriptions of the examples it is hoped that future scholars may yet be able to identify some of the more obscure selections. The bulk of Crotch's examples, however, come from major composers, for whom modern editions are readily available and which are far superior to the piano reductions of the *Specimens*.

Introductory Lecture 1818

The improvement of modern music, since the period usually assigned to its lowest state of decline,[1] is indescribably great; and the general advancement of the public taste in this country, and especially in this metropolis, since the commencement of the present century, clearly is perceptible. Instrumental music of every species is become more distinct in character from vocal. The passages distributed to various instruments are more congenial to their several properties. New and brilliant effects of composition have kept pace with or perhaps given birth to the increasing taste and execution of the performance. The accompaniments of vocal music have consequently become more varied and interesting. A gradual amendment in scientific writing is also to be discerned. And though a mechanical or pedantic style is not revived, we are no longer taught to regard contrivance and ingenuity with horror as something vicious (scelerato) and incompatible with elegance, expression and feeling.

To ascertain the precise period at which music was at its lowest ebb may not be an easy or a necessary task. It may have differed in various kingdoms.[2] In this nation it appears to have been about fifty[3] years ago, when a great musical revolution was attempted but, happily, not effected. A decided hostility was avowed by the lovers of modern music to all that was learned, serious and sublime. Our church music had lost its peculiar and devotional character. Oratorio composers were no more. Instrumental music was in its infancy; and the present Italian opera style was scarcely arrived at perfection, even in its vocal departments. The lovers of ancient and of modern music ranged on their respective sides, each party overlooking the merits of the opposite schools. A fugue was considered as Gothic and barbarous by the one while the other despised an Italian air as senseless and childish.

The lowest ebb of *public taste* was not, however, quite arrived but succeeded by a few years that of *musical composition*. The improvement of instrumental performance became so striking and captivating that it was no longer confined to professional persons, or the accom-

---

[1] Crotch includes the following calculation in pencil in the upper right-hand margin of the first page:

$$\begin{array}{r} 1818 \\ \underline{40} \\ 1778 \end{array}$$

[2] {or in the several composers of the same age}

[3] {forty}

plished few. To play became as indispensable a part of education as to read and write, and when the music thus generally performed consisted neither of the sublime productions in the church and oratorio, the beautiful refinements of the present opera style, or such ornamental pieces as we are accustomed to; but of inferior compositions now happily sunk into oblivion, then indeed the public taste in this nation was, in my estimation, at a lower ebb than at a still earlier period when the few who *could* play unostentatiously amused themselves with Alberti's[4] lessons or an opera song.

The introduction of Haydn's music into our concerts and of the productions for the chamber of Boccherini, Clementi and Kozeluch, in which harmony and imitation were cultivated, stamped a dignity on modern music which the admirers of the ancient school were disposed[5] to acknowledge. But when Mozart became the universal favourite, the long-desired[6] reconciliation between the parties necessarily followed. For the lovers of madrigals, anthems and choruses eagerly added[7] to their former store of amusement, the highly ingenious and elaborate vocal trios, quartets and finales from the operas of this extraordinary composer. On the other hand few, if any, are now found who affect to despise what is scientific and sublime.

The admirers of single authors also have altogether disappeared. We once had the exclusive votaries of Corelli, Purcell, Handel, Geminiani, Pergolesi and Hasse and of Haydn. But though Mozart be justly acknowledged to be on the whole and especially on account of his vocal productions the greatest of modern composers, yet he has not drawn off the attention from the former objects of regard, but rather by his own veneration for them and adoption of their styles has compelled us to enlarge and improve our taste. For we cannot consistently admire the works of Mozart and dislike what he esteemed. How, for instance, shall we vindicate a disapprobation of Handel, whom Mozart professed to hold in the highest regard (I speak from good authority) – some of whose works he adapted to German words for the use of his countrymen and the improvement of their taste, and whose style he frequently thought it no degradation to imitate? What is excellent in one master is equally so in another. And hence though a difference of opinions may still exist as to the relative merits of the ancient and modern schools or of the several composers of each, yet a division of the musical world into two great parties no longer exists.

---

4 {and Paradies}
5 {inclined}
6 {an unexpected}
7 {admitted}

The taste both of performers and auditors has of late years been greatly ameliorated by various circumstances. One of these is, that we frequently hear, in Concerts, not professedly consisting of Ancient Music, those never fading relics of former masters which have survived all that is inferior and stood the test, and obtained the approbation, of successive ages. In most Concerts,[8] which seemed formerly to consult rather than direct the public taste, pieces are now listened to, not with indifference but with deep attention and high approbation, which but a few years since were only known by the musical antiquarian. Foreigners also, from being accustomed to Mozart's style, soon acquired a taste for old music which is seldom heard on the Continent. It is true indeed that a diversity of tastes still exists. The Italian still prefers the vocal melody of his own nation. The German finds no instrumental effects like those produced by his modern countrymen. And the lover of canon and fugue, of all that is rich and magnificent, sacred and sublime still contends that the ancients have not been equalled much less surpassed; or rather that no approximation to their inimitable grandeur, has ever been effected. These several positions are true, and it is essential to the existence of good taste that they should all continue to be admitted. But they are no longer, as formerly, advanced in the way of opposition and hostility to each other. Whatever deductions may be made from a comparison of these styles, the above facts are all now pretty generally admitted, and this indicates a considerable improvement in the public taste.

Why then it may be asked was this not generally admitted *till lately?* Let us consider the habits and opinions of the contending parties already mentioned. The lovers of ancient music in this country had been accustomed to rich harmony, intricate contrivance and simple grandeur. And they justly continued to admire these notwithstanding the introduction, in the latter half of the preceding century, of a style, perfectly different in character, beautiful indeed but comparatively artless and trifling. On the Continent it has ever been the custom to perform the last productions of a favourite composer for a whole season and then lay them entirely aside. Thus the sublime style was superseded by the beautiful and ornamental. Italy was the mother of them all, but in her fondness for the younger offspring she had neglected and disowned her first born, who, however, found an asylum in this less fickle nation.

Ancient music has always had its firm friends. The admirers of novelty and especially of what they can readily comprehend, are ever numerous, and on that account the modern style could not want for votaries amongst our countrymen. But multitudes who were guided in all things by the fashions of the Continent, finding that foreigners

---

[8] {Even in some Concerts}

despised the productions of the old school, did not dare to do other-wise. And even our best critical writers seem to have regarded our art as totally dependent on invention for its charms. And while Painters were taught to venerate the old masters of *their* sublime schools, musicians were encouraged to regard every novelty as an improvement, every succeeding composer as greater than all who were gone before him! The attack was violent, and the defence vigorous. The Concert of Ancient Music and the performances at Westminster Abbey enabled the parti-sans of the old school to maintain their positions until the general pacification effected by Mozart so happily succeeded.

Another circumstance which was conducive to the improvement of the public taste of this kingdom was the establishment of Salomon's and afterwards of the Philharmonic Concert – [concerts] directed by profes-sional musicians, consisting of the music *they* admire, and in some degree embracing a variety of excellencies, at least uniting the best vocal and instrumental modern music. Here these musicians of two descrip-tions, I mean of the German and Italian schools, meet together and learn to appreciate the opposite merits of the beautiful and ornamental styles with a considerable though inferior portion of the sublime. And by making popularity a consideration of inferior moment, they lead instead of following, they correct instead of flattering the public taste.

Another cause of the increased diffusion of taste among our dilettante players appears to me to be the more general performance on the piano forte of music originally intended for an orchestra, either when read immediately from the score or from a correct adaptation. It is evident that the productions expressly intended for the piano forte, or songs with an accompaniment for that instrument only, form but a very small portion of the ample abundance of all that is admirable in our art. A keyed instrument was originally intended to be a guide to many parts: the first use of the organ was to organize or regulate the voices, and this is still its noblest employment. The peculiar characters of the harp, harpsichord and piano forte naturally suggested the invention of music calculated to display their tone and expression. In proportion, however, as the performer cultivates this display of his instrument he necessarily neglects the study of score and all the higher branches of the art. Hence so many ladies who have in their early years attained an extraordinary degree of execution, afterwards lay music wholly aside in disgust. Their judgement and taste were never interested; they never thoroughly un-derstood and enjoyed music. Let, however, the keyed instrument become a little domestic orchestra and it will be constantly resorted to that the imagination may be reminded of all that has given delight in the church oratorio, opera or concert. And thus to sonatas and canzonets may be added chants, psalms, anthems, madrigals, glees, overtures, songs, vocal and instrumental duets, trios, quartets, and quintets, concertos, sinfonias and choruses.

And it is not only from the quantity and variety but also from the quality of the music that the gratification of the performer will be enhanced. For, as a general position and with very few exceptions, it may be asserted that the greatest composers have produced far better music in score than for the piano forte or any other single instrument. Playing from score therefore amply repays any inferiority of execution which may be the natural consequence of its acquirement. Wherever this art is attained in an eminent degree it demonstrates indeed a more than ordinary capacity and disposition for music and cannot therefore be expected from *all* who play well, but surely the performance of well-adapted music may. I therefore notice with pleasure the superiority of many late adaptations of songs, overtures, symphonies and choruses, as unequivocally tending to diffuse and establish a preference for the best music.

The task of adapting has until lately been very ill executed. I shall not enter at present into a review of the several causes of the failure. Skill and fidelity were certainly required. Skill was sometimes wanting, but fidelity, the more valuable of the two, was rarely found.

Another improvement in some of the most excellent recent publications, is the introduction of rich harmony into music originally and expressly composed for the piano forte; an improvement naturally resulting from the increased attention to full music. That such instruments as the lyre and organ should continue for a length of time amongst their inventors to be played with only one hand, whilst enlargement alone was wanting to admit of both hands being employed, can only be accounted for on the supposition that music in parts was not yet invented. And when music for keyed instruments consisted of only a treble and bass it indicated no great predilection for harmony in its author. Composers for the organ and harpsichord at the age which I have assigned to the perfection of the art abounded with passages which resembled full music. Handel's lessons and Sebastian Bach's fugues and most of the German productions for the organ consisted generally of three and frequently of four real parts. The invention of modern music reduced them again to a treble and bass, and the latter often consisted of an arpeggio division of the chord adopted on almost all occasions and no fitter for one piece of music than another. The German composers after this occasionally indulged us with a few passages of harmony but it was not till very lately that we met with a continuance of them through the greater part of a movement.

Exercises or practices for the young performers, instead of consisting, as formerly, wholly of passages of execution, calculated merely to give rapidity to the finger, now prepare the hand, the eye and the mind for score, directing the attention to rich and ingenious contrivances rather than to the charms of melody alone. In illustration of the latter remarks I shall adduce a few specimens from two works intended for the improvement of piano forte playing by two eminent masters who at the time of writing these remarks were absent on the Continent. I mean the *Gradus ad Parnassum* in two Volumes by Clementi and the *Dulce and Utile* of Cramer.

That by Clementi consists of fifty Exercises, in the strict and in the free styles.[9] These are all excellent for the uses intended. But I pass by those *principally* meant to strengthen and equalize the fingers and improve the execution, though these are highly wrought and very masterly, and I shall rather perform two which are eminent both for richness of harmony and elegance of melody.[10] The fourth movement does not wear the appearance of a mere exercise but is a regular & interesting composition, no less calculated to improve & gratify the taste than to strengthen & expand the fingers. *(Ex 4 Clementi)*

The eighth example is an Allegretto producing in its accompaniments many effects which remind us of the Orchestra. It is short and seems to pretend to nothing but contains a finishing & accuracy which demonstrate the science of an able master *(Ex 8)*

Canons and fugues of intricate construction appear in this volume and although the predominant style of this Author and that wherein he chiefly excelled was a combination of the beautiful and the ornamental, it is evident that he could occasionally adopt one that was laboured, ingenious and learned.

Cramer's[11] *Dulce and Utile*[12] consists of six detached movements or regular compositions – not mere practices but answering rather to the

---

[9] Clementi's *Gradus ad Parnassum* was published in three volumes between 1816 and 1825. The final version consisted of one hundred pieces, not fifty.

[10] Crotch used this lecture on later occasions, for which he chose different examples from Clementi's collection. For later uses, he attached the following to the original manuscript:

The 42nd Example is directed by the composer to be played with energy, passion and fire and this describes its character sufficiently. The predominant style is tragic but sweet passages in the minor key are not wanting. The modulations are very ingenious and the whole is a fine study. (Ex. 42 page 58)

The above specimen is the first of three movements belonging to each other, but I shall prefer on the present occasion going back to the 38th Example which is in the major key – of an opposite character and in our author's happiest style. Here we have execution and brilliancy most happily blended with scientific counterpoint. (Ex. 38 page 32)

[11] *Studies were intended for the same purpose as the work I have just quoted and are too well known and adopted to need an encomium from me on the present occasion. His work called …*

[12] In 'A Feud Between Clementi and Cramer', *Music and Letters*, 54 (1973), 282, Alan

exploded denominations of Rondos. The first is extremely elegant although abounding with full harmony and uncommon modulation. Here are no rapid passages of execution but the whole is calculated to improve the expression and touch of the performer while it delights and soothes his ear. *(Ex. I Cramer)*

The second Movement is yet more elegant. The idea seems to have been taken from an adagio in the fourteenth Opera of Clementi, now inserted as one of the exercises of his late work. This resemblance was probably accidental and at all events immaterial and unblamable.[13] For though the key, the harmony, the cadences and the metre are the same, the melodies, time and the treatment of the subjects are different.[14] The musical composer must collect not invent materials. Whatever is wholly and rigorously new must be very disagreeable. *(Ex. 2nd)*

The performance of the other movements of this work is reserved for the following lecture where I shall likewise resume the consideration of the present state, both of the music usually performed in this country and of the public taste, which may indeed be regarded as the principal subject of the present course of lectures.

Fine.

Tyson reports that Cramer's collection was published in London on 19 December 1815 as Op. 55. Its original title was 'Dulce et Utile, Consisting of Six Movements Intended as (moderately difficult) Practice for the Piano Forte'. Other editions were also published in Leipzig and Paris. This date supplements Jerald C. Graue's 'before 1818' in 'Cramer Johann [John] Baptist', *The New Grove Dictionary of Music and Musicians*, ed. Stanley Sadie, 20 vols (London: Macmillan Publishers Ltd, 1980), vol. 5, p. 21. *Dulce et Utile* was reviewed anonymously in *Allgemeine Musicalische Zeitung*, 20 (1818), col. 167.

[13] The complex circumstances surrounding this apparent borrowing are discussed at length in Alan Tyson, 'A Feud Between Clementi and Cramer', 281–8 (with musical examples) and in Jerald C. Graue, 'The Clementi-Cramer Dispute Revisited', *Music and Letters*, 56 (1975), 47–54.

[14] {For though the key, the harmony, the cadences and the metre are the same, the melodies and the time are different}.

Lecture II 1818

The improvement of modern music, and the general advancement of taste both of performers and auditors, in this country, within a few years formed the subject of the preceding lecture. I then endeavoured to shew that when the composers of modern music first attempted to make it supersede the ancient, and to substitute the inferior styles for the superior, their taste was at its lowest ebb. And that such was the state of the public taste, *when* a general cultivation of the performance on keyed instruments prevailed without a correspondent acquaintance with the best authors. The present amelioration I ascribed chiefly to the introduction of Mozart's works which were admired both by the lovers of ancient and of modern music, who had long been at variance. I likewise mentioned as other causes of the same effect the more frequent performance of the relics of the ancient great masters in our miscellaneous concerts, the formation of a Concert in which Professional Musicians consult their own tastes rather than that of their auditors, the more general acquaintance with full music either performed from the score or well adapted as it now sometimes is, the reprinting of old music, the importation of foreign new music in score, and the introduction of fuller harmony into our piano forte music. Examples of the latter were adduced from the first volumes of Clementi's *Gradus ad Parnassum* and of Cramer's *Dulce and Utile* works intended to form the hand, to strengthen the fingers and to improve the execution, but calculated at the same time to direct the attention to what is worthy of study, and to make a useful rather than a dazzling performer.

I proceed now to offer some more specimens of the latter work. The third movement is lively and brilliant. Its subject opens with the gaiety of a French dance, but we are afterwards frequently reminded of the ancient style. Passages remarkable for their novelty and originality are mixed with others which resemble Mozart. Some are calculated to display the execution, others to elicit the peculiar properties of the instrument. The whole is well put together, and is much superior, in many respects, and especially in richness of harmony, to the generality of modern productions. *(Ex III Dulce etc.)*

The six movements which constitute this work are admirably varied in character; and though it has been said generally of them *all* that they are rich in harmony and elegant in melody, yet there are shades of difference which elude the powers of verbal description, but which a refined judgement will readily discern. The fourth movement, like the first is delicate and slow but more melodious. Like the second, it is tender but less grave and elevated; passages of execution are wholly excluded; and the modulation, though sufficiently varied and interesting, is remarkably simple and unaffected. *(Ex IV)*

The fifth movement is grave and pathetic.[1] The minor parts are beautifully opposed by passages in the major key in which a wavy motion is heard, somewhat like that which Handel has so happily used to elucidate Milton's description[2] in the song 'hide me from day's garish eye'[3]

> and let some strange mysterious dream
> wave at his wings in airy stream
> of lively portraiture display'd
> softly on my eyelids laid.

The variations of the melody and accompaniment are excellent, and the conclusion happily conceived. *(Ex. V.)*

The last movement is called 'Toccatina' and is manifestly intended as an exercise for the improvement of the execution and has consequently less melody and contrivance that the foregoing and yet sufficient, it is trusted, to establish the positions already laid down. *(Ex. VI[4])*

But while we hail this new dawn of improvement, let us not forget the superior splendours of the day that is past. Much yet remains to be effected which will require a length of time. The instrumental style is indeed much improved; but the vocal, even that of the opera seems to have past its zenith while the oratorio and church styles are much neglected. But the increased admiration of what is excellent in every style will it is hoped stimulate the rising composers to the restoration of every department of the art. The most difficult task will be for church composers to regain anything like the pure sublimity of the ancients. If this were effected it[5] might have a considerable influence on the oratorio and madrigal styles, and a much greater proportion of rich and scientific passages would be found in our music for keyed instruments.

---

[1] {<its subject is said to> <two lines indecipherable>}. The over-scored sentence probably concerned another instance of supposed borrowing.

[2] {of the Wings of a dream}

[3] Milton, *Il Penseroso*, lines 141 and 147–50.

[4] *The following movement from a Sonata by Beethoven called Letter A, is composed in a style far above that of Piano Forte music in general. The Master seems to have despised the applause of the multitude and merely to have written for himself and the best critics. It is, like much of this author's works wild and original. But it is replete with fine harmony, modulation, feeling and expression.*

(Vol III P.F.)
Beethoven

[5] {would}

Indeed, the majority of our late publications for the piano forte are airs with variations, consisting chiefly of difficult and extraneous, rather than of scientific or beautiful passages. The neatness of execution which they are meant to display, or the novelties and eccentricities with which they abound may surprise and amuse us as long as they are new, but in reviewing and weighing their merits as compositions, we cannot but lament that there should be so little for the mind to dwell upon, so little that we desire to have repeated or protracted. I am not now contradicting my former statements. There is indeed much more that is excellent than there formerly was, but desirable would be the acquisition of yet more.

But perhaps it may here be asked, if the discrimination of the peculiar qualities of the several instruments be admitted as an improvement in modern music in general, why should the piano forte be excluded? The fashionable music of the day is surely calculated to display its powers! This I admit; but I do not consider the piano forte as an instrument which is in general to be heard together with other instruments. In that case I should approve of a more immediate attention to its *peculiar* properties, as in the works of the elegant and judicious Kozeluch. This creates an agreeable contrast and prevents the deficiency of tone in the piano forte (as compared with the protracted sounds of the violin) from disappointing the ear. Yet, Mozart who was confessedly a far greater genius than Kozeluch neglected this, which he possibly deemed a minor consideration compared with the strict and scientific treatment of his subjects. He frequently gave the same passages, without the slightest variation, alternatively to the piano forte and the violin.

When the Piano Forte is to be heard *alone* however, the case is materially altered. Composers of solos, or solo concertos for other instruments generally endeavour to combine every possible variety of style and expression, while those who write for the piano forte seem afraid of exposing its defects and only display its peculiarities – though perhaps the piano forte is as susceptible of varied expressions as any other instrument. But if we consider the piano forte as an amusement for the chamber – a domestic orchestra, however inferior it may be to other instruments – we cannot consent to give up the sublime and beautiful styles for the ornamental, to neglect the higher and cultivate only the *lower* walks of the art. For when the piano forte is heard alone the imagination is called in and most willingly supplies every deficiency. It not only enjoys the rapid passages but seems to hear holding notes, can fancy the 'pealing organ' – can not only distinguish soft and loud passages but also discover the tones of different instruments, nay even seem to hear the words of a madrigal or chorus, previously known. And thus the mind, as well as the ear, not only of the experienced connoisseur but every lover of music, is delighted and amused.

This pleasure is analogous to that derived in a sister art through the organ of sight when the imagination has always more or less to supply the details. Few pictures will be found on a close examination to be so highly wrought as they appear to be when viewed at a proper distance. It is asserted by the great lecturer on that art, that too much finishing destroys this delightful employment of the imagination, and he thus partly accounts for the high gratification produced by the slightest sketches of the great masters.[6] In our art, those pieces for keyed instruments which have the least execution, are frequently if not generally the best compositions. The harmony and melody are most neglected when the author is chiefly anxious to astonish an audience by the brilliancy and rapidity of the performer. Hence also the tuttis of a solo concerto are in general so much better than the solos.

But I will cease for the present to argue on this subject and once more make my appeal to the ear. The following air with variations is published as the tenth number of that species of composition by Gelinek. Its superiority over the other numbers was first pointed out to me by a professed admirer of modern piano forte music, who naturally conceived it to be the production of Gelinek as the real author's name is unaccountably omitted in the English editions. It is, however, wholly the composition of Haydn and is adapted with tolerable accuracy from one of his quartets.[7] I shall perform this as a proof that I am not singular in supposing that the various tones and qualities of different instruments are not always requisite in the performance of what was originally intended for them. Haydn has treated his subject in three variations with his usual superiority in his own fanciful, ingenious, and peculiar style, giving the subject alternately to the several parts. He concludes with a spirited fugato movement in the ancient style on two subjects, the first of which is the exordium of the air itself. *(Haydn No 10 Gelinek) ms. page 20*

The last specimen I shall give in this lecture of the full and scientific style which, I trust, will eventually prevail, is a Russian air with Variations for the Piano Forte by Jean Pierre Theodore Nehrlich originally published in Russia and now reprinted in this kingdom. All the variations are extremely ingenious and very remote from vulgarity. Some of

---

[6] Sir Joshua Reynolds takes up these issues in several places, especially *Discourses on Art*, ed. Robert R. Wark (New Haven, CT, and London: Yale University Press, 1975), IV and XI.

[7] The quartet in question is Hob. III:80 (Op. 76/6) in E flat. See Milan Postolka, 'Gelinek, Joseph' in *The New Grove Dictionary of Music and Musicians*, ed. Stanley Sadie, 20 vols (London: Macmillan Publishers Ltd, 1980), vol. 7, pp. 222–3, and G. Proier, 'Abbe J. Gelinek als Variationenkomponist', (PhD dissertation, University of Vienna, 1962).

them are in three, others in four distinct parts. At one time the subject is heard in Canon. At another, it becomes the subject of a fugue and is used in augmentation and inversion. At last it terminates in the solemn style of a psalm tune or chant. *(Nehrlich vol. III)*

I beg leave to caution the student who has attended my former courses of lectures not to suppose that any change has taken place in my sentiments concerning the comparative merits of the several styles on account of my not having as yet pressed the arguments on which they were before established. I have preferred an endeavour of arriving at the same conclusions by a different path. I will however terminate the present lecture by repeating a short method of appreciating the comparative value of the style of which any piece of music consists, which the student will find simple, infallible and easy to remember. Let him consider in what manner the music affects him. Does it surprise and amuse him? Does it soothe and tranquilize him? Or does it elevate his mind and fill it with serious admiration? Whatever, in our art or indeed in any other art, produces merely surprise and entertainment, is inferior to what excites our complacency and love, and both are surpassed by that which awakens in us awe and wonder and veneration.

FINE.

Lect. IIIrd 1818

The superiority, both in quantity and quality, of full music over that composed expressly for the piano forte we now consider is an admitted fact. Nothing therefore seems more likely to improve the public taste than a still greater and more general familiarity with this music, either in score, or well adapted; and accordingly it is intended to offer in the present and following lectures, an illustration of this principle. If the opinions of the generality of my audience be at variance with these sentiments I cannot feel surprised. By attending a lecture, however, *they* assume the character of *students* not critics. And to *such alone* the present lectures are addressed. Many individuals now present may indeed be experienced critics, able composers, or amateurs who have long been in the habit of attending the best musical performances and require no assistance of the kind here offered. But such cannot, it is presumed, constitute the majority of any large audience. Nor would much material difference of opinion be apprehended from such experienced hearers.

Contrariety of sentiment usually springs from a confused and imperfect knowledge of the subject in at least one of the parties. For there is a kind of *Truth* even in matters of taste which will ultimately prevail. In presuming therefore to discover this Truth, a lecturer claims no ascendancy over other critics, he assumes no natural superiority of judgement. He well knows how long it took to cultivate his own taste and how much he was indebted to the strength and guidance of others. He only requests to point out to the young and inexperienced student what has been shown him by the oldest and most able judges. I shall, as I intimated in my last lecture, endeavour occasionally to give a direction to the principles of young composers. But the subject now proposed addresses itself rather to performers on the piano forte, who according to the prevailing system of teaching are acquainted with no music but such as was expressly composed for the instrument and if they occasionally hear full music at the concert or opera seldom or never delight and improve their minds by examining, analysing and dwelling upon it [in their] retirement.

Hence it should not cause surprise if the sentiments and opinions advanced on this occasion do not coincide with those of the student. Were a lecture on painting in general to be read to the mixed assemblies which frequent a public exhibition of new pictures, how astonished would the majority be at the comparatively little mention made of the contemporary productions which they had been accustomed to admire and prefer. Or if these were made the subject of the lecture, how much mortification and disappointment would they feel when informed that in appreciating the comparative merits of even these they had not formed a correct judgement. That what was most dazzling and attractive, most gay and brilliant, was considerably inferior to pieces which they would scarcely have noticed. It is true that the audience who are in the habit of frequenting scientific lectures are a very different description from what I have just alluded to and bring with them far better capacities for improvement.

Yet, making this allowance the cases will be found somewhat similar. The immortal works of Bird, Luca Marenzio, Carissimi, Palestrina, Stradella, Alessandro Scarlatti and other ancient composers are perhaps as little or even less known to the majority of my hearers than the ancient painters are to the admirers of an exhibition. And setting aside, for the present, these venerable founders of our art, which are necessarily most out of the reach of general investigation, how little is known of the finest productions of modern times by persons fully capable of performing and enjoying them. The quartets and quintets for stringed instruments by Boccherini, Haydn, Mozart and other eminent modern masters are seldom heard at all by the young performer on the piano forte. The full scores of some of these have been published on the Continent, but are rarely seen in this kingdom. Correct adaptations of them are seldom found. Incorrect adaptations indeed are unhappily, not wanting. However inferior the quartets of Pleyel may be to those of Haydn, Mozart and perhaps many other masters, they could not, I conceive, have sunk into that contempt and oblivion which have awaited them in this kingdom but for the disgraceful editions of these compositions for the piano forte by Lachnit and others.

I do not wish to oppose any opinion formed of these works by persons who know them in their original state. But I caution all others not to pass a hasty censure. Let them examine the score and they will find much that is excellent, and which they never could have expected from the adaptation. The quartets of Haydn have been no less disgraced by an incorrect arrangement for the piano forte in a work called the Beauties of Haydn.

The adaptation of full music to a single instrument may be compared to a translation from one language to another. Translators are certainly required to know the different idioms of the languages employed, and are therefore authorized to make any *necessary* deviations for the sake of preserving the spirit of the author. But having this commission given them, if they abuse their privilege and do not make the translation as literal as it *might* be without injury, they are *justly reprehensible* and it is the same with the adapters of full music.

I have already remarked that *want of skill* on the *one* hand and *want of fidelity* on the *other* are [the] leading defects [of incorrect adaptations]. Want of skill is manifest when a passage in the score which cannot be performed on the piano forte at all, or not without considerable difficulty, remains unaltered, or when any alteration which is necessary on account of the impossibility or difficulty of execution is not so contrived as to preserve as much as possible of the original intended effect. Here the translation is *too literal*. But this is a far more venial and less common error than want of fidelity. For if the passage cannot be *easily* executed, or even not at all, still the author's meaning may be seen. The performer may judge of the effect designed. But want of *fidelity* – the wanton, capricious, unnecessary alteration of passages which might easily be played on a keyed instrument as they originally stood, the extraordinary and total perversions and misrepresentation of every particular, of the notes, of the expression, of the chords, of the melody, of the situation of notes on the scale, of the number of bars, of the very passages themselves, some being entirely omitted, others inserted which were not in the original – this is intolerable. For this I can scarcely conceive any censure *sufficiently severe*.

Yet thus have the finest full pieces both of the ancient and modern schools, been mutilated and disfigured. Thus have all Purcell's, all Corelli's, all Handel's, and the greater part of Haydn's and Mozart's works been obscured transformed and disguised. So general has been the practice that to enumerate what has been thus spoilt would be an endless task, while to mention the really faithful and unexceptionable adaptations would be, at least comparatively, easy. Indeed it is only within a few years that an improvement in adaptations has become visible, and I sincerely rejoice at the symptom of improving taste. By the performance of *more* and *better* music on the piano forte the judgment of the student *must* be improved. By directing his mind more to the music and less to the performance (less, I mean, to the difficulties of execution, not less to the expression) more delight *must* be derived.

With the view of elucidating these positions I shall now proceed to give some specimens from modern quartets. The following is an animated movement by Haydn from the first in the small score printed at Paris; it is equally characterized by gaiety of style, skilful treatment of the subjects, and judicious modulation. *(Ex. Quar. G)*[1] *Page 1*

The Adagio of the same quartet commences with a subject somewhat resembling the celebrated March in Mozart's opera of the Zauberflote. This is opposed by fanciful and playful responsive passages between the

---

[1] Crotch gives the incipit of Haydn, Quartet in G major Op. 76 No. 1, first movement.

treble and bass, fully exemplifying the genius and originality of this inventive author. *(Adagio in C)*[2]

The middle movement of the second quartet of the same set is an elegant Siciliana. The returns to the subject are peculiar, wearing the appearance rather of experiments than of selected ideas. Our author indeed frequently seems to have taken pleasure in recording whatever presented itself to his fertile imagination. The variation is masterly and interesting though of a species by no means uncommon. The subject itself is remarkably tender and expressive. *(Ex 6/8 in D)*[3] *Page 10*

The motivo of the following finale seems to have been suggested by the imperfect recollection of some national tune or other production of a period much anterior to that of our author. Its character reminds us of the species of dance called the Hornpipe. It abounds with novelty. The parts are all busily employed in sustaining portions of the subject, and the whole is an excellent sample of the unity of science and invention, gravity and gaiety, elaboration and effect. *(Finale in B^b page 18)*[4]

From the quartets of Mozart the student may likewise select many pieces calculated to refine his taste and increase his love of harmony. The following movement is replete with new and elegant conceptions. The style of the whole is not that of Italian beauty or of the ornamental and humorous manner of Haydn. A greater degree of gravity and sobriety than is usual in modern instrumental music pervades the whole, rendering it somewhat less attractive at the first hearing though not less interesting on a longer acquaintance. On the contrary, as there are states of the mind which will not endure to hear any music at all, so there are some in which it could only bear sacred and ancient music; and again there are others in which the pleasantries of Haydn would give pain but the elegant ingenuities of Mozart would interest and delight; and the repetition of his music only winds it closer around the heart. It arrests and commands the attention but does not surprise by difficulties of execution or excite a smile by its levity and eccentricity. The subjects are treated with profound skill; many passages are in strict canon, and the modulation, though perfectly natural, is interesting and masterly. *(Mozart G page 24)*[5]

That Mozart could occasionally adopt the manner of Haydn may be seen from the following andante, where a few notes forming only a

---

[2] Crotch gives the incipit of Haydn, Quartet in G major Op. 76 No. 1, second movement.

[3] Crotch gives the incipit of Haydn, Quartet in D minor, Op. 76 No. 2, second movement.

[4] Crotch gives the incipit of Haydn, Quartet in B flat Op. 76 no. 4, fourth movement.

[5] Crotch gives the incipit of Mozart, Quartet in G major K. 387, first movement.

small portion of the principal subject are so frequently repeated as to become a striking feature. This is in a degree ornamental. It is even witty, yet it is not trifling or gay. It is not *L'allegro* but *Il Pensieroso*. Some of the modulations are sudden and unexpected and some of the melodies exquisitely tender and impressive. *(Ex Andante in F)*[6]

The last specimen of quartet music which I shall produce is a Rondo by Kreutzer adapted for the piano forte with an appropriate introduction by Cramer. This is the finale of a quartet[7] performed at the Philharmonic Concert by Vaccari where the beauty and cheerfulness of its style were deservedly admired.[8] *(Kreutzer)*

I shall conclude the present remarks by anticipating an objection which will naturally arise in the minds of many. I mean that quartet and other full pieces do not produce so much effect on the piano forte as on the instruments for which they were originally designed. To this I would reply that they will not be the less frequently performed on those instruments on account of their being also played on the piano forte. The fact is admitted. Engravings are not equal to paintings, but they are an admirable substitute. And to this I may also add as a weight in the opposite scale that such passages as require great precision in the time are generally more accurately rendered on one instrument than on four. If, however, it be admitted that the knowledge and study of this music refines the judgement that is daily increasing, I hail this indication of improvement in the public taste and would wish it to be furthered by every possible means and therefore earnestly recommend it to the attention of every composer, every performer and every lover of the art.

---

[6] Crotch gives the incipit of Mozart, Quartet in D minor K. 421, second movement.

[7] {lately}

[8] Crotch provides no incipit for this work, which does not appear in the Philharmonic's programmes as recorded in Miles Birket Foster, *History of the Philharmonic Society of London, 1813–1912: a Record of a Hundred Years Work in the Cause of Music* (London: John Lane, 1912).

Lecture IV. 1818. Sinfonias

If a comparison be made as in the preceding or present lecture between music composed for the piano forte and that for other instruments, it will prove as I have already remarked not very favourable to the former. It must I fear be confessed that the cultivation of the peculiar qualities of this brilliant and expressive instrument has induced those who exclusively compose for it, to sacrifice in too great a degree, what is grand and elegant for the sake of decoration and effect. And thus they have rendered piano forte music in general less worthy of study than all other kinds of writing. Composers should ever consult the mind as well as the ear. All passages that do not more or less gratify both the one and the other should be wholly expunged, or at least not suffered to predominate and form the peculiar characteristic of the style and leading feature.

The excuse usually offered, that the practice of rapid passages gives a command of the instrument and facilitates the execution of such as are easier, appears to me very fallacious. *This* kind of practice adds nothing to the expression and but little to the precision of slow passages. Those who have spent much time in vanquishing these needless difficulties can seldom boast of any other attainment. Such performers generally fail in an Adagio. They are unable to read well much less to play *correctly at first sight* even the *easiest* music. They seldom hear or relish what is sublime or beautiful. They seldom are acquainted with the various clefs. They cannot read from score. They cannot be denominated able and well-grounded musicians.

It may perhaps appear a bold assertion, but I hesitate not [to] affirm that those who have with the most unequivocal success surmounted the greatest difficulties of *execution only* are deceiving themselves and their admirers, unless their sole object be to dazzle and surprise *for the moment*. The deception is indeed extraordinary. It is *so great* that I no longer feel myself competent to judge of the real proficiency of a pupil from the performance of a piece thus practised. I have frequently heard the most difficult music played to perfection by those who were, as I afterwards found, wholly ignorant of what they were doing and incapable of performing the most simple air correctly without the previous instruction of a master and much practice.

Ornamental passages are indeed peculiarly suited to the genius of this instrument. But the predominance of the ornamental style in any kind of music, as well as in poetry, painting, architecture or sculpture is ever an indication of inferiority and decline. Another species of decoration with which piano forte music is encumbered to excess, is exaggerated expression: the rapid succession of loud and soft passages;[1] the rinforzando, or sudden crescendo and diminuendo; and the sforzando, or loud note in the midst of a soft passage, abound more than in any other style of music. A monotonous uniformity of tone is indeed fatiguing and uninteresting and may be justly compared to the want of chiaro oscuro or light and shade in a sister art, but too much opposition of the kind already mentioned resembles the distraction of lights justly complained of in the old French school of painting.[2] The intermixture of a profusion of discords with concords, though justly chargeable on the generality of modern music, is I fear peculiarly predominant in that for the piano forte. This destroys all definition of character, rendering this style capricious, affected and obscure. Hence it seems undeniable that the delight of the student would be increased and his taste improved by an enlarged knowledge of all other kinds of music, in addition to that for the piano forte.

In asserting the *general* superiority of other music, however, it is not meant that the various species are all alike, all equally superior or even that < > are inferior. Solos, duets and perhaps trios for other instruments seldom contain much that deserves high commendation. They are generally inferior to quartets, and are frequently less full and scientific than the piano forte sonatas of Haydn, Mozart and Beethoven,[3] many of which disdain the peculiarities of an individual instrument and seem to emulate the rich effects of the orchestra. Much that is worthy of study may be found in the tuttis of concertos, but, it is feared, not so much in the solos, which are chiefly intended to display the execution. Of quartets, I have already adduced specimens. But sinfonias for a full orchestra, overtures to operas or oratorios, and all such vocal music whether choruses or songs, ancient or modern, sacred or secular as will produce any *tolerable* effect on the piano forte (however inferior to that originally intended) is worthy of deliberate and attentive study, as being in general more sublime or more beautiful, more rich in harmony, or more skilfully treated, more chaste and unaffected and more calculated to improve the public taste than what is expressly written for a keyed instrument.

Of the various kinds of modern Instrumental music that which possesses most grandeur, beauty and science must upon the whole be superior. Such appears to be the Concert Sinfonia. Here we hail the triumph of the modern[4] school. However inferior to the ancient in pure sublimity,

---

[1] {and what is yet worse}

[2] Crotch may have in mind Reynolds's *Discourse* IV, 63–4, where French academicians are mentioned in the context of criticizing Paul Veronese for the fault mentioned.

[3] Only the first two composers were originally mentioned in this sentence.

[4] {German}

in chaste beauty, in all that is *purely* vocal and belongs to the higher walks of the art, yet, in the instrumental department modern music is confessedly unrivalled.

The Concert Sinfonia usually consists of five movements: a short introductory adagio, an allegro, a slow movement, the minuet with its second minuet or trio, (a term to me unintelligible as applied to the second minuet) and the finale. The introduction is less necessary to the constitution of a Sinfonia than the other movements, yet it is often the sublimest part of the whole. Sometimes it is tragic and impassioned; at other times it is plaintive and inclined to elegance. The allegro is the most scientific and laboured of the quick movements. The slow movement is ever interesting to the mature judgement, for in this is found the greatest degree of *beauty* – the most studied finishing, the most refined expression. After this the composer seems generally to cease writing for himself and the more[5] experienced hearers and to think it necessary to arouse and amuse the majority of his audience. The minuets are agitated and eccentric – the trios melodious, contriving some pleasing solo or concertante passages. The finales are capricious, rapid and wild. Such is the general description of a modern sinfonia.

I have selected two[6] as specimens for the present occasion, both from the works of Haydn, an unrivalled composer in this species of music. The first, called from its concluding movement La Chasse is one of his early productions and not so long in duration or intended for so complete an orchestra as some of his more recent works. The score not having been published in this kingdom, and the adapted copy conveying but a faint idea of its original excellence, this sinfonia is scarcely known, but it is one of those extraordinary efforts of genius and taste in which the treasures lie somewhat beneath the surface and only seem to increase by being sought. It may please the first time of hearing, but it will require much repetition to discern all its excellence and if I may judge by my own experience, it is never likely to disgust by becoming familiar and most intimately known.

The introduction is not so much distinguished for its grandeur as its originality. The exordium is soft and mysterious. The loud unaccented

---

[5] {mature}

[6] This lecture shows the effects of an unusually large number of revisions, with additional pages having been attached to the notebook. The symphonies of Haydn that Crotch used for this part of the lecture varied considerably. In what seems to have been the earliest version, he compared what he thought of as an early work, No. 73 ('La Chasse'), with one of the London symphonies, No. 99. Later, he used two London symphonies, the '7th and 8th sinfonias of Salomon's Set' (i.e., Nos 104 and 103 respectively). Finally, Crotch replaced Symphony No. 73 as his example of an early work with Symphony No. 85 ('La reine').

notes produce a novel and peculiar effect. The allegro is not one of the quickest kind but abounds with semiquavers, which in more modern music have been supplanted by scarcely less rapid quavers. The first subject commences with the chord of the Subdominant or fourth note of the key, which is far from being common but produces a fine effect. Its melody is elegant. It is treated with profound skill, becoming in one part a species of fugue. It is admirably contrasted by various passages, some of which are grand, others beautiful and pathetic. The modulations are all interesting. We meet in the second part with that experimental kind of writing in which the composer seems to hesitate as uncertain how to proceed. One passage near the conclusion consisting of slow notes which remind us of the organ, suddenly interrupted by the full orchestra is[7] sublime and masterly. *(Introduction and fugue of La Chasse)*

The andante is constructed on a very simple and unaffected subject, chiefly remarkable for the long delay of the first and final cadence. The variations are not of any uncommon species, but by the aid of the minor key and the other modes, connected with it, the interest is maintained and the ear delighted throughout. *(Andante)*

The minuet and trio of this sinfonia though not so pleasing as many others by our author are yet worthy of his pen. The subjects are skilfully treated. The trio contains a solo for the oboe. The finale (La Chasse) is spirited, fanciful and original. Its subjects, modulations and peculiar effects amply reward the minutest investigation and closest study. *(Minuet and Presto)*

As a contrast to the foregoing early production of our author I have chosen my second Specimen from one of his latest works, number ten of the twelve sinfonias composed for Salomon's Concert or number three of the score printed at Leipsic. That one of the inventors of this species of music, while it was of shorter duration and composed for fewer instruments, should be continually striking out novel effects was worthy of our admiration. But after a career of twenty years, when the orchestra was enlarged and the length of the sinfonia was increased, when such pupils as Mozart and Beethoven had mainly endeavoured to surpass him in this species of writing, but in vain, and after he had himself produced so many great works of the kind, to find him still as new – cheerful, interesting, learned, pathetic and dignified as ever, is truly astonishing. The Introduction is very sublime, quite original, and contains an ingenious and unexpected enharmonic modulation. The allegro is at once elegant, spirited and grand. Some irregularities in the resolution and want of resolution of the more ordinary discords should not be regarded as authorities for the practice and imitation of the

---

[7] {most ingenious}

young composer. No length of time would, I apprehend, render them
familiar or agreeable to the ear. They produce surprise, the leading
feature of the ornamental style, the undue prevalence of which, in all
arts is as we have said the fatal indication, perhaps we *might* say, the
cause of decline. *(Introduction and Allegro No. 10)*

The Adagio is, in every respect far above all praise. The subjects are
peculiarly graceful and elegant. The modulations ingenious, and all its
contrasted effects resulting from the opposition of slow and quick, loud
and soft, high and low passages, are striking and admirable. The minuet
if compared with those of the sinfonia already performed contains a
greater variety of subjects and bolder modulations. Yet they are inferior
to those of many other sinfonias in beauty of melody. The finale reminds us of that of Mozart's celebrated sinfonia in the same key and
was probably a designed imitation. For science and skill it could not
exceed Mozart's, but for ease, spirit, gaiety and instrumental effects, it
is superior. *(Minuet and Presto)*

The peculiar object of the present lecture has been to shew that much
of the highest and most laboured species of instrumental music, the
concert sinfonia, may be heard and understood on a keyed instrument,
though some of the peculiar effects must unavoidably be lost. Enough
may be preserved to render it an object worthy of attention; and from
the science with which it abounds the study of it is eminently calculated
to refine and improve the public taste.

[Second version]

[I have selected two as specimens for the present occasion both from the
works of Haydn, an unrivalled composer in this species of music. These
are] the seventh and eighth sinfonias of Salomon's Set. The seventh
commences with a sublime introduction in the minor key of D. The
allegro following it is the major, a most brilliant and animated strain
in which the novelty of the subjects themselves and their masterly
treatment equally demand admiration. *(Introduction and Allegro No.7)*

All the slow movements of Haydn are deserving of peculiar study and
attention. He seems to have been the first who introduced into them the
combined use of all the instruments in the orchestra. That this has
improved the movement abstractly considered will scarcely admit of a
doubt. But whether the general effect of the whole sinfonia can be
improved by that which destroys the contrast of the several movements
may well be questioned. *(Andante)*

In the minuets the tempo-rubato or seeming mixture of common and
triple times and the unexpected modulations in the trio are remarkable.

The finale seems to imitate something in the Russian or Asiatic style of national music. The whole sinfonia may be reckoned one of this author's most happy productions. *(Minuet and Finale)*

The eighth sinfonia is in the key of E flat major. Its introductory adagio commences with a roll on the drum and a passage for the basses in unison after which the wind instruments and the violins and other instruments are gradually introduced till they are all heard in the allegro, which consists of compound triple time but not of the < > <species?> and is admirable for its masterly and scientific treatment of the various subjects and for the recurrence of them all and even of the introductory movement. This ought to furnish young composers with a useful hint that repetitions judiciously managed are among the most important arcana of the art of composing. *(Introduction and Allegro No. 8)*

[Third version, on new leaves attached to original manuscript]

I have selected two as specimens for the present occasion, both from the works of Haydn, an unrivalled composer in this species of music; for although Mozart and Beethoven have carried their elaborations and refinements to an extraordinary length yet it is still acknowledged by the most experienced judges that the attention is more fascinated and amused by the performance of Haydn's sinfonias than by those of any other composer.

The first of these is one of his earlier productions and is not so long in duration nor intended for so large an orchestra as most of his more recent works. The score not having been published that I know of, and this sinfonia not having been adapted till lately it is not generally known. It is now, however, the ninth of a set which the lecturer is still continuing to bring out at the Royal Harmonic Institution called by its author 'La Reine de la France'. It is one of those extraordinary efforts of genius and taste in which the treasures lie chiefly beneath the surface and seem only to increase on being sought. It may perhaps please the first time of hearing, but it will require many repetitions to discover all its excellence, and if I may judge by my own feelings it is not likely to disgust by being most intimately known. The Introduction is in that[8] grand style,[9] for which our author was so remarkable. The allegro is very singular in its subject and general character. The modulations in the second part are very unexpected, but the principal feature is the masterly treatment of the subjects which is even greater than usual in

---

[8] {mixed style of}
[9] {and yet playful}

our author, justly celebrated for skill and learning. *(Introduction and first Allegro Crotch's Haydn)*

It may generally be said of all the slow movements of the great master that they are almost all in the least fallible species of composition. Quick movements may be vulgar and grow antiquated and out of fashion, they often contain trifling, unstudied thoughts; they are generally in the ornamental style, abounding with novel ideas which have no merit after they cease to be new and they are written to please untutored ears.

Lecture V. 1ˢᵗ Act of Don Giovanni

The superiority of vocal music over instrumental is so obvious that it only seems surprising that it should ever for a moment be questioned. The human voice if unaccompanied by instruments, even when not articulating words, or only such as are in a language not understood, is more beautiful in tone than any instrument whatever. The harmonious combination of a few voices forms the most perfect intonation and accordance imaginable and is capable of the most delicate refinements of expression. A full chorus of voices without instruments is the most sublime of all effects; but if to a voice or voices the varied and manifold contrasts of instrumental accompaniments are added, this very addition must render that which still retains the appellation of vocal music, superior to instrumental. For even if voices were *inferior* to instruments, which can only be allowed for the sake of argument, the variety they afford would improve the effect. But in the higher walks of the art, in sublimity and especially in beauty, vocal music has ever been pre-eminent while the ornamental style, confessedly inferior to the others, predominates only in Instrumental music. But when the words of vocal music are in a known language – when the union of poetry with her sister, adds sense to sound, gives a meaning to pleasure and calls in the attention of the Mind as well as of the Ears – we can surely no longer withhold our assent to the proposition.

For let us consider: what *are* the powers of instrumental passages? What *can* they represent? They may express certain qualities of objects but they cannot convey any idea of the objects themselves. We hear something tranquil, agitated, cheerful, or sad – as it may be in the Church, Pastoral or Military Styles. But why it is so we are left to conjecture. A French writer in attempting to analyse the eighth sinfonia of Haydn [from] Salomon's set, which commences with a roll of the drum and a slow passage for the basses, talks about a congregation in Church being alarmed by a thunderstorm and afterwards going out to dance, with other absurdities too ridiculous to deserve attention.[1] I also once heard a celebrated admirer of Haydn who seemed to imagine I had not done justice to the slow movement of the same sinfonia by my feeble praises, suggest that in a certain bold modulation near the conclusion the

---

[1] Crotch refers to a measure-by-measure analysis in Jérôme-Joseph de Momigny, *Cours complet d'Harmonie et de composition*, 3 vols (Paris, 1806). See, Malcolm S. Cole, 'Momigny's Analysis of Haydn's Symphony No. 103', *The Music Review*, 30 (1969), 261–84.

composer seemed to start at the sight of a sudden glory as if he had caught a glimpse of heaven's inmost recesses and *then* ... He was going on but suddenly stopped in the recollection, as I suppose that this *sublime passage* (for such it certainly is) returned abruptly to the military march which forms the subject of the movement and of which transition he was not prepared to give a satisfactory account and said no more.

Music is of itself a language of adjectives without substantives. It awakens affections but can create no images. Call in the aid of poetry and all becomes clear and interesting. Then not only the voices but the very instruments speak an intelligible language and the overture is no longer a mere instrumental piece of no meaning performed before the drama commences, but is intimately connected either with the first or some other important scene. In vocal music we are enabled to criticize the manner of expressing the words which the composer has adopted; in instrumental music his transitions are arbitrary or made only for the sake of contrast and variety. Having in the former half of the present course of lectures treated of instrumental music, I shall dedicate the remaining part to the consideration of vocal. The specimens I have selected are from the works of Mozart and Handel, who were respectively unrivalled in the opera and oratorio styles.

But before I proceed to the investigation of their several merits I must be permitted once more to caution my hearers not to form their judgements from the *effect* which their performance on the present occasion may produce as that will necessarily have a contrary tendency to what is meant. In exact proportion to the worthiness of the object held out to the contemplation of the student will be the failure of its representation. The quartet, when performed on a single instrument, loses much of its effect. The overture of sinfonia yet more. The absence of the voice in songs, duets, trios, quartets and other similar vocal pieces is irreparable. And if this be the case in modern music where the accompaniments are so attractive as to be almost principal, how great must be the failure of the attempt to convey any adequate idea of that style in which accompaniments are altogether subordinate, in which it is required not only to

'Wake the full Lyre' but 'swell the tide of song' –

Which even when performed as originally intended owes its greatness to something vastly higher than mere effect. The audience must supply by their imaginations the inevitable deficits of the portrait. The lecturer, like the Bard, calls on them to

piece out his imperfection by their thoughts –[2]

---

[2] William Shakespeare, *Henry V*, prol. 24: 'Piece out our imperfections with your thoughts'.

Had the design of the Lecturer been merely to amuse his hearers or had that been his *principal* aim, or even one about which he thought it his duty to be very anxious, he would naturally have confined his subject altogether to instrumental music and especially that composed for the piano forte. But his object has not been entertainment but instruction. Not to flatter but to further the improvement of the public taste. Unable himself by immediate experiment to demonstrate his theory he refers the student for this kind of satisfaction to those Concerts which profess to unite excellences of various kinds, where he will hear both ancient and modern instrumental and vocal full music. But he should not only hear it in public but contemplate its excellence in his retirement, for its superiority over mere piano forte music is a sufficient compensation for the loss of effect when performed on that instrument.

Thus, the student is in a sister art admonished to view, whenever it is possible, the finest collections of painting and as he cannot possess these himself to place engravings from them continually before his eyes. For though Engravings must, *as copies*, fail in exact proportion as the original painting depends on colouring for its excellence, yet much positive beauty of outline and shading will be retained. And his imagination and memory will derive no small amusement and improvement from the constant endeavour of supplying the deficiency of colour, which from the nature of the case was unavoidable.

The opera of the *Don Giovanni* has been so frequently performed at the Italian Theatre of this metropolis that the detail of the fable will be altogether unnecessary and on account of its immorality and indecorum will as much as possible be supprest. I may perhaps have overstepped the bounds of my proper sphere in thus noticing the department of the poet, but I cannot but regret that a fable in which degrading vices are treated with such unbecoming levity should have been the subject of such general amusement owing doubtless to the importance which has been conferred on it by the music of Mozart. I am aware that it may be urged that the moral of the fable is good because the Libertine is destroyed, and I am willing to admit that vice should be held up as an object of abhorrence as well as virtue, of imitation. My complaint is that vice is rather rendered interesting and amusing, that the tendency of the whole is baneful and by no means counteracted by the visit of a Ghost or the ending the guilty wretch to keep company (as it is expressly said in the finale) with Pluto and Persepine. Happily, our innocent art is incapable of contamination from its having been connected with vicious poetry. And the *music* of Mozart to this opera is amply deserving of the extraordinary admiration it has at length universally excited. It is, I believe, generally esteemed his finest production. I must confess my own preference for *La Clemenza di Tito* on account of its grandeur, which is an indication of superiority though it would have been improper for a comic opera.

The overture to Don Giovanni commences with a slow introduction abridged from the music of the principal scene of the piece in which the animated statue of the Commendatore whom Don Giovanni had slain, comes, agreeable to his invitation, to sup with him, and counsels him, but in vain, to repent. This scene I shall be obliged to omit in its place, and therefore take the present opportunity of praising the happy conception of these extraneous combinations, these supernatural and terrific melodies. The second movement seems from one of its passages intended to allude to the finale, and was probably suggested by it according to modern practice, this overture having been written after the rest of the opera was completed. Other subjects in the allegro remind us of Handel, Leo, Corelli and even earlier masters whom it is clear our author held in due veneration. Mozart frequently adopted (and in this opera especially) the dramatic form of uniting one movement to another for which Glück was so celebrated.

Then, the overture wanders from its original key to introduce the song by Leporello, 'Notte e giorno faticar', which is very lively, pleasing and characteristic. The trio in which Donna Anna endeavours to detain and discover Don Giovanni, though well written, is not particularly expressive of distress and seems protracted to an unnecessary length before the Commendatore comes to the aid of his daughter, after which the music becomes more interesting. The combat is well portrayed and the death of the Commendatore is particularly fine. The accompanied recitative in which Donna Anna returning to the succour of her father discovers his dead body and swoons over it, is an unparalleled masterpiece of pathetic expression. Her lover Don Ottavio takes this opportunity of causing the body to be removed from her sight and on her recovery endeavours to console her and swears to revenge her father's murder. The contending passions of grief and love are finely depicted in the following duet 'fuggi crudele fuggi', which though far less attractive and popular than the rest of the opera is deserving of the most careful attention and study. The polished beauty and refinement of Italian melody is indeed still unequalled, but in the representation of the stronger emotions, in chromatic melodies and elaborate harmonies, the German composers are superior, and our author unrivalled. *(Duo. fuggi –) Page 68*

The Trio 'ah chi mi dice mai' introduces Donna Elvira indignantly complaining of her wrongs and seeking Don Giovanni who had forsaken her – This movement is in many respects peculiarly excellent – its melody in particular is so elegant and vocal as fully to establish the character of Mozart as the greatest of modern composers, for had he confined himself to instrumental music, Haydn must not have been suffered to yield the palm to our author, as he is known to have done with the most genuine modesty and cheerfulness. *(Ah chi mi dice. Page 88)*

Leporello's song 'Madamina, il catalogo è questo', in which he shows Donna Elvira a list of his master's favourites, is humorous and pleasing, but depends very much on the effect of the accompaniments, especially in the first movement. The second is in the style of the Minuet and one of its passages reminds us strongly of D^r. Arne's finale to the overture to Artaxerxes.[3] *(Madamina il catalogo)*

The duet of Zerlina and Masetto with the chorus of villagers celebrating their approaching nuptials, 'Giovinette che fate all'amore', is a remarkably lively and expressive pastoral, resembling in its style the French national music. This movement like some others in this opera being, as I am informed, generally played much faster than seems to be required, induces me to make my protest against this very common error of exaggerated expression. Most of our adagios are played too slow, most of our allegros too quick. *(Giovinette 121)*

In the late representations[4] of this opera many airs were necessarily omitted on account of its length. Masetto's song 'Ho capito, Signor si', which seems admirably calculated for stage effect, was of this number. The Duet 'Là ci darem la mano' is a universal favourite. The first movement admirably expresses the suspicion and hesitation with which Zerlina at first receives Don Giovanni's offer of marriage, but the fear of being deceived and her reluctance to wound the peace of her former suitor Masetto give way to the vanity of being courted by a nobleman and the prospect of immediate advancement to high rank, and her consent is playfully conveyed in the last movement which abounds with original and graceful melodies. *(Là ci darem 133)*

Donna Elvira now enters and exposes the real character of Don Giovanni to Zerlina. The Song 'ah fuggi il traditor' (omitted in the representation) is remarkable for its striking affinity to the style of Handel. Several passages may be traced to his works. Its subject is also like a well-known Spanish air, and the resemblance was probably not accidental as the scene of the drama is laid in Spain. *(Ah fuggi – 143)*

Another song for Donna Elvira with a preceding accompanied recitative, inserted in the Appendix but omitted in the representation, I should have supposed to be intended for the close of the scene in which

---

[3] *Artaxerxes*, an opera in 3 acts to Arne's translation of Metastasio's *Artaserse*, premiered in London in 1762.

[4] This originally read 'representation', suggesting that Crotch's observation applies specifically to the first London performance.

she first appears. But I follow the English translator, who assigns it this place. The recitative is extremely expressive and original, especially in the accompaniments, and the air is peculiarly elegant and flowing for a production of the German school. The modulations and the management of the instruments are superior to those of Italian composers. The divisions for the voice, though not rapid, are very difficult. The subject is beautifully sustained by answers and imitations throughout, and the whole is one of the finest productions of a composer, who in this style at least was unrivalled. *(Mi tradì – Appendix Vol. II No.5)*

The quartet 'Non ti fidar' is full of dramatic effect, rich harmony, and elegant melody. The recitative 'Don Ottavio' abounds with scientific harmonies. The air 'or sai chi l'onore' is spirited and dignified.

The subjects of the air 'Dalla sua pace' are beautiful and the modulations very original. These, however, and many others, partly for want of time but chiefly from the difficulty of conveying the intended effect, will only be mentioned. 'Fin ch'han dal vino', however, a little comic air in which Don Giovanni gives orders for a feast and a dance, is so distinct in character, so animated and pleasing, that I cannot pass it over. *(Fin ch'an [sic] 186 Vol I)* –

The air 'Batti, batti, O bel Masetto' in which Zerlina endeavours to pacify her lover's jealousy is well known and most deservedly admired. But those who have not seen the score or heard it performed in an orchestra can form no idea from the adapted copy of the exquisitely beautiful and fanciful accompaniment for the violoncello which pervades both the movements of this song. *(Batti, batti 186)*

After this, a succession of movements takes place without interruption, highly dramatic and full of effect, but which would be less interesting when deprived of the words than such as are brought to a regular termination, and therefore will be omitted on the present occasion. It is almost impossible to enumerate the several excellences of this long scene. One, however, is too curious to escape notice. A dance is heard at a distance played in common time and in this the principal characters agree to join. It is discontinued, however, and the drama proceeds. Soon after, a minuet is heard, and Donna Anna, Donna Elvira and Don Ottavio, who attended the feast in Masks for the purpose of detecting and counteracting the designs of Don Giovanni, sing a beautiful slow trio accompanied only by wind instruments.

At length the minuet is commenced by a complete orchestra on the stage and danced. While this is proceeding, a second orchestra tunes and commences the former air in common time, which is also danced, while the minuet continues. Then a third orchestra tunes and a Waltz is danced, and these three all continue together for some bars till interrupted by the rescue of Zerlina from Don Giovanni by the principal characters, who unmask and reproach him for his baseness and in the following spirited finale of the first act threaten him with the vengeance of heaven. He is at first confused and alarmed, but his rash courage returns and he sets heaven and earth at defiance. All this is admirably expressed by the music, which in the performance must produce a most terrific effect. *(Finale 275) last 2 movements*

From the foregoing imperfect sketch of the first act of this opera no adequate idea can be formed of the impression which the various combinations of voices and instruments must make on the mind in the performance of the music independent of all the aids of dramatic representation. But if the transcendent excellence of its harmonies, melodies and modulations, and the masterly treatment of the subjects have been felt and acknowledged, the principal intention of the lecturer will have been fully accomplished.

Lecture VI. 1818.
2nd Act of Don Giovanni[1]

Italy, as we have before remarked, was the inventress of all that is admirable both in harmony, melody and science. The sublime style sprang from her chants and other church music. The beautiful was next adopted and afterwards superseded. The ornamental style, to which we are indebted for all instrumental music, originated in the accompaniments and symphonies of her songs. But at length[2] she neglected the sublimity and science which she herself had invented and would suffer nothing to draw off the attention from the voice. The English judges, however, still admired the sublime and scientific styles, and hence their ready and lasting admiration of Corelli, Purcell, Handel, Graun, Hasse, Haydn and Mozart. These remarks may serve to prepare the answer to a very natural question which arises out of the consideration that the opera of Don Giovanni was performed in the year 1787 at Prague but not in this kingdom for many[3] years after.

Why was it not heard in England before? In answer to this we may observe that Mozart's music in general did not reach us for many years after it was composed. I do not remember to have seen his operas till about the year 1800.[4] The Italian opera singers who were the principal suppliers of modern vocal music to this country were not enthusiastic admirers of scientific harmony. Their exclusive predilection for melody has by no means been universally countenanced in this nation from the

---

[1] The original beginning of this lecture read as follows: Every musical audience may be supposed to comprehend at least two descriptions of persons, those who are real judges, and those who merely approve or censure according to their feelings, without assigning a reason for their opinions, or criticizing upon sound principles. It rarely happens that these are both equally delighted at the same time; and when this is the case, it is no proof of elevation of style and consequently of superior excellence in the piece performed, but rather indicates a clearness of melody, a justness of expression and a vigour of effect. A more refined melody, more scientific combinations and more sublime effect would in a great measure confine the admiration to judges alone. While, on the other hand, a deficiency of science and incorrectness of harmony, which the true critic would justly despise would not be detected by the mere lovers of the science. And thus, a great deal of indifferent music is admired exclusively by the ignorant while much of the best can only be relished by those who have acquired some knowledge & experience – and some may be enjoyed and even understood by all.

[2] {this fickle nation disapproved of}

[3] {near 30}

[4] The date Crotch originally included here has been written over. The first date is unreadable but may have been 1805.

first, and a division of the musical world into two distinct parties was, as I have before shown, the unavoidable result. The singers and composers of Sacchini's school were less disposed to approve of Mozart's style than the lovers of ancient music. They found it difficult of execution and less calculated to display the powers of the voice than the music of their own country. Had the opera before us been performed here as soon as composed, it would, I doubt not, have met with the same success and admiration which at present it so deservedly enjoys.

But still it may be inquired why *this opera in particular*, which is by many esteemed our author's finest production, should be presented to us so much later than the *Zauberflote*, *Così fan tutte*, *Le nozze di Figaro* and *La clemenza di Tito*, of the same master? Italian singers, even after they had begun to acknowledge the merits of Mozart, could not be indifferent to their own opportunities of attraction, and a Catalani or a Banti would naturally prefer an opera of Cimarosa or, Paisiello (in which the whole attention of the audience would be riveted to her voice) to any of Mozart's (in which all the singers are of nearly equal importance and the instruments of no less consequence than the voices). So when the increasing reputation of Mozart's operas rendered it necessary for the Italians to introduce them into this country, they commenced with such as were most simple, popular and easy to perform. And hence Don Giovanni seems rather to have been demanded by this nation than pressed upon us. The opera of Idomeneo by the same author is yet more abstruse and scientific, and not being comic or containing many graceful and intelligible arias, is still less likely to be performed on the stage and be generally admired though it will form a rich repast for the private contemplation of the student of harmony. We are informed by the preface to the English translation of Don Giovanni that Mozart considered it as less adapted for the people of Vienna than for those of Prague and professedly to have written it principally for the amusement of himself and *friends*, by which, of course, we are to understand his pupils, his professional brethren, his musical friends and admirers.

The second act opens with the following lively little movement 'Eh via buffone', a duet for the Don and his servant, who, tired of the ill treatment he receives, declares his intention of quitting his master's service. *(Eh via 294)*

The trio 'Ah taci, ingiusto core' is extremely elegant in its melody and chaste in its style, but the principal excellence lies in the admirable management of the accompaniments. The modulation from E major with four sharps to C major, is striking and masterly.[5] And the union of

---

[5] Crotch apparently refers to a section in C major, mm. 35–48.

the three voices near the conclusion after so many detached solo passages produces a most beautiful effect. *(Ah taci 304)* –

After the preceding movement, in which Don Giovanni had prevailed on the too credulous Donna Elvira to listen to his professions of penitence and while she descends from the balcony of her house, he changes dresses with his servant, whom he obliges to pass for himself, and then frightens them away together.

After this, he sings the following air 'Deh vieni alla finestra', accompanying himself on the Mandoline. The subject of this very artless and pleasing ballad is formed out of a passage in the foregoing trio. The style, the harmony, and the modulation are superior to what is generally found in notturnos and canzonets; but I was particularly struck on first perusing the score, with the consistency of the accompaniment, which in the adapted copies of this air, is wholly lost and obliterated although by no means difficult of execution on the piano forte. Such unnecessary and unmeaning alterations in the works of the greatest masters cannot be too frequently or too strongly reprehended. *(Deh vieni 319)*

The air 'Metà di voi quà vadano', which the hero of the piece in Leporello's dress sings to Masetto, is very remarkable for the playfulness of the accompaniments. That of 'Vedrai, carino', which Zerlina sings to console Masetto for the severe chastisement he had just received from Don Giovanni, is too well known to require much commendation from me. Its melody is confessedly beautiful and its harmony rich and sonorous. And the adapted copies of this air are unusually faithful. Its resemblance of style and even of whole passages to Handel is not however generally remarked, because Handel's opera music is so little known, and so unjustly depreciated by the lovers of modern music. It must be confessed indeed that Handel had no talent for the production of playful and comic effects which are the chief characteristics of the modern school. Many of his opera songs and overtures are certainly fitter for sacred than secular subjects. But his songs of 'Misero' quel vago volto' in Radamisto and 'Charming Beauty' in the Triumph of Time and Truth are not only very like the song before us but scarcely inferior in vocal elegance. *(Vendrai carino 338)*

The sestetto 'Sola, sola in bujo loco' is replete with all that variety of effect and scientific treatment of the score for which our author is so justly celebrated. In the commencement of it, Leporello, still disguised as his master, is endeavouring to escape from Donna Elvira. He is, however, suddenly beset by Don Ottavio, Donna Anna, Masetto and Zerlina, who are determined on killing him. Donna Elvira then intercedes for him as her husband. Finding that they are bent on his death, Leporello discovers himself to the astonishment of all. Part of the slow movement resembles the ancient style and in the spirited allegro 'mille torbidi pensieri' the experienced ear will perceive transitions and[6] harmonies of a similar description. To such imitations of the old school our author probably alluded in declaring that he had written this opera rather to please himself and friends than the public at large. *(Sola sola 347)*

Leporello's song 'Ah pietà signori miei' in which he endeavours to manifest his innocence presents us with many pleasing novelties. This likewise contains a passage bearing a considerable resemblance to one in Handel's overture to Parnasso in festa afterwards prefixed to the oratorio of Athalia. *(Ah pietà 385)*

In the Appendix, Zerlina is made to arrest the flight of Leporello, then bind his hands and revenge herself for the beating she supposed him to give her lover Masetto. This is admirably expressed in the following duet 'per queste tue manine', which was omitted in the representation. This is an excellent sample of Mozart's peculiar style, containing many passages which he has frequently used in other parts of his works. *(Per queste 571)*

Don Ottavio's elegant air 'Il mio tesoro intanto' commences *con sordini*, with mutes on the violins, which are seldom used in our English concerts though the effect is extremely different from that of playing soft without them. Our countrymen seem[7] to dislike the peculiar tone thus produced, but surely the opinions of such masters as Haydn and Mozart ought to preponderate and render the presence of the sordino in every orchestra indispensable. *(Il mio tesoro 397)*

In the celebrated scene where Don Giovanni and his servant conceal themselves near the tomb and equestrian statue of the Commendatore, the slow chromatic notes performed by wind instruments to the words which the statue speaks must, if played with a mysterious softness, produce an awful effect. Then a duet follows in which Don Giovanni obliges his servant to go up to the statue and invite him to supper. The statue nods his head and afterwards answers Don Giovanni in the affirmative. The music is perhaps somewhat more gay and elegant than the words seem to require. The air for Donna Anna 'Non mi dir, bell' idol mio,' with its very appropriate introductory recitative, in the accompaniments of which the subjects of the song are anticipated, are worthy of much attention on account chiefly of the beautiful Italian melody, such as our author usually assigns to his principal female singers. The accompaniment consisting of octaves between the second violin and tenor is, I believe, rather uncommon. I do not remember to have seen it any where other than the Pastoral Symphony in the Messiah. *(Non mi dir 432)*

---

[6] {melodies}
[7] {affect}

We are now arrived at the last scene, of which I shall very briefly notice the most remarkable particulars. Don Giovanni sits down to supper while music is performed for his entertainment and several airs are acknowledged by the characters on the stage to be taken from modern operas, some the production of Mozart himself. This absurdly makes the hero of the piece, not a grandee of barbarous times whose memory was faintly preserved by tradition and who furnished subjects for dramas in the early part of the seventeenth century, but one who lived in the time of our author and who had heard *La Cosa Rara* and *Le nozze di Figaro*. This concert is interrupted by the entrance of Donna Elvira, who on her knees entreats Don Giovanni to change his course of life, but her suit is rejected with insolence, contempt and ridicule. As soon as she has left him, she is heard to scream. Leporello is sent to discover the cause, and returns terrified, affirming that the 'White Man, the Man of Stone' stands knocking without. Unable to persuade his servant to admit him, he himself opens the door. And the statue of the Commendatore enters and to the horrific strains already performed in the introduction to the overture counsels the profligate to repent, but in vain. The spectre then quits him and immediately furies hurry him down to perdition.

The symphony which terminates this chorus is very like that of Handel in which Samson pulls down the edifice on the head of himself and his enemies. In the late representation of this opera this catastrophe (as I conceive from the book of the words) formed the conclusion of the piece. But the original has three more movements. In the first, Leporello relates the fate of the Libertine. The second is a beautiful slow duet for Don Ottavio and Donna Anna. And the third is the following finale, 'Questo è il fin di chi fa mal', sung by all the characters who previously denominate it a very ancient song. Its style is accordingly that of the old school. It commences in the manner of a fugue, and the general effect of the whole, from the great prevalence of long notes, is extremely grand. Mozart knew how to avail himself of what was truly great in other masters, though himself so notorious for originality. In one passage of this movement our author seems to have had in mind Handel's last chorus in Samson at the words 'Endless blaze of light' and in the next passage, the beautiful movement 'Ecce mulier filius tuus' in Haydn's Passione Stromentale. The loud and soft passages are admirably contrasted and the termination is at once dignified, simple, and uncommon. *(Questo è il fin 519)*

Such is Mozart's music to Don Giovanni, in which so many varied excellences are united, that if it be inferior to any of his own works, it is yet superior to those of all other cotemporary and preceeding masters and is abundantly sufficient to justify the assertion that he is the greatest of *all modern composers*. FINIS.

Lecture VII 1818.
Alexander's Feast. Handel

The sublime style comprehends several shades of character, particularly the simple, the terrific and the intricate. It acquires also by combination with the beautiful[1] and the ornamental styles a difference of quality. The beautiful seems to me very nearly allied to the simple, as is also the pathetic to the terrific and the ornamental, in general, to the intricate species of sublimity, though the sublime style is not necessarily combined with any of these. For instances of the purest sublimity, which is neither[2] terrific nor intricate, we refer to the most ancient Church music. For terrific sublimity, neither simple, nor magnificent, see the chromatic choruses of Handel's oratorios, especially those in Israel in Egypt. For intricate sublimity, neither[3] terrific nor simple, see his full choruses in general. A combination of sublimity and beauty may be found in Gibbon's services and anthems. Pathetic sublimity in Carissimi's Jeptha or in his motet 'Hodie Simon Petrus'. Grandeur and ornament are heard together in Glück's overture to Ifigenie and in that to La clemenza di Tito by Mozart, for Modern Music is frequently grand and magnificent but rarely contains simple sublimity.

Sublimity and grandeur are indeed frequently used as convertible terms. Sublimity, elevation and loftiness are strictly synonymous but appear to be somewhat different from grandeur and magnificence, which, I conceive, imply something splendid and attractive. I am not now presuming to assign to these expressions their proper or original sense, but merely take advantage of the difference of meaning which seems at present attached to them. A military man well knows the difference between the magnificence of a parade and the sublimity of a real battle.

Having in the present course of lectures endeavoured to persuade the student to cultivate the performance of full Instrumental music on the piano forte, as containing more science and beauty than that expressly composed for this instrument, by first introducing him to quartets and then to the sinfonias in which there is much ornamental grandeur, then proceeding to *vocal* music, and first to Mozart's operas, in which there is much beauty, pathos and magnificence, with occasional indications of terrific sublimity but in which the ornamental style still predominates

---

[1] {the pathetic}
[2] {pathetic}
[3] {pathetic}

over the beautiful and both over the sublime, we would *now* conduct him still higher: To music in which the sublime, beautiful, and ornamental preserve their due order, an infallible criterion of pre-eminence. This combination seems to have prevailed in the works of the greatest composers of the former part of the eighteenth century. The Italians disturbed this order of styles by giving an undue predominance to the beautiful as the Germans did to the ornamental. The one thereby improving vocal and the other, instrumental music, yet neither of them improving the *art upon the whole*. In painting, we are taught to ascribe pre-eminence to Raffaelle, though colouring and other inferior branches of the art have been much improved since his time. Neither was he the most sublime of all painters, for then the palm would rather have been bestowed on Michael Angelo. But Raffaelle excelled by uniting the styles and preserving their due subordination. Thus *in our art* Bird, Purcell and Sebastian Bach were undoubtedly more sublime than Handel, but Handel seems to be our *Raffaelle*. We therefore deem him the greatest of all composers.

The frequent repetitions of these general principles with the result to which they led will, it is trusted, be excused by such as are weary of hearing them, for the sake of some to whom they may be *altogether new*. Such praises might perhaps appear extravagant and partial if not supported, as we trust they are by sound principles. The application indeed of the principles may be questioned. It may be perhaps denied that Handel did excel in all the three styles preserving their due subordination, but we confidently insist upon the *principles themselves* as common to the fine arts, the result of the sound reasoning long experience and refined taste of the best judges. And if the characters we have given of the several composers be but accurate, our conclusions are established.

The subject of the present Lecture is Alexander's Feast or the Power of Music, an Ode written for Saint Cecilia's Day by Dryden and set to music in 1735 by Handel. I shall beg leave to offer my remarks, as usual, without any studied arrangement, merely as the thoughts presented themselves on perusing the score.

The overture consists of three movements. The introduction is a happy union of majesty and grace. The subjects are sustained without rigour. The predominance of the sublime is relieved by an elegant pastoral passage for the stringed Instruments and also by the unexpected soft conclusion. In the tutti's, the first violins are reinforced by the oboes playing in unison with them and giving by their vocality a consequence and predominance to the melody of the upper part. The fugue is constructed on a natural and unaffected subject, at first answered strictly, and afterwards with energetic freedom and amusing variety, not fatiguing the attention by its length or cloying it with obvious repetitions. The minuet is airy and vocal and its subjects cadences and modulations are not at all impaired by age, but are still interesting and agreeable. *(overture Alexander's Feast) 16 < >*

The first recitative "Twas at the royal feast for Persia won', is highly expressive of the words. The change of style and key at the description of Thais is particularly well conceived. The song

> Happy happy happy pair
> none but the brave deserve the fair

is constructed on an impressive subject which, if we have previously heard it sung, never fails to remind us of the words. The orchestra for which Handel originally composed this ode was probably numerous. The air before us was made for Beard, a powerful tenor singer, yet it is specified that one violoncello, one double-bass and the harpsichord are to accompany the voice while the symphonies are marked tutti. Complaints are still made that the accompaniments in all Concerts are too loud for the voice. Yet the best remedy for this evil is not making a part of the band silent but in training the whole to play very soft when required, which produces an inimitably beautiful effect. Considerable skill is manifested by our author in the variety given to so long a movement, set to only two lines of poetry. The following chorus to the same words is further diversified by obbligati passages for the principal treble and tenor voices, by a judicious treatment of the subjects and an interesting maze of modulation. *(Air and Chorus. Happy Pair Page 11)*

In the following Chorus,

> The listening crowd admire the lofty sound,
> A Present Deity they shout around,
> a Present Deity the vaulted roofs rebound

the words are forcefully expressed, the protracted sounds of the voices conveying an idea of echo and reverberation to the acclamations of the multitude while the accompaniment maintains throughout the whole, its elegant wavy motion.

The first symphony consists of two passages, the one, soft and for a few treble instruments, the other loud and full. In the concluding symphony, the order of the two passages is inverted and the whole ends with a diminuendo which forms a striking and happy contrast to the full tide of harmony, which precedes it. The impression which the performance of this admirable movement by a full band leaves on the mind is a pleasing astonishment unmixed with terror, indicating that the style is a union of the sublime with the beautiful and ornamental. It is a temperate and chastened grandeur, not produced by noisy and warlike instruments or by rapid passages. All is clear, calm, dignified and sonorous. *(Chorus the listening Crowd 21)*

The song 'with ravish'd ears/the monarch hears' has the merit of equalling in lightness and grace most of the Italian airs of the same age. Indeed, some of the passages are copied from the Numitor of Porta, one of the earliest operas performed at the Royal Academy of Music under Handel's direction, and from which he frequently extracted sweets for his own use. The divisions of this song are elegant, but too long. Here we also have another of the frequent instances of our author's judgement in making the introductory and final symphonies different from each other and suitable to their respective stations.

We pass on to 'the praise of Bacchus'. Much as the forbearance of Handel in not making an intemperate use of the warlike instruments in the generality of his compositions is to be commended, it would be difficult to account for our not hearing them, at least in a short flourish, when Timotheus cries, 'The jolly God in triumph comes:/sound the Trumpets, beat the Drums'. This is the more extraordinary as the command of Timotheus, 'now give the Hautboys breath!' is attended to in the symphony which introduces the bass song 'Bacchus, ever fair and young'. Obligati passages for the horns are also introduced and the contrast between these concertante passages, the soft accompaniments of the song, and the loud tutti's are very striking. All the bold and triumphant melodies of this air are expressive and masterly; that which occurs at the mention of 'pain' – in a minor mode – is peculiarly so. The semichorus or trio which follows the song conduces to the variety and enables the composer to protract the movement considerably and repeat many of the passages without fatiguing the ear. The last symphony is, as usual, a judicious curtailment of the first. *(Bacchus ever fair 37)*

Timotheus having raised the vanity of the monarch even to the defiance of heaven and earth not by the power of Music, for that has no such bad tendency, but of poetry, now 'chang'd his hand and check'd his pride/ He chose a mournful muse/soft Pity to infuse'. Perhaps the greatest effort of pathetic sublimity which exists in the musical world is the recitative 'heu mihi filia mea' in Carissimi's Oratorio of Jephtha. I can conceive Handel, after many unsatisfactory attempts to rival the pathos of this venerable production, boldly taking the notes themselves as the best examples of the power of music, making such alteration alone as were necessary for the accommodation of the words, accompanying the whole with instruments, and attaching to its appropriate ritornello or symphonies. Thus the great architect of our Metropolitan Cathedral not only copied the general form of Saint Peter's at Rome but incorporated into his design the Sibyl's Temple, the double range of pillars in the Colosseum, and the windows of the Capitol, which he converted into Doors. Thus and thus only, according to the precepts and example of the great lecturer in a sister art, genius and invention become fertile and inexhaustible.[4]

The simplicity and solemnity of the measure and subjects of the symphony and accompaniments of the exquisitely beautiful and expressive air 'he sung Darius, great and good' are worthy of the highest admiration. Yet the second movement, 'deserted at his utmost need', is, if possible still finer. Here our musician rivals the poet, and without the aid of words these strains would speak of woe. It may I think be fairly questioned whether a representation of the fallen and deserted Darius could affect the feelings of the best judges of painting with such *force* as this music does the true lovers of our art. I could say much for the vocal melody and responsive accompaniments of this movement, but I shall merely mention these and the simplicity and pathos of the whole, which are the chief source of its charms. *(He sang 51)*

In the accompanied recitative 'With downcast looks the joyless victor sat', the composer, by unexpected modulations and chromatic harmonies, forcibly depicts the monarch now melted into tears and 'awaking in his alter'd soul/the various turns of Chance below'.

The chorus 'Behold Darius great and good' differs from the air to the same words in its modulations, and in its fugue on a double subject to the words 'fall'n, and weltring in his blood'. The soft conclusion of voices alone with the gentle symphony at its termination are beyond all praises and the whole is one of the finest specimens extant of pathetic expression. *(Aria he sang 51; chorus 'Behold' 55)*

The air 'softly sweet in lydian measures' for a soprano voice accompanied with the violoncello is formed on the plan of the Italian canzonet in which Allessandro Scarlatti, Cesti, Stradella and their contemporaries excelled. And in spite of all the changes of fashion and the indubitable improvements which the modern school has introduced, this species of song displays the tones of the voice and violoncello better than any modern production whatever. *(Softly sweet. 64)*

The air for a tenor voice 'War he sung is toil and trouble' is expressive of a restless unsatisfied and weary spirit. The accompaniment is ingenious and masterly. The minor key forms an excellent foil to the major key of four sharps in which the following popular chorus 'the many rend the skies with loud applause' is composed. The first movement is written on a ground bass or subject of five bars, which is repeated fourteen times with so much variety of accompaniment that many persons well acquainted with its other merits have overlooked its

---

[4] Reynolds's most extended treatments of the practice of borrowing or imitation are found in *Discourses* VI and XII.

artful construction. The second movement is a species of not very strict fugue on a simple and obvious subject remarkably easy of management. But our author has infused sufficient variety into this animated movement by means of accompaniment and second subjects. The air 'The Prince, unable to conceal his pain' having been adopted as a Concert Song by some of our principal singers and received with unbounded applause, I shall leave it in full possession of its popularity not regretting however that I am not expected to vindicate its title to such a reception. The act terminates with a repetition of the last mentioned chorus. *(The many rend. 72)*

The second act commences with an accompanied recitative 'Now strike the golden Lyre again' followed by the Chorus 'Break his bands of sleep asunder', in which the poet thought to pay a compliment to the power of music by employing it to awake from sleep his intoxicated Monarch. The composer, determined not to fail on his part, has rendered it sufficiently noisy in the printed score. Our ears have, in modern times, been assailed in the midst of soft passages by a violent blow on the drum, and in some of the latest sinfonias of the German school pistols are to have been fired, but our author, in one of his performances of this ode, actually had a discharge of small cannon which, however, for the honour of good sense and propriety seems never to have been repeated. *(Now strike 105)*

The Bass song 'Revenge Timotheus cries' is decorated with a rich and busy accompaniment and its whole effect is spirited and dramatic. The slow movement 'Behold a ghastly band' is of the highest order of the great school. The tossing of torches and the strangely mournful notes, seeming to proceed from 'the voices of the dead', are painted with a masterly hand. Timotheus cries 'give the vengeance due to the valiant crew'. The Torches are tossed more vigorously. 'The princes applaud with a furious Joy/and the king seiz'd a flambeau with zeal to destroy.' The song to which the latter words are first set is chiefly remarkable for its playful accompaniment. They are again used in the following Chorus which succeeds the song 'Thais led the way', in which the expression has been censured as too feeble and tame. But I think the objection is rather hypercritical. *(Chorus The princes 135)*

The recitative accompanied 'Thus long ago' is perfectly original and its soft simplicity is admirably calculated to set off the rich extraneous harmony and scientific fugue of the Chorus 'At length Divine Cecilia came'. There follows the unrivalled fugue on four subjects, 'Let old Timotheus yield the prize', in which the ease and dexterity of management are so great that we forget we are listening to an artful and laborious species of music. He had used three of these subjects in one of his early productions, and he only who has attempted to add a fourth subject equally interesting with three already composed, will be able to form a *just* idea of our author's extraordinary powers of writing. *(Let old Timotheus 149)*

Here ended Dryden's Ode, and this was the termination of the music as first printed. Later editions, however, contain the following Chorus in praise of Saint Cecilia 'your voices tune', which, though it would not confer immortal fame either on the poet or the composer, is not without interest and contains some fine passages. *(Your voices tune)*

Enough, it is trusted, as been noticed that is pre-eminent in this composition to awaken in the musical student not only a wish to hear it performed in public but also to make it the object of his minute and private study, to become thoroughly acquainted with its merits, and to learn from its effects what and how *great* are '*the Powers of Music*'.[5]

---

[5] The following conclusion was apparently added for a lecture series beginning on 28 April at the Royal Institution as described in *General Account*: The principal object of the present course of Lectures has been to recommend to the musical student the performance of all full music whether ancient or modern instrumental or vocal. I conclude therefore with once more congratulating him on the manifest improvements which have taken place even within the last year or two, in the adaptations of full music in general. I hail it as a most favourable indication of the real and rapid amelioration of the public taste.

Lecture VIIIth.
The Dettingen Te Deum

The invention of the sublime style is considered as the greatest effort of the human mind, and it is consequently to be preferred to the beautiful and ornamental when regarded separately. For the value and rank of every style bears a correspondent proportion to the mental labour employed in its formation and the mental attention required for the enjoyment of its performance. The sublime inspires awe, the beautiful is tranquilizing and the ornamental amuses. The sublime therefore, or a union of that with the beautiful, or at least a considerable preponderance of these over the ornamental, is best calculated for sacred subjects, and accordingly composers of the ancient school who excelled in church music have ever infused a considerable predominance of the sublime style in their works. The ornamental has but little if any affinity to sacred subjects, the Beautiful is at best neutral, but we may say with the poet

> To heavenly themes sublime strains belong –

We readily allow that when some of these early writers flourished, neither the beautiful nor the ornamental had been brought to perfection and that consequently the difference between grave and gay, between sacred and secular subjects does not seem always to have been *sufficiently* marked. Instances may not infrequently be found in which ancient madrigals and even canzonets would, in our opinion at least, have been better calculated for serious subjects than for absurd love ditties.

To the ears of those, however, who were accustomed to the examination not only of every phrase of melody, but of every note of each phrase throughout a whole piece, a difference between what was sacred and secular might have been clear, which to us is become imperceptible. In thus extolling the inventors of scientific music, who like those of other arts commenced with the sublime, we by no means would detract from the merit of those who afterwards excelled in the beautiful and ornamental. But we assert that these early masters are still the great and unrivalled models of all that is sublime and sacred in our art, and that it is only by a judicious adoption of their mode of teaching and even a quotation of their very thoughts that modern composers can hope to excel in church music. In the choral or oratorio style, however, the beautiful and ornamental may contribute their subordinate aid. It is not the adoption but the undue prevalence of these styles which has checked the growth and hastened the decline of the art. All that is beautiful in vocal melody, with all of the decoration of instrumental accompaniment of which both songs and choruses are susceptible, may be considered as a valuable acquisition, and for a composer to excel in all the styles is, accordingly, regarded as a test of superiority. Each style may be made to preponderate according to the nature of the subject. A predominance of beauty in the opera style and of the ornament in instrumental music may be expected, but the most awful of subjects demands the greatest elevation of style.

The most rational, the most worthy, the most indispensable of all our employments, the very end of our existence, *the praise of God*, surely claims our best services, the full exertion of our noblest faculties. And we rejoice that the demand has not been wholly made in vain. The finest productions of many arts have been consecrated to *this best* of uses. The noblest edifices, the loftiest poems, the grandest paintings, the sublimest of musical compositions have been *sacred*. The pre-eminence of these several efforts do not indeed appear to have always sprung from *personal religion in their authors*. I dare not say of a musician as a writer in painting once said of an artist, that if he would excel in his profession he must necessarily be a *good man*. But I think every good man must take delight in seeing the finest productions of all arts dedicated to religion; so that the mere enquiry after what is *most excellent* will lead to the subject which ought to be uppermost in the minds of all. Thus, in calling the attention of the musical student to the *best* music, (*best because* it *contains most of the sublime*) I am likewise inevitably directing it to sacred subjects. I cannot aid his conception of the meaning and expression of the composer without quoting the words he has been setting. And by pursuing the same course in his retirement, the student will find music not merely an innocent amusement, but a profitable and I had almost said a heavenly employment.

Of the Te Deum of Handel which we have selected as a specimen of sacred choral music was composed for the victory at Dettingen, and on this account perhaps commences with a flourish of military instruments. The subject of the next passage for hautboys and bassoons is (like various others, in this composition, and in the oratorio of Saul) taken from a Te Deum by Padre Uria of Bologna. Various *concertante* effects are produced in this first movement by the different combinations of the instruments. After a considerable delay, the burst of voices to the words 'We praise thee O God', in slow and solemn notes while the accompaniments move rapidly, produces an unparalleled effect. The full parts are relieved by soft symphonies, and by solos for the principal alto voice accompanied by the trumpet. These subjects are then used in the way of fugue in full chorus. At the words 'We acknowledge thee to

be the Lord' the ornamental grandeur becomes more sublime, the harmony and modulations are less martial and more in the cathedral style.
But the violins continue their playful accompaniment.

After this, the former passages are repeated with the requisite
abridgments and alterations, the whole constituting an unequalled specimen of rapturous and devout praise. *(We praise thee)*

The symphony of the chorus 'All the Earth doth worship thee' is on a
subject by Padre Uria which our author has also used in the admired
duet in Israel in Egypt 'The Lord is a man of war'. The soft passages are
beautiful and form a striking contrast to the fuller parts. At the mention
of 'the father everlasting' a solemnity of expression is employed. The
character of the whole seems to represent the Christian church in a state
of joy, exultation and triumph. *(All the Earth)*

The words 'To thee all angels cry aloud' are expressed by the minor
key. This has been censured as false expression resulting from a misap-
prehension of the meaning of the word '*cry*'. But though Handel, as a
foreigner, was liable to occasional errors of this kind, I do not imagine
he would have been ignorant of the true sense of any part of the Te
Deum. Our own countryman Purcell has done the same in his admirable Te Deum, and our author has set the same word in the very next
movement and the same sentence in another of his Te Deums in the
major Key. I should rather imagine, therefore, that the minor key is
used *solely* for the sake of *contrast* to the surrounding movements; just
as the voices of the Cherubim and Seraphim are represented by trebles
that the effect of the Tenors and Basses may be heightened in expressing
'The heavens and *all ye powers* therein'. The uniformity of rhythm in
the accompaniments, the passages for many voices in unisons or octaves,
and the simplicity of the notes employed are all productive of the purist
sublimity.

That many composers have in general exceeded Handel in this style
has been frequently admitted, but in some *few instances* he seems even
in this respect inferior to none. And I cannot but coincide in an opinion
of the late Mr Malchair of Oxford, that this passage is both the greatest
effort of *this* master and far beyond what any other composer has ever
conceived. In the next chorus 'To thee Cherubim and Seraphim' the
scientific treatment of the fugue to the words 'continually do cry' and
the solemn simplicity of the holding note 'Holy Holy Holy Lord God of
Sabaoth' are productive of different descriptions of the sublime. And at
the words 'Heaven and earth are full of the majesty of thy glory', the
plenitude of effect resulting from the vast compass of scale, the fullness
of harmony and the dignity of rhythm attains the same object in a still
higher degree. Indeed, this movement seems a compendium of the various excellencies which we have been accustomed to admire. The subject

'Holy Holy', particularly where the treble voices strengthened by the Trumpet ascend diatonically, remind us of the Hallelujah Chorus in the Messiah.

The passage to the words 'continually do cry' is used in the Funeral Anthem in a passage of simple harmony near the end. And the threefold repetition of the word Holy to the same notes (doubtless in reference to the awfully mysterious doctrine alluded to in the words) reminds us of the 'Wonderful, Counselor' in the chorus 'For unto us a child is born'. In both these movements the mind is presented with the grandest image that can possibly fill it, that of the heavenly host praising God as described in the book of Revelations and thus rendered by the poet:

> All the multitude of angels, with a shout
> Loud as from numbers without number, sweet
> as from blest voices, uttering joy, heav'n sung
> with jubilee and loud Hosannas filled
> The Eternal regions –

(To thee all angels and To thee Cherubim)

The next movement is a semichorus or trio, or at least is generally performed as such, and is ushered in by a most elegant symphony with a bass accompaniment in quavers. The bass voices repeat the same solemn notes to the words 'The glorious company of the Apostles', 'the goodly fellowship of the prophets', and 'the noble army of martyrs'. These seem to be some fragment of a chant or other ancient Ecclesiastical melody, and were used to the words 'the father everlasting' in a preceding chorus. The sudden transition from the key of B minor with two sharps, to that of B major with five [and] also from a continuity of motion to the slowest time at the words 'The father of an infinite majesty', is another extraordinary effort of sublime expression. The allegro 'thine honorable true and only son' is perhaps somewhat inferior to the rest of the composition. The subjects are short and the style is inexpressive of the words. The passage 'Also the Holy Ghost the Comforter' is a subject of Padre Urias to the same words and our author seems blamable for having followed his model too closely. He had better in this instance have trusted to his own invention. In general, Handel has evinced himself a most skilful plagiarist, converting whatever he touches into gold. The student would be astonished at the dullness and unpromising aspect of the ore from which his riches are extracted. Uria's Te Deum has but little sublimity, less magnificence and no beauty. In the hands of our author, however, his subjects usually grow up into the perfection of Music. *(The glorious company)*

The Bass Song 'Thou art the king of glory O Christ' is accompanied by the trumpet obbligato, and its simplicity is admirably opposed to the fullness of the Chorus which follows. A passage of canon occurs in the latter, which is also inserted in the beautiful chorus 'Then round about the starry throne' in Samson. Indeed, the thought may be traced back (for its harmony) at least to a celebrated madrigal by John Wilbie 'Flora gave me fairest flowers'. It is one of those successions of chords that must ever give delight with whatever melody it may be clothed. No part of this movement seems copied from Uria except one of the cadences in the song. The style and expression are remarkably lofty and worthy of the subject. *(Thou art king)*

The Air for a baritone or high bass voice 'When thou tookest upon thee to deliver man' is eminent for its beauty. Its melody is graceful, its harmony clear, its modulations peculiarly varied and interesting, and the whole expressive of the wondrous love and condescension described by the words. The style is that of the best Italian composers of the old school. But it has suffered nothing from age and would not have disgraced the pen of a Mozart. *(When Thou tookest)*

Handel has adapted the words 'When thou hadst overcome the sharpness of death, thou didst open the kingdom of heaven to all believers' to two movements, the first, grave, mysterious and pathetic, the second lively and triumphant. *This also* has been censured as false expression, because both the members of the sentence are speaking of a period in which our Lord *had already* surmounted and triumphed over all his sufferings and death. But we protest against this objection as frivolous and hypercritical. For on what does the mind fix its attention on reading the words? Is it not on the *pangs* felt? Can the very idea of the words *'sharpness of death'* set to lively and rapid notes, be tolerated? The composer now, however, makes the whole transaction pass before us as in a drama: Our Redeemer *first suffers*, then opens the kingdom of heaven to all believers. *(When thou)*

The trio 'Thou sittest at the right hand of God in the glory of the father' is remarkable both for the scientific treatment of the voice parts and for the variety and effect of the accompaniments. The violins, after giving out the subjects in the symphony, sustain the chords of the harmony in long holding notes in a manner which Mozart has frequently adopted, the oboes playing little symphonies to relieve the solo voices.

When the vocal parts become fuller, the instruments are altogether confined for a time to short ritornels until at length they seem to emulate the richness of the voices, increasing the number of the real parts of the score and extending the scale to an extraordinary compass. *(Thou sittest –)*

The conclusion of the foregoing trio would be justly considered as abrupt were it not immediately succeeded by other movements which I am obliged to omit – reluctantly, however, as they are justly ranked amongst the finest parts of this admirable composition. After the words 'We believe that thou shalt come to be our judge' a solemn pause is unexpectedly interrupted by the sound of the trumpet calling the world to Judgement. The Chorus 'We therefore pray thee help thy servants Whom thou hast redeemed with they precious blood' is in the pure sublime style on a subject Carissimi[1] also quoted by our author in his choruses of 'Hear Jacob's God' in Samson and 'father of mercies' in Joshua. The effect afterwards produced by treble voices without any accompaniment to the same words is most pathetic and plaintive. The transition from this earnest prayer for '*help*' to that bolder petition which evinces the *full assurance of faith*, 'Make them to be numbered with thy Saints in glory everlasting', is most happily conveyed by the music, and the rest of the words are as, D[r] Burney justly remarks, admirably rendered.[2] These, then, are the movements which I would especially press upon the notice of every student, and particularly of the young composer, as being far more worthy of study and imitation than those which are the most striking, splendid and attractive.

The Chorus 'Day by day we magnify thee' reminds us a little of Purcell's manner of setting the same words. Part of the Trumpet passage is from Padre Uria, as is also the subject of the spirited fugue 'And we worship thy name ever world without end'. *(Day by day etc.)*

The air 'Vouchsafe O Lord to keep us this day without sin' is very remarkable for the pathos and expression of the vocal melody and the erudition and science of its chromatic harmonies and Enharmonic Modulations, forming a strong contrast to the plain diatonic scales of the adjacent movements. The last strain of this admirable composition 'O Lord in thee have I trusted, let me never be confounded' is worthy of the minutest investigation. Its subject, which ascends gradually whilst its bass accompaniment forms a second subject by descending, is first heard on two trumpets. These are then joined by the rest of the instruments, with the exception of the drums which are judiciously withheld until the principal alto voice has gone through the several subjects with soft accompaniments. Then they aid the full Chorus, in which all the subjects are managed with the most consummate skill. One of them, to the words 'let me never be confounded', is used by our author in the chorus 'And the Glory of the Lord' in the Messiah, in the song 'With pious hearts' in Judas Macchabaeus and other places.

The judicious treatment and intermixture of these subjects and the effects produced by the various combinations of instruments *and by the*

---

[1] {frequently}

[2] Charles Burney, *An Account of the Musical Performances in Westminster-Abbey* (London, 1785; New York: Da Capo Press, 1979), Part I, pp. 28–31.

solemn pause before its slow termination, render this movement in no degree inferior to any of the kind extant, forming a sublime and satisfactory conclusion to the whole piece by

> Untwisting all the chains that tie
> the hidden soul of harmony –[3]

It is then in the higher walks of the art that we must trace the footsteps of the greatest masters, in the sacred and sublime styles that we must seek for the greatest of all composers. And if Handel is allowed to be the best of oratorio composers, this very circumstance places him above all his competitors.

Having guided the steps of the student to this lofty summit, I now leave him to contemplate the grandeur of the prospect and enjoy the enlargement of his views. He must now surely look down on the first stages of his ascent the scenery of which, though once admired, is comparatively so limited and humble. He may not indeed choose to *dwell* on this eminence, and descent in every direction is always easy. But it is hoped he will frequently revisit these higher walks which raise him far above all earthly and common sounds, and in their stead substitute sublime and sacred strains which (as Milton expresses it),

> dissolve him into extacies
> and bring all heav'n before his eyes –[4]

---

[3] Milton, *L'Allegro*, lines 143–4. Burney concludes his brief discussion of the *Dettingen Te Deum* in his *Account*, Part 1, p. 31, with this quotation from Milton.

[4] Milton, *Il Penseroso*, lines 165–6: 'dissolve me into extacies/and bring all Heaven before mine eyes'.

Bibliography

Materials concerning William Crotch at the Norfolk Record Office

NRO, MS 5288 Manuscript notebook
NRO, MS 5289 Manuscript notebook
NRO, MS 5294 Manuscript music book
NRO, MS 11090 Memoir by C. F. Kitton
NRO, MS 11099 Observations on Dr Crotch's Works
NRO, MS 11200–11213 Notes by A. H. Mann
NRO, MS 11214–11226 Crotch's correspondence vols 1–13, 1801–45
NRO, MS 11234 Collection of marches and waltzes by various composers
NRO, MS 11242 Anthem books
NRO, MS 11244 Memoirs
NRO, MS 11246 Copies of works by various composers
NRO, MS 11253 Crotch's copy of J. S. Bach, *The Art of Fugue* with annotations

Additional correspondence in Royal Institution manuscripts

CL 1/35 WC to J. P. Auriol 2 February 1808
CL 1/36 WC to J. P. Auriol 22 February 1808

Crotch's lectures

NRO, MS 11063 Eight lectures 1820
NRO, MS 11064 Fifteen lectures
NRO, MS 11065 Eight lectures
NRO, MS 11066 Five lectures
NRO, MS 11067 Three lectures
NRO, MS 11228 Thirteen lectures
NRO, MS 11229 Ten lectures
NRO, MS 11230 Nine lectures 1806 and 1817; General Account of all the Courses of Lectures
NRO, MS 11231 Eight lectures
NRO, MS 11232 Twelve lectures
NRO, MS 11233 Seven lectures
Col/7/43–53 (formerly Colman 644) Ten lectures

Published works by William Crotch

Elements of Composition; Comprehending the Rules of Thorough-Bass and the Theory of Tuning, 3rd edn, London, 1856.

Specimens of Various Styles of Music Referred to in a Course of Lectures read at Oxford and London, 3 vols, London: Royal Harmonic Institution, *c*. 1806.

Substance of Several Courses of Lectures on Music, London, 1831; Clarabricken, Co Kilkenny, Ireland: Beothius Press, 1986.

'W. C.' [William Crotch], 'Remarks on the present State of Music', *Monthly Magazine*, 10 (1800–1801), 125–7, 505–6.

A list of published transcriptions, original compositions, and minor pedagogical works by Crotch not listed here is found in *Substance*, pp. 171–5.

Published works by Charles Burney

'Account of an Infant Musician', *Philosophical Transactions of the Royal Society of London*, 69 (1779), 183–206.

An Account of the Musical Performances in Westminster-Abbey, London, 1785; New York: Da Capo Press, 1979.

A Catalogue of the Valuable and Very Fine Collection of Music, Printed and MS, of the late Charles Burney, London, 1814; Amsterdam: Frits Knuf, 1973.

A General History of Music, with critical and historical notes by Frank Mercer, 2 vols, London, 1935; New York: Dover, 1957.

Memoirs of the Life and Writings of the Abate Metastasio, 3 vols, London, 1796; New York: Da Capo Press, 1971.

The Present State of Music in France and Italy: or the Journal of a Tour through those Countries, undertaken to collect Materials for a General History of Music, 2nd edn, London, 1773; New York: AMS Press, 1976.

The Present State of Music in Germany, the Netherlands and United Provinces, 2nd edn, 2 vols, London, 1775; New York: Broude, 1969.

Review of *Essays, Historical and Critical on English Church Music*, by William Mason, *Monthly Review*, 20 (1796), 398–408.

Review of *The Four Ages*, by William Jackson, *Monthly Review*, Series II, 26 (1798), 109–99.

Review of *Historical Memoirs of the Irish Bard*, by Joseph Walker, *Monthly Review*, 77 (1787), 425–39.

Review of *Historical Memoir on Italian Tragedy*, by Joseph Cooper Walker, *Monthly Review*, series II, 29 (1799), 1–15.

Review of *An Inquiry into the Fine Arts*, by Thomas Robertson, *Monthly Review*, 74 (1786), 191–8.

Review of *The Life of Samuel Johnson, L.L.D.*, by Robert Anderson, *Monthly Review*, Series II, 20 (1796), 18–27.

Review of *Melody the Soul of Music: an Essay towards the improvement of the Musical Art*, by Alexander Molleson, *Monthly Review*, 27 (1798), 189–94.

Review of *Musical and Poetical Relics of the Welsh Bards*, by Edward Jones, *Monthly Review*, 74 (1786), 49–63.

Review of *Observations on the present State of Music, in London*, by William Jackson of Exeter, *Monthly Review*, 6 (October 1791), 196–202.

Review of *Poems by William Whitehead, Esq ... To which are prefixed, Memoirs of his Life and Writings*, by W. Mason M. A., *Monthly Review* 78 (1788): 177–82.

Review of *Poems on various Subjects*, by R. Anderson, *Monthly Review*, Series II, 29 (1799), 104–5.

Review of *Principles and Power of Harmony*, by Benjamin Stillingfleet, *Critical Review*, 31 (1771), 458–63, and 32 (1771), 15–24.

Review of *Principles and Power of Harmony*, by Benjamin Stillingfleet, *Monthly Review*, 45 (1771), 369–77 and 477–84.

Review of *Reliques of Irish Poetry*, by Charlotte Brooke, *Monthly Review*, Series II, 4 (1791), 37–46.

Review of *A Treatise on the Art of Music*, by William Jones, *Monthly Review*, 75 (1786), 105–12 and 174–81.

Books and articles

Addison, Joseph, *The Spectator*, ed. Donald F. Bond, 5 vols, Oxford: Oxford University Press, 1965.

Allen, Warren Dwight, *Philosophies of Music History: a Study of General Histories of Music 1600–1960*, New York: American Book Company, 1939; New York: Dover, 1962.

Andrews, C. Bruyn, ed., *The Torrington Diaries; Containing the Tours Through England and Wales of the Hon. John Byng (Later Fifth Viscount Torrington)*, 4 vols, London: Eyre and Spottiswoode, 1935; New York: Barnes and Noble, 1970.

Anonymous, 'Dr. Crotch's Lectures', *The Harmonicon*, 7 (1829), 160.

Anonymous, 'Memoir of Haydn', *The Harmonicon*, 1 (1823), 17.

Anonymous, 'Memoir of William Crotch, Mus. Doc.', *The Harmonicon*, 9 (1831), 3–6.

Anonymous, 'Review of New Musical Publications', *Gentleman's Magazine*, 83 (1813), 354–6.

d'Arblay, Frances (Burney), *Memoirs of Doctor Burney*, 3 vols, London, 1832.

Avison, Charles, *An Essay on Musical Expression*, 2nd edn, London, 1753; New York: Broude, 1967.

Bacon, Francis, *Essays, Advancement of Learning, New Atlantis, and other Pieces*, ed. R. F. Jones, New York: P. F. Collier, *c.* 1937.

[Richard Mackenzie Bacon]. (Anonymous), 'The Philharmonic Society', *QMMR*, 1 (1818–19), 340–50.

——. 'Plan of Work', *QMMR*, 1 (1818–19), 1–2.

——. ('Vetus'), 'On the Character of Musicians', *QMMR*, 1 (1818–19), 284–5.

——. (Anonymous), 'The Royal Academy of Music', *QMMR*, 4 (1822), 370–400.

Barrington, Daines, 'Some Account of Little Crotch', in *Miscellanies*, pp. 311–25, London, 1781.

Bate, Walter, *From Classic to Romantic: Premises of Taste in Eighteenth-Century England*, New York: Harper and Row, 1946.

Battestin, Martin, *The Providence of Wit: Aspects of Form in Augustan Literature and the Arts*, Oxford: Clarendon Press, 1974.

Beattie, James, 'An Essay On Poetry and Music, as They Affect the Mind', in Beattie, *Essays*, pp. 347–580, Edinburgh, 1771; New York: Garland, 1971.

Beedell, A. V., *The Decline of the English Musician 1788–1888*, Oxford: Clarendon Press, 1992.

Bell, C. F., 'Thomas Gray and the Fine Arts', *Essays and Studies by Members of the English Association*, 30 (1944), 50–81.

Bennett, J. R. Sterndale, *The Life of William Sterndale Bennett*, Cambridge: Cambridge University Press, 1907.

Betz, Siegmund A., 'The Operatic Criticism of the *Tatler*, and *Spectator*', *Musical Quarterly*, 31 (1945), 325.

Blake, William, *Complete Writings*, ed. Geoffrey Keynes, London, Oxford University Press, 1966.

Bond, Donald F., ed., *The Spectator*, Oxford, Oxford University Press, 1965.

Bonnet-Bourdelot, Pierre, *Histoire de la Musique et de ses effets*, Paris, 1715.

Brocklesby, Richard, *Reflections on Antient and Modern Musik, with the Application to the Cure of Diseases*, London, 1749.

Brown, John, *A Dissertation on the Rise, Union, and Power, the Progressions, Separations, and Corruptions, of Poetry and Music*, London, 1763; New York: Garland, 1971.

Brownell, Morris R., 'Ears of an Untoward Make: Pope and Handel', *Musical Quarterly*, **62** (1976), 554–570.

Buelow, George J., 'The Case for Handel's Borrowings: the Judgment of Three Centuries', in Stanley Sadie and Anthony Hicks, eds, *Handel Tercentenary Collection*, Ann Arbor, MI: UMI Research Press, 1987.

Bumpus, John S., *A History of English Cathedral Music 1549–1889*, 2 vols, London: T. Werner Laurie, 1908.

Burgh, Allatson, *Anecdotes of Music, Historical and Biographical*, 3 vols, London: Longman, 1814.

Burke, Edmund, *A Philosophical Enquiry into the Origin of our Ideas of the Sublime and Beautiful*, ed. James T. Boulton, Notre Dame, IN: University of Notre Dame Press, 1968.

Burney, Fanny, *The Journals and Letters of Fanny Burney*, eds, Joyce Hemlow, Patricia Boutilier and Althea Douglas, 8 vols, Oxford: Clarendon Press, 1973.

Busby, Thomas, Review of *Melody the Soul of Music*, by Alexander Mollesen, *Analytical Review*, **28** (1798), 395–7.

———. *Concert Room and Orchestra Anecdotes of Music and Musicians Ancient and Modern*, 3 vols, London: Printed for Clementi & Co., 1825.

Butler, Charles, *Reminiscences of Charles Butler Esq. With a Letter to a Lady on Ancient and Modern Music*, 4th edn, 2 vols, London, 1824.

Cazalet, Revd W.W., *The History of the Royal Academy of Music*, London: T. Bosworth, 1854.

Clark, Caryl. 'The Lectures of Dr. William Crotch: Conservative Thought in English Musical Taste at the Turn of the Nineteenth Century', MA, McGill University, 1982.

Clark, J.C.D., *English Society 1688–1832: Ideology, Social Structure, and Political Practice during the Ancien Regime*, Cambridge: Cambridge University Press, 1985.

Clark, Kenneth, *The Gothic Revival: an Essay in the History of Taste*, New York, Humanities Press, 1970.

Cole, Malcolm S., 'Momigny's Analysis of Haydn's Symphony No. 103', *The Music Review*, **30** (1969), 261–84.

Corder, F.A., *A History of the Royal Academy of Music from 1822 to 1922*, London: F. Corder, 1922.

Cosgrove, W., 'Affective Unities: the Esthetics of Music and Factional Instability in Eighteenth Century England', *Eighteenth Century Studies*, **22** (1988–89), 133–55.

Cox, H. Bertram and Cox, C.L.E., *Leaves from the Journals of Sir George Smart*, London, 1907; New York: Da Capo Press, 1971.

Coxe, William, *Literary Life and Select Works of Benjamin Stillingfleet*, London, 1811.

Cramer, Richard, 'The New Modulation of the 1770's: C.P.E. Boch in Theory, Criticism and Practice', *Journal of the American Musicological Society*, **38** (1985), 551–92.

Cudworth, C.L., 'An Essay by John Marsh', *Music and Letters*, **36** (1955), 155–64.

Czerny, Carl, *School of Practical Composition*, trans. John Bishop, 3 vols, London, 1848; New York: Da Capo Press, 1979.

Daniells, Roy, 'The English Baroque and Deliberate Obscurity', *Journal of Aesthetics and Art Criticism*, **5** (1946, 115–21.

Day, Thomas, 'A Renaissance Revival in Eighteenth-Century England', *Musical Quarterly*, **57** (1971), 575–92.

Dean, Winton, *Handel's Dramatic Oratorios and Masques*, London: Oxford University Press, 1959.

Dennis, John, *Essay on the Operas after the Italian Manner, Which Are about to be Establish'd on the English Stage: with some Reflections on the Damage Which They May Bring to the Public*, London, 1706.

Dennis, John, 'The Grounds of Criticism in Poetry' and 'The Stage Defended, from Scripture, Reason, and the Common Sense of Man', in Edward Niles Hooker, ed., *The Critical Works of John Dennis*, 2 vols, Baltimore, MD, Johns Hopkins University Press, 1939–43.

Deutsch, Otto E, *Handel: a Documentary Biography*, New York: W.W. Norton, 1955.

Dibdin, Thomas, *The Reminiscences of Thomas Dibdin of the Theatre Royal, Covent Garden, Drury Lane, Haymarket, etc.*, 2 vols, London: Henry Colburn, 1827.

———. 'Poetry and Music in Eighteenth-Century Aesthetics', *Englische Studien*, **67** (1932–33), 70–85.

Diderot, Denis, d'Alembert, Jean le Rond and Mouchon, Pierre, eds, *Encyclopédie ou Dictionnaire raisonné des sciences, des arts et des métiers 1757–1772*, 35 vols, Paris, 1757–80; Stuttgart-Bad Cannstatt, Frommann, 1966.

Draper, John W., 'Queen Anne's Act: a Note on English Copyright', *Modern Language Notes*, **36** (1921), 146–54.

———. *William Mason: a Study in Eighteenth-Century Culture*, New York: New York University Press, 1924.

Dynes, Wayne, 'Gothic, Concept of', in Philip P. Wiener, ed., *Dictionary of the History of Ideas*, New York, 1973.

Edwards, F.G., 'Music in England in the Nineteenth Century', *The Musical Times*, **42** (1901), 88–9.

Fisk, Roger, 'Concert Music II', in H.D. Johnstone and R. Fisk, eds, *The Blackwell History of Music in Britain*, vol. 4, *The Eighteenth Century*, Oxford: Blackwell, 1990.

Fleming-Williams, I., 'William Crotch, Member of the Oxford School and Friend of Constable', *The Connoisseur*, 159 (1963), 140.

Foster, Myles Birket, *History of the Philharmonic Society of London, 1813–1912: a Record of a Hundred Years Work in the Cause of Music*, London: John Lane, 1912.

Frankl, Paul, *The Gothic: Literary Sources and Interpretations through Eight Centuries*, Princeton: Princeton University Press, 1960.

Fubini, Enrico, *Music and Culture in Eighteenth-Century Europe: A Source Book*, trans. Wolfgang Fries, Lisa Basbarrone and Michael Louis Leone, ed. Bonnie J. Blackburn, Chicago and London: University of Chicago Press, 1994.

Fuller-Maitland, John Alexander, *English Music in the XIXth Century*, London: Grant Richards, 1902.

Furniss, Tom, *Edmund Burke's Aesthetic Ideology: Language, Gender, and Political Economy in Revolution*, Cambridge: Cambridge University Press, 1993.

Gerard, Alexander, *An Essay on Taste*, Edinburgh, 1764; facsimile reprint, New York: Garland, 1970.

Gilpin, William, *Three Essays: On Beauty; On Picturesque Travel; and on Sketching Landscape: To Which is Added a Poem on Landscape Painting*, 2nd edn, London, 1794.

Graham, Walter, *English Literary Periodicals*, New York: Octagon Books, 1966.

Grant, Kerry S., *Dr. Burney as Critic and Historian of Music*, Ann Arbor, MI: UMI Research Press, 1983.

Graue, Jerald C., 'The Clementi-Cramer Dispute Revisited', *Music and Letters*, 56 (1975), 47–54.

———. 'Cramer, Johann [John] Baptist', in *The New Grove Dictionary of Music and Musicians*, ed. Stanley Sadie, 20 vols, London, Macmillan Publishers Ltd, 1980, vol. 5, p. 21.

Greene, Donald, *The Politics of Samuel Johnson*, New Haven, CT: Yale University Press, 1960; Port Washington, NY: Kennikat Press, 1973.

Hadley, David W., 'The Growth of London Musical Society in the Nineteenth Century: Studies in the History of a Profession', DPhil, Harvard University, 1972.

Harris, James, *Three Treatises: The First, Concerning Art, The Second Concerning Music, The Third Concerning Happiness*, 2nd edn, London, 1765.

[Sir John Hawkins], *An Account of the Institution and Progress of the Academy of Ancient Music with a Comparative View of the Music of the Past and Present Times by a Member*, London, 1770.

Hawkins, Sir John, *A General History of the Science and Practice of*

Music, ed. Othmar Wessely, 2 vols, London, 1776; London, 1875; Graz, Austria: Akademische Druck- u. Verlagsanstalt, 1969.

[William Hayes]. 'Remarks on Mr. Avison's Essay on Musical Expression, wherein the Characters of several great Masters, Both Ancient and Modern, are rescued from the Misrepresentation of the above Author, and their real Merit asserted and Vindicated', in Otto E. Deutsch, *Handel: a Documentary Biography*, pp. 731–34, New York: W.W. Norton, 1955.

Heartz, Daniel, 'Classical' in *The New Grove Dictionary of Music and Musicians*, ed. Stanley Sadie, 20 vols, London, Macmillan Publishers Ltd, 1980, vol. 3, p. 453.

Hilles, Frederick Whiley, *The Literary Career of Sir Joshua Reynolds*, Cambridge: Cambridge University Press, 1936.

Hipple, Walter John jr, 'General and Particular in the *Discourses* of Sir Joshua Reynolds: A Study in Method', *Journal of Aesthetics and Art Criticism*, 11 (1953), 231–47.

———. *The Beautiful, the Sublime, & the Picturesque in Eighteenth-Century British Aesthetic Theory*, Carbondale, IL: Southern Illinois University Press, 1957.

Hogarth, George, *Musical History, Biography and Criticism*, London, 1835; New York, 1848; New York: Da Capo Press, 1969.

———. *The Philharmonic Society of London; From Its Foundation, 1813, To Its Fiftieth Year, 1862*, London, 1862.

Holbrook, W.C. 'The Adjective *Gothique* in the XVIIIth Century', *Modern Language Notes*, 56 (1971), 498–503.

Honour, Hugh, *Neo-classicism*, New York: Penguin Books, 1977.

Hooker, Edward Niles, ed., *The Critical Works of John Dennis*, 2 vols, Baltimore, MD, Johns Hopkins University Press, 1939–43.

F.W. H[orncastle], 'Plagiarism' *QMMR*, 4 (1822), 141–7.

———. 'Plan for the Formation of an English Conservatorio', *QMMR*, 4 (1822), 129–33.

Horne, George, *The Works of the Right Reverend George Horne, D.D.*, 2 vols, New York, H. M. Onderdonk & Co., 1848.

Hughes, Rosemary S.M., 'Dr. Burney's Championship of Haydn', *The Musical Quarterly*, 27 (1941), 90–96.

Hughes, William, *Remarks Upon Church Musick, to which are added Several Observations upon some of Mr. Handel's Oratorios and other Parts of his Works*, 2nd edn, Worchester, 1763.

le Huray, Peter and Day, James, eds, *Music and Aesthetics in the Eighteenth and Early-Nineteenth Centuries*, Cambridge: Cambridge University Press, 1981.

Hurd, Richard, *Letters on Chivalry and Romance*, London, 1762; New York: Garland, 1971.

Husk, William Henry, *An Account of the Musical Celebrations on St. Cecilia's Day in the Sixteenth, Seventeenth, and Eighteenth Centuries*, London, 1857.

Hussey, Christopher, *The Picturesque: Studies in a Point of View*, London: G.P. Puttnam's Sons 1927; Hamden, CT: Archon Press, 1967.

Hutcheson, Francis, *An Inquiry into the Original of Our Ideas of Beauty and Virtue*, London, 1726; New York: Garland, 1971.

Irving, Howard, 'Haydn and Laurence Sterne: Similarities in Eighteenth Century Literary and Musical Wit', *Current Musicology*, 40 (1985), 34–49.

Irving, Howard, 'Richard Mackenzie Bacon and the Royal Academy of Music', *International Review of the Aesthetics and Sociology of Music*, 21 (1990), 79–90.

———. 'William Crotch on Borrowing', *The Music Review*, 53 (1992), 237–54.

———. 'Classic and Gothic: Charles Burney on Ancient Music', *Studies in Eighteenth Century Culture*, 23 (1993), 243–63.

———. 'William Crotch on *The Creation*', *Music and Letters*, 75 (1994), 548–60.

Irving, Howard and Riggins, H. Lee, 'Advanced Uses of Mode Mixture in Haydn's Late Instrumental Works', *Canadian University Music Review*, 9 (1988), 104–35.

Jackson, William of Exeter, *Thirty Letters on Various Subjects*, London, 1784; New York: Garland Press, 1970.

———. *Observations on the Present State of Music in London*, Dublin, 1791.

———. *The Four Ages; Together with Essays on Various Subjects*, London, 1798; New York: Garland, 1970.

Jacob, Hildebrand, *Of the Sister Arts; an Essay*, London, 1734.

Johnson, Fredric, 'Tartini's Trattato di Musica Seconda la Vera Scienza dell'Armonia: an Annotated Translation with Commentary', PhD, Indiana University, 1985.

Johnson, Samuel, *Lives of the English Poets*, ed. George Birkbeck Hill, New York: Octagon Books, 1967.

Johnstone, H. Diack and Fisk, Roger, eds, *The Blackwell History of Music in Briton*, vol. 4, *The Eighteenth Century*, Oxford: Blackwell, 1992.

Jones, Edward, *Musical and Poetical Relics of the Welsh Bards*, London, 1784.

Jones, William (of Nayland), *Physiological Disquisitions: or Discourses on the Natural Philosophy of the Elements*, London, 1781.

———. *A Treatise on the Art of Music, in which the Elements of*

HARMONY and AIR are Practically Considered ... , Colchester, 1784.

Kassler, Jamie Croy, 'British Writings on Music, 1760–1830: a Systematic Essay Toward a Philosophy of Selected Writings', PhD, Columbia University, NY, 1971.

———. *The Science of Music in Britain 1714–1830: a Catalogue of Writings, Lectures, and Inventions*, 2 vols, New York: Garland, 1979.

———. 'The Royal Institution Music Lectures, 1800–1831: a Preliminary Study', *The Royal Musical Association Research Chronicle*, **19** (1983–85), 1–30.

Kerman, Joseph, 'A Few Canonic Variations', in Robert von Hallberg, ed., *Canons*, pp. 177–95, Chicago and London: University of Chicago Press, 1984.

———. 'Theories of Late Eighteenth Century Music', in Ralph Cohen ed., *Studies in Eighteenth-Century British Art and Aesthetics*, Berkeley and Los Angeles: University of California Press, 1985.

Kidd, Ronald R., 'Jackson, William', in *The New Grove Dictionary of Music and Musicians*, ed. Stanley Sadie, 20 vols, London: Macmillan Publishers Ltd, 1980, vol. 9, pp. 439–40.

Kivy, Peter, 'Mainwaring's *Handel*: Its Relation to English Aesthetics', *Journal of the American Musicological Society*, **17** (1964), 170–78.

———. *The Seventh Sense: a Study of Francis Hutcheson's Aesthetics and Its Influence in Eighteenth Century Britain*, New York: Burt Franklin, 1976.

Klima, Slava, Bowers, Garry and Grant, Gerry S., eds, *Memoirs of Dr. Charles Burney 1726–1769*, London, NB: University of Nebraska Press, 1988.

Kollmann, A.F.C., *Essay on Musical Harmony*, London, 1796.

———. *Essay on Practical Music Composition*, London, 1799.

———. 'A Retrospect of the State of Music in Great Britian, since the Year 1798', *Quarterly Musical Register*, **1** (1812), 6–28.

Krehbiel, Henry Edward, *Music and Manners in the Classical Period*, New York, 1898; Portland, ME: Longwood Press, 1976.

Langley, Leanne, 'The English Musical Journal in the Early Nineteenth Century'. PhD, University of North Carolina, Chapel Hill, NC, 1983.

———. 'Burney and Hawkins: New Light on an Old Rivalry', paper presented at the annual meeting of the American Musicological Society, Austin, Texas, October 1990.

Large, David C. and Weber, William, eds, *Wagnerism in European Culture and Politics*, Ithaca, NY, and London: Cornell University Press, 1984.

Leppert, R. and McClary, Susan, eds, *Music and Society: The Politics of*

Composition, Performance and Reception, Cambridge: Cambridge University Press, 1987.

Levine, Joseph M., 'Ancients and Moderns Reconsidered', *Eighteenth-Century Studies*, 15 (1981), 72–89.

———. 'Edward Gibbon and the Quarrel between the Ancients and the Moderns', *Humanism and History: Origins of Modern English Historiography*, pp. 178–89, Ithaca, NY: Cornell University Press, 1987.

———. *The Battle of the Books: History and Literature in the Augustan Age*, Ithaca, NY: Cornell University Press, 1991.

Lightwood, James T., *Samuel Wesley, Musician: the Story of his Life*, (London: Epworth Press, 1937).

Lipking, Lawrence, *The Ordering of the Arts in Eighteenth-Century England*, Princeton, NJ: Princeton University Press, 1970.

Lippman, Edward, *A History of Western Musical Aesthetics*, Lincoln, NB and London: University of Nebraska Press, 1992.

Locke, John, *An Essay Concerning Human Understanding*, ed., Peter H. Niddeth, Oxford: Clarendon Press, 1975.

Lockman, John, Preface to *Rosalinde, a Musical Drama. To which is prefixed. An Enquiry into the Rise and Progress of OPERAS and ORATORIOS, with some Reflections on LYRIC POETRY and MUSIC*, London, 1740.

Longueil, Alfred, 'The Word "Gothic" in Eighteenth Century Criticism', *Modern Language Notes*, 38 (1923), 453–60.

Lonsdale, Roger, 'Dr. Burney and the *Monthly Review*', *Review of English Studies*, 14 (1963), 346–58 and 15 (1964), 27–37.

———. *Dr. Charles Burney: a Literary Biography*, Oxford: Clarendon Press, 1965.

———. 'Johnson and Dr. Burney', in James Marshall Osborn, ed., *Johnson, Boswell and their Circle: Essays Presented to Lawrence Fitzroy Powell*, pp. 21–40, Oxford: Clarendon Press, 1965.

Lovejoy, Arthur O. 'The First Gothic Revival and the Return to Nature', *Modern Language Notes*, 27 (1932), 414–46.

———. *Essays in the History of Ideas*, Baltimore, MD, Johns Hopkins Press, 1948.

Lovell, Percy. '"Ancient" Music in Eighteenth-Century England', *Musical Quarterly*, 60 (1979), 401–15.

Luckett, Richard, '"Or Rather Our Musical Shakespeare": Charles Burney's Purcell', in Charles Cudworth, Christopher Hogwood and Richard Luckett, eds, *Music in Eighteenth-Century England*, pp. 59–77, New York: Cambridge University Press, 1983.

Lysons, Daniel, *History of the Origins and Progress of the Meeting of the Three Choirs of Gloucester, Worcester and Hereford*, 3rd edn, London, 1865.

Mace, D.T., 'Musical Humanism, the Doctrine of Rhythmus, and the Saint Cecilia Odes of Dryden', *Journal of the Warburg and Courtauld Institute*, **27** (1963), 271–92.

Mackerness, Eric David, 'Fovargue and Jackson', *Music and Letters*, **31** (1950), 231–7.

———. 'William Jackson at Exeter Cathedral, 1777–1803', *Devon & Cornwall Notes and Queries*, **27** (1956–57), 7.

———. *A Social History of English Music*, London: Routledge and K. Paul, 1964.

Mainwaring, John, *Memoirs of the Life of the Late George Frederic Handel*, London, 1760; New York: Da Capo Press, 1980.

Malcolm, Alexander, *A Treatise of Music Speculative, Practical, and Historical*, Edinburgh, 1721; New York: Da Capo Press, 1970.

Malcolm, James, *Anecdotes of the Manners and Customs of London during the Eighteenth Century*, London, 1808.

Manfredini, Vincenzo, 'Defense of Modern Music and Its Celebrated Performers', in Enrico Fubini, *Music and Culture in Eighteenth-Century Europe: a Source Book*, trans. W. Fries, L. Basbarrone and M.L. Leone, ed. B.J. Blackburn, Chicago and London: University of Chicago Press, 1994.

Mann, A.H., *Lectures Read by Mr. Crotch*, NRO, MS 11230.

[John Marsh]. 'A Comparison Between the Ancient and Modern Styles of Music in Which the Merits and Demerits of Each are Respectively Pointed Out', *Monthly Magazine*, supplement to vol. 2 (1796), 981–6.

———. *Hints to Young Composers of Instrumental Music, Illustrated with 2 Movements for a Grand Orchestra in Score*, Chicester, n.d.

———. 'Hints to Young Composers of Instrumental Music', edited and with an introduction by Charles Cudworth, *Galpin Society Journal*, **18** (1965): 57–71.

Mason, John, *An Essay on the Power of Numbers, and the Principles of Harmony in Poetical Compositions*, London, 1749.

Mason, William, *The Poems of Mr. Gray to which is prefaced Memoirs of his Life and Writing*, York, 1775.

———. *Essays Historical and Critical, on English Church Music*, York, 1795; London, 1811.

Matthew, James E., 'The Antient Concerts, 1776–1848', *Proceedings of the Royal Musical Associations*, **33** (1906), 55–79.

Matthews, Betty, 'Addenda and corrigenda to Brian Pritchard and Douglas Reid, "Some Festival Programs of the Eighteenth and Nineteenth

Centuries: 1. Salisbury and Winchester"', *R. M. A. Research Chronicle*, 8 (1970), 23–33.

McGeary, Thomas, 'Music Literature', in H.D. Johnstone and R. Fisk, eds, *The Blackwell History of Music in Britain*, vol. 4 *The Eighteenth Century*, Oxford and Cambridge: Blackwell, 1990.

McKendrick, Neil, Brewer, John and Plumb, J.H., *The Birth of a Consumer Society: The Commercialization of Eighteenth-Century England*, London: Europa Publications, 1982.

McVeigh, Simon, *Concert Life in London from Mozart to Haydn*, Cambridge and New York: Cambridge University Press, 1993.

———. *Calendar of London Concerts 1750–1800* (London: Goldsmiths College, University of London, 1993.

Milligan, Thomas B., *The Concerto and London's Musical Culture in the Late Eighteenth Century*, Ann Arbor, MI: UMI Research Press, 1983.

Molleson, Alexander, 'Melody, the Soul of Music', in *Miscellanies in Prose and Verse*, Glasgow, 1806.

de Momigny, Jérôme-Joseph, *Cours complet d'Harmonie et de composition*, 3 vols, Paris, 1806.

Monk, Samuel H., *The Sublime: a Study of Critical Theories in XVIII-Century England*, Ann Arbor, MI: University of Michigan Press, 1960.

Neubauer, John, *The Emancipation of Music from Language: Departure from Mimesis in Eighteenth-Century Aesthetics*, New Haven, CT, and London: Yale University Press, 1986.

North, Roger, *Roger North on Music: Being a Selection from his Essays Written during the Years c. 1695–1728*, ed. John Wilson, London: Novello, 1959.

———. *Roger North's The Musicall Grammarian 1728*, Mary Chan and Jamie C. Kassler eds, Cambridge: Cambridge University Press, 1990.

Oldman, C.B., 'Mozart's Scena for Tenducci', *Music and Letters*, 42 (1961), 44–52.

———. 'Dr Burney and Mozart', in *Mozart Jahrbuch 1962–1963*, pp. 75–81, Kassel, Germany: Internationale Stiftung Mozarteum Salzburg, 1964.

———. 'Dr Burney and Mozart: Addenda and Corrigenda', *Mozart Jahrbuch 1964*, pp. 109–10. Kassel, Germany: Internationale Stiftung Mozarteum Salzburg, 1964.

'Oxoniensis', 'Remarks on the distinctive Character and essential Qualities of Good Musick', *Gentleman's Magazine*, 88 (1818), 414–16, 30–32.

Parke, William, *Musical Memoirs*, 2 vols, London, 1830.

Polier, Charles, 'An Essay on the Pleasure which the Mind Receives from the Exercise of its Facilities', *Memoirs and Proceedings of the Manchester Literary and Philosophical Society*, 1 (1785), 110–34.

Postolka, Milan, 'Gelinek, Joseph', in *The New Grove Dictionary of Music and Musicians*, ed. Stanley Sadie, 20 vols, London, Macmillan Publishers Ltd, 1980, vol. 7, pp. 222–3.

Price, Sir Uvedale, *An Essay of the Picturesque as Compared with the Sublime and theBeautiful; and, on the Use of Studying Pictures, for the Purpose of Improving Real Landscape*, London, 1794.

———. *Essays on the Picturesque, as Compared with the Sublime and the Beautiful* … , 3 vols, London, 1810; Gregg International, 1971.

Pritchard, Brian and Reid, Douglas, 'Some Festival Programs of the Eighteenth and Nineteenth Centuries: 4. Birmingham, Derby, Newcastle upon Tyne and York', *RMA Research Chronicle*, 8 (1970), 1–22.

Probyn, Clive T., *The Sociable Humanist: the Life and Works of James Harris 1709–1780*, Oxford: Clarendon Press, 1991.

Rainbow, Bernarr, *The Choral Revival in the Anglican Church 1839–1872*, New York: Oxford University Press, 1970.

Raeburn, Michael, 'Dr Burney, Mozart, and Crotch', *The Musical Times*, 97 (1956), 519–20.

Rees, Abraham, ed., *The Cyclopaedia; or, Universal Dictionary of Arts, Sciences, and Literature*, 39 vols, London, 1802–19.

Reid, Douglas J., 'Some Festival Programs of the Eighteenth and Nineteenth Centuries: 2. Cambridge and Oxford', *RMA Research Chronicle*, 6 (1966), 3–22.

Reid, Douglas J. and Pritchard, Brian, 'Some Festival Programs of the Eighteenth and Nineteenth Centuries: 1. Salisbury and Winchester', *RMA Research Chronicle*, 5 (1965), 51–79.

Rennert, Jonathan, *William Crotch (1775–1847): Composer, Artist, Teacher*, Lavenham, Suffolk: T. Dalton, 1975.

———. 'William Crotch (1775–1847) – Worth Reviving?', *The Consort*, 31 (1975), 116–25.

———. 'William Crotch, 1775–1847', *Musical Times*, 116 (1975), 622–3.

Reynolds, Sir Joshua, *Discourses on Art*, ed. Robert R. Wark, New Haven, CI, and London: Yale University Press, 1975.

Ribeiro, Alvaro, S. J., ed., *The Letters of Dr Charles Burney*, vol. 1 *1751–1784*, Oxford: Clarendon Press, 1991.

Ritter, Frederic Louis, *Music in England*, New York, 1883.

Robertson, Thomas, *An Enquiry into the Fine Arts*, London, 1784; New York: Garland, 1971.

Rogers, Pat, 'The Critique of Opera in Pope's *Dunciad*', *Musical Quarterly*, **59** (1973), 15–30.

Rousseau, Jean-Jacques, *Dictionnaire de Musique*, Geneva, 1767; Paris, 1768.

The Royal Institution of Great Britain, *Minutes of the Manager's Meetings 1799–1900* in facsimile; with an introduction by Frank Greenaway, Menston: Scolar Press, 1971.

Rumbold, Valerie, 'Music Aspires to Letters: Charles Burney, Queeney Thrale and the Streatham Circle', *Music and Letters*, **74** (1993), 24–38.

Sadie, Stanley, 'Concert Life in Eighteenth Century England', *Proceedings of the Royal Musical Association*, **85** (1958–59), 17–30.

Scholes, Percy A., *The Great Dr. Burney*, 2 vols, Oxford: Clarendon Press, 1948.

Schueller, Herbert M., '"Imitation" and "Expression" in British Music Criticism in the 18th Century', *Musical Quarterly*, **34** (1948), 544–66.

———. 'The Pleasures of Music: Speculation in British Music Criticism, 1750–1800', *Journal of Aesthetics and Art Criticism*, **8** (1950), 155–71.

———. 'The Use and Decorum of Music as Described in British Literature, 1700 to 1780', *Journal of the History of Ideas*, **13** (1952), 73–93.

———. 'Correspondences Between Music and the Sister Arts, According to 18th Century Aesthetic Theory', *Journal of Aesthetics and Art Criticism*, **11** (1953), 334–59.

———. 'The Quarrel of the Ancients and the Moderns', *Music and Letters*, **41** (1960), 313–30.

Shaw, Watkins, *The Succession of Organists of the Chapel Royal and the Cathedrals of England and Wales from c.1538*, Oxford: Clarendon Press, 1991.

Shedlock, J. S. 'Handel's Borrowings', *The Musical Times*, **42** (1901), 450–598.

Simpson, Christopher, *A Compendium: or, Introduction to Practical Music. In Five Parts*, London, 1678; 6th edn, London, 1714.

Spingarn, J. E., ed., *Sir William Temple's Essays on Ancient and Modern Learning and On Poetry*, Oxford: Clarendon Press, 1909; Folcroft, PA.: Folcroft Press, 1970.

Spink, Ian, ed., *The Blackwell History of Music in Briton*, vol. 3, *The Seventeenth Century*, Oxford: Blackwell, 1990.

Stevens, Richard John, *Sacred Music for one, two, three & four voices from the works of the most esteemed composers, Italian, & English, selected, adapted and arranged by R. J. Stevens*, 3 vols, London, 1798–1802.

———. *Recollections of R. J. S. Stevens, an Organist in Georgian London*, ed. Mark Argent, Carbondale, IL: Southern Illinois University Press, 1992.

[Benjamin Stillingfleet], *Principles and Power of Harmony*, London, 1771.

Stock, R. D., *Samuel Johnson and Neoclassical Dramatic Theory: the Intellectual Context of the Preface to Shakespeare*, Lincoln, NB: University of Nebraska Press, 1973.

Swedenberg, H. T. Jr, ed., *The Works of John Dryden*, Berkeley and Los Angeles: University of California Press, 1976.

Temperley, Nicholas, 'Instrumental Music in England, 1800–1850', PhD, Cambridge University, 1959.

———. 'Handel's Influence on English Music', *The Monthly Musical Record*, 90 (1960), 163–74.

———. *Haydn: The Creation*, Cambridge: Cambridge University Press, 1991.

———. 'Mozart's Influence on English Music', *Music and Letters*, 42 (1961), 307–18.

———. Introduction to William Crotch *Symphony in F Major* in Barry Brook and Barbara B. Heyman, eds, *The Symphony: 1720–1840*, 60 vols, New York: Garland, 1984.

Thomson, William, *An Enquiry into the Elementary Principles of Beauty in the Works of Nature and Art*, London, 1798.

Toynbee, Paget and Whibley, Leonard, eds, *Correspondence of Thomas Gray*, with corrections and additions by H. W. Starr, 3 vols, Oxford: Clarendon Press, 1935.

Tovey, Duncan C., ed., *The Letters of Thomas Gray*, 3 vols, London, G. Bell and Sons, 1900–12.

'Triest, Herr', essay in *Allgemeine Musikalische Zeitung*, 24 (1801), cols 405–8.

Trowbridge, Hoyt, 'Platonism and Sir Joshua Reynolds', *English Studies*, 21 (1939), 1–7.

Twining, Thomas, *Aristotle's Treatise on Poetry Translated with Notes on Translation, and on the Original; and Two Dissertations, on Poetical, and Musical, Imitation*, London, 1789; New York: Garland, 1971.

Twining, Thomas, *Recreations and Studies of a Country Clergyman of the Eighteenth Century*, ed. Richard Twining, London, 1882.

[Thomas Twining], (Anonymous), Review of *An Account of the Musical Performances in Westminster Abbey ... in Commemoration of Handel*, by Charles Burney, *Critical Review*, 59 (1785), 130–38.

Tyson, Alan, 'A Feud Between Clementi and Cramer', *Music and Letters*, 54 (1973), 281–8.

Uphaus, Robert W., 'The Ideology of Reynolds', *Discourses on Art*, *Eighteenth Century Studies*, 12 (1978–79), 59–73.

'Veritas', 'The Concerts of Ancient Music Vindicated', *The Harmonicon*, 8 (1830), 276–7.

Vines, Sherard, *The Course of English Classicism from the Tudor to the Victorian Age*, New York, Harcourt, Brace, and Co., 1930; reprinted New York, Phaeton Press, 1968.

Walker, Arthur D., 'Addenda to "Some Festival Programs of the Eighteenth and Nineteenth Centuries: 1. Salisbury and Winchester"', *RMA Research Chronicle*, 6 (1966), 23.

Walker, Ralph S., ed., *A Selection of Thomas Twining's Letters 1734–1804: the Record of a Tranquil Life*, 2 vols, Lewiston, Queenston, Lampeter: Edwin Mellen Press, 1991.

Wallis, John, 'A Letter of Dr. John Wallis, to Mr. Andrew Fletcher; concerning the strange Effects reported of *Music* in *Former Times*; beyond what is to be found in Later Ages', *Philosophical Transactions of the Royal Society*, 20 (1698), 297–303.

Walton, Izaak, *The Complete Angler: or, Contemplative Man's Recreation*, ed. Sir John Hawkins, London, 1760.

Walpole, Horace, *Anecdotes of Painting in England*, 4 vols, London, printed for J. Dodsley, 1782.

——. *The Yale Edition of Horace Walpole's Correspondence*, ed. W. S. Lewis. New Haven, CT: Yale University Press, 1937–83.

Warton, Thomas, *The Poetical Works of the Late Thomas Warton*, 5th edn, 2 vols, Oxford, 1802.

Watson, George, ed., *John Dryden: of Dramatic Poesy and other Critical Essays*, 2 vols, London, J. M. Dent, 1962.

Webb, Daniel, *Observations on the Correspondence Between Poetry and Music*, London, 1769.

Weber, William, *Music and the Middle Class: The Social Structure of Concert Life in London, Paris and Vienna*. New York: Holmes and Meier Publishers, Inc., 1975.

——. 'Mass Culture and the Reshaping of European Musical Taste, 1770–1870', *International Review of the Aesthetics and Sociology of Music*, 8 (1977), 5–21.

——. 'Intellectual Bases of the Handelian Tradition, 1759–1800', *Proceedings of the RMA*, 108 (1981–82), 100–14.

——. 'Wagner, Wagnerism, and Musical Idealsim', in David C. Large and William Weber, eds, *Wagnerism in European Culture and Politics*, Ithaca, NY and London: Cornell University Press, 1984.

————. 'The Rise of the Classical Repertoire in Nineteenth-Century Orchestral Concerts', in Joan Peyser, ed., *The Orchestra: Origins and Transformations*, pp. 361–86, New York: Charles Scribner's Sons, 1986.

————. Review of *The Emancipation of Music from Language: Departure from Mimesis in Eighteenth-Century Aesthetics*, by John Neubauer, *Eighteenth Century Studies*, 21 (1987), p. 243.

————. 'The 1784 Handel Commemoration as Political Ritual', *Journal of British Studies*, 28 (1989), 43–69.

————. *The Rise of Musical Classics in Eighteenth-Century England: a Study of Canon, Ritual, and Ideology*, Oxford: Clarendon Press, 1992.

————. 'The Intellectual Origins of Musical Canon in Eighteenth-Century England', *Journal of the American Musicological Society*, 47 (1994), 488–520.

Wesley, John, *The Works of the Rev. John Wesley, A. M.*, 3rd edn, 7 vols, New York, n. d.

————. 'Thoughts on the Power of Music', in *The Works of the Rev. John Wesley, A. M.*, 3rd edn, 7 vols, New York, n. d., vol. 7, pp. 455–7.

————. *The Journal of John Wesley*, ed. Percy Livingstone Parker, Chicago: Moody Press, 1974.

Wesley, Samuel, Lectures, BM Add. MS 35.014.

W. G. [William Gardiner], 'Defense of Modern Music', *Monthly Magazine*, 31 (1811), 133–6.

Whitney, Lois, *Primitivism and the Idea of Progress in English Popular Literature of the Eighteenth Century*, Baltimore: The Johns Hopkins Press, 1934; New York: Octagon Books, 1973.

Will, Frederic, 'Blake's Quarrel with Reynolds', *Journal of Aesthetics and Art Criticism*, 15 (1957), 340–49.

Willetts, Pamela, 'The Ayrton Papers: Music in London, 1786–1858', *The British Library Journal*, 6 (1980), 7–23.

Wilson, Ruth M. *Anglican Chant and Chanting in England, Scotland, and America 1660 to 1820*, Oxford: Clarendon Press, 1996.

Wolcot, John, *The Works of Peter Pindar, esq.*, 5 vols, London, 1812.

Wollenberg, Susan, 'Music in 18th-Century Oxford', *Proceedings of the Royal Musical Association*, 107 (1981–82), 70.

Wotton, William, *Reflections on Ancient and Modern Learning*, 2nd edn, London, 1697.

Wright, Herbert, 'William Blake and Sir Joshua Reynolds: a Contrast in Theories of Art', *The Nineteenth Century*, 101 (1927), 417–31.

Zon, Bennett, *The English Plainchant Revival*, Oxford: Clarendon Press, 1998.

Zottes, Paul Eustace, 'The Completest Concert or Augustan Critics of Opera: a Documentary and Critical Study in English Aesthetics' (PhD, University of Pennsylvania, 1977).

Index